For Kings and Planets

The Palace Thief
Blue River
Emperor of the Air

For Kings and Planets

ETHAN CANIN

Rec by Wistons buy

Sarah Haxter 4/05

BLOOMSBURY

First published 1998 in Canada by Random House

First published in Great Britain 1998

This paperback edition published 1999

Grateful acknowledgement is made to the following for
permission to reprint previously published material.

Harcourt Brace & Company: Three lines from "The Quaker
Graveyard in Nantucker" from *Lord Weary's Castle* by Robert Lowell.
Copyright © 1946 and renewed 1974 by Robert Lowell.
Reprinted by permission of Harcourt Brace & Company.

Random House, Inc. Six lines from "Musée des Beaux Arts"
from *Collected Poems: W. H. Auden* by W. H. Auden,
edited by Edward Mendelson. Copyright © 1948 and copyright renewed 1968
by W. H. Auden. Reprinted by permission of Random House, Inc.

Bloomsbury Publishing Plc, 38 Soho Square, London W1V 5DF

A CIP catalogue record is available from the British Library

ISBN 0 7475 4400 X

10 9 8 7 6 5 4 3 2 1

Printed in Great Britain by Clays Ltd, St Ives plc

For Barbara, and Amiela Rose

ACKNOWLEDGMENTS

Much gratitude goes to Neil MacFarquhar, Alex Gansa, Claire Ferrari, Lisa Canin, Bob Hoffman, Sue Schuler, Chard deNiord, Julie Colhoun, Dan Geller, Dayna Goldfine, Jon Maksik, Leslie Maksik, Judith Wolff, Po Bronson, Anne Lamott, Ellie Dwight, Meaghan Rady, Jean-Isabel McNutt, Kate Medina, and, of course, Maxine Groffsky.

One

I

Years later, Orno Tarcher would think of his days in New York as a seduction. A seduction and a near miss, a time when his memory of the world around him—the shining stone stairwells, the taxicabs, the sea of nighttime lights—was glinting and of heroic proportion. Like a dream. He had almost been taken away from himself. That was the feeling he had, looking back. Smells and sounds: the roll and thunder of the number 1 train; the wind like a flute through the deck rafters of the Empire State Building; the waft of dope in the halls. Different girls, their lives coming back to him: hallways and slants of light. Daphne and Anne-Marie and especially Sofia. He remembered meeting Marshall Emerson on his second day at college, at dawn on the curb of 116th Street and Broadway, the air touched with a memory of heat that lingered in the barest rain. It had reminded him of home.

New York: he'd driven with his parents, arriving in three days from Cook's Grange, Missouri, cabs honking and speeding by them as at last they pulled onto the West Side Highway late in the afternoon on the first day of September, 1974; the cornices of midtown skyscrapers ablaze in sunlight above his father's homburg as he inched along in the right lane. Hugging the wheel of the Chrysler like a man on a tractor. Orno was in the backseat, coming to Columbia University, the first in his family to go east for an education. He remembered his father, driving like a farmer. His mother in her flowered dress.

He himself was in corduroy pants and a tie, upright in his seat with hopes of deeds and glory. That evening, after his parents left him, he wandered downstairs and sat on the dormitory steps in the warm air, eager to offer aid to anyone moving in. But three days remained before the start of registration and nobody appeared for him to help. He went for a walk in the direction of the Hudson instead, coming out at last onto the high bluffs. They reminded him of the Mississippi until at sunset the lights began to come on across the water. Streams of red and yellow on the throughways. Buildings clumped like stars. He returned to the dormitory again, still not having spoken to anyone and suddenly remembering that he was not to walk out alone after dark; he went upstairs to his room, where he read *Look Homeward, Angel* until he became used to the sounds of traffic and slept. Fear entered him and replaced his hope of glory, fear that he had erred badly. He remembered thinking: I am no longer among my own.

The next morning he woke early, a habit from Missouri. He showered before dawn, left his hair wet, and walked down to the west gate of campus. On the park bench the guard dozed and a young boy sat unbundling newspapers. A misty rain was settling, no more than a touch of cool on his skin. In the distance he heard a garbage truck shrieking and clanging as it came to intersections, muffled when it moved behind the apartments. Then he was aware that someone was saying his name: another student, possibly his own age, in a smoking jacket. Friendly in a sly way. "Well," he said. "Did I get it?"

"My name?" said Orno. "Yes you did. How'd you know?"

"The book of pictures they gave us. The face book."

"You're a freshman, too?"

"Yes, I'm embarrassed to say." He put out his hand. "Marshall Emerson."

"Orno Tarcher."

"As I said."

"As you did."

"You're up early, too," said Orno.

Marshall smiled. "Hardly." He rubbed his hands. "We're in the same hall, you know. Four hundred of us hungry dogs. I think you're right downstairs from me. You're in 318. I'm in 418."

"How'd you know all this?"

"I told you. It was in the face book."

"There are hundreds of pictures in that book."

"Well, I was right, wasn't I?"

"I guess so," said Orno, holding out his hand. "Let me see your picture."

"I tossed the thing weeks ago. Sorry. But I'm from here," he said. "Manhattan." He pointed up around him. "And I didn't let them have my picture anyway. I sent them a drawing. But they didn't use it. Now you know my name, anyway."

Orno smiled.

"You know what I love?" Marshall said. "I love the way at this hour you could be anywhere on earth. Before it wakes, the world is the same everywhere. In Istanbul now you would be hearing the first call to prayer. This rain reminds me of it." He put his hand to his mouth and made a chanting noise. "*Allahu Akbar. Ashadu an la ilaha ill Allah.* The muezzin." He smiled. "In the minarets."

"I've never been," said Orno. "Have you spent much time there?"

"In a way. A beautiful and mysterious city. I once saw a man there feed a house cat to his snake. *Ashadu anna Muhammadur rasul Allah.* It means, God Is Great. In practice it means, get out of bed."

Orno laughed. His whole life he would remember this moment: the world opening. "I'm glad to see you wake up at this hour, too," he said. "Where I'm from, everybody does, but around here nobody seems to."

Marshall stared at him. "Oh, you're really not kidding, are you?"

Orno looked back, smiling unsteadily.

"I'm not waking up," said Marshall. "I'm getting home."

———

"They make these like this so we can't jump out of them," Marshall said, trying to force open Orno's window. It was later that day, early afternoon sunlight bouncing in from the gray stone walls. "You can't open them wider than your hand, you know."

Orno walked over and pushed. "I'll be darned."

There was a flatness to the light off the granite, like heat. Marshall had come downstairs to visit, knocked once on his door and then opened it. That and the fact of New York out his window: he could see the cornice of a prewar building across the street, green copper thirty stories up, maybe a roof garden. It was thrilling. There was still almost nobody else in the dorm, though now through the window he could see them starting to arrive. Cabs at the curb. Boxes. All day his mood had risen and fallen wildly. At Clarkson College, where his father and uncles had gone, the windows were huge, wood-paned rectangles that spun on pivot hinges: dusty sunlight and prairie wind and yellow jackets in the high corners of the rooms. Just as quickly fear rose in him. He touched the glass again. "My folks are out to drop me off," he said. "We're going to lunch."

Marshall kept looking out the window.

"I mean, if you want to come."

"What are your folks like?"

He had no answer for that. It was odd. "I mean," he said, "I doubt it will be fancy or anything." He thought of his father. "But still."

"Out from where?"

"We're from the Midwest."

"Where in the Midwest?"

"St. Louis." He was looking down at Broadway, knowing his father would pull past in the yellow Chrysler.

"The face book says Cook's Grange."

"I thought you threw out the face book."

"I did. Where's Cook's Grange?"

"Two hours from St. Louis."

On the street the Chrysler drove by: Orno glimpsed his mother's hat, red flowers at the brim, the camera on her shoulder. "You probably have better things to do."

"No," said Marshall. "I'd love to come along."

They walked outside into the glancing light. Getting into the car Marshall said, "I've never been in a private car in Manhattan in my life."

"Is that right?" asked his mother. "Where does your family reside?"

"East Sixties."

She smiled blankly.

"The Upper East Side of Manhattan," said his father. "Across the park."

Orno said, "Mother, Father, this is Marshall Emerson."

His father lifted his hat, a country gesture. "Drake Tarcher," he said. It could have been the opening of a crop-insurance pitch.

"How do you do?" Marshall answered, a phrase Orno himself had never used. He made a note of it.

His mother smiled.

They went to lunch on Broadway at a place Marshall knew: plate-glass windows opening on to a scene of rush—streams of taxis, roofers next door hauling tar pots up a rickety ladder, women in heels, a policeman clomping midstreet on a rebelling mare. The menu made his mother laugh: sandwiches named The Brooklyn Bridge (Wanna Buy It?), The President Nixon (We Can Explain Everything), The Big Apple (But I Wouldn't Want To Live There). The waiter introduced himself, and his mother asked him where he was from, while somehow his father and Marshall continued a discussion of World War II that they must have started on the street. Orno's father had seen action in the Philippines and Marshall seemed to know about all the battles there: Corregidor, the China Sea. Orno had heard of them too, but he'd never paid attention. He felt envy, his father talking this way.

His mother said, "My, you certainly seem to know a great deal. What does your father do?"

"Both my parents are professors."

She raised her brows. "Both of them?"

"Yes, ma'am."

"What does your father teach?"

"Vertebrate biology."

"And what is that exactly?"

"Fish mostly, in his case. He studies a genus of Teleostei, at Woods Hole. That's where we go in the summer. But in general the field is any animal with a backbone. For some reason it's a distinction biologists make." He smiled thinly. "Ironically enough."

"And Mrs. Emerson?"

"Anthropology." He nodded. "She uses her own name, by the way. She goes by Pelham, not Emerson."

"Oh dear," said his mother.

His father taught at Columbia itself, it turned out, a fact Marshall seemed to admit with the same unease Orno had felt that morning saying he was from Cook's Grange. His face reddened, a quick flight of color. Then he was pale again, one long arm out on the table. Orno ate ravenously, hungry with envy. He finished his sandwich and ordered a salad. Maybe it was more than envy; maybe it was less. He wanted things, could feel himself on the verge: a new half of the world. He started tapping his feet. Everything was brimming—the windows, the conversation, the stream of walkers, the white stone architecture across the street, on fire in the sun. Marshall was telling them about his mother now. She studied a village in Turkey and a primitive tribe in the South Pacific, the first woman ever to venture alone into the island jungle.

"The South Pacific?" said his mother. "It must be lovely. Are there really such beautiful waterfalls?"

Orno could feel the smallness of his own life.

"Not really," Marshall said. "Not where she goes. And in any case, it wasn't so lovely for her children."

———

Orno and Marshall were in a history class together—a great relief to Orno, because as school started and he walked the diagonal paths between the halls of classrooms he was swept with thoughts of smallness. The trees were at their late summer peak, the humid, stretched leaves, the magnificent span of boughs among the buildings; height everywhere, everything seeming older and more permanent than himself. The other students seemed to know one another, moving in packs through the brass-bottomed swinging doors, talking in whispers. To find Marshall in his history class was a comfort, deeply so.

It was an introductory course: History 120. Ancient Greece and Rome. An old professor in an old black suit, shiny at the belly and shoulders, a bald head of scolding hugeness, a cane unused against the podium like an umbrella. His name was Winthrop Menemee Scott, all three names spelled out anew on the blackboard the first and second and third days of class, a slanting unsteady hand on the dusty slate, the letters huge to Orno in the first row and obviously degenerate from disease.

Marshall didn't appear until the fourth day, looking stricken as he entered to find Orno where he was, one seat off the aisle, the closest student in the hall to the orating professor. Marshall looked up the rows of slanting burgundy seats, hesitated, then sat beside him. Winthrop Menemee Scott paused for a moment and then nodded. Marshall waved back, a small gesture, his hand not leaving his lap.

When class was over Marshall told Orno that Professor Scott knew his father, and after that he tried to get Orno to sit high in the auditorium with him, well back in the rows of ill-cushioned seats where the armrests had been scratched with initials and the upholstery smelled like medicine cut ineffectively with lemon. Flea powder, it was said to be. Orno obliged and for several days moved back in the room, high up over the sea of bodies that sometimes daunted him, 220 downturned heads of hair, 220 notebooks, the frightening obliviousness of other people's hopes. Private-school students, most of them, he knew from looking at the face book: Groton, Deerfield, Hotchkiss. He wondered what that meant. Sitting high up, his attention wandered out into the fall sky over the quadrangle: splendid, a darker blue than Missouri, nearly cobalt—it lacked opacity, some evidence of earth in it, the blown dust of the summer sky back home. Forty yards away the marble friezes of the academic buildings sat in eerie relief that vibrated in his eyes: pigeons strutting jerkily on the sills, dandelion fluff spinning at outrageous heights. His attention wandered and snapped back, then turned to the rows of heads and the sound of pages being turned. He told Marshall he had a hard time hearing so far away and went back to sitting in front.

In a week they'd covered the Minoans and the Mycenaeans and moved into the Age of Solon. Each night there were a hundred pages to read before he could even turn to his other classes; it seemed Professor Menemee Scott must have been trying to scare them. Coming out of class into the suddenly cool afternoons he tasted metal in his throat: a dry hesitance that didn't ease until he was most of the way through the short, dining-hall dinner. He brought his book bag with him to the cafeteria and set it below the table, saving perhaps ten minutes, then left for the library with two plastic cups of coffee, one in a paper bag to drink later, lukewarm. In the library he stacked his books in front of him and set about the work. He was counting on the belief that he could study harder than the other students he saw through the round-topped windows overlooking the grass. They filtered out over the remainder of the dinner hour, smoked cigarettes sitting on the steps below the statue of Alma Mater, sauntered in twos and threes through the wrought-iron gates onto Broadway. A hundred yards away from them he sat with two feet on the floor for posture and his jacket off to ward away sleepiness in the air-conditioned stacks. He looked down: on a sheet of notebook paper he'd written, *Don't be afraid.*

He didn't know what he planned to major in, but there was some feeling at home that it would be history, like his uncle Clarence in Centerville, a lawyer and the only one in the family with books in the house; but every night he read through Menemee Scott's own book on the Greeks and felt the words skid: "The solipsistic Athenians, surrounded on two sides by the bellicose Spartans and the bellicosely commercial Carthaginians, internally confined, it could be said, by their own static harmonies, failed to grasp—" The library lights made a humming noise and now and then the air conditioner changed pitch and he would tumble from his reverie, the page unturned. What did he care about these thoughts? He looked up into the maze of colored ceiling tiles and out through the now dark windows. There were no private schools in Cook's Grange; there were none until St. Louis. On the other hand he was used to the struggle of discipline. He welcomed it, really; it was as familiar to him as waking in the black Missouri winter. But the field of history itself, coupled with Menemee Scott's trembling voice and the recounting of lives that seemed to him in essence to be squandered, touched him with panic. And the others, 220 of them, all eager. A distant past, obscured and generalized and reworked for him to commit to memory. It seemed not the kind of thing he could retain. He had often doubted his intelligence, but now for the first time he began to doubt his resolve. He looked around, gazed hungrily at the other students chatting in the stairwells. Then he set to work again. He was taking freshman composition as well, and courses in chemistry and physics that, to his great relief, yielded to his discipline. He had applied to Columbia without telling his parents.

———

Every night when he came back from the library he would stop by Marshall's room, in which it seemed Marshall didn't study at all. Two huge speakers stood against the back wall, playing Steely Dan or the Grateful Dead, and Marshall himself lay reclining on the wide tasseled pillows on the floor. He'd built the speakers himself, he told Orno; now he listened to them with wary, proprietary attention. Orno never saw him reading. Other students moved in and out, wandering in when the libraries closed, taking off their shoes outside and arraying themselves across the pillows. Bottles of schnapps and beer stood on the windowsills; joints lay in the brass ashtrays. Orno had never smoked before, but one night he did, feeling nothing as the joint was passed to him. Usually they skipped him over, the joint moving in a half-circle toward Marshall and then back again, nobody offering to him and Orno not asking. But now, suddenly, it was in his hand and he drew on it, feeling the bite in his throat. An obscure change seemed to come over the room and he grew quiet and watched the others.

They exhaled bluish smoke and debated Marshall over small points of music history, narrow-eyed like cats. He waited for more to happen. The next night he tried it again, again waiting. It struck him that he had the wrong character for it, something immovable inside him, immune to the effects he saw everywhere else. The others talked languorously or tapped their fingers. He was embarrassed at his own stolidness and closed his eyes for effect. He felt the word *Missouri* written on his forehead. He tried to concentrate on the music, but he kept thinking instead of his father, waking early to fetch the newspaper.

But for some reason Marshall took to him. Orno didn't need a lot of sleep—it was how everyone lived where he was from—and it wasn't hard for him to stay late into the night in Marshall's room, picking up a conversation after most of the others had gone back to their own beds. Marshall didn't really confide anything in him, he realized later, but he had an ease about him that invited confession. Orno would come back when the library closed, drop his books in the hall outside Marshall's door and leave his shoes there, then come in and take his place amid the ruins of the evening. Sometimes other students were asleep against the wall. The pillows smelled of smoke; bottles had worked their way between the mattresses. Marshall told him he never slept before 4:00 A.M.—he was usually asleep when Orno came back from his morning chemistry class—and for as long as Orno was willing to lie there on the pillows he maintained an intermittent run of conversation, pausing for certain riffs in the music at which he would raise his hands and close his eyes. He had a vigilance at night that he lacked during the day.

In his room the group talked about the other freshmen in the dorm, conversations Orno enjoyed in part because they felt illicit. He'd always assumed that people were good, that they worked hard for any number of things that required self-interest but that certain boundaries prevailed: decency, respect for others, truth. He couldn't have said this before he came to Columbia, but several times in his first few weeks there he was made to, late at night in Marshall's room, with its shifting cadre of onlookers. The easterners had sway here; that much was clear. He knew that he didn't want to become one himself, but he also knew that he was envious, and his envy shamed him: their quick words; their outlook; their comments. One evening a girl actually laughed at a point he'd made in earnest, that each generation improved upon the mistakes of the last. She claimed it was a midwestern outlook. He laughed along with everyone else but of course the comment stung him.

Marshall himself subscribed to a theory of character taken from a book called *The Enneagram* and from two thinkers named G. I. Gurdjieff and Oscar Ichazo, who seemed like cultists to Orno but whom Marshall liked to cite at astounding length in his conversation. The first time Orno heard him quote one of them he nodded, put his beer bottle to his lips and feigned comprehension, then spent the next afternoon in the reference room searching for most of an hour before he even stumbled on the correct spellings of the names. From the short articles he read, both men indeed seemed like mystics or perhaps cranks. Yet Marshall seemed to hold them in a reverence that hinted at a conspiracy against their social ideas and, by extension, against his own as well. Marshall had already lived a life of spectacular worldliness.

Late at night in his room he liked to tell Orno about his childhood, part of which he'd spent in Istanbul, living in the Hotel Luxor with an Irish governess while his mother carried out her research in the countryside. He remembered the life of the city with perfect clarity and would describe it to Orno reverently—the crumbling Theodosian walls, the shaded gardens of Süleymaniye, the meals of börek and beyaz peynir, the pink blossoms of the Judas trees along the Bosporus and the deep-riding ferries struggling crosscurrent between two continents. Orno loved to listen, though at times the stories worried him because he felt obligated to counter them with exoticism from his own past; but soon he understood he wouldn't have to. When it was his turn to talk, he recounted simple memories of Missouri winters, commonplace tales he exaggerated only slightly, snow high enough to build tunnels through, escaped steer frozen like statues onto the irrigation canals. Marshall laughed at all of it, a loose, uncomplicated laugh that seemed to transmit amazement and filled Orno with pleasure.

Of his own childhood days in New York, Marshall told stories about dinners and drinking and carrying on in his parents' apartment with people like Margaret Mead and Harlan Ellison and Francis Crick, friends of his parents and evidently of his own as well.

The stories made Orno feel giddy, as though he himself were somehow part of them, or soon to be. The world of influence seemed astoundingly close and even more astoundingly pedestrian, tossed off by Marshall with a nonchalance that Orno soon found himself cultivating. One afternoon, as they walked on Columbus Avenue, they passed the actor Steve McQueen, whistling and looking up at the second-story windows, and it was Orno who was able to point him out to Marshall, calming himself enough to mention it nearly offhandedly, as they were about to turn the corner.

———

Marshall explained the tenets of *The Enneagram*. There were nine basic roots of character, and he went through the dormitory systematically, talking about each of the other students as a mixture of two or three of them: core of four, wings of three and five; core of nine, wings of eight and one. A certain girl especially, Phoebe Lyall—whose full name, Marshall said, was Phoebe Allison Morgan Lyall—fascinated him. At night he usually returned to her after he'd discussed a few others, granting her special consideration, a complexity that he did not acknowledge in the other students. Sometimes he called her a cross between the Performer, the Observer, and the Tragic Romantic; other times she was the Giver, the Performer, and the Perfectionist. In Orno's opinion she was shy and polite, simply enough, like a lot of girls he had known at home; but she had a narrow mouth and tapered cheekbones that made most people think she was aloof, especially after Marshall let it be known that her ancestor was J. P. Morgan. This seemed a bit cruel to Orno—Marshall's announcing to a group at dinner, which did not include Phoebe Lyall herself, who her great-grandfather had been—but he didn't say anything to stop it. He merely asked aloud if Marshall knew the genealogy of everyone in the dorm. Marshall laughed, along with the rest of the group, but Orno was aware of having transgressed. Later, he apologized; afterward he waited to see if Marshall and Phoebe Lyall would begin seeing each other.

Once, near the middle of the term, on a still night when the cool had first turned to cold and the leaves on the ground had become brittle, crackling underfoot, he came to Marshall's room after spending six hours at the library reviewing the order of monarchy of the Greek and then the Roman emperors. It was late October; the dormitory heaters had come on, clanking through the night and heating the top-floor rooms to such uncomfortable temperatures that the students left their doors and windows wide open. When Orno came in, Marshall was pushed back against the wall, legs splayed. It was only after Orno had taken his place among a set of pillows across the room that he noticed Phoebe next to the window. She was lying quietly with her eyes closed, listening to the odd music that was on the stereo, a moody piece on which Orno, too, concentrated. It was hard to classify—avantgarde jazz, perhaps, although it could have been classical even, a mixture of strings and lower-register bells that in the cool autumnal air seemed to exactly personify sadness. It wasn't the kind of thing Marshall usually listened to. They all had midterms the next morning.

Phoebe nodded at him.

"Where have you been?" Marshall asked.

"Studying the Greeks and Romans. Hi, Phoebe."

"Ah, the Greeks and Romans," said Marshall. "Menemee Scott is teaching us all the wrong things, you know, company man that he is. Let's see," he said, rubbing his chin, "let me see what I remember. 'From the division of the Roman Empire into east and west in AD 395 until the fifteenth-century conquest of Greece by the Ottoman Turks, Greece shared the fortunes and vicissitudes of the Byzantine empire.'"

Orno took the book from his bag and opened it. "Darn, Marshall, that's word for word."

Phoebe stood and came over next to Orno. "Try this," she said, flipping through the pages. "Page ninety-two."

"Oh, come on, I can't do that."

"Try it."

"What's it start with?"

Phoebe held the book up. "'These colonies had a great influence on the history of the Greek mainland—'"

"'—where the city-states were developing in quarrelsome freedom,'" said Marshall.

"Was he right?" said Orno.

She was staring at Marshall.

"Well, did he get it right?"

"Exactly," she said. "My Lord, that's rather amazing."

"No wonder you don't wake up for class."

Marshall lifted a bottle of schnapps from the mattress and took a drink. "It's a gift," he said, "that's all. Something I've been given. But a lot of the Emersons can do it. It's not that big a deal in my family. Not *all* the Emersons can do it, I guess. My mother and my sister can't. But my father and I can, and my father's father could, too. He was a civil rights attorney. He used to argue before the Supreme Court and cite the exact holdings on any case in American or British history. In that profession it's a useful gift, but in other ways it's a hindrance."

"Some hindrance," said Orno.

"One of my uncles can do it, too. My father's brother, who was one of JFK's close advisers, but he has Asperger's Syndrome, which is a kind of autism. His field was the space program. He saw Kennedy every month to bring him up to date, but he had to wash his hands every time he touched somebody. It's weird."

"You don't do that, do you?" said Phoebe.

Marshall looked at her. "So far, nothing like that." He smiled.

"So how's it a hindrance?" said Orno.

"I remember too much of my life."

"What's wrong with that?" said Phoebe.

"I don't think I'd be able to explain."

"That's how you knew my name the first day," said Orno. "Isn't it?"

"I guess that's right."

"You don't have to open a book for the test tomorrow, either. Do you?"

"Not really," he said, "except if you mean that yes, I had to read it at one point." He took another drink. "But I've already finished it."

Phoebe eyed him. "When did you read it, Marshall?"

"What do you mean?"

"I mean, how long ago did you read Professor Scott's book?"

"Why do you ask?"

"I believe I know the answer," she said.

"I think I read it in grade school, actually. I think it was on my parents' shelf."

"That's what I thought."

"I think I'll go home," said Orno. "I think I'll go right back to Missouri. I'll just go to my room now and pack."

"I'll pack, too," said Phoebe. "I'll catch the eleven o'clock to Hartford."

"That's why I didn't tell you," said Marshall. "The thing is, if you could do it yourself you wouldn't be so impressed. We're amazed at a dog's sense of smell, but the dog isn't."

"Yeah, but all the dogs can do it," said Orno. "You're not going to have to study at all the whole time you're in college, are you?"

"He's right, isn't he?" said Phoebe.

They both looked at him.

A week later, when the midterms were graded, Orno went with Marshall to pick them up. Orno had a B−, an eighty-one, which stung him, and Marshall had a perfect score, an A+ circled on the front of his blue exam book. Professor Menemee Scott was in the office when they came by and he gestured to Marshall through the half-open door. "Just like the old man, I see, eh, Mr. Emerson?"

"Yes, sir," said Marshall, and on the walk home he dropped the test into a trash can.

———

Marshall loved buildings. Whenever he could, he convinced Orno to walk with him, the two of them quiet as they meandered, sometimes all the way to midtown, an entire loop around the New York Central building or the Chrysler Building, looking up; sometimes they went just a few blocks from school, east to St. John the Divine with its bays unfinished after a hundred years, or west to Grant's Tomb, where Marshall told him the history of the satrap Mausolus and the crypt in Halicarnassus. The short Doric columns cast angled shadows where he liked to stand gazing at the cupola, cut in half by sunlight; or south on West End Avenue, then east to the Pythian Temple on Seventieth Street, with its strange seated row of pharaohs. Sometimes he liked to walk a few blocks slowly, other times they strode together for hours, covering huge distances, all the way down to Wall Street once on a Saturday, then all the way back. Orno had two hours without classes on Wednesday afternoons and three on Thursday mornings, the only day Marshall woke early. They would walk together down to Riverside Drive, where Marshall told him the history of the Dutch colonizers and the city then that was no longer: New Orange by name and not New York, a stately camp on a river.

———

For Thanksgiving, they went to Marshall's family's house on the East Side, the morning brilliant as they walked all the way down from Columbia, crossing Central Park at West Seventy-ninth Street, where the trees had turned but not yet dropped their leaves. In his hand Orno carried a bouquet of lilies for Mrs. Pelham and a bottle of scotch for Professor Emerson. He was filled with a sense of friendship. Near noon they came out onto the East Side, where Fifth Avenue flowed with taxicabs honking their horns and the sidewalk bustled with walkers in their winter coats; it was like stepping from a forest into the bright shining center of the world. The stone buildings gleamed. The mantels and granite window wells cast upward a great sheet of light.

Marshall wore a black shirt beneath his black wool overcoat, but Orno wore a jacket and tie, as all his family did for holidays; no doubt Mrs. Pelham would appreciate the acknowledgment. Their house turned out to be a brownstone on Sixty-third and Lexington, the near corner in a row of brownstones of the same size but differing exquisitely in the details of their architecture, in their roof lines and friezes and stone staircases that ran up to mid-landings and wrought-iron newels and railings. They entered through the service door, set a couple of feet below the street; inside was a narrow basement hallway and quarters for servants now filled with a washing machine and an ironing board and an old upholstered armchair; from it rose an elderly black woman whom Marshall embraced and then held in his arms as Orno waited behind them.

Then without any more conversation Marshall released her and set out down the hall again. She was Olivia, the housekeeper who had raised him, he said over his shoulder; she still stayed in the downstairs apartment, though she had long ago stopped working in the house. Orno followed, trying to act at ease. In Cook's Grange he'd occasionally heard of using a cleaning woman after a party, but other than this people cleaned their own houses and they certainly raised their own children. Marshall was too big for the narrow hallway. He seemed to have led a complicated life.

The walls of the staircase to the main house were hung with frames that he stopped to admire as they climbed, partly because his own father for safety reasons had always forbidden brooms or shovels or clutter of any sort along their stairs in Missouri; here, on either side, hung dozens of small drawings, exotic carved figures of black wood, Lucite boxes containing tiny sea animals mounted on cork. He wanted to study them, but Marshall stood waiting at the top. Upstairs they had to step among piles of books to make their way to the kitchen, and even there he found shelves stacked heavily with plants and art books and at the far end of the room underneath the window a carved, primitive table that looked like the whole trunk of an ebony tree. A young woman was standing in the light of the window; she crossed the room to embrace

Marshall, stepping into and then out of the shaft of sunlight. Marshall said, "Simone, my baby sister."

At dinner everyone was intent on talking to him. Marshall seemed to have told his family nothing of his life at Columbia, and Orno kept looking over at him to see whether it was all right to tell Professor Emerson, who looked like Marshall in the same strong line of his brow, about what classes Marshall was taking, or Mrs. Pelham—Orno remembered to call her this—about the other students who passed the time with them at night in Marshall's room. Simone was at the far end of the table and she laughed now and then at what was said, but she was not quick to speak herself. When Marshall spoke, though, he seemed to speak to her.

"So you're taking Winthrop Menemee Scott's course, are you?" said Professor Emerson to Marshall after Orno had mentioned it.

Marshall nodded.

Professor Emerson put down his fork.

"Now take it easy, Walter," said Mrs. Pelham.

"That man is a grifter and a fraud," said Professor Emerson. He clasped his hands together on the table.

"Walter, leave it alone."

"The man's name is Irving Greenstein," he said. He turned to Orno. "Did you know that? His name isn't any Winthrop Menemee Scott. He's a—he's a Jew from Queens, he's the son of a hat salesman."

"Daddy," said Simone, "why do you keep doing that?"

"I like the class," said Marshall, spooning cranberries onto his plate. "I like to sit up front with Orno."

Orno looked at him.

"Stop it, you two," said Simone. "Please? Marshall can take whatever class he wants."

Professor Emerson picked up his fork and took a bite of the turkey. Nobody spoke, and then suddenly the cloud that had been over the table passed. He reached for the potatoes.

Finally, Orno said, "I was wondering if you'd show me something, Professor Emerson. Marshall says you can all do what he does, the memory trick."

"Not all of us," said Simone.

"Almost all of you, I guess."

"So Marshall showed you? He doesn't usually show people," said Mrs. Pelham. "He must like you."

"Don't know if I was the one he was showing it to," said Orno. Marshall glanced at him. "They forced it out of me," he said.

"Can you do it, too, Professor Emerson?"

"Oh, it's nothing." He coughed. "Nothing, young man."

"Oh, show him, Walter," said Mrs. Pelham.

Professor Emerson seemed to be composing himself. "Fair enough," he said. "Go get out—get out a book from the shelf."

"Which shelf?"

"Any one," said Simone. "That's the point."

Orno rose from the table and retrieved a volume from a set on the wall of the dining room, a novel called *Josephine's Way*, an old hardback with gilded edges.

"Ah," said Professor Emerson. "Old Josephine. Now, you might as well learn something from this, Orno. This is called eidetic"— he coughed—"eidetic memory, which is what your pal Marshall and I are fortunate enough to possess. As is my brother and as was my father. And some say that Ralph Waldo Emerson had it, too, though he's only a distant relation."

"Ralph Waldo Emerson was your relative?" said Orno.

"Apparently," said Professor Emerson. "We descend from the brother of his father, William Emerson, a family of clergymen." He coughed again. "Now, eidetic memory is to be distinguished, to be distinguished from what's thought of—"

"Come on, Daddy," said Simone. "Just show him."

"All right, then. Where shall we start? At the beginning, say?"

Orno opened to the first page. Marshall stood and went into the kitchen, where Orno heard him rummaging in the cabinets as Professor Emerson began reciting the opening of the novel, every word correct, adding theatrical twists to the sentences and flourishing his hands in the air whenever the prose was overdone. He ended by asking Orno if there was still a stray mark on the page, a black fleck of printer's ink near the signature binding above the title heading.

"Indeed there is," said Orno.

"It looks like a goose," called Marshall from the kitchen. "If you stare at it. Heading away from you with its wings out."

Professor Emerson closed his eyes for a moment. "Indeed it does," he said.

For the rest of dinner Orno was shy to speak, though the Emerson-Pelhams still prodded him with questions about Marshall's life at school, and though he still answered them as carefully as he could, glancing at Marshall for direction, steering his stories away from what really went on in his room, the dope and late nights and pillows spread along the floor. Marshall had come back from the kitchen with a tall glass and he sipped it as Orno told his parents a mild version of their lives together at college.

Suddenly Simone said, "All you're doing is asking him about Marshall. I'm sure he'd rather talk about other things, such as his own life, for one. Please excuse us, Orno."

"That's okay," said Orno. "Marshall's fun to talk about, aren't you?"

"Of course he is," said Mrs. Pelham, "but Simone's right. We can be like that sometimes, although it's only because Marshall won't tell us anything himself. He wouldn't tell us himself if he won the Nobel Prize."

"Well," said Marshall, "I haven't."

"But you'll tell us if you do?" said his mother.

"I promise."

"Well then, Orno," said Professor Emerson, "I understand you're from Missouri."

"Yes, sir."

"Marshall says your family knows the Vanderbilts."

"Marshall says what?"

"I said he knew someone named Helen Vanderbilt," said Marshall.

"Oh, Helen Vanderbilt," said Orno. "She used to live in New York City. I guess I must have told you about that. She's a friend of my uncle's. She was the one who encouraged me to apply to Columbia."

"I see," said Professor Emerson. "Well then, what is St. Louis like? I was there during the—during the war for a time. Damn," he said, touching his throat. "I believe I'm developing a stutter."

"Don't be silly," said Mrs. Pelham.

"Anyway," he said. "I remember St. Louis. A broad city, expansive, no high-rises to dilute the sunlight. Dusty air, though. I remember the dusty air. It used to cling to everything, cover everything." He cleared his throat. "Does my voice sound funny to anyone?"

"It sounds fine, Daddy," said Simone.

"I've actually never been to St. Louis," said Orno.

"Orno's not much of a traveler," Marshall said into his glass.

"Well then," said Professor Emerson. He coughed.

"Come on, everyone," said Simone, "that's not all we can come up with to say, is it?

Orno looked down.

"What classes are you taking, Orno?" said Mrs. Pelham.

He told them, and then when she asked what he planned to major in he discussed that too, telling them first that his father thought medicine was a noble and reliable profession, but not going further, about his uncle Clarence or the law, because he could tell that Professor Emerson wasn't interested; he was pinching the skin on his own neck. Mrs. Pelham asked him about Cook's Grange and he was even more brief about that. Only Simone seemed to be listening, really, nodding her head as he spoke; when she looked at him now, he saw that her eyes were like Marshall's, a deep lower rim and the trace of a distant, Asiatic fold.

As soon as the meal was done, Marshall told his parents they were due back at the dormitory for a party, and to Orno's surprise the whole family disappeared into different parts of the house while the dishes were still out on the table. Mrs. Pelham said she had some letters to write and climbed the stairs; Marshall told Orno he needed to collect some things before they could go back to school, then left him in the dining room and disappeared toward the rear of the house; Simone smiled at him, then went into the kitchen with a few of the dishes in her hands. Orno was left alone in the dining room with Professor Emerson, unable to think of what to say. In Cook's Grange his sister cooked and it was his own job to clean up: he rose and began gathering plates. Professor Emerson sat watching him for a moment; then, without speaking, he too rose and left.

In the kitchen Simone had filled the sink with soap and was scrubbing pots. "You shouldn't do that," she said without turning around. "You're a guest."

"Not at all."

"It's the servants' day off."

Orno went back out to the dining room.

"I was just kidding," she said when he returned, not looking back at him but nodding toward the wall. "They're just pretending they're used to servants."

"You never know."

She rolled up the sleeves of her blouse and tucked her hair under her collar, which made her look older. "Marshall was raised in a barn," she said.

"Where I'm from that's a compliment."

She turned around. "Oops. Sorry. Is it really?"

"No." He went to the bookshelf and examined its rows of expensive travel books, one on Istanbul. He pulled it out and touched the lacquered photograph on the cover: he recognized the Haghia Sophia.

"I don't think any of us have even been *near* a barn," she said. "That's why you're so exotic."

"That's why I'm so *what?*"

"Exotic."

He laughed. "*I'm* exotic?"

"Yes. A tiny bit."

He opened the book to a picture of the Egyptian market called Misir Çarşisi, which Marshall had once described for him: the spices from all corners of the globe, the teeming domed chambers. He fingered the smooth page. "Did you go with them?" he asked.

"Where?"

He pointed. "Here."

She looked at him.

"To Istanbul," he said.

She turned back to the sink. "No," she answered. "I stayed right here, doing the dishes."

He put the book back, then made several trips out to the table, returning to scrape the bones into the trash and then arrange the china behind her into stacks of cups, saucers, and plates. He'd erred, he realized, by bringing it up: she seemed suddenly chilled. But he wondered why she hadn't gone along; perhaps she'd been too young. Each time he came in with his hands full he wanted to say something funny, or something that truly *was* exotic; but even the kitchen, with its odd-colored crockery and hanging paraphernalia, robbed him of ease; she was working intently at the sink and he was aware of overstepping. "That's it," he said finally. "Table's done."

"You were sweet to help out."

"Learned it in the barn."

"I didn't insult you did I? I didn't mean to."

"Not in the least. You flattered me. I thought I might have insulted *you*."

She turned around and leaned against the sink. "Marshall talks about you a lot," she said.

"Well, Marshall's great."

She raised her eyebrows. "I think so too," she said. "But don't be too impressed with him, either."

"How do you mean that?"

"Oh, you seem sweet, that's all. Not everybody around here is."

"What do you mean?"

"I apologize for what my father said about Professor Menemee Scott."

"You don't have to. It didn't bother me. Your father's amazing."

"My father works at being amazing."

"I think he succeeds, don't you?"

Just then, before Orno had heard any footsteps, Marshall burst through the swinging door into the kitchen. "I suppose my sister's giving you the lowdown," he said. He was wearing a velvet smoking jacket Orno didn't recognize.

"At least Orno helps out," she answered. "Maybe he could teach you some of that. Maybe you should consider a little independent study."

"Orno's studying too much already," said Marshall. He leaned forward and kissed her on the cheek.

"You would be the one studying, Marshall," said Simone.

"I'll consider it."

Orno wanted to talk more to her but Marshall pulled him toward the door. Then they were in the hallway and all he could do was call out his thank-you to Mrs. Pelham before Marshall grabbed both their coats and led him out into the cold evening. He flagged a cab and when they arrived back at Columbia paid the driver from a roll of bills unfurled from the pocket of the jacket.

There were parties that night, but Orno stayed in. It was his first Thanksgiving away from home, and instead of going out he wrote Mrs. Pelham a thank-you note and then a letter to his sister at Clarkson, telling her story after story of his time in New York. He closed by writing, *and they think I'm exotic. Happy Thanksgiving to you.* He was breathless as he sat at the Masonite desk by his window, overwhelmed with the sense of a tremendous, brilliant world through the glass that none of the Tarchers had ever seen. The whole thing was stupendous to him—the Emerson family, about whom he was already composing in his head a heated, braggardly letter to his parents; the polished stone buildings of Manhattan; the never-ending thrum of buses and taxis outside, all the way through till the morning; the freshmen in black trousers and black shirts; Marshall's stereo speakers, so light they could have been hollow inside. And they *were* hollow actually, or nearly so, Orno discovered later that night, when Marshall used his roach clip to pry the cover off one of them and hide his new roll of bills there. They had just smoked half a joint and Orno was waiting for some movement inside of him. He didn't ask where the money was from. Marshall was affectionate when he was high, and he chatted and laughed as he worked the bills into a notch in the narrow cabinet. With the grill removed the speaker was nothing but a black plastic sheet with a round concavity in the middle; Orno stared at it with detached fascination, a rubberish, indented diaphragm

whose simple vibration produced the stupendous screaming gui-
tar solos and the low pounding beat of the bass drum that he felt
in his bed every night downstairs, a rubber hammer tapping the
floor as he drifted off to sleep, the high-hat crashing on the off-
beat like shattering glass.

That winter Marshall gradually disappeared from Orno's life. The cold settled in and the teeming walkers vanished from the streets; people wrapped themselves tight and darted from the buildings to the subway banisters, scarves flapping; steam billowed from the manholes as though underground the city were burning. It was a cold winter, everyone said, but Orno kept walking. It was nothing like Missouri: a salt dampness to the air but not the deadly freeze, the wind-rounded, iced earth he'd known back home. Now much of the time he walked alone. Routes he knew from his days with Marshall—streets that took him away from Morningside Heights or Harlem, buildings whose histories he recited aloud, thinking of his friend.

Marshall in the meantime had begun seeing Phoebe Lyall: Orno first noticed her in his room, then he saw them walking through the quadrangle together or sitting on the campus steps beside the statue of Alma Mater, never among the knots of students who had their places there as well; they sat off by themselves, leaning close. After a while, whenever Orno passed her, her face took on a brooding look. When they spoke, she gave off an expectant, charged air; but something between them missed, rupturing the expectancy; he found himself embarrassed—he didn't know why; and then, by the descent of winter, with the sun barely cresting the unbroken gray above the roofs of the prewar apartments, Marshall fell right out of his life.

He wasn't there in his room anymore when Orno returned from the library; or sometimes he *was* there but the door was locked. Orno liked Phoebe Lyall, but now he resented her, and then he chided himself; his embarrassment around her worsened; it was good for him to spend time alone and he resolved to attack his studies more diligently. Sometimes he had to pass Marshall in the hall, too, and now and then this was awkward. It was a knife blow. Orno didn't really have other friends in the dormitory, and by that time there were groups already and he didn't find himself among one. People liked him—they always had; but he'd grown used to spending his day with his friend. Christmas came and he was excited to go home.

His grades were good—he did little but study now—and on a bitter cold morning in Cook's Grange a week before Christmas he showed his first-semester's transcript to his parents; they looked out at a wet snow that had covered the land the night before and settled thickly over the maple trees. He was glum. He wanted to tell them of his astonishing adventures in New York City, but he could only show them a report card. A fierce wind had come up in the morning and massed the snow into drifts.

"Marshall is dating J. P. Morgan's great-great-granddaughter," he said.

His mother was mixing bread dough in a bowl and she paused a moment. "A nice girl?"

"Don't think it matters."

His father laughed, but his mother looked up.

"Sorry," he said. "She's nice enough."

"That must be a trial for her, when people find out."

"Yeah, you're right, but I think Marshall likes people to know about it."

"That's unkind."

"I don't know. He comes from this amazing family. They're all either brilliant or have traveled everywhere in the world. There's letters on his wall from John F. Kennedy and Lyndon Johnson. His mother talks on the phone with Margaret Mead. They're friends with writers and artists, and I just kind of got the idea that she was part of it. That it was part of what he liked in her."

He went to the window and looked out; his father probably hadn't read a book in five years and his mother had carried an Instamatic over her shoulder everywhere she went in Manhattan. Below him, the acreage sloped down from the house to the frozen creek bed in the distance. It wasn't beautiful, but he tried to imagine Marshall seeing it for the first time: the wind that had blown the snow into ice, then blown waves into the ice: a still river. Marshall would have noticed that; it wasn't something you saw in Manhattan. He tried to imagine what he would have said to Marshall about his parents. It was strange: he was embarrassed for them.

Did that mean he was embarrassed for himself? He turned and without saying anything went out into the field. He didn't have a coat on and you didn't venture far in weather like this even in the daytime, but he couldn't stand being in that room. He walked into the frosted pasture, his hands pulled up into his sleeves, his arms crossed against his chest. It was these easterners who had mistreated him; he knew that perfectly well—they had brought him close and then shunned him. But it was exactly their view he found himself harboring against his own parents. They sat inside the kitchen a hundred yards up the slope from him, his father smoking his pipe and no doubt still looking at his report card so he could tell his brother Clarence about it on the telephone, grade by grade; his mother kneading bread dough in a bowl her own mother had made from clay.

When he came back in, his father said, "It's what they call the East Coast establishment, Orno."

"I can only imagine what they think of *us*, then," he answered.

"And what might that be?" said his father.

"You know," he said—"hicks."

His mother stiffened, but his father lit his pipe and laughed. "They're the ones who don't know how to drive a car," he said. He blew out the smoke. "And remember, you can work harder than they can."

———

Clara came home from Clarkson for the end of the vacation, and Orno, thankful for the distraction, spent his last days with her. After dessert each night the two of them drove out to the House of Pancakes on the interstate and sat drinking coffee in a window booth, watching the truckers and farmers eat late-day dinners. Clara was a steady girl, had always been sure of her desires— more like their father in that way, though she looked just like their mother, a frail turn to her bones but a hardy, not unpretty face. She always loved a story. Now she listened to him the way nobody else in the world did, devouring what he told her about New York City while her eyes alternately squinted and widened across the table. When he asked her if she ever wanted to move east, though, she didn't hesitate but shook her head and said, "It's not for me." That was the sureness; it was irritating in a way, not that she felt it but that he himself didn't. He said, "Well, *I* might, you know." She looked back at him solemnly and he felt mean for saying it, not sure whether he'd meant it or simply wanted to shock her. Driving back home later on the still roads that led into Cook's Grange, he gazed ahead into the long tracks of salted freeze and felt pangs for all of them, for his sister next to him and his father and mother out here in land that never broke the eye's gaze; above them the sky was black and the plowed snow beyond the paint of his head-lights was blacker still. In a few days he was returning to Manhattan. He couldn't have called the feeling pity; not loss either, and not nostalgia; it was a sorrow, really, a sorrow of familiarity; there was no basis for it other than that, he understood, and its appetite scared him. As he drove in the familiar night, it seemed to be coming right in through the vents of the car, undiluted by the heat, a cold earthen smell: prairie in winter, all the years of his life.

I I I

One night in February Marshall phoned and told Orno to come to an address on Fifth Avenue. It was late, Orno hadn't spoken to him in two months, and the glum deep chill of late winter had finally arrived, blowing in from the north, covering the curbs in dark ice and freezing newspapers to the sidewalks. He was studying chemistry, flash cards of the elements whose properties he was trying to learn, halogens and noble gases, concepts the professor moved past rapidly, but that he was keeping up with now, given his studious days and nights. He had an exam at the end of the week. He looked out the window. Crystals of frost clouded the glass, but there was a glee in Marshall's voice that he found himself drawn to. "It's awfully cold," he said. "I'll come in the morning."

"Come now. Take a cab. I'll pay."

"Where are you?"

"You'll want to see it."

"What is it?"

"Just come, O."

He picked up a flash card. "What's the atomic weight of fluorine, Marshall?"

"Will you come if I tell you?"

"No."

"It's 18.998."

Orno turned over the card, picked up another. "What about selenium?"

"78.996."

"I'll think about it then," Orno said. "Got a lot of work to do."

"How unusual."

"Got exams coming up, Marshall. Some of us have to study for them."

"We'll study over here."

"Don't count on me."

"I have to count on you, O."

He stayed at his books, the frosty air creeping in the edges of the window. Marshall had been insistent. Insistent and unrepentant, and it occurred to Orno that he had only imagined the distance between them. He rubbed the glass and looked out at the skinny trees: couples still walked on the paths. The street, though drab, still had life: cabs, hawkers, bums. After a time he cleared his desk and sat there watching his bit of New York, above it the stolid Pantheonic dome of Low Library.

He took the subway finally, shivering as he crossed beneath Broadway in the howling tunnel, changing trains in the maze of Times Square and Grand Central and then walking the last few blocks to Fifth Avenue from Lexington with his head pulled down into his collar. He could never resist Marshall. A neighborhood of gray stone edifices and green awnings on brass rails; jewelry stores at street level with windows of half-inch glass; doormen inside atriums. Across the street was the park. It was after midnight, but he passed a Mexican doorman walking two Irish wolfhounds as tall as his coat pocket. The wolfhounds bounded at him and he took off his glove and gave them his hand, which they bumped with their skeletal snouts while the doorman looked down at the edge of the sidewalk. He was being treated like a rich man. He made a comment about the cold, but the doorman kept his eyes on the curb. He put his glove back on. The address Marshall had given him was in the Seventies, and when he set off again he realized it had to be Phoebe Lyall's house: he wondered why Marshall hadn't just said so.

He wished he'd worn nicer shoes. Now, as far as he could see, there was no one else on the street, a sight he'd noticed only a few times since Cook's Grange. The wind here came unhindered from the west, and the cold made him lengthen his stride. A couple of cabs waited at a red light, but otherwise New York was quiet, a sleeping city on a park. At Seventy-second he found the address, granite columns at street level and doors that reached to the second story. He paused in front and checked the number and suddenly the door opened. It startled him, but he recovered and went inside, pulling off his gloves in the doorway and stamping his feet the way people did back home as part of greeting. The doorman eyed him, half-smiling and deferential, but still wary, waiting for him to shake out his hair and pocket his gloves. Orno introduced himself and the doorman touched a button and said into an intercom, "Mr. Tarcher for you." Then he opened the elevator door and pushed a button. Orno went up, looking at his plain face in the mirror, wishing it otherwise. He pulled off his coat and after a moment the door opened and he walked into the living room of an apartment that looked like the Metropolitan Museum of Art. "Oops," he said. "What happened to the hallway?"

"Can't charge rent for a hallway," said Marshall. He sat barefoot on a sofa next to Phoebe, a champagne glass in his hand. On the walls hung oil paintings the size of pool tables. Suddenly Marshall and Phoebe burst out laughing.

"Sorry I'm so late," Orno said. "Hi, Phoebe."

"Hi, Orno."

"Nice walk?" said Marshall.

"Took the subway."

"What did I tell you?" They laughed again.

"Good for you, Orno," said Phoebe. She reached for the glass in Marshall's hand. "I hope Miller didn't give you a difficult time downstairs."

"Miller's the doorman?"

"Miller's the spy," said Marshall.

"Whose spy?" Phoebe said.

"Your father's."

She laughed. "Wouldn't that be a thought!"

"He was very nice," Orno said.

"He must be ill then," said Marshall.

"Just a good judge of character," said Phoebe.

"I suppose he has to be." Marshall smiled. "Wonderful you could make it, O."

Orno still held his coat in his hands. "So am I. Is this your house, Phoebe?"

"It's my parents' house."

"It's ours for the night," Marshall said, rising from the couch. "Come look at this."

"Now, don't." Phoebe started to get up but her heel caught in the rug and her shoe fell off. "Damn." She smiled at Orno. "We shouldn't be doing this."

"Maybe I should go."

"No, no," she said, waving at him as she fiddled with her shoe strap. "I didn't mean it like that. It's fine. Maybe you'll be a good influence."

"Look here," Marshall called from the next room. He had his hand against the stonework of the hallway and when he reached with his foot and touched the baseboard a hidden door swung away in front of him into the wall. It was dimly lit inside, but Orno saw pale blue light coming up from below. "The dungeon," Marshall said. He wiggled his fingers like a snake charmer. "We're going to put you in it."

"For what?"

"For studying too much."

"Come on, Marshall," said Phoebe. "Close that door."

"Oh, couldn't I show him? He's our best friend."

"Do what you want, then."

"Come here, O."

"That's all right. We shouldn't be poking around your parents' house."

"Oh, it's fine, Orno," said Phoebe. "See how polite he is, Marshall? Maybe he could teach you some of that."

"Uninquisitive is what he is, if you ask me," said Marshall. He was making faces back at them that Phoebe couldn't see.

Phoebe turned to him, looking expectant again. Orno really wanted to go with Marshall, but it seemed rude. "Curiosity killed the cat," he called.

"Well-heeled is what he is," Phoebe called back. "Go ahead," she said to Orno. "It's just a pool. My father had it put in. He has a ruptured disc so he needs to swim."

"I'm sorry."

"Don't be," Marshall called up from inside the door. "As far as I know, curiosity never killed any cats."

"You won't be sorry when you see the pool," Phoebe said. She covered her mouth. "Oh that was pretty indiscreet wasn't it? See? Marshall's got me drunk."

"I'm not much of a swimmer," said Orno.

He stood there unsure of what else to say. Phoebe leaned down and adjusted her shoe again. What he wanted was to go ahead and see the pool. A secret door! The blue light shimmered on the ceiling. Marshall put his head back through and when Phoebe waved Orno on he finally followed, down a short flight to the water that sat in a dark tile bed in a greenhouse: windows at the end gave onto a snow-covered outdoor atrium; he could see prehistoric ferns the size of garage doors, their fronds bouncing pendulously in the mist. Marshall stood grinning at the far end, his foot in the water. He lifted his glass. "Not bad, is it?"

"Jeez."

"Phoebe was nervous about it. I told her you were used to this kind of thing."

"Right. Like our secret pool at home, except for the dark bottom. Gets too hot for that in Missouri."

"That's what I told her."

"So, I haven't seen you in a while, Marshall. Is this where you've been?"

"More or less. It's amazing. They have a place in Litchfield with thoroughbreds. I played polo and fell off a horse." He laughed and took a drink of champagne. "Her father doesn't like me."

"You get hurt?"

"No broken bones, if that's what you mean. Luckily I couldn't get the damn thing to go faster than a walk."

"How's everything else?"

"Good. Phoebe's in love with me, I think."

"That's what I call good luck, M."

Marshall raised the glass. "To good luck then," he said, sipping.

"Are you in love with *her*?"

"When we're drunk I am."

Orno laughed. "And otherwise?"

"I don't know what it means."

"Come on."

"I *don't*. I like her. I think she's beautiful. And she seems to think well enough of me."

"All right," Orno said. "Things are going well, though?"

"It's a little embarrassing how well." He gestured toward the pool.

"Guess I'm not going to be studying tonight."

"We can go in the water if you want. There's a sauna behind that wall, and a Jacuzzi."

"Does Phoebe have any friends for me?"

"Come here," Marshall said. He stepped to the back wall of the greenhouse, where the windows looked onto a courtyard. "Look at that," he said. "The old man had it built this way. He's an old bastard, but he loves the same things I do." He pointed up to where a gap in the cornice let through the view of Central Park and across the dark river of treetops the lighted pinnacles of the Upper West Side. "How can you not love this?" he said. "Look at that. Look at those buildings. The Dakota. The San Remo. The Majestic. Gangsters lived in the Majestic. Meyer Lansky and Lucky Luciano." He took a drink. "They called the Dakota the Dakota because people said it might as well have been in the Dakotas. That's how far uptown they thought it was. Now look at it. Look at how they built things in those days." He pointed into the clear black night. "In Istanbul, there's a huge water cistern below the city, filled with columns and arches that nobody ever sees. It's called Yerebatan

Saray, the Sunken Palace. It was hidden for a thousand years until someone realized that the peasants caught fish through holes in their cellar floors. Isn't that exquisite?"

"It is," said Orno.

"That human beings would build such monuments. Like climbing Everest, if you ask me. The human urge to build. Sublime. To be close to God."

"I can understand that. It being close to God."

"It's the one thing the old bastard and I have in common," Marshall said. He came away from the window. "Otherwise he can't stand me."

"So you've been spending a lot of time here?"

"Only when her father's gone. They're coming back tomorrow."

"Why doesn't he like you?"

"Why? Because he's a villain. A villain can spot another villain." Orno laughed.

"It's the truth." Marshall walked back across the deck and stood next to the pool with his back to Orno. He shifted his pants and in a moment Orno heard him peeing into the water.

"Come on, Marshall!"

"This is from me," he said to the ceiling. "Lyall, you old bastard!"

"Phoebe's right outside."

The stream continued. Marshall turned around grinning. "Don't worry," he said. "It's all very polite around here." He had been pouring out his glass of champagne. "Besides, I wouldn't waste this if I didn't know there were a hundred bottles downstairs."

A moment later Phoebe came into the room; she turned down the lights and they went swimming. She wore a bathing suit, but Marshall and Orno skinny-dipped. Orno watched her in the water—there was a seriousness to her, half-derailed by the alcohol, that made her suddenly seem unhappy to him. She dove in at one end and started a lap in a well-taught stroke, trying to resist Marshall, who bumped her from below. She stopped and wrapped her legs around him, then thought better of it and kicked back into her stroke; Orno crouched in the shallow end with his eyes at the waterline, watching them. He was cuttingly aware of being an outsider looking in on Marshall, but it was also clear that Marshall was looking in on Phoebe. He wondered what Phoebe herself was feeling, what exactly was the expectancy he always seemed to feel around her. He also wondered if she really was in love with Marshall. Alone she continued her laps, while Marshall pulled himself off to the side and sat on the edge, watching. A servant opened a door and looked in, then closed it: a moment later a fan came on, pulling the mist into ducts on the ceiling. The door opened again and a stack of towels was laid on the deck. After Phoebe finished her laps they all took a sauna together and it was near dawn when Orno finally dressed to head back to the dorm. Phoebe offered to give him a bed but he declined: he wanted to go home. Marshall guessed the reason and laughed, but then he rode down with him in the elevator and in the lobby told him he was sorry he'd taken him away from his studies for so long. "You're my best friend, O," he said. "That's all. Let's do things together." Then he reached over and hugged Orno. When he stood again, Orno walked out into the frozen night, covered inside his coat with the warmth of the sauna that lasted several blocks into the cold, though not as far as the subway.

I V

Then Marshall drifted away again. After that night, Orno heard nothing from him, saw him only in the hallways of the dorm or in the low-ceilinged dining hall where the students waited in lines at the rows of steam servers and ate their meals in clusters at the long shellacked dining tables. At dinner, dozens of the tables were spread about the enormous room, so that almost never again did he find himself at the same one with his friend; all he knew of him now was the music he could still feel in his own room downstairs.

Orno signed up for the next history class in the Western Culture series, which brought him to the Enlightenment by the end of the winter. The crocus bulbs were coming up all across the campus, and New York suddenly took on a very surprising beauty to him, a chrome-colored shine he never thought he would see there: the streets gleamed; the long views down the avenues continually took him unawares, the great majestic corridors that narrowed in the distance as though all the structures there made by man, the colossal skyscrapers and shining granite department stores as bright as mirrors, were pointing toward the monumental buildings downtown, the great human feats of steel and engineering. He missed his walks with Marshall. The beauty of the city had entered him, but it was a beauty he still heard in the voice of his friend: San Remo; Majestic; Dakota. It was odd, carrying inside him someone else's amazement.

He didn't know which classes Marshall was taking and he never saw him in the history lectures anymore, though he heard that he was still auditing. He also heard that Marshall was routinely scoring the top grade on exams. One day a girl in their dormitory told him that Marshall was actually auditing courses all over campus and scoring brilliantly, but signing his tests with a different name. It was a strange story, but soon Orno heard it again from someone else. Nobody could tell him what name he was using. He looked for him on exam days, but on those mornings the class was divided between two rooms and he couldn't be sure whether Marshall was even there. The rumor was that he was taking physics and biology and political science courses, not even going to class, then throwing off the curve for everybody else by scoring perfect marks. According to the story, certain professors had begun adding questions just for him; but he answered these as well. Orno didn't quite believe it. Yet he couldn't stop thinking about it. Students were always exaggerating things, but he also knew that if Marshall wanted to do something like that he could probably come close; he imagined him chuckling to himself, tapping his fingers as he raced through the questions.

———

As the weather warmed he began to feel unmoored, on the verge of change. It was an uncertain feeling, a sense of his own diminishment before the driven commerce of humanity; walking south of the university now by himself, jostling among the throngs of Spanish-speaking street vendors, he felt himself without purpose, less gripped by his own destiny than the men selling colored soaps from bins or the old women pointing down at cheaply dyed tablecloths on the sidewalk. He knew he could be convinced by the merest look—imploring glances from anyone: children, old women, infirm men. So he walked with his eyes cast down, the only way he could defend himself.

His studies became his certainty. The time he passed in Butler Library now went by without the feeling of drift, and he began to spend all afternoon there, then all evening in the sciences library near a window that looked out over a light well. The cold through the glass kept him awake and there was no view to distract him from his work. For his physics class in the morning he arrived an hour early and read in the empty auditorium.

Soon he decided on engineering, and when he wrote home with the news his father approved. It was not medicine, but it was of use to society and commanded respect. With labor, he found he could maintain himself in the middle of the curve of the large classes, which filled the lecture halls and gave off a nervous air that his history and literature classes had lacked; the professor wrote in yellow on the black chalkboard and Orno struggled to understand each equation before the next one came up in the relentless argument of mathematical logic. Sometimes he panicked, but he learned to defeat panic with diligence.

With Marshall gone he preferred being alone to trying to mix with the groups of other students that had already formed friendships. He had always been easy by himself. In midtown anonymity he walked, gazing up at the skyscrapers. To him they were forgotten pieces of art: the weightless fretwork of the Chrysler Building a thousand feet above Lexington Avenue; the boasting spires of the Woolworth Building and the odd, saddened figure of Woolworth himself, cut in stone, counting dimes; the vertiginous lift he felt every time he rode to the top of the Empire State Building and paid to stand on the observation deck, the overpowering views filling him with fear not of falling but of flying upward. It was a strange obsession—he returned now and again through the semester as the light changed from dim winter to the limpid higher sun of spring, and each time he stood listening to the wind rushing through his legs he feared himself so inconsequential amid the looming steel and concrete that he imagined he might be picked up like a sycamore seed and carried aloft. Here was where he had decided on engineering—he considered architecture for a time, but as a profession it seemed too frail—and here he had returned over and over when he tired in the library that year, stowing his books and going underground to the number 1 train for the ride downtown to Forty-second Street. The train itself was a work of human genius, tunneled through rock; he thought of the pyramids. He thought of Marshall, gazing across the park at the glowing, distant Dakota. He imagined the lighted straits of the Bosporus, Europe on one shore and Asia on the other. Working ferociously, he struggled through his courses, staying near the middle.

———

Spring peaked early and inside him expectancy opened. A small transformation: on the street he now found himself buying wares from the vendors he used to avoid, the ones who somehow picked his face from the passing crowds. Who could say what it was? He bought a small rug, a watch. They could spot him in a crowd of dozens, his expression open in the way of a newcomer, his eyes willing. A bigger change was coming. He thought it was because his fear had passed. One morning he simply thought of New York as his own, a simple step, but one he hadn't known he would come to. He was in Morningside Heights, the streets washed from overnight mist and still cooler than the air. He'd been afraid of everything in New York, he realized, the whole time he'd been here, and now, suddenly, watching a dog nose hopefully among a row of galvanized metal flower containers, he realized he wasn't anymore.

One morning before his physics class he met a girl. Her name was Sofia and she'd arrived in the auditorium early and sat in the row below him. Somehow he spoke to her, leaning over the chair back: her reply was softened by an accent—swallowed sibilants that pierced him. She was Russian, the daughter of a physicist who had defected, her mother and sisters still in Leningrad. She was in engineering as well, one of a dozen girls in the classes of hundreds. All his fears had somehow been set aside. He asked her to come walking with him that evening.

Dear Clara—

Here I am back in the big city in springtime. I think if you ever came out here you'd change your mind about this place. How can I tell you what it's like? A new world, but more than that, a world I never knew existed. How can I describe stepping up out of the subway onto Lexington Avenue in a throng of walkers, every one of them bright and daring and reaching for the shining stars? The buildings are glittering canyons. They seem too bright to be true, like someone cleans the whole city every night, right up to the rooftops. I know that's probably not how you think of New York but it's how I see it.

Back home we never walk anywhere. You don't realize that until you come here. Where could we walk? Over to the Marjorrsons? Down to the creek?

I met a girl in class. She's very lovely and for some reason she seems to like me. We go on walks together, which is what I used to do with Marshall before he disappeared. (Has anything like that ever happened to you?) Sometimes I think I could fall in love with her, though we've only known each other a couple of weeks. Maybe it's New York. Maybe it's the spring. We walk for miles.

How is school for you? How are your own romances? How are Mom and Dad?

Love,
Orno

Dear Dad—

Work continues well here. I'm satisfied with the decision to take a try at engineering. I'm taking chemistry and physics, both of which are difficult but I am beginning to think they are not beyond me. I've found two spots in the library, one upstairs at Low where I can be nearly alone behind a row of stacks.

Engineering requires quite a few units to graduate and I am meeting with a counselor next week to plan out my years.

Spring is really here and the crocuses are coming up. Has the owl returned?

Love to Mom.
—Orno

———

Sofia was immediately devoted. She was even more rootless than he had been at the start in New York, the city utterly foreign to her; he showed her his own life, the toiling hours in the chilly downstairs of the science library, the subway rides, the respites at the observation deck of the Empire State Building, where he grew silent and she responded in exactly the same way, although he suspected she was thinking of different things. It was as though she hadn't had a life before he met her and now she had his; at restaurants she ordered whatever he did.

He was a virgin but she was not, and soon he wasn't either. His grades declined and he felt himself begin to drift again. In class now and then he came awake with a start. He hadn't been daydreaming, but he hadn't been paying energetic attention either. After he left her at night he still went to study, walking down Broadway to a twenty-four-hour grill where he read his course books, ate Danishes, and drank black coffee, getting up when he grew tired to circle the run-down block despite the warnings they were given about Morningside Heights. He recognized the locals now, and they didn't scare him. He was hungry all the time. It was one of her effects, along with a restlessness that brought him to take her all over Manhattan on the subway and then Brooklyn and Hoboken too. Sometimes he wondered if it was because he didn't know what to say to her—he hadn't known much trouble and she'd already known so much—and it was easier for the two of them to move than to stay still. He felt it most when he was alone with her in an elevator; there was nothing for them to look at. He would take hold of her and kiss her in order to hide his eyes. Her own were sorrowful, sorrowful when they walked hand in hand around the boisterous aviary in Central Park, sorrowful when they stood at the rail of the tourist ferry in New York harbor, sorrowful when they giggled together at the breathtaking peak of the Empire State Building, gazing out at night over what seemed to him the most exquisite city in the world. Her irises were dark and her lids hung at a Tatar's hooded slope. She wore a fur collar at her neck that ended in the tiny predatory mouth of a lynx; above it her own mouth, the small sharp tips of her teeth unsheathed when she tilted up her head to kiss him.

They made love every day, although he tried not to miss any classes for it, coming to her room at noon after his physics course and an hour at the library. She wore sheer black leggings and lace underwear that took away his breath and returned to him in dreams back in his own dormitory at night, staggeringly exotic. Thinking about her in class, his mouth grew dry. She had an electric grill in her room and cooked soups from vegetables bought on Broadway in the corner markets; they were simmering when he arrived with his books on his back. She kept a bottle of vodka on her windowsill. At the tops of her boots he could see black edges of lace.

———

Dear Orno—

Of course the owl has returned. I suspect there will be a good supply of field mice, as the snowpack was unusually deep this winter, and now with the warm spring the topsoil is soaked to bedrock.... Olaf Marjorrson has cleared another ten of willows and will plant roses as an experiment! Evidently there is a market.... The house needs new siding at the basement door. Flashing rusted clean through. I should have noticed but only your mother uses that door. Plan for next year is to use all the doors in the house.... Engineering is a great profession and has put us where we are on this earth. I applaud the decision.

—Dad

One rainy day in April he happened to pass through a different corridor of the physics building on his way to class, and up on the wall was a graph of scores for an exam; well above the mass of students was a single dot indicating someone who'd scored 100 percent. There were no names, however. He stood in the low hallway for a long time, looking at the circled blue point, wondering what it meant; he hadn't spoken to Marshall in weeks, but he couldn't help thinking that the mark really was his and—strangely—that he was doing it for him. There was no reason he should have thought this, but he did. It was a joke, he somehow realized, between the two of them, and alone in the dusky hall he let out a laugh.

Over Easter vacation he decided not to go home and instead took the train with Sofia down to Washington, DC, where they stayed in the apartment of some other Russians. There had been a pause on the line when he told his mother he wasn't coming back to Cook's Grange. He and Sofia wandered around Washington for five days, visiting the National Gallery, the Smithsonian, the Phillips Collection, and the Air and Space Museum, walking down to see the cherry blossoms before they were fully out, taking a bus back that drove by the Pentagon, where Sofia grew pensive looking out at the monumental walls. She didn't tell him until the day before they left that she had an appointment at the State Department. She had to spend the afternoon there and he felt a chill when she told him; she was lobbying to bring the rest of her family from Russia. It was understandable, of course, but she'd obviously planned the trip with that in mind and hadn't told him; he had thought it was just a vacation together and now he felt naive. Walking by himself down Pennsylvania Avenue trying to look at the buildings, he wondered whether she'd just been biding her time with him. Suddenly he was scared again. A year of his college career was gone and he didn't yet have a set of friends.

After they came back from Washington, though, the feeling vanished. They spent the last weeks of spring walking around New York the way they had before they'd left—riding the trains to Staten Island and City Island and Coney Island like tourists. And in a giddy way Orno felt like one again. It was his second time learning the city and he saw it now from his place of ease, Sofia next to him. At night especially, sitting arm in arm in a swaying subway car, the feeling that he'd first had on Pennsylvania Avenue would come back to him—that he and Sofia were only biding their time—but then he would turn to her and bury his face in the sweet black pelt of her hair.

V

n the autumn of his sophomore year he enrolled in European History. Again it was a large class, and again he found himself unsuited to the discursive discussion, sitting high in the creaking seats and looking out the dusty windows at the buildings. It reminded him of his freshman year with Marshall, the same slope of heads cascading below him in the auditorium, the same frightening devotion in everyone but himself.

He'd gone through a period when he felt wounded by Marshall. The feeling was remarkably strong, an unseemly emotion that he did his best to quell—but with Sofia in his life it had diminished, and then sometime between his first college summer, when he went back to Cook's Grange for two months and worked in his father's insurance office, and the fall of his sophomore year, when New York was clean again and shining and he woke up late afternoons with a breeze in the window and Sofia's dark hair on his shoulder, it slipped completely from his mind. She contained the world. They ate together, walked together, made love together in her single bed, pushed up against the wall below her window. Marshall had moved into an apartment in Morningside Heights,

Orno knew, but that was all he'd heard. His own studies were in limbo; he had slid down to the lower half of the engineering cohort and for the first time in his life he lacked the will to pull himself up.

After the first midterm in European History he waited a few days before picking up his test, and when he finally did he came in at night. The exam books lay in two boxes in front of the professor's door. The building was empty except for a guard, who stood behind a corner in the atrium. Orno had never done anything dishonest in his life. He leaned down quickly and sorted through the first box. Most of the marks were low—these were the students who never picked up their work—but then he looked through his own box—*M* through *Z*—and there, one below his own 83 amid the handful of ragged booklets was a test with a perfect score. Again he laughed out loud. He picked it up and slipped it under his coat. The name on it was Diogenes Mendelsohn, and that night, as he expected, the Columbia University operator told him that there was no student enrolled under such a name.

The next morning he returned and tacked up a note above the boxes:

M—
    I have your exam. Nice work by the way.

—O

———

Fall lasted late. The afternoons were still warm in October and the evenings fine enough to walk without a coat, the streets cleaned of their summer rot and not yet laced with cold. If he wasn't with Sofia now he was alone. One day, just after he'd come in from a differential equations exam on which he'd found himself half panicked and wandering from question to question as time ran out, the phone rang. Marshall said, "I need you."

"What's the matter? Where are you?"

"You need to come over here now." He gave an address on

Broadway, high up, half a mile north of school. He sounded strange; his voice was plaintive and at the same time uninvolved and when Orno tried to talk he was distracted by Marshall's hard breathing. Orno had his physics class in an hour, so before he set off uptown he put his books in his bag; then he left, mindful of where he walked even though it was two in the afternoon. Of course he'd been surprised, but as he made his way up toward 129th Street he reconsidered: perhaps he should have been cooler toward him. Where had he been for so long?

The address was missing a numeral and Orno walked the block twice to find it: up a flight of steps, a dented metal door with three locks set in a column, one at the bottom edge. He knocked. He knocked again. He went down to the street and looked for a window then came back up when he heard the bolts turning and a bar sliding along the floor. Marshall looked pale, nearly white. He was panting. "Nice place, isn't it?"

"Hi, M," said Orno. Inside, a narrow staircase went up too steeply.

"I don't live here. I left Phoebe. It's a friend of mine's."

"I wouldn't have mistaken it for Phoebe's."

Marshall didn't smile. "That's no longer."

"You were living with her?"

He took a few breaths. "I was. Not anymore." He put his head out and glanced up the street. "Obviously."

He started up the stairs, but halfway up he turned and fell, crumpling to the carpet. Orno just had time to bound up and catch him before Marshall went down backward. He tried to stand, but his knees buckled.

"I'm damn glad you're here—"

"What's going on? Are you sick?"

"I didn't mean to disappear, O. Phoebe had something about you."

"What's the matter with you?"

"Phoebe made me stay away. I think I can make it upstairs."

"Are you drunk? Tell me what's the matter."

"She didn't want us to be friends."

"I'm carrying you." He gripped Marshall under the shoulders

and hauled him up, one stair at a time, to a room with a mattress in the corner and a card table in the middle of the floor. Marshall's legs were dragging. Orno laid him on the mattress. "What the hell have you been drinking? Did you take something?"

"It's going to be all right. Good. Fine." His eyes were closing.

"I'm getting you some water." He shook him. "Come on, Marshall. Wake up."

"Call a doctor. Call a professor."

There were no ashtrays in the kitchen, no bottles in the refrigerator, nothing in the drawers. On the card table were two aspirin bottles. He looked inside. "What was in these?"

"Good work."

"Marshall, did you take something?" He shook the jars. "What did you take? Are you sick? Marshall, wake up and talk."

"Aspirin."

"What else?"

"Nothing."

There was no phone. Orno ran out and found one on the street, where he called an ambulance. Back upstairs, Marshall was breathing drowsily, long pauses between breaths. He didn't look drunk. Finally they heard the sirens.

"I knew you'd come, O."

"Of course I did. Keep talking."

"Phoebe Lyall had a smile, nearly knocked me out. But when I found her—" He took a panting breath.

"Keep going."

"When I found her, all around her—"

"Yes?"

"—a limerick."

"Go on. Come on, Marshall, what's next?" He sat him up against the wall and shook his shoulder. "What's after that?"

"A lime rickey." His head drooped.

"Tell me about Istanbul."

He shook him again.

"Where did you shop for food? Tell me about the Bit Pazar."

"They kicked me out. They tried to keep me out."

Suddenly the ambulance attendants were in the apartment. One was shaking Marshall and shouting in his ear; another put an IV into his arm. Orno gave them the two bottles of aspirin, told them it was probably some drug he'd taken, though he didn't know which; they looked around the apartment, opened all the drawers that Orno had already looked through; one of them went into the bathroom and took everything out of the medicine closet. He called something back to the other one, who was holding the IV bag over Marshall's head. They took him out strapped to a stretcher. Orno followed, sat in the back of the ambulance as it weaved through traffic. Marshall's head was rolling so that the attendant had to hold it down to the side as he spoke to Orno.

"Does he have a history of medical problems?"

"I don't know," Orno answered. "I don't think so."

"He's not sick?" He put the stethoscope on his chest and listened. He pumped up the blood-pressure cuff. "Does he take medicine?"

"I don't think so."

"What were you drinking?"

"I wasn't there."

The paramedic looked up. "How'd you find him, then?"

"He called me."

"Did he say he was drinking?"

"No."

"Drugs?"

"Yeah. Probably. He didn't say."

"Which ones?"

"I don't know. Dope, maybe. Marijuana. I mean, he used to. I don't know what he was doing lately. You're not going to tell anybody?"

"No."

"Truth is, I don't know what happened."

The man wrote something down. "I'm not a cop."

"I know. I just don't know what he did."

"Was he depressed?"

"I don't know. I haven't seen him in a while. He called me today and told me to come over. We're both students."

"What time was that?"

"What time was what?"

"When did he call you?"

"An hour ago."

"Are you sure?"

"Yeah, about."

"That's good."

"Why's that good?"

He didn't answer.

"He might be sick." Orno said. "I'm not sure. I know a girl who knows him. She could tell you. They just broke up."

"They just broke up?"

"Yeah."

"Has he ever tried to hurt himself?"

"Hurt himself?"

"Has he ever tried anything self-destructive? Overdosed? Anything like that?"

"No, nothing like that. I don't think so. He's always seemed fine. He's brilliant. He has a photographic memory."

"Let's hope he lives to remember this, then."

"I can call his girlfriend. I can call his parents, too. His father's a professor."

"You do that. Call the parents and call the girl too. Ask them everything I just asked you."

"I'm not sure I remember everything."

The doors opened: they were at Columbia-Presbyterian. Men were there pulling the stretcher out, its wheels snapping open.

"Is he okay?" Orno asked.

"I don't know."

Orno followed them into the lobby but then they were gone through another set of doors and a nurse stopped him. She pointed at a sign. Orno tried to go through, but she took his arm. She said something, pointed up again, and held him there.

"Come on, Marshall," he said, and watched him disappear through the tiny window. Then he understood that the nurse was asking him the same questions he had just been asked in the ambulance. She looked at him as though he should have known the answers.

He called Marshall's parents, but the line was busy; then he called the operator to find Phoebe Lyall's number, but it wasn't listed; he called the Emersons again, and it was still busy, so he called Sofia, who wasn't home. There was a line behind him now at the phone booth in the dirty waiting room, so he tried the operator again and asked her to break into the Emersons' line. Mrs. Pelham answered and told him she'd meet him in the hospital cafeteria; she was already leaving.

Orno made his way there, wandering the labyrinth of corridors, asking directions that took him down then up again on short, dark staircases and through the crowded hallways. All kinds of buildings seemed to have been joined together to make the hospital. Fearful sights everywhere he looked: white machines being wheeled, slit windows in the metal doors, figures in gowns pushing past. He seemed to be a great distance from where he'd left Marshall. This suddenly scared him: perhaps he should go back. But Mrs. Pelham would be waiting; he wasn't even sure he could find the emergency room again if he needed to return.

At last he found the cafeteria, but she wasn't there; he bought a pastry and took a seat at a window table where he could see the cab stand, wondering if he'd missed her. He waited. What if Marshall was in trouble? What if Marshall died while he waited in the cafeteria, eating a cherry Danish? He stood and paced, kept his eyes on the dirty windows, returned. He bought another pastry. Mrs. Pelham might have already come and left; but there was the ride uptown, twenty minutes even in a taxi. He went back to the table. She must have gone to see Marshall first. He thought of the emergency room, the view through the double doors: women groaning in chairs, a man in handcuffs. He took out his books and tried to look at them. Marshall falling backward on the stairs: his wet arms shaking.

He wondered what the doctors were doing. Chill came through the glass and fear unsettled him; somehow it was already evening. He found himself next to the phone, thinking of his parents: he wanted to call them; he wanted to hear his mother's cheerful optimism and his father's goading rigor. He had the sudden desire just to tell them he was all right, that he was safe in this city that at the moment seemed a city of horrors. He picked up the receiver, returned it to the hook. To call them seemed to be running from Marshall, somehow, abandoning him in his need. He was cold, even inside. He picked up the receiver and called the hospital operator instead, but she didn't have any information. He called again, using a different voice. Still he could find out nothing. Finally, after dark, Mrs. Pelham walked in with Simone. "God," Mrs. Pelham said, embracing him. "Thank you for bringing him. My poor Marshall."

"Have you seen him?"

"For a minute. They were doing something ghastly."

"They were giving him charcoal, Mother." Simone turned to Orno and hugged him quickly.

"What did they say?" said Orno.

"He's going to be fine," said Simone. "The doctors are sure." She stood between them, looking from one to the other.

"It seems he swallowed aspirin," said Mrs. Pelham. "Such a strange thing to do."

"He knew Orno would find him in time."

"It was pure luck," said Orno.

Mrs. Pelham took his hand. "You were a hero."

"I did what anybody would have done."

"It wasn't luck," said Simone. "Of course you were sweet and came to help him. But he knew just what he was doing."

"No, he didn't," said Mrs. Pelham. "Don't be absurd."

Simone pulled out a chair next to her mother, and Mrs. Pelham sat. Orno regarded the two of them. He knew Simone was only seventeen, but it was hard to make sense of the fact.

"Did he give you any warning?" asked Mrs. Pelham.

"I can't say he did, but in truth I wasn't seeing him as much. He really disappeared this fall when he moved off campus. I don't know if anybody saw him a lot, at least not lately."

"That's what he always does."

"You don't know that, Simone," said Mrs. Pelham.

Orno waited for them both to look at him again. "I didn't think there was any warning," he said, "other than that he disappeared, but that was a while ago. Here," he said, pushing the pastries toward them. "Have these."

"Do you know what he was doing?" asked Simone.

"You mean when he disappeared?"

"Yes."

"Apparently he was with Phoebe Lyall. I actually don't know."

"She's the Morgan, isn't she?" said Mrs. Pelham.

"J. P. Morgan's great-great-granddaughter." Orno looked at her to see if she knew about Phoebe, or where Marshall had been living lately.

"Orno," said Simone, "do you know that my brother's done this before?"

"You don't have to bother anybody with that, Simone."

"I'm telling Orno the truth. Things are difficult for Marshall."

"Things are difficult for everybody, honey."

Simone looked at Orno. "Not the way they are for my brother."

"Well, we don't need to embellish Marshall's life like that. What's important is that Orno was there when he was. We all thank you for that."

"Please," said Orno.

"Marshall likes you a lot," said Simone. "He told me that."

"Well, I like him, too."

"I hope you'll always be there for him, then," said Mrs. Pelham. She reached across and took Orno's hands in hers. "But the truth is," she said, raising her chin, "we must be ready for the worst. We must harden our hearts."

They sat like that while the busboy came by and took away the plates of pastries. Orno was silent. Mrs. Pelham's face seemed to vacillate between weeping and proclaiming the importance of rectitude. "It was good of you to come," she finally said, letting go of his hand. "We're going over to see him again now. It's been two hours. The doctors say they think their timing was good. It just takes time now for his system to clear." She stood up to leave.

"I'm never going to harden my heart," said Simone.

Orno regarded her. "If you need anything," he said, "either of you—"

"You're so kind," said Mrs. Pelham. She pulled on her hat, then moved with Simone through the small aisle to the door. "By the way," she added, "Professor Emerson sends his best to you. He's out of town."

He saw Simone start to say something.

I won't harden my heart either, he wanted to say to her.

"Say hello to him then," he said instead, and he rose and stood in front of the cafeteria, watching as they left him and walked south on Fort Washington Avenue, finally hailing a taxi at the corner, where Simone, just before she ducked inside, turned around and looked back up the street at him.

———

The next day Orno visited Marshall in a room guarded by a watchman reading a magazine. The bed was surrounded by a curtain; on the other side, another bed in which a man lay talking to himself, his hands tied to the railing. "They're watching me," Marshall said. "I talk to a shrink twice a day."

"Is it interesting?"

"What could be more interesting than talking about yourself?"

"I suppose."

"That's what we think in the East, at least. Maybe it's different in Missouri."

"What do they ask you?"

"They ask me if I think of hurting myself again. And they ask me if I have a plan for next time. I think they're going to let me go tomorrow."

Orno looked down. "What do you say when they ask?"

"I say I wouldn't do it again."

"Is that the truth?"

"Yes," he said. He looked up at the watchman, who went back to his magazine. Then he said, "No. I mean, how can I say?" He turned away toward the curtain. "It's strange, though. As soon as I did it *you* came to mind." He took a sip of water. "I took the aspirin and as soon as it was down—it's not so easy to take something like that, by the way, you start to gag—but as soon as I'd swallowed it I suddenly felt very clear-eyed, like a bird looking down, like I was alive for the first time in my life. Alive enough to understand everything. So I called you. I was thinking about Phoebe and I realized you were my true friend and she was a bloodsucker. But the pills were already down, so I called you."

"You can always count on me."

"I know. I knew you'd come."

"Of course."

"If I'd have called Phoebe, she would have been busy or something."

"She would have come too, Marshall. Anybody would have."

"It's funny," Marshall said. He shook his head. "You're so Christian, in a way. You always have an excuse for everybody else."

"I guess I do, but it's not necessarily Christian."

"I mean, it's nice. But I guess the Emersons just aren't used to it. I don't think Phoebe would have been so kind to *you*, if it was reversed."

Orno looked at the window that opened only narrowly at the top: outside, a light well and a dingy grating. He didn't know why Phoebe Lyall would dislike him. He'd always been decent with her. He'd always assumed they liked each other. "By the way, I've been meaning to ask you," he said. "You're Diogenes, aren't you?"

"Who?"

"Diogenes Mendelsohn. The guy who's taking all the exams."

"No, but I've heard that plenty of people think I am."

"Come on, I know it's you."

He laughed. "Well, it's not. I think it's some professor who didn't get tenure. It's the kind of thing those guys do."

"Come on."

"Suit yourself, O. I wish I *were*. Then I wouldn't have to do this kind of thing."

"What do you mean?"

Marshall smiled. "To get you to visit."

Orno looked out the window. "Come on, M," he said. "You're the one who disappeared." He was suddenly embarrassed. He could feel Marshall's affection, like a child's, suddenly out from hiding. "I didn't even know you could do damage with aspirin," he said at last. "It doesn't seem right. How'd you find that out?"

"Oh, aspirin," Marshall answered. "Tylenol, too. Lots of stuff. It's no big secret. I know it all. We all do."

———

For three days Marshall was at Columbia-Presbyterian; then he came back to school and moved into a dormitory suite with a group of transfer students. He'd been spending his time with a crowd Orno had never come across before, a small clique who thought of themselves as poets and artists and gathered every evening in a Lebanese café near campus, called The Odalisque; he began taking Orno along. The others there were appraising him, Orno knew, and from the start he felt he didn't meet their approval. They were thin dark-haired boys in old double-breasted coats and pale girls in dresses from the forties; it all seemed sarcastic. Orno wore what he always wore, denim trousers with a T-shirt or, if he'd had a seminar class that afternoon, a plain-colored button-down shirt and ironed slacks. Fashion made him think of rot. The first evening he came, Marshall introduced him around and then said he would recite some poetry in his honor, which turned out to be Keats's "Ode to a Nightingale," which Orno recognized from high school, and then a prelude by T. S. Eliot, which he didn't. During the poems Marshall kept his eyes on him, and when he finished he raised his glass and said, "To my friend."

They all raised their drinks. The room was dark and they were in its darkest corner, back away from the warped windows at an oblong table behind the bar; in the shadowed faces behind the raised tumblers and snifters Orno saw what seemed suddenly to be a gallery of suspicion and rivalry; Marshall was smiling, enjoying the aura of his recitation as though nothing unusual had happened to him in the previous days, but in the other faces Orno felt no real welcome. It would have been entirely different if this had been a group of engineering students; in their matter-of-fact expressions he would have seen a certain passive friendliness—not exuberant, but not caustic either. Here there was rivalry and posturing, a distilled version of what he'd first discovered in his dormitory.

But it was clear right away that Marshall was the leader of the group, and in this Orno felt comfort; the appraising faces around him leaned away into the shadows but in Orno's mind he saw Marshall in the hospital bed, his head emerging timidly from the gown, his eyes clear with affection. Orno wasn't certain if anyone knew what Marshall had done, or where he'd been. It felt like a secret, and Orno could keep a secret well.

Some time after he'd recited his poetry, Marshall stood up from his end of the table again, raised his snifter of bourbon and said, "The Toasting of Idiots." The table became quiet. They all raised their glasses once more. Then Marshall proceeded to lay into one of the crowd who was sitting right below him, a wet-haired boy in an overcoat whom he mimicked harshly with his glass raised, producing several word-for-word reenactments of things the boy had evidently said over the year, making them sound so foolish that as Marshall recited them Orno turned away; but the boy simply sat smiling with his own glass raised and when Marshall was done the conversation resumed.

It was a strange spectacle. It horrified Orno, but he also knew that he was privileged now in Marshall's eyes, that as Marshall stood at the shadowy head of the table with his glass raised he was looking all the time in his own direction. He was doing it for him, somehow. It was odd, exactly what he'd felt in the physics building.

Nonetheless, he began coming regularly, if only because he liked passing the time with his friend. Whenever Sofia was busy he would call Marshall and meet him outdoors by the tall iron gate that separated Columbia from the trash-strewn uptown streets; soon he was doing this even if Sofia was available, stopping later to see her on his way home. There were late nights. He started to enjoy the moment when the drink eased his wariness and he began to feel the beginnings of calm among the other students as well, sitting across the table amid the stench of cigar and clove-cigarette smoke that cleared for a moment whenever the doors opened onto Broadway and then regathered when they closed. The group came together three nights a week at the same large table in the back and ordered a bottle of cognac and a bottle of bourbon. Orno began to enjoy the cognac especially. He and Marshall developed a signal: whenever someone said something ill-considered, Marshall would touch his forehead and glance over; then Orno would touch his own in return. This was how Marshall gathered material for the toasts. The whole procedure was uncomfortably cruel, but Orno also felt he was now on the inside of it.

One day, as they were walking home, Marshall stopped him and said, "I'm never going to pick on *you*, right? You know that, don't you? Because *you're* not a pretender."

Below them a set of subway stairs plunged into darkness. "Well, thank you," said Orno.

"I just didn't want you to worry. You're different."

"That's a relief."

"It's a trick of Gurdjieff's, that toast. He discovered what it did."

"What does it do?"

"It exposes the hidden shadow of personality. And no matter how uncomfortable people get with it, that kind of exposure is irresistible, at least to certain people. That was Gurdjieff's point."

"It surprises me that everyone takes it."

"Interesting, isn't it?"

"I suppose so, but I'm glad you're not planning to do it to me."

"I couldn't do it to you, Orno. That's the point. You've got nothing hidden. You're too sincere. You, my friend, would have stumped Gurdjieff."

"Thank you."

Marshall laughed. "Which proves it again."

———

There was a literary conceit to the evenings. Paperbacks lay here and there on the table and the group would read passages aloud to one another, sipping from their mismatched glasses. Each night, as well, one of them would read a few of his own poems or occasionally a story and then there would be a period of commentary in which as the bottle circled the table they insulted one another with shocking nonchalance. Orno of course had nothing of his own to recite and though he was growing comfortable he felt no basis for criticizing the work that the other students read aloud. He was quiet when they discussed it; but under the influence of drink he felt a growing benevolence, and after a glass of cognac he would sometimes try to say something if the talk turned to any of the books he'd chanced to have read before; the conversation would pause and the others would look up with their hooded eyes while he made a comment about a writer he knew from high school, Fitzgerald or Dos Passos or Sherwood Anderson. Sometimes Marshall would chime in to save him, turning his point into an esoteric one that Orno barely recognized. "This is what my friend is getting at," Marshall would say. Orno couldn't help thinking of what his father would have thought of the whole scene: these sharp-tongued, dismissive students, fine arts majors and literature majors, drinking late on money wired from afar.

One night after someone had mentioned *The Great Gatsby* he found himself speaking up: "Gatsby isn't about ambition," he said suddenly in a loud voice that grabbed the zigzagging attention of the table, "I think it's about the salves of the ambitious." The ease with which he formulated the words shocked him: he sounded like someone else. He'd forgotten himself really, stepped for the first time right into the fray without fear; the others fell silent, looking down the length of stained wood at him. Then they began speaking again and his self-consciousness returned. "Bullshit," someone said from out of the dark.

"Not bullshit," Marshall answered. "Original thinking."

Then the debate started, but Orno fell away, thinking only of his consternation at speaking. His point might or might not have been a good one, but what shocked him was that the words had come from his mouth unbidden—as though he too had such thoughts resting inside him. He walked home that night aware of the stars and trees and the curbs shining in the moonlight. In bed he lay awake thinking of his moment.

The possibility of another such event began to attract him: he started coming along with Marshall two and three times a week, now stopping off to see Sofia beforehand, leaving his books back at the college and meeting Marshall at the gates at ten o'clock, when commerce on the quadrangle had dwindled to the few students returning from the libraries and the handful of guards making their early rounds on the footpaths. He had a feeling of emancipation: it was late fall and brittle leaves lay in the gutters. On the first chill evening in November, Marshall brought along a fedora, which he handed to Orno just before they entered. The others looked at him when he took his seat. He had never worn anything in his life that he would have considered an affectation; many times over the course of the evening he found his hands going up to the brim or the ribbon, lifting it and replacing it on his head; he brought it to his lap and examined it, the feltish warp of the fabric, the stiff insewn brace; he had a mind to hand it back to Marshall but one of the other boys had a panama hat and another had a beret.

He kept it. He wasn't yearning for the approval of these self-congratulatory types, but it became important to him that he be able to stand on his own among them. He wore the fedora every evening and under the small shadow it made over his eyes he began to feel some of the bold anonymity that he had seen in the others; their looks didn't frighten him anymore. Gradually he began to feel acceptance around the table, and the world he found at night after leaving Sofia in her dormitory room seemed to contain any number of possibilities. On his strolls home with Marshall he would ask about the names of writers he hadn't recognized during the evening, and Marshall would dazzle him with recitations. Night after night, wandering up Riverside Drive, Orno gazed below at the boat lights on the Hudson while Marshall recited Whitman and Eliot and Pound, stepping to the edge of the promontory and bellowing verse until someone in the apartment buildings shouted to silence him. "I knew a man, a common farmer, the father of five sons," he called, his voice dropping low, turning to Orno. "And in them the fathers of sons, and in them the fathers of sons."

————

One evening Sofia asked to come along. He took her down to the gate with him that night and Marshall seemed pleased; yet as they set off down Broadway Orno was aware of a change in him. Marshall and Sofia had met before in his own room, but the three of them had never been out together. Marshall walked between them pointing out nightclubs and coffeehouses along Broadway, thrusting his arms up to point out the buildings so that his long coat flew open and the stiff wind ruffled his shirt; he was garrulous. Sofia exclaimed at the bits of history he recited, hurrying to keep up. Near The Odalisque, Marshall stopped on a corner and turned away from Orno to point at the sky.

"My God," Sofia said.

Marshall bowed.

"No," she said to him, "it is good. The accent is very good."

She took Orno's arm. "He says the moon is beautiful, Orno. In beautiful Russian. That is incredible, Marshall."

He turned and said something else, held his arm up and spoke a piece in pausing, sibilant phrases.

"It is Yevtushenko," she said.

"Of course it is," said Orno. "Nothing amazes me anymore."

"I only know a few words. It's a Pelham talent. We fake languages."

"Oh, no, it is a very good accent and not faked." She leaned up and kissed Marshall on both cheeks and Orno put his arm over his back. Later, he would remember the moment: the three of them like that, their upturned faces beneath the gibbous moon. When they reached The Odalisque, Orno held the door and watched Sofia pass before him into the building, small and mysterious and as darkly radiant as he'd ever seen her.

"They are all children," she said the next afternoon in his bed. "Drinking with their fathers' money and proclaiming everything."

"They're trying to be writers, Sofia. Marshall likes them. He says a couple of them are good."

She made a spitting motion. "They know nothing. In Russia you would not find them."

"Marshall is serious about literature."

"Marshall is different. The rest of them are making postures."

"Posing," he said.

She got up from the bed. "Yes, exactly. They are posing only." She went to the bureau and reapplied the dark lipstick that was her only makeup. "I wish you had a mirror," she said. "You are the only student of Columbia University without a mirror."

"I don't need one. I know what I look like."

"You are very handsome."

"Not as handsome as Marshall."

She raised her eyebrows. "I am supposed to say that you are more handsome, but really it is not the truth. He is as handsome as you are."

"We're equally handsome."

"Right," she said, laughing for some reason at the words, then coming to the edge of the bed and kissing him. "Orno and Marshall are equally handsome."

She wouldn't come back with him to The Odalisque that evening, and he left her in his room, feeling that the short walk from the entrance hall of his dormitory down the stone steps into the night was a repudiation of what she had said about Marshall's friends, though he himself knew that she was correct. He waited until he was outside to put on the fedora. Making his way down the angled footpaths to the gate, he thought of his parents too; back home, the grain would already have been sold at market. Families would be tallying their gains and his father would be on the road, hopeful, if it had been a good year, that the farmers would have enough money after seed and crop hands to buy their insurance. Marshall was outside the gate on Broadway, reading the newspaper. It pleased Orno somehow that Sofia found them equally handsome: they would share the world.

———

When the bottles came around that night, Orno changed from cognac to bourbon and after his second glass he began to feel the room slip away. There was a girl who came every night, Daphne, and suddenly he saw her across the table in a sequined blouse, her eyes on him whenever she drew on her cigarette or touched her fingers to her glass. His own reactions puzzled him: how had he not noticed her before? He thought of Sofia's words about this crowd and tried to resist the feeling that crept forward. At a break in the discussion he went outside for a cigarette with Marshall and when they returned he found himself next to Daphne, talking garrulously. He was surprised that he'd sat down there. Then Marshall was behind him with his hands on his shoulders; he was leaning over to pour both of them more drinks. Sofia's words returned again, but now they were beyond his grasp. There was a feeling of shame, but it was underneath. Marshall poured again.

Even walking home with Daphne, gripping at the parking meters to feel their staunch presence, he was aware of the world still moving away. She would appear ahead of him, waiting at a lamppost under a cone of shining mist, and he would hurry to reach her; then she would be farther up the street again. He thought he detected shyness, but the drinks clouded it. Marshall had disappeared. Where to? Orno looked at Daphne for a reflection of his own eagerness, an invitational glance or a lingering with her shoulders; when he thought he found it in her eyes on a corner outside the first metal fencework of the university, he leaned forward and kissed her. They were in sight of Sofia's dormitory, across a narrow lawn from her small darkened window that looked down over the street. What on earth was he doing? He moved Daphne behind a fence post. Then she took his hand and was leading him. At the door to her building she kissed him again and slid his hands up along the sequins; she was smoky-tasting and her body pushed at the curves of the blouse. "Marshall told me you were shy," she said touching his lip with her finger; he didn't know what to say, so he kissed her again.

Her roommate was asleep on the foldout couch in the living room, so they sneaked into the bedroom and smoked a joint without speaking. Things were not at the distances they seemed: doorways, tables, the edge of the dark blue bed. Daphne sat there and Orno moved next to her. They still hadn't spoken more than several words. Orno tried to fill the silence, asking her about her studies until she put either hand on the shoulders of her blouse and then with a single motion pulled it up over her head. He had been with two girls now. Sofia was athletic and matter-of-fact; Daphne was languorous. She smelled of cigarettes and booze and didn't want to talk even after they lay looking out the window at the moon, still white and shining. His thoughts went dismally to Sofia.

Daphne got up and came back with a cup, setting it betwee
on the headboard. He thought it was water but it turned out u
more bourbon.

———

He felt like someone else. Coming across Broadway at sunrise in
the broken silence of the distant, clanking garbage trucks and
speeding taxis, he felt like a man inhabiting another man's life,
as though he could be upstairs now in one of the dark windows
above him looking down through the parted curtains at the rum-
pled figure hurrying to get home before daylight. The buses had
begun to run, but the sun was still only faint to the east. Sofia was
an early riser as well, and he circled the campus at 119th Street
and came in from Amsterdam Avenue. It struck him as blatantly
evasive: by themselves, his legs began to run. He had to stop them.
He walked to his dormitory and to prove himself walked once
more around it as the sky brightened, then went upstairs and
showered and changed his clothes and left again to study. He
wanted to go right to Sofia's room but he felt criminal.

In the science library he sat in the cool window of the light well,
but even there the view of ducts and vent stacks distracted him: a
rosy light had come up, and from above a filtered pink lit the thick
paint on the jointed industrial fittings. Abruptly the smell of
Daphne's perfume came back to him and he turned around startled
to the empty carrels. There was nothing murky or internal to him
about guilt: it was simply a finger of accusation—his father's, his
junior high school principal, Mr. McKinstry's—a finger pointing at
him unwaveringly. But he'd enjoyed himself—that was the more
difficult fact—and, as he remembered Daphne's smell in the library, he now enjoyed it once again. Smoke, oranges, liquor. His
legs felt loose and he kicked them out underneath the desk. He re-
arranged his books and stared down at them, but even in the static-
charged chill of the library basement he felt loose-limbed and
athletic and aroused. He prayed it would pass before afternoon.

It did: by the time he went to see Sofia the exhilaration had wearied him and his physical quirks had become betrayals. In the hallway of her building his hand shook and he suddenly could not remember the rhythm with which he customarily knocked on her door. She was waiting for him, reading a novel. He tried to act forthright, aware of his feet and how his shoulders seemed to turn on their own away from her so that his face was hidden. They made love as usual—his second girl in the same day—and in the evening he went back to his own room and sat down by the window. He began to tremble. He looked down at his own knees shaking; he lifted his hands to the glass and watched them quiver against the darkening backdrop of Riverside Church. He called Marshall and suddenly he was laughing as he told the whole story on the phone. Marshall laughed as well and told him not to worry. "I'm sure Sofia has it in her as well," he told Orno, and in an instant the shaking went away.

VII

Later, he would remember those days as ones of longing—the afternoons still warm, filled with the last heat left over from Indian summer but no longer truly hot; the evenings colder and bearing the faint smell of water. Everything seemed on the brink—the change of seasons, the coming of possibility. It was going to be winter soon, but for now every warm day came upon him startlingly, the morning chill when he woke containing summer and winter both. Washed breezes blew in over Manhattan from the east. The buildings stood out as though the bright Atlantic air had cleaned them. He and Marshall walked late at night after going to The Odalisque, and in the east-west corridors of the uptown streets, where gusts from the Hudson lifted the brim of the fedora, Orno told him about his exploits with Daphne; he still saw her regularly, unsure of what drove him. He was still seeing Sofia as well, and Sofia knew nothing. Marshall nodded, gazing at him thoughtfully.

Again for Orno it was as though he were watching himself; or, not watching himself but watching a young man he partially recognized, taught one way his whole life but now behaving in another; he was adrift in an ecstasy. There were more days when he went from Daphne's room back to Sofia's, showering in between. At night he ran the short blocks home to school, crazily energized by his misdeed. Marshall laughed, deeply pleased by this kind of moral ruin; he goaded Orno to talk more. Orno was sick at bragging but he did it anyway because Marshall had hold of him, somehow. They walked together, Orno speaking when his mood, as it always did on their walks home, suddenly bloomed. He started the stories shyly but then he began exaggerating, while Marshall made little appreciative comments next to him, laughing with his head turned up to whichever stars shone brighter than the glow of the towering buildings.

One night Marshall said, "I've never told you about Penny McRary."

"Who's Penny McRary?"

A trio of yachts was moving north on the Hudson below them. "She was my nanny," Marshall said. "In Istanbul. My governess, is what my mother called her. She was an Irish girl my mother knew somehow, from one of her friends in Europe. When we went to Turkey, my mother hired her. She stayed at the Luxor with us." He looked over the edge of the escarpment. "Those boats remind me of the Bosporus."

Orno looked over. The yachts were moving swiftly against the outline of the New Jersey shore, their lights reflected across the water like a line of moons.

"My mother's work in those days was outside Istanbul. In the ruined monasteries of Heybeli, in the Princes Islands. The Princes Islands are in the Sea of Marmara, not too far away. For days when she was in the field I stayed home with Penny McRary at the Luxor. She was the age then that we are now," he said, looking out at the silent boats below. "It's strange to think of that."

"How old were you?"

"Twelve."

"And what happened?"

"When my mother was away from town, Penny McRary was supposed to stay with me, and the rule was we had to stay inside the grounds of the Luxor. It wasn't hard, because the place was huge. Behind the hotel there was a long, tropical garden, maybe the size of a football field, and in the summer we would sit out on the veranda under the orange trees—they had the smallest oranges, like red lemons. They used to make drinks with those oranges—they were blood oranges. All the drinks were red. We used to watch the diplomats and the expatriates drink themselves silly under the awnings. Sometimes they would shout at each other, which I loved, and the waiters would come running out from the kitchen. I thought they were there to break up the fights, but now I think they probably hoped they would see a good one. The American ambassador used to drink there, and he used to come for walks with us sometimes. I guess I was pretty young. I used to think he probably missed his son, or something. I used to think he liked walking with me."

"You don't think he did?"

"Of course not. He wanted to walk with Penny McRary. She was absolutely beautiful. Black Irish, you call it. And if the ambassador had any sons, I'm sure they were there in Istanbul with him."

"All right."

"But I guess after a while Penny McRary got bored with the walled garden, or maybe the ambassador started to scare her. All the other diplomats were eyeing her anyway, I have to figure. But she stayed close to me. I remember being flattered by that, even though I didn't understand it. For whatever reason, one day she decided to take me into the city. I guess anybody would have done that after a few weeks, even though my mother expressly forbade it. We started by walking in the neighborhood around the Luxor, which was very elegant. It was the only place in Istanbul where you could be alone on a sidewalk."

"Did you ever get caught?"

"No. Never. And of course it was no more dangerous than walking on the East Side. Soon we were going to the Topkapi Sarayi and the Hamam of Roxelana. My favorite was the fortress of Rumeli Hisari, all the battlements running to the sea. One morning she took me to the Kapali Çarşi—that's the market. The stalls there are like a labyrinth, and suddenly I realized I could get lost and never find my way back. She must have realized it too, because she took my hand as we walked. I was twelve, remember, but I looked older."

"Don't tell me."

"The Turkish men were always stopping to talk to her. They stopped their bikes, you know, they leaned from their car windows, they came out from the market stalls. I think because she was beautiful and in a way she looked like one of them, with her dark eyes and black hair. They used to offer her date rolls and apricots covered with sugar. I would stand there, trying to look old. Soon she was taking my hand whenever one of them approached. After a while I knew she wasn't trying to protect me anymore, though. She was asking me to protect her."

"And what happened?"

"She was a friend of my mother's, O. I mean, besides being her employee. I was in love with her but I knew she would never take anything farther."

"I thought you didn't know what being in love was."

"I don't. But I thought I did, then."

"So nothing happened?"

"No. Something did."

"What, then?"

"We became close."

"What does that mean?"

"Turkey is a strange land." He laughed. "Like New York."

"Don't be cryptic," said Orno. "What happened?"

"What usually happens? One morning we were on the Galata Bridge, which is the bridge between the two halves of the city, sitting in a café looking at the boats. We were at an outside table—all the cafés are lined up on the bottom story of the bridge—one of the ferries was moving away from the dock and while we were sitting there watching it an old man on the top deck somehow got pushed toward the rail and went right over, thirty feet down into the water."

"You're kidding."

"I remember thinking for a second that nobody was going to do anything. Like, life was so cheap in that city that an old man over the rail wasn't cause for alarm. Of course one of the stewards went right in after him off the gangplank, and a boat came from the bridge to pick them both up. It was an odd experience, though."

"Why?"

"Because of what happened with Penny."

"What did happen?"

"Evidently she was shaken by it. We sat there finishing our tea and *lokmas*—I'll find you a *lokma* sometime in New York. I used to love them, sugary little doughnuts we'd eat with cream. But Penny's expression was different. Somehow I picked up on it. As we were walking back to the Luxor—my mother was getting back that evening; even though her boat came in right near the Galata Bridge we didn't wait there because she didn't know we were leaving the hotel—so anyway, as we were walking back to the hotel a beggar with no legs called up to us. Penny McRary gave him some change from her pocket—usually she didn't; she was the daughter of a baker with nine other kids, I think, a working-class girl from Dublin. She figured everyone could work, just the way she did—even an old man with no legs. But he was also covered with some kind of sores—I guess that tipped the balance. You saw all kinds of things like that in Istanbul. There were no wheelchairs, you know. If you were crippled, you dragged yourself along on a piece of cardboard on the sidewalk. Anyway, Penny gave this beggar her change and then took my hand. But she didn't let go. We walked back the rest of the way through the city instead of taking a taxi, which we ordinarily would have done at that hour, and she held my hand the whole way. Even when we got back near the Luxor, where we were the only ones on the street."

Orno looked up from the river. "Was that the end?"

"No, as a matter of fact. We got back to the hotel and I knew there were still a couple of hours before my mother's boat was in. You could see the ferries on the Bosporus from the Luxor balcony, and I knew how to recognize my mother's from the smokestacks. From the time I saw it I knew we had an hour and fifteen minutes until she was back at the hotel. We sat there on the balcony, and I was watching Penny and at the same time watching for my mother's boat. I could tell Penny was still upset about the two men."

"Who was the second one?"

"The old man who fell in."

"So what happened?"

"I was twelve, but it was a moment I understood. The complicated thing women have. The fear they have of men and at the same time their need to protect them. The beggar was perfect—frightening but pitiable. So was the old man falling in. It was the steward who went in after him, the guy in the uniform, who changed my life. That's what I think. Some young Turkish guy in a white jacket and a seaman's hat. Somehow she connected him with me, that young men were coarse and predatory but also heroic. We were sitting on the balcony watching the Bosporus, and I just realized all of this in an instant."

"So, what did you do?"

"I kissed her."

"How did you know how to do that?"

"Movies. We watched a lot of movies in Istanbul. There was a theater in the basement of the Luxor."

"What did she do?"

"She kissed me back. I have to admit I was surprised. We became lovers. What a story, isn't it?"

"How did you do it?"

"My mother was gone five days out of the week. We were in the most exotic city in the world. In a first-class hotel. It wasn't difficult. It didn't last long, though."

"Why not?"

"She left early," he said. "I guess it became unbearable to her, lying to my mother. A few weeks before we were supposed to go home she just disappeared. She did it at night while my mother was there with us, so that I wouldn't be left alone the next day. In some ways Penny still treated me that way, like her charge, even with what was going on. She came in and said good-bye to me while my mother was asleep on the other side of the courtyard. There were courtyards in the upstairs rooms in those days. She woke me and we went to stand outside, looking at the lights of Üsküdar. Üsküdar is the beginning of Asia. It's an eerie feeling.

You stand there looking from Europe into the East. I think she was trying to tell me that if I wanted to, I could come with her. Wherever she was going to go." He looked out again at the river. "But I knew I wasn't going to leave. It just wasn't a possibility. I was twelve, remember. She was wearing a gauze gown, and when she leaned against the railing I could see the lights through it from the other side of the Bosporus. Anyway, later that night she took her bags and went back to Dublin. I mean, I guess she went back to Dublin—I never actually found out where she went. I never told my mother why, either. My mother thought she'd stolen from us. That morning, when Penny didn't come down to breakfast, my mother went back up to the room and took out all her necklaces and bracelets. But she never found anything missing. It made me mad, but I also knew it was good cover for what had happened. For the last few weeks I walked around Heybeli with my mother, thinking about Penny McRary. I was in a fever."

"You must have been heartbroken."

"No. It wasn't like that. It was a different kind of fever. She had just woken up an appetite in me. Not just for girls. It was much more. An appetite for the world. For life. My mother was forced to take me along to Heybeli, so I walked around and my thoughts of Penny made everything interesting—all the piles of Byzantine rock, the green dust from the old copper mines, the ruined monasteries. It all seemed exquisite in my eye. There's no other word for it. Here we were in such a strange land and I'd done this powerful thing." He watched the boats move out of sight under the George Washington Bridge. "And to this day," he said, turning from the river, "it's the most extraordinary thing that's ever happened to me. That's why I'm telling you. I was in a shell, but from then on it was opened."

"What do you mean by that?"

"All kinds of things. It's going to happen to you, too, you know. Being here in New York, doing what you're doing."

"What am I doing?"

"You're doing things you would never have done if you'd stayed with the world you knew."

"Maybe."

"But I haven't even told you the most amazing part—the most amazing part is what happened after."

"I can't imagine," said Orno.

"I was walking around Heybeli with my mother. I told you everything was so exquisitely clear to me. In my eye, somehow. Things just looked brighter. It was like I'd never seen colors before and now I saw them. The copper dust, for example—I don't know if it looked green to everybody else. I think to my mother it was just brown. But I could see the green in the earth. It wasn't green, actually; it was more like the suggestion of green, a funny buzz in my eye that was like seeing color. I can't describe it any better than that, but I could tell when we were reaching the head of one of the old mines because I started feeling this buzz when I looked down at the path. And the mine openings were hidden by a hundred years of dirt and brush. They'd all caved in decades before. Most of the ones they knew about had been dug by British archaeologists in the fifties. It was a big event to find one, and after one day I just knew that I knew how to do it. I could see this thing that nobody else could. They had kits to test for copper, but it was laborious and they hardly ever took them out."

"Did you find any mines?"

"I found one, but then the other thing happened, which was even more amazing. At least to me. One night we were waiting for the ferry to come back from Heybeli, and there was a big sign painted on the wall of the pier with all the tariffs and the destinations—it was in Turkish, of course. I'd never paid attention to the language when I was there. I knew a few words from being in the Kapali Çarşi, but everyone at the hotel spoke English, which they practiced on me and Penny. You know, if I said 'teşekkürederim,' they said, 'You're welcome, young sir.' We got on the ferry; it was a two-hour ride and we sat up on deck because even though the sun had gone down the weather was still beautiful. The end of a *lodos* was blowing, and it was still very warm. There was a napkin on the table and I took out a pen and wrote out the ferry sign I'd just seen. In Turkish. Every word of it. My mother looked at it and broke into tears. She was really weeping. I didn't understand it. She spoke Turkish, obviously."

"Why was she upset?"

"That's the thing I've never told you. Before that day I'd just had a regular memory, like every other kid. I never had the photographic part. That was the moment it changed. The eidetic memory—it just came to me that afternoon."

"All at once?"

"In a flash. From then on I remembered everything I saw. It was something neurologic, I think—that's why the colors, too. How else do you explain it? Poof. Just like that."

"Did your mother know what was happening?"

"Of course she did. It's the way it had happened to my father, too, you know, when he was young." He turned from the river and moved back up to the path. "That's why she was weeping," he said.

VIII

They were walking again, occasionally in the mornings but usually after midday. The air was cold now, and they kept a good pace, the wind arising in the afternoons when they headed south on Broadway or Amsterdam; calming for their return so that at the fall of evening there was a moment of stillness, the breeze ceasing as the air shifted to its nighttime weight; then picking up again from the east. At dinnertime came a lull: on Central Park West the cabs thinned, almost disappeared; the sidewalks emptied; the San Remo, the Beresford lit themselves as they watched, the lights blinking on unevenly across the broad, dappled faces. In the yellow windows, figures paused to look out at the minarets of the Museum of Natural History, or across at the dark outline of the park. They'd been up and down the same routes before but now Orno began to see small sights he'd missed: the carved cupids and foxes of the row houses on Seventy-first Street, the Tiffany windows of St. James Episcopal, the fossils in the red limestone of the Tishman Building. "Brachiopods and Crinoidea," Marshall told him, lazily fingering the rock. "A few goniatites." Orno no longer was amazed.

He had come a distance. He slept less now than he even had before, awoke early with a feeling of hunger; every morning he was drawn to the window of his room just to see the sight—a small patch of Broadway and a corner of the black gates of the university. It still thrilled him. The sun coming up over Avery Hall as though over the peak of a mountain. The shining dew on the transom.

I was in a shell, but from then on it was opened.

———

One night, walking up Broadway after their evening at The Odalisque, Marshall said, "I'd like to see Sofia, you know."

Orno looked over.

Marshall was grinning. "I mean, given what's happened."

"You'd like to what?"

"See Sofia."

Orno kept walking. "Darn, Marshall. You don't mean what I think you do."

"Yes, I do. But I'm asking you, you know. I won't if you don't want me to."

"Is that why you set me up with Daphne?"

"I didn't set you up, O. You did that on your own."

"You were pouring the bourbon."

"All you have to do is say no and I'll never mention it again."

"That's not the point. You just shouldn't have asked me."

"Oh, come on. It's not Missouri."

"You just shouldn't have asked."

Marshall shrugged. "Okay. Forget it."

They made their way uptown. There was something about Marshall, the most unreliable person he'd ever been friends with, that kept bringing him back. He drank you, really; that's what it felt like. Orno never knew what the rules were going to be. There was charisma in that, in the fixed points in Marshall's world that were not the fixed points in his own. Marshall stopped and held out his hand. "Ezra Pound shared his women," he said.

"I thought you said you dropped it, Marshall."

"I'm a salesman. Like your dad. We don't give up. Ideas, old gossip, oddments of all things."

"What's that mean?"

"It's Pound. Strange spars of knowledge and dimmed wares of price—"

"Ezra Pound was crazy."

"But generous."

Orno wouldn't shake his hand. "More crazy than generous."

"Tragical?" said Marshall, looking at him. "No. You preferred it to the usual thing."

"Stop," he said. "You have me beat."

"I'm just trying to teach you. That's 'Portrait d'une Femme.' "

"Thank you." He stopped at a corner. "So, you just want to have an evening out with her?"

"That's all," Marshall said. "Think of Penny McRary."

"What's it got to do with that?"

"Open your world," he answered.

Orno looked up at the struggling moon. "Well, I guess I don't own her," he said. "She's different, though. You better know that. She's very devoted. She's from a completely alien world, you have no idea. Her mother and sisters are in Leningrad."

"I know all that."

"How do you know it?"

"She told me."

"When?"

"The other night. At The Odalisque."

"Where was I?"

"I think you were thinking about electrical engineering."

"Damn, Marshall."

"You were distracted."

"I don't know. The whole scene is funny for her."

"She enjoys it. It's European."

"She has her own thoughts about it."

"I'll be nothing but a gentleman."

"I don't know."

"I knew you'd agree."

"I haven't agreed, M."

Marshall stepped into a doorway, fished around in his coat, and pulled out a joint. He lit it. When Orno came over, he held it up between them at eye level. "A toast," he said. "To friendship," and he held it out until Orno took it from his hand.

————

The next morning Orno bought a bouquet of chrysanthemums from a gypsy on Amsterdam Avenue and knocked on the door of Sofia's apartment. It was not yet noon and she eyed him. "You are early."

"These are for you."

"Oh no, thank you." She took them from him and smelled them.

"The weather's beautiful," he said. "Let's walk."

"To where?"

"Who knows? Let's just go."

"They are beautiful, Orno. How much did they cost?"

He laughed. "That's a funny question. They're for you. They're chrysanthemums. They're in our garden at home. They remind me of you."

"Chrysanthenons."

"Chrys-an-the-mums."

"Chrysanthemum." She smiled, then turned and rustled around the small kitchen until she found a jar. "Expensive I think." She looked over her shoulder at him.

"Not too."

"They are nice, my Orno." She placed them in the jar, fanned open the stems, and set the arrangement on the windowsill. "But you should not anymore."

"Why?"

"They waste your money."

"Not a waste at all."

"You are sweet to me." She moved the flowers farther into the light and stepped back to regard them. "But do not."

"Let's walk."

"How come you are not studying?"

"I want to walk with you."

"Oh yes, flowers and we walk in the afternoon. What is it?"

"Nothing. But if I want to bring you flowers I will."

"Yes, okay. Not expensive, though."

"Okay, not expensive."

He took her hand and they walked out into the West Side. At a dive uptown they ate eggs and toast and then continued down through the midafternoon bustle of the Spanish stores. He was wearing his fedora, and now and then people looked at him for a moment, interested, then turned back to their doings. He was on edge to be with her, knowing that Marshall wanted her, too; the fact of it made him nervous, and he fought it by walking fast, moving through the parting crowds with Sofia holding on to his hand. But all the commerce swelled him, also—made him remember that he had come to a far end of the earth. At Seventy-second Street they descended into the subway, where they stopped to watch a man play a trumpet made from milk bottles and scrap metal; then they got onto the big, hurtling express that barreled through the dark toward Times Square, the two of them standing at the swaying rear watching the flicker of workmen's lights in the caverns.

Later, as they stood together on the platform of the Empire State Building watching a bank of clouds move past the Hudson, he said, "Marshall was mentioning something."

She eyed him.

The wind was whistling and he took off the fedora and held it in front of his waist, a posture he instantly recognized as his father's, talking to a farmer; he moved it under his arm. "He's fond of you," he said.

She found a cigarette in her purse and turned to him. "Oh, I see," she said. "This is why the flowers." She lit the cigarette. "He has already asked."

"He did what?"

"He asked me if I will like to see him."

"I can't believe he did that."

She went back to gazing over the city. "I said I will ask you."

"How did he do it?"

"I asked him if he meant it in the innocent way and he said no, he didn't."

"When was this?"

"At The Odalisque."

"When at The Odalisque?"

"You know I have only been there once, Orno. He is very direct," she said. "Your friend."

Orno was shocked. Marshall had asked her weeks ago. "Well," he said. "Do you want to?"

He turned and she gave him her Russian stare. "Yes," she said. "I do."

He looked away.

"Oh, Orno. You know that you and I are only for a time. You are not so naive. And you know about Marshall, too, or you would not be friends with him. He is so extraordinary."

"That's—"

"You must not be hurt, my Orno."

"Well, I am."

"Then why are you asking me if I will see him?"

He couldn't answer. He looked out at the clouds stacking up against the wall of cold air over the harbor. "I don't know," he said. It was ridiculous: he was trying to shake up his life; he was trying to do the unexpected. But he couldn't say this to her. He didn't know if he even believed in it. "I guess I thought maybe you'd say no," he said.

"My sweet Orno," she answered. "Marshall is formidable. Neither of us can resist him."

Winter, late in coming, wouldn't end. The sky was gray every day and the city, which had shone like zinc in the first cold light of December, now reflected nothing; the cornices of the downtown buildings receded in the shade of the overcast and the windows were the color of lead. Orno ventured out to the Empire State Building by himself and tried to summon the grandeur and fear he'd known, but it wouldn't come; the lobbies were stifling and the tourists were gone. On the street, pigeons hid from the wind. He knew Marshall was seeing Sofia, but any more than that was concealed from him. Neither of them said anything, and he became aware of how little he knew of the very world in which he traveled. Sofia and Marshall had their own lives and he circled them; he began to feel wary. He saw Marshall all the time and he even saw Sofia now and then, but it was like the beginning of a children's game in which a scarf had been tied over his eyes, he had been spun and set in a closet, and now he had to chase everyone around like a blind man. Sofia was stoic in her Russian way: now when he chanced to see her on the campus she looked at him over her books implacably. To him this meant she had fallen in love. He did not want to compare himself. After he saw her, he would wander for blocks trying to sort his thoughts, reminding himself that envy served no one. Missouri was thirty degrees colder, but he walked huddled in his coat.

He tried to return to his studies. He refused to call Sofia himself, but every now and then she would call him and he would walk over disconsolately to her dormitory late in the evening and take her out for tea. He did this because he could not resist; he knew it was useless and would put him into a state. That she herself called him seemed like something that might happen in wartime or famine; it was strange, so far from what he expected that each time it occurred he thought she was ready for a pronouncement, perhaps that she was returning. But none came. She invited him once to a film and once to a play. They even had a long kiss one evening when she invited him in—she'd been out with Marshall beforehand and smelled of whiskey—but she wouldn't let him stay. His sadness seemed to amuse her, and this served to lighten it, because it was of course trivial by her standards. She cooked him soup that night; she pulled at his hair gently to wake him when he fell asleep on her couch. He asked if Marshall was on his way over to see her again and she only laughed. Her feelings were impenetrable to him now, but he was aware of this only because for the first time he wanted to know them. When they had been together her stolid expression had been a comfort; now it hid what he wanted. Sometimes she was gentle; other times there was a distracted fury behind her gestures. He recognized his friend's effects. Marshall said nothing.

At the same time he continued to go to The Odalisque, and though the world he knew there seemed to move farther and farther from what he was accustomed to and from what he thought he had wanted, he nonetheless felt a proprietary claim whenever he and Marshall were together in the dark bar, far away from Sofia; and even more so when they walked home each night along Riverside Drive reciting poems above the Hudson. Marshall called him "O" now all the time, and he called Marshall "M." If the subject of

Sofia ever came up, Marshall would laugh and shake his head as though they had an agreement not to speak of her. After a time this seemed like a wise course even to Orno. They walked slowly, stopping to lean on the railings. Orno had begun keeping late hours again the way he had freshman year, finding himself out on the streets after they had emptied of traffic. He was tired in the mornings now, but the fatigue was pleasant; it helped him forget Sofia. It also heightened his senses. He could feel them enlivening each night after the cognac at The Odalisque, the world dropping its veil. The streets were misty, and over the steaming manholes hung pockets of smells, rotting garbage and the thawing piles of leaves from the ginkgoes. The corners echoed.

Over the course of the winter, Daphne showed up at The Odalisque one night a week, sometimes two, and he would walk her home and then go upstairs to her cluttered bedroom; but he didn't see her any more than that. By March, with polluted ice melting and refreezing in the doorways, he began to feel unashamed of what he had before thought of as his corruption; and before long another girl at The Odalisque drew his attention. Her name was Anne-Marie. She wasn't pretty, but there was a concealed seductiveness about her that one day she showed to Orno like a spotlight; and after a time he was sleeping with her as well. He had always needed comfort in winter. Daphne was aware of her—they were friends—but Orno was allowed to move between them. Thoughts of Sofia raised themselves and he quelled them. He could not have imagined such a life. *I was in a shell*, he thought to himself, *but from then on it was opened.*

But he couldn't concentrate on his studies. He was sitting aimlessly in his engineering courses now like a soldier in a church, snapping back in class with memories of drunkenness and his trysts in the two smoky apartments. The classes met three afternoons a week, and he could sense the nervous ambition of the other students who'd made it this far, where diligence and willingness and sharpness of insight were at last going to reward them; but he couldn't muster his own ambition. How could equations interest him? The lectures droned. He watched the rows of Chinese and Korean and Indian students working below him in the auditorium; he thought of the cognac; he thought of Daphne, of the rows of photographs in her bedroom, of the tears that sometimes brimmed from under Anne-Marie's eyelids when she slept.

X

Spring came and his father, sensing something wrong, called and said he was coming to visit. He took the train all the way from Missouri and then the subway from Penn Station, bounding up the filthy steps onto Broadway on the first warm afternoon in April. From his window across the quadrangle, Orno spotted him admiring the iron gates of the university. Everything about Drake Tarcher set him off from the commerce and hurry of the street—his gait, his upright posture, his hat under his arm. Orno felt a stone in his heart.

Perhaps in the two years at Columbia he himself had become a New Yorker. Below him on the quadrangle clusters of students lay on the grass, and though he could still recognize their posed nonchalance and the dismissive irony of their clothing—all black: pants, shirts, skirts, and shoes—it had somehow become what he himself wore, and, in a way he suddenly recognized, now that his father stood in his view, what he himself felt about the world. In the closet behind him was the fedora and now a velvet smoking jacket as well, black with satin lapels. At the gates his father set down his valise and rubbed his hands together like an actor playing an eager businessman or a rube. One of the guards eyed him. Orno waited a moment, then retrieved the smoking jacket from the closet and walked out to greet him.

They went to dinner at the same restaurant they'd visited on his parents' first trip, and this time Orno saw what Marshall must have known then—the wide brass handrails at the mezzanine and the pictures of actors on the walls: *it was a tourist joint.* His father ordered a sandwich called The Big Apple, and as he spoke to the waiter Orno burned with shame. He'd only realized it now, two years later: Marshall had been making a joke.

In his room that night his father said, "I see you've become a dandy."

Orno wasn't sure he'd heard correctly, so he didn't answer. But his father brought it up again. "I'm just seeing what I see," he said, sitting at the edge of the mattress removing his shoes.

"Well, screw that," said Orno. He was shocked at his own words and had to turn away. He rarely fought with his father and when they did they were civil, like business partners. His father's voice was low and slow and Orno had to keep his own from rising as he paced around the bed he'd given over to him. "I'm sorry," Orno said. "I shouldn't have spoken."

His father didn't pause in the work of removing his socks, then setting them inside his shoes. "Your grades are poor. You're wearing a velvet jacket. There's an ashtray in here."

"My grades are fine."

"They're poor. Your desk is in disorder. You've given up on medicine."

"I've what?"

"As far as I can see, you've given up on medicine. It's the most honorable of professions. I would have studied it myself if I'd had the opportunity."

"I'm studying engineering."

"But you had the opportunity to study medicine."

"A year ago you were happy I was going to be an engineer."

"Indeed I was. I didn't know there was an ashtray in your room and that you wore velvet dinner jackets. I hope you didn't decide important things about your life out of idleness."

"That's ridiculous."

"Possibly," he said. He stood, removed his pants and straightened them, then went to the closet. "There are beer bottles in here."

"You shouldn't snoop in my room."

"I'm hanging up my pants, Orno. I don't care what these other students are doing; you are here for your education. You should learn to hang your pants too, while you're at it. They'll last longer. You don't come from the background these other students might. Marshall is Marshall," he said. "You are Orno."

"You sound like—jeez."

His father returned to the bed and set his shoes underneath it. "I see," he said.

"This isn't Clarkson College."

"Yes, I know. On my checks I write 'Regents of Columbia University.' "

"I'm going to pay my own loans."

"As you well know, they don't cover everything."

"It's a lot harder here than at Clarkson."

"I know that too, which is why we're willing to pay for it. And now you've learned that your parents are hayseeds."

"I never said that."

"You were prepared to."

Orno sat down. His father hadn't mentioned medicine since his freshman year and at the time he'd seemed just as enthusiastic about engineering. Orno had set down two folded blankets on the floor next to the bed and now he pulled off his jeans and lay back across them. It appeared that the discussion had ended. Since knowing Marshall in New York, he'd gotten into bigger arguments in taxicabs and restaurants, but in those exchanges both sides raised their voices—waiters and drivers and maître d's; his father, on the other hand, seemed interested only in a quiet reprimand, as though as soon as he'd pointed out a few missteps Orno would understand the course of his error. It infuriated him. Nobody in his family had ever lived in a city larger than St. Louis. He pulled the blankets over him and tried to push it from his mind, but his thoughts seemed to light upon all the insults and slights of his memory. He kept thinking of Marshall bringing them to that restaurant as a joke; then he thought of his father. As soon as he forced away the thoughts they returned, and before long he was sitting up. Engineering was as useful as any profession and certainly difficult enough. There was a flask of brandy in his boot in the closet and he rose quietly, pretended to go in there to hang up his pants, and drank from it. Then he lay down again. His father's arms were folded over his chest and his face was unbothered. Orno heard his breathing begin to slow. Then he was snoring. He rose and slipped out the door and went to see Daphne, returning at four in the morning after he'd awakened her and made love angrily, then wandered by himself for block after block in the misting early morning; he knew his father rose at five.

That day his father walked to lunch in the dining hall with him and that night treated him to dinner at another restaurant. He didn't mention their argument, and as with all disagreements Orno had known in his house he seemed to have forgotten it without a trace. He insisted on coming to Orno's engineering classes, so Orno took him to two of the lectures; his father sat next to him, paying rigid attention to the diagrams and equations on the overhead screen, although of course he understood none of them; Orno took notes and nodded occasionally but in fact it was once again difficult to pay attention: he was drawn to his father's face. There seemed to be a structure to it that set it apart not only from those of the students around him but from all of the faces in New York City; he imagined him with long hair, in rakish clothing or a hat from the 1940s; he imagined him late for a train and pushing his way through a crowd, but there was a sensibility to his expression that was distinct. It was staunch, mildly weary, and imperturbably optimistic—Orno's own face, of course—hardy like a farmer's or a fur trapper's but not refined or intelligent. He watched it at the edge of his vision, aware of each familiar movement. The fact was that he was ashamed of it. He'd been ashamed of it in himself every night at The Odalisque, despite the fedora and the smoking jacket, so excruciatingly apparent in its simplicity that a year ago he had removed the mirror from the door of his room. It had only showed him how ordinary he was.

————

His father wouldn't take a taxi to Penn Station, so Orno saw him off at the subway. He descended the steps with his valise under his arm and his hat on his head, waving over his shoulder as he disappeared into the darkness. Orno waited upstairs for the rumble of the subway cars, and only when he felt it a few minutes later, shaking the street where he stood, did he turn and set off in the direction of Daphne's apartment.

When he arrived she was on the fire escape outside her window, on the far corner of the platform that gave her a small, broken view to the Hudson. He stepped outside next to her and gazed over the dilapidated rooftops; her apartment looked down on the back of an Indian restaurant where a dog was eating between two overflowing cans of garbage. He ducked back in and returned with the bottle of bourbon from her shelf. She stood and kissed him. He'd never drunk before during the day, and after two shots he stood and had to hold the handrail; she seemed to be better on her feet and helped him climb back in through the window. They went to bed and kept drinking. They began to make love, but his attention wandered. The phone rang for a long time until she rolled to the edge of the mattress and kicked it off the cradle. His anger turned to sadness. He was drunk, but he reached across to the night table and took another drink; the sadness moved to the edge of his grasp. His father's train would be moving west already, passing out of New York into the suburbs and by night at last into farmland. This was no doubt a comfort to his father, but to Orno it was only more sadness. He slept, not waking until the evening bells of St. John the Divine; the apartment was hidden in darkness.

His knees and elbows ached, and when he sat up he found he was still tipsy. Daphne was next to him, her arm hanging over the edge of the bed, and he rose and went to the bathroom for a wash-cloth; he cleaned her face with it, then gave her a glass of water that he held to her mouth. She was asleep again a moment later and he climbed out on the balcony to find fresh air; he tried to shake the drunkenness from his head, but it was still there; behind the Indian restaurant the dog trotted to the fence and looked up at him. It was a street animal with thin haunches like a hyena's.

He sat down on the metal platform and leaned his head against the building. There was always a din in New York, so many horns and sirens and engines that he could tune his ear to different lay-ers of them; at night in Cook's Grange he used to sit under the maple and not hear a sound until the horned owl came out from the laurels to look at him. Below him the dog started to whimper; he didn't want to look. Then, briefly, he felt tears come to his eyes. He blinked and was looking up at the dark stripe of the river, lit at its edge by the lights of North Bergen, when it came upon him with clarity that his father was right: he had lost his way.

XI

He had two years left in college. From his desk he took his file of grade reports and sat on his bed to look at them. A minuses his freshman year; then, the semester he met Sofia, his first B; then two C's this last semester, when, for the first time in his life, he had begun during the day to look forward to the glass of cognac at night. Was this all the character he had? His great-grandfather had walked to Missouri from Georgia through the territory of the Cherokee Indians; now, in two years in New York, he'd let his own determination go slack under the influence of dilettantes and libertines drinking on their fathers' stipends. He called Marshall and told him he wasn't coming out that night. Marshall showed up at his room.

"What's the problem, Casanova?"

"I'm not coming, M, that's all. I was looking at my grades. They went off a cliff."

Marshall chuckled. "Your father put you up to this."

"He's got nothing to do with it."

"My mistake then. I don't know why I thought he did. Coincidental, I suppose, his being out here."

"He mentioned it, but he was right, you know."

"So maybe you need to work harder."

"That's why I'm staying home from now on."

Marshall went to the window. "From now on?"

"That's right."

"Grades don't matter *that* much, Orno."

"Not to you, maybe."

"You can do whatever you want, O. That's the point of this place—you're training your mind not to need Columbia—that's the reason you went here, you know. A well-trained mind can find its own education."

"I need a job when we get out, Marshall. Have you ever thought about that? Have you ever thought about what you're going to do when you graduate?"

"I'm not going to graduate."

"What's that supposed to mean?"

"I quit. Two months ago. I canceled my registration."

"You did not."

"Yes, I did. I don't need it."

"You're not in school?"

"I'm going to write a novel," he said. He took a cigarette from his pocket.

Orno went over to his desk and sat down. His engineering texts were arranged there, where he'd set them out to study later. "I don't understand you," he said. "Why didn't you tell me?"

"It didn't seem important."

"Not important that you dropped out of school?"

"Not to me."

"My God, Marshall. If I dropped out my father would walk to New York to find me."

"My father wouldn't walk across campus."

Orno moved a pad around on the desk. He wondered if Marshall was right. "What are you going to do instead?"

"I'm going to California. I have an uncle in Los Angeles. A very cool man."

"When were you planning to tell me?"

"I wasn't planning to go until you asked."

"But now you are?"

"Yeah. Especially if you're not coming to The Odalisque tonight. You're really not going to?"

Orno hesitated. He thought of his father. "Not tonight," he said. "Not tomorrow night."

Marshall looked intently out the window. "Well, you're leaving me to heal the broken hearts."

"A tough job, but someone's got to do it." He tried to laugh.

Marshall pointed through the glass and when Orno stood and moved next to him he saw that he'd been watching a group of girls in halter tops walking toward the gates on Broadway.

"Ah, fair Columbia," said Orno.

"The women come and go, talking of Michelangelo."

They grinned at each other.

"So, when are you planning to leave?"

"I hadn't thought about it, actually," Marshall answered. "Perhaps tonight," he said, and winked.

———

Marshall wasn't in his room for several days, and Orno began to wonder if he'd actually left New York; then one morning he received a note from him saying he was on his way to Los Angeles and would call when he arrived. The postmark was Las Vegas. In the light of his desk lamp he held the letter and felt hemmed in by the small reach of his life. Impossible: to walk away from everything in an afternoon. He put the envelope in the back of the drawer and went to the window: evening, the campus quiet. He watched a girl cross from the dormitory to the library carrying a load of books. He was deeply envious of Marshall for the unencumbered haste of his deeds; it seemed otherworldly.

But he had work to do himself; he would have to set his mind firmly against influence. To begin with, he stopped going to The Odalisque. Then he cut his contacts. He wrote Daphne a letter apologizing and explaining that it wasn't her fault, it was his own weakness that obligated him to be alone. He told her that for him she had been a beacon on a rough sea and the next evening, writing to Anne-Marie, he was tempted to use the same explanation again but didn't. He imagined each of them receiving the letters: Daphne reading hers outside on the fire escape; Anne-Marie taking her own to the park on Riverside Drive, where the statue of Kissuth stood among ginkgoes and straggling grass. Anne-Marie had been his temptress and not his comfort. She would probably laugh; she had brothers and understood boys without rancor; she would assume that in time he'd come back, and writing her he could not help but wonder so himself. He was aware that it probably showed in his letter. More of his own weakness, he thought.

He worried over Daphne. She took a morning art history lecture and for a few days he stopped by the class and looked in from the hallway, down the rows of sloping seats to the side aisle up front where she sat, her long hair pulled up inside a barrette. Then he went again to study. He had timed it well in this instance; somehow, his work appealed to him again—there was redemption in sacrifice for a cause. As he sat in the library carrels, beneath the windows with their intricately warped sashes that looked out over the trunks and limbs of the courtyard maples, he suddenly felt reverent again; the problems yielded. There was symmetry in nature, a common organization he saw in the zag of lightning and the spherical propagation of a wave and the branched hyphae of a fungus, whose picture he lingered over one afternoon in a biology text. Once again he thought of medicine. Soon a memory of devotion emerged, a wonder and abiding calm that brought to mind the white walls and the tall curve-topped windows of his family's Methodist Church in Cook's Grange, the glass placed high on the wall there, too, so that one could only look up through it, to treetops and sky. He read more biology. Nature yielded again and again to a set of simple patterns: branching division, motion as vector, the boundless repetition of small event. He realized Daphne was tougher than he was and he stopped checking on her. He pulled his grades up. Spring crested and lit his eye again with the peculiar light of the big city, flatter and more silvery than in Missouri; it seemed distilled by mirrors.

In May he saw a counselor and asked about the possibility of medicine. The same white-sashed windows opened above them onto the shadowed cleft of an elm and Orno gazed at the leaves while the woman looked through his transcript. There were two C's in the sciences, an emphasis on engineering and not a good preparation in biology or even chemistry. She was stern and frowned at him, yet opened her eyes wide to take him in. She said he needed another year of course work in biology and even then his chances were not good. She asked if he'd considered dentistry.

He laughed. "No," he said. "Everyone hates dentists."

"I happen to like mine," she answered.

He stumbled out into the afternoon. He walked through the campus, looking first at the brick and granite edifices and then at the streams of students—where was he going to find his calling? He phoned his parents and told them he was going to stay on in New York for summer session. He told them Marshall had left school and his father said, "I'm not surprised," annoying Orno. But he said nothing.

He found a job washing dishes in a French restaurant and didn't go home until August, when only a week remained before his fall classes. Clara picked him up at the airport, embracing him as he came up the stairs from the tarmac, and he felt mean for having stayed away. They stopped for a soda on the way home and she told him their mother had cried when she'd found out he wasn't coming home in June.

"But she never said anything," said Orno.

"She never would. She wants you to do what you want."

"I don't know what I want. That's why I stayed in New York."

"Don't tell her that," she said. "It sounds mean."

"What's mean about it?"

"It just *is*. It's very ambitious. You sound like you're from there, already."

"Well I don't feel like it. When I'm in New York I feel like I'm still from here."

"And what do you feel like when you're here?"

"Like I'm from New York."

"That's what I thought. Don't tell Mom that. She'd cry again."

She pointed out the window. "Doesn't this feel like home to you anymore?"

He looked. There it was: the horizon, damp with heat, a pale blue bowl of simplicity around the car. The answer was yes. "No," he said. "Not really."

———

He had a week with his family and, secretly, he began looking at their mouths; it seemed shameful, an admission of failing. He watched them over coffee cups in what he hoped seemed like a distracted manner as they talked. His father's: tight, disapproving, set hard, it seemed, against difficulty; a web of lines pursed above the incisors—the *vermilion border* is what a dentistry text had called it. His mother's: fleshier, with the sleek aspect of a plum, a dark bulb in a translucent skin. His sister's: soft and edemic. One evening at dinner he said, "It looks like medicine isn't in my future, but I'm thinking of dentistry."

The moment he said it he thought of Marshall in a bungalow in Santa Monica, sorting through a bowl of hashish. His father set down his fork.

"They don't see you as a candidate for medicine?"

"Had two C's." He saw Marshall writing at the bungalow window looking over the Pacific.

Across the table Clara seemed startled.

His mother turned halfway to the window. "You do whatever you think is right," she said.

"Dentistry, then," said his father, and picked up his fork.

XII

Back at school a package arrived from Los Angeles. He picked it up at the post office, went upstairs to drop off his books, then set off for Central Park. On a bench by the reservoir he opened it and laid it across his lap. He put the note aside and flipped through the pages; there were a hundred and twenty, numbered in pencil; a poor photocopy but readable. The joggers on the path didn't even look at him. The note read:

O—

Well I miss you but I knew I would. I live surrounded by the culture of greed and men in hairpieces inquiring after my screenplay—of course I'm not writing one—and I even met someone who wanted me to work on a *treatment* if you can imagine such a word applying to art. My uncle is a repellent sort it turns out so I am living in someone's basement. Nicer than it sounds, near the beach, with a window at ground level that looks a hundred and fifty yards into the waves. I am reading Borges and Faulkner. Here is my novel so far. What do you think?

He turned it over—there was no more, no signature even. The first sentence of the novel read:

Estophius Adams returned to the land of his home on a day of pulchritude and fervent heat, his brow dotted with humidity, his legs bowed up beneath him in the metal bus seat that had clanged and rattled two thousand miles north into Texas from the collapsing straw eaves of the barrio huts of Panama City, Panama, on the burning, glass-clear coast of two oceans.

He read for three hours straight and finished the section. "I have looked up 'pulchritude,' " he wrote to Marshall that night from a carrel in the library, "and of course I should not have doubted you; it makes perfect sense where it is. The novel read slowly but I think it is very good so far, the part I've read."

———

All of September, he heard nothing from Marshall. Thinking he had insulted him, he wrote again; and once more, no response. The heat still cast a dulling blanket over the commerce and ambition of the city; the skyscrapers softened by haze, all the colors of metal washed by white; the leaves of the ginkgoes stilled by dust. He narrowed his world further. He was taking physical chemistry and organic chemistry and a mid-level course in circuits. It was a heavy load, and he entered a rhythm of serious work unlike any period he had ever known. The library was cool and its basement air felt prickly with static from the huge air conditioners humming in the vents. He found himself unbothered by Marshall's silence and actually thankful to be alone in the strange uptown tropics of the city. Work was his savior and he lost track of all else.

As he made his rounds between the science library and the quiet Italian pastry shop on Amsterdam Avenue where he went for a nightly cannoli before retiring, he was actually heartened by the habit and progress of his solitude—his grades had come up, and though he had missed A's in his two chemistry courses he had done respectably well in both. Yet at the same time he was sometimes ebbingly aware of missed opportunity. Around him the seasons ran through their muted course; the fall crowds somehow making the heat less vivid than in Missouri; the winter cold dirtied and warmed by a thousand rushing cabs; then Christmas back home, and the long early months of the year; spring finally arriving haltingly. He was aware that life at The Odalisque continued, that Daphne and Anne-Marie still went there at night and might now and then think of him, that Sofia still cooked soups on her small stove and sat in her window to study. He didn't see her at all anymore: with Marshall gone those days seemed perilous. A feeling occasionally rose in him that he had misplayed the course of his years here—now and then, crossing the campus, he stopped and imagined himself twenty years older, a fearful nostalgia bluntly wearying his discipline. But he persisted through habit. He moved into a university apartment and lived alone. He added an afternoon walk to his schedule. It was a small act, though among such days it meant a lot; it took him away from his books but not for long, and the river air braced him. A few Italian graduate students in engineering frequented the same pastry shop he did, and he sometimes stayed late to talk with them or watch soccer on the snowy television above the door. He felt strangely like a foreigner himself.

He was perfectly content, really. By the end of his junior year he understood quite firmly that he did not have the intelligence to compete in the advanced chemistry and biology courses; he knew he could work as hard as anyone but even with his discipline he occupied a spot only slightly upward of halfway in the class. There were Jewish and Chinese and Pakistani kids who simply drank down the material he spent hours battling, reading and reading and reading. He went back to see the counselor, who frowned when she held his transcript: there had been improvement, but still his chances were not good. It was a cloudy day and the room was glum. She told him he might as well apply to medical school but to keep alternatives in mind.

That summer he went home and looked around him again. His

father drove off every morning to his office and returned every evening exactly at six, whistling as he traversed the short section of driveway in his suit; he visited his uncle Clarence in his paneled anteroom, glass bookcases lining the walls but barely a soul coming through the door for the entire afternoon; he walked over the hill and watched Olaf Marjorrson in his tractor next door, rumbling among the swaying aisles of corn. The commerce of the world seemed bleak. But when he considered his own life it became clear to him that it was not freedom he desired—he thought of The Odalisque, of Daphne and Anne-Marie, of Marshall in a seaside bedroom; it was discipline; it was work; it was the steady, small progress of a day.

XIII

Senior year he made his applications to schools of dentistry and to four medical schools as well, and in the spring he heard what he had more or less expected: all of the medical schools declined; so did six of the dental schools. March passed and he heard nothing more, and by the beginning of April, with winter still heavy in the stone walls of campus, he began to wake wide-eyed in the middle of the night, afraid. What if no place accepted him? He thought of his father, crossing the porch at six in the evening; he thought of Clara, driving the dusty road to Level.

Dear M,

Well, what is your life like out there? Here the winter refuses to die. It snowed this morning and already the slush is brown, ready to be thrown by cabs. New York is so different without you. My grades are better at least. (But I'm beginning to wonder how far that will get me.) How is the life of a writer? I haven't seen the novel in a long, long time.

—O

Every afternoon he checked his mailbox; every afternoon he found it empty. Then:

Dear O,

It is winter here too (the bougainvillea are blooming), and believe it or not I think I have found a calling. I am working hard on the book and though it is not easy work it does come with time and diligence. I will send it along soon. But anyway why don't you come out here when you're done? There is a juice bar on my corner and for a dollar and a quarter they will put a whole pineapple into a blender.

—M

———

Then at the end of April two letters in his mailbox on the same afternoon: acceptances from the dental schools at the University of Missouri and the State University of New York at Stony Brook. He took them up to his room and held them to the window: through it his view of the black gates and the hurrying street, the orange of a fading afternoon. He was relieved, but not completely. He fanned them out across his desk and found he was somehow sorry when he looked at them; his eye went to the window, to the city he was now leaving. How odd, he thought to himself, to have stumbled backward into a life.

Yet he had always feared an uncharted path, and now his own lay charted before him. He had two classes left for his engineering degree, but instead of studying for them he began to read biology texts. It was the emergent channel of his thought; there was no logic or foresight to it, as there had been in engineering, but to everything there was an elegant yet incomplete explanation, cogent but less than whole, that prickled him. One night in the library he found himself thinking that the insufficiency, perhaps, was God; and again he had memories of the Methodist Church with its windows abutting the ceiling; he was stirred. From a neurobiology text he copied the sentence, "Yet it is a long way indeed from the action potential in the myelinated axon of the giant squid to the passion of a Chopin nocturne." He wrote his parents, telling them that he'd been accepted at Stony Brook but omitting the University of Missouri. "I am embarking on an adventure," he wrote. "It is a long way indeed from the study of a cell to the great works of man." His father wrote back, including in the package his own father's wristwatch, which Orno slid over his wrist on a warm evening in May, then sauntered out onto Broadway.

He found himself passing The Odalisque but it was not difficult to avoid entering; the wristwatch was gold with a flexible metal band from the 1940s and a straightforward mechanism, and amid the unkempt storefronts the gift of it from his father made him feel courageous, that he was permanently beyond The Odalisque and the sophomoric literary debates of Marshall's friends inside. He suddenly saw their behavior as trepidation couched in scholarly gesture; he himself was about to learn a trade and a science: it had everything he needed, wonder and practicality and authority. His skin bristled. For the first time in months, in years even, he was buoyed.

He walked all the way downtown debating whether to tell his parents about the University of Missouri, deciding at last as he came out into the theater district that there was still a world here in the East of which he'd had only the smallest glimpse; he wasn't ready to return home—perhaps he'd never be. He decided to write them again thanking his father for the wristwatch and telling them he'd accepted SUNY Stony Brook for the DDS degree, starting in the fall.

———

Marshall sent him a revision of the first forty pages along with a postcard: *I'll be going to the Emerson-Pelham cottage at Woods Hole for June. Why not come up for a couple of weeks? We can investigate the sun and catalog the flora. You'll say yes I hope.*

There was no mention of their long estrangement, nor of the two unanswered letters from the year before; there was no further letter inside the manuscript even, just the jovial invitation on the other side of a photograph of Mann's Chinese Theater and the stapled pages of the novel, which he took without hesitation to a bench beneath a lamp, high above the Hudson. He knew he had a right to anger, but in his own life he'd never felt betrayal; it didn't arouse his wrath. Evening was half-descended: the dark river touched him with nostalgia.

He read the pages eagerly, but in truth did not know where they had been changed; fearing his own ignorance he delayed in writing back. He waited a few days, then read the manuscript again and finally sat down to compose a reply. He was encouraging—the book was obtuse but he felt incapable of saying so—and at the end of the letter he told Marshall about Stony Brook and wrote that he would love to come to the Cape when school was done. He wondered how Marshall would take the mention of his graduation and imagined that it might be difficult, although at the same time he suspected that Marshall did not care at all about such affairs.

———

O—
    You're really going to be a *dentist?*

                                                    —M

———

M—
    Yes, it looks as though I am.

                                                    —O

———

On a raining morning in June of 1978 he graduated from Columbia, saddened by the fact that there were no parties to take his parents to and stumblingly aware that if the pageant had not been alphabetical he would not have had a comrade with whom to march to the proscenium. It had never happened to him before; in high school he'd had a dozen friends. Now in New York he'd given himself first to Marshall and then to Sofia, and four years had fled by; Marshall sent a telegram that said CONGRATULATIONS STOP NOW STOP STUDYING STOP. He heard nothing from Sofia.

At the end of the proceedings, as the graduates spread out from the auditorium pulling their gowns off over their shoulders and moving away into the melancholy afternoon, he saw Anne-Marie in the distance. That night, after he returned from dinner with his family, he called her and went to see her, aware of the humility he was obligated to feel. He offered to help her move out of her apartment, which she was leaving for the summer. She was kind to him. He'd always thought of her as unhindered by the weight of the world, a girl who stood next to the beer keg at parties and lost her voice every weekend from cigarettes, but now he saw that she was also solicitous. She knew what he was feeling. She hadn't packed yet so there was nothing to move: she seemed amused by his intent. He professed it several times but they ended up making love anyway, startlingly like friends, and he woke up early in the morning and looked out her window onto the neighborhood he would now be leaving, aware of it keenly as the harbor of his missed opportunities. She expected nothing from him, asking him matter-of-factly where he was going for the summer and what he was doing next year. It was the benevolent levelheadedness of a girl with brothers. He dressed, kissed her, and went out into the world.

Two

XIV

He took the northbound local to Providence; from there he transferred to the bus, moving from the damaged industrial towns west of the Cape Cod Canal out through the first gray clapboard fishing villages turned to tourist havens and from there onto the arced heel of the Cape, through Falmouth alongside Buzzards Bay, until the stunt end of the peninsula was so narrow he could feel the sea on both sides of him, and then at last to Woods Hole, the end of the land, where he got out, crossed the road, and stood on the waveless shore of the inlet. He felt light in the world. He had packed one small bag and he set it in the sand. College was behind him and he had come away from it with a certain practical resignation and a future, even if neither one was what he'd expected, and now the smell of brine and the prospect of a month here were tonics. The beach spread around him in a broad half-circle and he suddenly understood what must have been the excitement of the Pilgrims—the land even at first glimpse had an aura of frontier about it and the sense that beyond the low stand of maples and larches lay an expansive country of coast and inland forest, threatening but bountiful: as fertile as

Missouri, as promising as New York City. A vision of the future came to him: living on this peninsula, somewhere among these broadly shadowed coves of maples and the winding roads that led inland behind them, skirting the scrubby low hedges and the seashore.

He took a taxi to the address and was paying the driver when Marshall walked down the path from the side of the house. At the same time the screen door opened and Simone came out onto the front porch, waving; then Marshall was upon him, shaking his hand. He had lost weight in California and his hair had lightened. Orno took in these things only halfway aware of them and was not even sure what he said in greeting. Marshall pulled him close with the handshake and hugged him.

"Nice hairpiece, M."

Marshall laughed. "Let me show you my treatment."

He led Orno back up the walk, gesturing at the house and telling him the history of its owners, a list of merchants and clergy from the eighteenth century and a governor of Massachusetts from the nineteenth, while Orno looked up at the huge, grayed, clapboard amalgamation of rooms and porches that ran like battlements over the hilly yard. The land was bare in places to the sand below and covered elsewhere with dune grass blown low. His own bag was taped where the zipper had pulled apart and he turned the tape inward against his leg and followed, walking all the way around the house behind Marshall before they returned again to the front and went inside.

"The old folks are here this week, but after that it's ours," Marshall said and steered Orno by his elbow around to the back, where a second-story deck looked out over a steep beach and a slanting run of waves. He hadn't seen Mrs. Pelham since the hospital. "You remember Orno," Marshall said.

"Of course," she said, rising.

Professor Emerson looked up from his book and took a drink from his tumbler. He shook Orno's hand and then returned to the book.

"Orno just graduated," said Marshall.

"That's lovely," said Mrs. Pelham.

"Sensible is all," said Professor Emerson.

"I don't need it," said Marshall.

"Perhaps you don't."

"That's enough," said Mrs. Pelham.

Marshall walked to the edge of the deck and looked out. "You don't need a degree to be a writer," he said.

"I'm simply suggesting you finish what you started."

"Please excuse them, Orno," said Mrs. Pelham. "Marshall and his father have been having a disagreement."

"Tell my dad what you're doing next year, Orno," said Marshall.

"I'm sure we can talk about it later."

"Just tell him."

"Going to graduate school," said Orno. He looked down. "I'm going to dental school."

"He's going to be a dentist."

"Good for you," said Mrs. Pelham.

"I didn't get into medical school."

"I'm sure that's their mistake," said Mrs. Pelham.

Marshall folded his arms.

Professor Emerson said, "Well, good. My rear molar has been bothering me."

Marshall looked at him.

"Orno is Orno," said Professor Emerson.

"Exactly my point," said Marshall.

The door opened then and Simone came across the deck, her hands flattening her billowing sundress. "Good for you about dental school," she said.

"Simone's a junior at Bard," said Mrs. Pelham. A boy appeared in the doorway.

"I'll be a junior in the fall, actually," she said, "although I'm sure nobody cares."

"I do," said Orno.

"Thank you, Orno."

"Orno, this is David Bridges," said Marshall, "Simone's boyfriend."

He walked onto the deck and they shook hands. He was probably in her class, a young-looking boy who moved awkwardly, like an animal testing a clearing. He was wearing yellow boat shoes. "Congratulations," he said.

"It's not medical school," said Orno, "but I decided late."

"You can always transfer into medicine," said Mrs. Pelham. She raised her eyebrows.

"He might not want to transfer," said Simone.

"We'll see how it goes," said Orno. "I think I'll be perfectly happy."

"Maybe *I* should go, then," said Professor Emerson without looking up. "If it will make me perfectly happy. Maybe we should all go."

"Father—"said Simone.

"Don't worry," said Marshall, "I'm not going to let him go." He punched Orno on the shoulder. "I'm going to talk him out of it while we're up here."

"Orno, the striped bass are running," said Mrs. Pelham. "The men were planning to go out this evening and catch our dinner. You and Marshall will be sharing a room. Marshall, did you put out a towel?"

"Yes," said Marshall.

"I doubt it," said Simone. "I'll get one."

Marshall kissed her on the cheek.

"I've never fished in the ocean," said Orno.

"Just a big lake," said Professor Emerson. "Except the fish have teeth. You'll like it."

"He will?" said Simone.

"Big teeth," said Marshall, snapping.

"Well, he won't know if he doesn't try," said Professor Emerson. "Will he?"

Nobody answered, so after a moment Orno said, "Well, I suppose teeth are going to be my specialty. So I might as well try it."

———

Marshall's room was at the back of the house, looking out underneath the deck between the high dunes; everything in it had been eaten by salt—the splitting thresholds of the windows, the fraying carpet, the small desk in the corner that had turned gray over the years, and the two thin quilts on the beds, both worn through at the thread lines. Orno unpacked his duffel but there was no room in the bureau drawers. He set his things down on the floor in a corner of the closet, and when he looked up Simone was in the doorway. "What are you doing there?" she said.

"Just putting my stuff away."

"Is that how you do it in Missouri? You can use a drawer, you know."

"There's no room in the dresser."

"Marshall!"

"It's fine. I'll keep my things right here."

"Marshall! What did you expect your friend to do?"

Marshall appeared in the doorway. "Sorry, O."

"That's fine, M."

"My brother has the manners of a pack animal."

Marshall butted her with his head. "My sister has the manners of Queen Victoria."

"Really," Orno said. "It's no problem."

"Yes, it is. Marshall, clean him out a drawer. Look," she said, stepping to the bureau. "What is all this stuff? It hasn't fit you in years." She threw a handful of bathing suits onto the bed. "And what about towels? Did you get Orno a towel?"

"I thought you were going to do that."

"I'll get my own," said Orno. "Don't worry about me."

"No, you won't," said Simone. "Marshall should have gotten everything ready beforehand."

Marshall leaned next to her and put his arm over her shoulder. Then he nuzzled her neck. "All right, all right," she said, pushing away his head. "I'll get the towels. But I want you to clear him a drawer. All right?"

"All right," said Marshall.

"Do you see this, Orno?" she said, turning from the room. "He has us all eating from his palm. Don't you let him do this to you."

In the late afternoon they drove out to the harbor. Professor Emerson's boat was moored alongside huge motorboats and sailing yachts: a low skifflike hull that to Orno's surprise needed paint, with a small enclosed cabin and gunwales that sloped away to the rear like a tug or a vessel made for specialty work. Professor Emerson must have used it for his research; it looked out of place, riding so low between two cabin cruisers that Orno hadn't even noticed it until they were in front of its berth. On the back was the name *Chesterton*, in a low arc. The deck smelled of fish and when the engine started a billow of blue smoke churned up.

He had never been on the ocean before and in the low-riding stern as they passed through the rough surf they were so close to the waves that he had to keep his gaze on the dark line of land to the west to quell his fear. The sun was moving low and he felt it would be dark within the hour. Professor Emerson darted the boat up behind the surf so that Marshall could cast his line into the running curl beneath the foam; Orno and David Bridges were on the other side, fighting the slant of the deck and the eruption of spray when the hull pitched sideways on the backs of the waves. The craft bobbed up toward the shoreward wall and if it topped at the crest Professor Emerson lurched it into reverse and pulled it down again along the seaward edge; Orno was queasy and when his own side turned toward the shore the blowing spume soaked him and the crash of the breakers was like a pistol. Soon he was drenched and his feet were slipping in his shoes. He knew how to fish on a lake but it was difficult to keep his balance here well enough to get his line to the target; his hands were so cold he had trouble letting out the line. He and David Bridges barely spoke and it became obvious that either Professor Emerson was testing them or was oblivious to their fear. The boat pitched. Across the deck Marshall stood with one knee against the gunwale, casting across the top of the curls, placing the heavy lure into the clear belly of the waves; twice Orno saw the pucker and white flash of a fish near Marshall's line and finally as the wind came up fiercely and the waves began to run both ways, shoreward at their bases and seaward at their crests, Marshall hooked a striped bass and pulled it in. He netted it, threw it onto the deck, pulled a rolling pin from the bait chest and stilled it with a blow behind the head. Then he went to the stern and began cleaning it as Professor Emerson turned the boat out to sea again and to Orno's relief they motored home.

David Bridges sat on the gunwale with his hands on his knees. The sun set as they crossed into the channel. Marshall was tossing the entrails into the churning wake behind the engine, where seagulls dived at the remains. Orno had never seen him do anything physical with confidence before, but now he used the knife in quick cuts that flayed the fish in a few moments, his face marked with the same grave silence he'd shown as the boat pitched in the surf. David Bridges wasn't talking either. To Orno he looked frightened or perhaps seasick. When the boat finally pulled into its slip Marshall jumped ashore and tethered it to the dock, fore then aft, while Professor Emerson revved the engine to full throttle and then killed it, striding out of the cabin and then jumping ashore so that he was already in the gravel parking lot beside the station wagon before Orno and David Bridges had climbed out of the boat.

Back at the house, Marshall led the way, holding the fish as the four of them walked through to the deck, where Simone pointed to Orno's leg and said, "Oh my, what happened to you?"

He looked down. Blood soaked his pants around the ankle; instantly seasickness rose and he sat back on a chair. Simone knelt: "Here, let me see what they did to you."

She pulled up his pants leg: his shin was slashed and the skin curled away. There had been no pain until that moment, but now he was nauseated with it. Mrs. Pelham came out of the kitchen with a dishtowel and wrapped it. "You're going to the clinic," she said. She turned to her husband. "Didn't you see this?"

Professor Emerson looked out at the waves. "I was driving the boat and then I was driving the car." He glanced at Orno. "It's not as bad as it looks."

David Bridges said, "I was going to mention it on the boat but it didn't look so bad then."

Simone looked at him.

"It's not too bad," said Orno.

"Don't move a muscle," said Marshall, "I'll get Simone's sewing box."

"I think I'll take the clinic, M."

"There's always a lot of blood from the shin, Marshall," said Professor Emerson. He had a glass in his hand. "I wonder if you can name the muscle."

"Peroneus longus," said Marshall. "The blood in his socks comes from the popliteal veins." He offered Orno his tumbler. "It looks like it hurts."

"Kind of does."

"It's awfully deep," said Simone.

"I thought he knew about it," said David Bridges.

"You still should have said something," said Simone.

"Blue thread," said Marshall, "to match his lips."

"See," said Simone, resting her hand on Orno's shoulder, "the fish *do* have teeth."

"To future clients, then," said Marshall, raising his glass. He turned toward the kitchen. "What the man needs is his own scotch, though, *before* he goes to the clinic." And as Mrs. Pelham and Simone helped him hobble to the car, that is what he brought him.

———

The spume on the beach that night was phosphorescent and behind them as they walked he could see the glow of cocktail parties in the windows and the small cloudy glow of bonfires along the dunes. The sand was still warm from the afternoon, and they took off their shoes but stayed high on the beach away from the water: Orno had taken two dozen stitches, and the doctor had cautioned him against getting them wet. When the suturing was done the nurse had given him a tetanus shot, and after she wiped his forearm with alcohol she had asked quietly, "Is there anything you didn't want to tell the doctor?" He shook his head, wondering himself how he could not have felt such a wound on the boat.

Now it throbbed, and his arm hurt from the shot, and as he and Marshall walked slowly along the shore and looked out at the rumbling dark mass of breakers the time on the boat seemed once again frightening and, as he'd felt in the clinic, somehow sinister. It seemed that Professor Emerson had been trying to pitch them into the sea. Marshall was walking ahead of him. Orno wanted to ask him about it, but in the boat he'd been as fierce as his father; even on the ride back as he cleaned the fish there seemed to be an armor of silence around him that had made Orno feel like a stranger. Now, once again, five yards ahead of him on the sand, Marshall seemed to be forbidding him from speaking. As they passed the estates behind each stand of dunes, he turned around and told Orno who owned them, actors and writers and a man Orno recognized from the news as a confidant of the president.

"So, M, this is more of what you grew up with, eh?"

"I guess so."

"I grew up with farmers and insurance salesmen."

"I grew up with Kennedys and insurance salesmen."

"I grew up with pigs everywhere," said Orno.

"And we had that in common." He stopped and waited for Orno to reach him. "How's your leg?"

"Hurts like crazy."

"Here, we should slow down. I can't believe I didn't see it on the boat."

"I can't believe *I* didn't see it either."

"That's the way it is out there with my father."

"That's the way what is?"

Marshall looked at him. "That's how *he* is." He laughed. "I used to be scared to death."

"It was pretty hairy," Orno said. "I admit it. David Bridges was green."

"My sister is really in love with him."

"He doesn't talk much."

"Hah," said Marshall. "He doesn't need to. He's from the Lazard Frères family. He's a liar just like my sister."

"Your sister's a liar?"

"Wait and see," said Marshall. "She's a core of two, wings of eight and three. The Giver and the Performer."

Orno didn't know what to say. He had the feeling Marshall hoped he would ask about it, but he didn't want to; if anything,

Simone seemed like the one in the family who told the truth. He thought about it as they walked. "Who's Lazard Frères?" he asked finally.

"The investment bank. It's one of the biggest in the world. One of his grandfathers started it. Their family is a bunch of liars, too. That's how you make money on Wall Street."

Orno's leg was throbbing: he thought he should probably put it up. Marshall seemed to have learned a great deal about the world since he left Columbia; or perhaps it was simply knowledge that went with a childhood in this territory, the way Orno himself had knowledge of farm animals and weather. He felt naive again, cast behind from the secrets he'd first encountered his freshman year. "Well, that didn't seem to help David Bridges on the boat," he said, trying to keep up the conversation. "And Simone was pretty mad at him."

"How do you know that?"

"From what she said to him. That he didn't say anything about my leg on the boat."

"I told you, you can't believe everything my sister says." He leaned down and picked up a dark tangle from the sand, then carried it into the shallows, where he pulled it through the foamy water. "Look at this," he said. "*Phaeophycophyta*. Giant kelp. I think it's gorgeous. Don't you agree?" He turned it over in his hands and the bulbs glistened. "Sometimes I want to be in the sea. On the ocean floor a hundred miles out where it's covered with this, waving as though it's in the wind. I just think that would be incredibly beautiful."

"It would."

"I think I'll die in the sea."

Orno started walking again. "Don't talk about that, Marshall, unless you want me to take you seriously."

"Oh, don't worry, I'll never do that again. I just think that when it's my time I would like to end up in the ocean."

"I'll try to remember that."

"That would be kind of you."

Orno looked at him. "Do you go to the beach in L.A.?"

"Of course—everybody does. But it's a different ocean there

and a different beach. Here," he said, stopping at the waterline, "this ocean makes me nostalgic." He waved the kelp over the panorama of dunes and houses behind them. "In Los Angeles, it's temporary. It's hot as hell and you have the feeling that it goes on forever, the ocean there. There's nothing private about it, and nothing about it changes. Ever. You don't ever see it storming in winter. Every day is the same."

"So why did you go?"

"Because it's the place to write about America. I'm writing about America." He turned. "That's what America *is*."

They walked farther. "I guess your dad doesn't like it."

"I guess you noticed."

"It's not hard."

Marshall draped the kelp over his head so the fronds fell over him. "That's why I'm doing it."

"I hope that's not the only reason."

"Maybe it is," Marshall said. "Getting a college degree would be easy. My dad doesn't see beyond the one small thing he's done with his own life."

"Your dad's hardly done a small thing with his life. He's a professor. He's a well-known scientist."

"He's a scared man. That's why he tries to scare *us*."

"He's just worried about you."

"You don't understand."

"I'd be worried too if my kid dropped out of school to write."

"I'm telling you, you don't understand."

"Sure I do."

"You have no idea," Marshall said. He turned away from the sea. "I hate my father."

"You do not."

"And so does Simone."

"I don't believe that."

"What you don't understand is that my father and I are in a fight to the death."

"That's ridiculous."

"Possibly."

"It's paranoid, M. Your father loves you. That's the only reason he gives you a hard time."

"What makes you say that?"

"It's obvious."

"Why?"

"Because he's your father, that's why."

Marshall laughed. "See," he said, "you can't even consider it. You've lived this life—you just don't know—I can't tell you how much my sister and I would have loved your life. You can't even understand what ours is like."

The ferry pulled into view beyond the dunes and they watched it move toward the stone breakwater at the end of the beach.

"Your sister and you would like *my* life?"

"You have no idea."

"You'd trade this for Cook's Grange? Excuse me, but I find that a little hard to believe." He brushed aside the kelp on Marshall's shoulders. "Those smell like fish."

"It's the fish that smell like the kelp, O. See, you misunderstand my father. He's not worried about me getting along in the world. He's just terrified of me. That's all. He's afraid I'm going to outdo him. Think of what you'd be like if your own father was that way. Your dad wants a lot from you, but that's because he wants a lot *for* you. That's the difference. My father won't be happy unless I make him think he's done the right thing with his own life. It's got nothing to do with me. That's why he's happy you're thinking of dental school."

"What does that have to do with dental school?"

"I'll tell you if you want."

Orno picked up a handful of sand and let it drain through his fingers. The grains were still warm from the afternoon. "He thinks being a dentist is below him, I guess."

"That's right," said Marshall, "and *I* think it's below you, too, O. I really do."

Orno kicked up the sand in front of him. His face was hot. "I can't believe you're saying that."

"I'm an honest man."

Orno walked ahead. They had passed the houses now and were

on a spit of sand bordered by a tidal lagoon. "Funny," he said. "Of course I always suspected you thought that, and I thought I would be mad if you said it. But I'm not." He laughed. "I'm relieved, actually. *I* was ashamed of it, too. At first, that is, but I learned I was wrong. My dad sells insurance, M. If he didn't sell insurance he would sell well-diggers, and if he didn't sell well-diggers he'd sell tractor parts. There's nothing wrong with dentistry, despite what you think."

"You'll buy a house in the suburbs."

"I might. You'll buy a house in Los Angeles."

"You'll have two kids."

"So will you. And just the same we'll both die one day."

"In the meantime I'll be doing what I love."

"If it works out."

"You don't think it will?"

"No, I think it probably will. I think you can do anything, Marshall. You don't understand. You're brilliant. Everybody knows that. Until we got used to it, Phoebe and I used to talk about it twice a day. Sofia and I used to talk about it. You're extraordinary. The rest of us aren't. The rest of us are dentists and salesmen. You could be a college professor in your sleep."

"You don't like my book, O, do you?"

"What makes you say that?"

"What you just said, that I could be a professor. You were telling me not to be a writer."

"I like your book very much."

"Say that to my face, O, so I can see if you're lying." He took Orno's arm and turned him around.

"I like your book, Marshall."

Marshall looked at him closely, put his face right up to his and examined it. "Look," he said, "I don't care if you don't like it, but I want you to tell me the truth. I want to know that I have one friend in the world who will tell me the truth. Okay?" he said. "I'm waiting. I told you the truth about dentistry." He turned and looked at the sea.

"Who else has read it?" Orno asked.

"Just you and an agent."

"What does the agent think of it?"

"You're making me nervous now, O. Just tell me."

"All right," said Orno. "The truth is, I really do like it."

"You do?"

"Yes."

Marshall pulled the kelp off his head and tossed it into the waves. Then he turned around and walked up from the sea onto the dry sand, where he hugged Orno, full on, and Orno saw to his surprise that tears were on his face.

———

Marshall said to everyone at the table, "Well, I convinced him not to be a dentist."

They were eating breakfast. "Did you really?" said Mrs. Pelham. She was serving potatoes. "Well, that was easy enough, Orno."

"Good God," said Professor Emerson, "*too* easy."

Orno looked up at him. "Wait a second," he said. "I haven't decided not to go."

"Oh, come on, O. Anybody can be a dentist, not *you*. What a waste that would be."

"It's not a waste if he wants to do it," said Simone.

"A waste?" said Professor Emerson. "Pot calling the kettle black, to me."

"Dentist is a waste, writer is not a waste."

"Well, as you'd like," said Professor Emerson, smiling at the others. "By the way, Orno," he said, holding out his arms in front of him, "do both these arms look the same to you?"

"Yes, they seem to."

"Nothing's a *waste*," said Simone. "Writer isn't a waste, dentist isn't a waste. Why does everything have to be this way?"

"These are just people's opinions, Simone," said David Bridges. "They're just saying what they think."

Simone glanced at him. "Thank you, David," she said.

"It's not even true, necessarily," said Orno.

"Both of them?" said Professor Emerson, turning his palms up and holding them steady. "Identical?"

"Yes, I think so," said Orno.

"Simone's absolutely right," said Mrs. Pelham. "When your teeth ache, dentist is as important as it gets."

"Actually," said Orno, "I think the novel Marshall's writing is important."

"Well, the point is moot, anyway," said Professor Emerson, "because I think Orno's still got it in him to do dentistry either way, haven't you, Orno?"

"That's what I was trying to say. To tell you the truth, I haven't changed my mind at all."

Marshall looked stricken. "Come on, O," he said. "You can't."

"Please," said Simone. "He can do whatever he wants. Why do you care so much?"

"Because he's my friend."

"Well, I appreciate it," said Orno.

"Then you should want what *he* wants."

"The point is," said Professor Emerson, "at least your friend Orno will be earning a living." He put his hands down.

"I'm earning a living, too," said Marshall.

"Let's not start this again," said Mrs. Pelham.

"And how are you doing that?" said Professor Emerson.

It occurred to Orno that he didn't know the answer to this; he didn't even know if Marshall had a job in Los Angeles. He'd only pictured him writing, living in the apartment that looked out at the sea.

"I'm doing temporary work," said Marshall.

"Temporary work?"

"In the business. I'm answering phones."

"What business is that?"

"The movie business," said David Bridges. "That's what people mean in L.A. by the business. Right, Marshall?"

"That's right."

"You're answering phones at a movie studio?"

"Yes, jobs like that, for one example."

"Tell me, do the other operators have course work from Columbia?"

"I said that's enough of that, you two," said Mrs. Pelham, and she stood and took away Professor Emerson's plate, though there were still eggs on it, and most of his potatoes.

Professor Emerson put his arms back out. He looked at Orno. "I'll be specific," he said. "Do you see a tremor here?"

———

There were a figure and a carriage on the Cape that Orno had never seen before: gray hair in the old men, but long over the neck, and a back-leaning gait that implied ownership of the sand that stretched endlessly around; it was a confident, mildly weary walk, the hands clasped behind in the manner of psychiatrists or professors, the gaze turned up from the waterline toward the dunes, whose difficult footing was to be avoided; the wives wore sun hats and one-piece bathing suits ending in skirts; the nannies and children followed behind.

What was it—the boisterous children? The nannies? The strolling old men? Orno felt he was in a different country, a land of franchise and estate in which he was of no consequence. He simply had never conceived of such a world. It wasn't envy that he felt exactly, but some kind of lack in himself—not that he had never known such a life, rather that he had never even imagined one. *I am not a dreamer,* he thought.

He tried to let this comfort him. Even if the families here looked down on dentists, it was of consolation to know that his own people did not. He reminded himself that Marshall had told him of his and Simone's envy. What could it be for? For his simplicity? His humble hopes? For the paltry ambition that had at least allowed him an unroiled life?

He was walking with Marshall above the tide line. "You know," Marshall said, "I just said those things at breakfast because I wanted you to see what my father's like."

"I told you, he's just worried about you."

"So worried that he rides me like that. It's a little bullfight. I buck him away. He doesn't let up. I buck him again. My sister dances in and puts the lances in my shoulders."

"Your sister doesn't do that."

"How do you know?"

"Because I'm there, M."

"You just haven't seen yet. He needs his little picador. And it's not because he's afraid I'll fail as a writer, it's because he's afraid I'll succeed."

"Come on, you see the worst in everything. Simone only wishes well for you."

"For example," said Marshall, "you know why I said you were quitting dentistry?"

"To bug me."

"Nope. It's because I know that my father could get you into medical school by picking up the phone." He smiled. "He could do it in a second."

Orno looked out at the ocean. "No, he couldn't."

"It would take him ten minutes, two phone calls."

"I don't have the grades."

"Hah! You think that matters?"

"Yes, I think it does."

"Well, it doesn't."

They walked on. Suddenly Orno was struck with the possibility: he imagined calling home—his mother's hand going to her mouth, his father setting down his pipe. "Well," he said, "it doesn't matter. Because if that's how I got in, I wouldn't go."

"Come on, O, you're not in Missouri anymore."

"I wouldn't. It's got nothing to do with Missouri."

"Be smart, O."

"I *am* being smart." He picked up a rock, weighed it in his hand, and threw it into the sea. "That's all," he said, "I'm not talking about it anymore."

———

On the deck that afternoon, after they'd eaten a salad and drunk white wine out of chilled glasses, Orno fell asleep on one of the weathered Adirondack recliners facing the beach. When he woke the sun was low, a third of the way to the sea, warped at its shallow angle by the gauze of humidity at the horizon. He had a headache and his mouth was dry. He turned around and saw Simone working in the nasturtiums next to the deck.

"Good morning," she said.

He sat up straight. "What have I been doing? It's a sin to sleep in the afternoon."

"In my family there aren't any sins."

"Hah!"

"There *aren't*." She climbed over the railing and continued working from the inside of the deck. "I just want you to know," she said, "I think dental school is fine for you. Don't let Marshall talk you out of it."

"I wasn't planning to." He smiled. "But I'll consider myself warned."

"Good," she said. "That's my job. I warn people."

"What else do you have to warn me about?"

"Sunburn," she said. "Ticks. Sleeping in the afternoon."

He got up. The nasturtiums were growing crazily from planters set in the dunes, startlingly cheerful colors tumbling among the rails and pushing their way through the gaps in the deck boards. He began to pluck them with her.

"How's your leg?" she said.

"Not so painful but pretty embarrassing."

"Can I ask you something?"

"Please do."

"Did my father pull his usual display?"

"Where?"

"On the boat."

"What's his usual display?"

"Did he try to scare you?"

He looked up. "I think he did, actually."

"Is that how you got hurt?"

"To tell you the truth, I really don't remember. I didn't feel it till *you* saw it."

"That's my other job." She smiled, then turned away.

"I thought it was seawater in my shoes."

She was setting the flowers in pitchers. "Not exactly the sensitive sort, I guess." Her face was still turned away, looking out at the beach. She seemed to be teasing him.

"I'm not used to being on a boat, to tell you the truth."

"Oh, it's not just that," she said. "It's my father. If I'm along or my mother is, he drives like an old man, but when he's out with Marshall I'm scared. I've seen Marshall's face after he comes in from being pounded out there. It's like no other time with him, you know, he gets this look of mortal concentration."

"I know. I saw that look, too."

"But the whole thing is unsaid between them. My father won't admit he does it, and Marshall won't admit it scares him."

"He admitted it to me."

"He did? He must trust you."

"He said that he and your dad are still in a fight."

"He said that?"

"A fight to the death, is what he said."

"That's a bit extreme."

He laughed. "That's what I told him."

"My brother has a talent for exaggeration."

"Does he?"

She peered at him. "You've never seen it?"

"I don't think so."

"Oh, it's just another way he's like my father." She brushed back her hair and turned toward the house.

"How's that like your father?"

"You don't really want to know."

"Of course I do."

"Look at this house," she said, pointing. "He's a biology professor. Everyone else on the Cape comes from family money. He tries to make them think we do, too. Do you know how deeply he's mortgaged to keep us here?"

"All right, but Marshall doesn't do that."

"Maybe not now, but one day he will."

"Perhaps," he said. "But that's not exactly a logical argument."

She turned back to him. "What makes you think you can say that to me?"

"Sorry."

"You barely know me."

"But I like you," Orno said.

"You do?"

"Yes."

She turned to the beach again. "Orno, do you know what my father's father did?"

"He was a civil rights attorney."

"How do you know that?"

"Marshall told me, freshman year. He had a photographic memory, too. He argued in front of the Supreme Court."

"That's what I mean," she said. "I don't know if I know you well enough to tell you this."

"Come on," he said. "Trust me."

She tossed her hair. "I never believe that line from a boy."

She stood looking at the water; watching her from behind, he suddenly felt boldness come over him. When she turned back, he leaned across the railing and kissed her.

"Oh, God," she said. "What are you doing?"

"I don't know. Sorry."

"David is in the house."

"It was the way you said that, that you don't trust that line. It was irresistible." He had to fight himself; he couldn't tell whether she was angry or just flushed. They were looking at each other: he felt crazy, but the feeling only emboldened him again.

"Orno, look in there. I think David is right in there."

"I won't do it again."

"I want to believe that," she said. She smoothed her dress. Then she walked away from him, out onto the beach, where the spent waves ran up at her, one after another, as she headed north over the dunes.

————

That night, he lay awake trying to separate the sounds in the house from the slide of the surf that obscured them. Marshall was still playing backgammon with his mother behind the closed door of the living room, and the darkness around Orno was broken only by the glint of china and the tortoiseshell lamp shades reflecting the low moon through the window. He'd behaved badly: in his right mind he would never have kissed her. It had utterly surprised him; he hadn't even known he was considering it. The air had taken on a chill, and he still hadn't heard her come home. She'd gone out to dinner with David, wearing a straw hat and not even turning around to say good-bye to Orno, who'd found himself standing next to the door as they walked off together in the early evening.

He considered apologizing. He was as careless as Marshall, it seemed to him; but as he listened intently to the radio, to the creak of chairs, to the laughter and the dull clatter of dice in a cup, he again had the feeling that there was a hidden boldness inside of him. Then the thought began to trouble him that perhaps someone had seen him kiss her; David Bridges had a way of entering a room quietly—he might have been anywhere. He closed his eyes. If Simone asked him to leave he would go back to New York; he would go to a YMCA, and from there to Cook's Grange if he had to. He tried to distract himself. The chances were that nobody had seen and that Simone would just ignore it, or at worst mention it to David and then keep away from him for the rest of his visit. Orno had run into David in the hallway before he'd gone out, but he'd passed him too quickly to scrutinize his reaction; now, as he thought about it, he convinced himself that David had been the same as always—shy around him, and hesitant, moving against the wall to let him pass. For that he felt a moment of pity as well, lying in the dark. But what if she told Marshall?

Yet he'd felt so decisive on the deck with her, so different from how he'd ever felt with Daphne or Anne-Marie or Sofia, that he actually found himself proud of his recklessness. Maybe it was Marshall he'd learned it from, after all. There seemed to have been a hand guiding him, a mysterious agent of deliverance.

Through the window, whitecaps played offshore. He listened for the different footfalls in the house—for Marshall's careless flop, for Professor Emerson's bored shuffle, for Mrs. Pelham's optimistic, almost dancing step. Simone herself had a careful stride, but he didn't hear it, or David Bridges's quiet one. He was aware whenever the door opened to the living room because the radio grew louder, and then, as the door closed again, softer, and by this he felt he could track the commerce of the house. It was well into the early hours of morning before he heard her come home.

———

The next morning breakfast was nearly over when he sauntered out to the kitchen. Simone was at the table with David and Marshall, sipping her coffee with one arm pulled inside the sleeve of a Bard College sweatshirt. He stood by the window first, and then, feeling awkward, took the seat at the far end of the table, next to Marshall. She was wearing black jeans and a baseball cap, her hair in a rubber band beneath it. David Bridges's arm lay across the tablecloth, near hers. Everything seemed normal with them, and he tried his best to make it seem normal with him as well. He drank from a coffee cup, then realized it wasn't his. Marshall noticed him set it down again and smiled in a way that could have meant any number of things. Mrs. Pelham was at the kitchen window, loading the dishwasher and gazing out at the sea; Professor Emerson was standing outside the window in the dunes.

"Sleep well?" asked Mrs. Pelham.

"Fine, thank you." He felt himself blush.

"I think he's tired himself out up here," said Marshall. "He normally wakes at six. That's okay, O, I've already milked the cow."

"I always sleep well near the ocean."

"When have you ever been near an ocean?" Marshall smiled at him.

"It's his leg," said Simone. "He's tired."

"It's school," said Orno. "It's four years of studying."

"So why are you opting for four more then?" said Marshall.

"I'm sorry I didn't tell you about your leg on the boat," said David Bridges. "I thought you knew and were just toughing it out. I wasn't sure what you could have done about it out there anyway."

"He could have come in, for one," said Simone.

"That's fine, David," said Orno. "Don't trouble yourself over it."

"Marshall," said Mrs. Pelham, "I was hoping you and Orno could go grocery shopping this morning."

There was a silence. Orno found his gaze on David Bridges, who ate his cereal carefully, his elbow out, lifting the spoon of shredded wheat like hot soup. He felt sorry for him once again. Marshall tilted back on the rear legs of his chair and suddenly Orno thought of The Odalisque: there was something the same there in the predatory ordering and reordering of strength in the room.

"David and I will come along, too," Simone finally said.

"That's okay," said Marshall.

"No, really, we don't mind. We need to get a few things in town anyway."

"Then come with us," said Orno.

On the way to the store, Marshall drove and Orno sat in the front next to him, trying not to look at Simone or David. They were in the backseat, and from the corner of his vision Orno tried to discern her mood; she was looking out the window most of the time and her hand seemed to be near David's leg, but when he turned around he thought he caught her looking at him; but immediately she turned away again. What had been on her face? Expectancy? Defiance? He couldn't be sure, and now she wouldn't look at him again. He put his arm up along the back of the seat, but this suddenly seemed false, and he returned it to his lap.

In the store she finally came up to him at the dairy freezer and said, "I think what I'm going to say is that you should never do that again."

"I'm sorry," he said. He opened the door to the freezer. "I think I need to cool off."

"I didn't say you should be sorry."

He turned around. She might have been smiling; it was a frank expression. He didn't know what it signaled. "I shouldn't have done it," he said.

"You've confused me. You've put me in a difficult position, that's all."

"Is that encouragement?"

"I don't think so."

"It must be a warning, then."

"No, it's not that."

"I'm sorry again, then."

Her expression was still mysterious, different wills in it. He glanced back from the freezer. The store was busy, but he couldn't see Marshall or David. Clouds of cold were moving around them. Something about her: he felt bold again.

"Don't," she said.

"Don't what?"

But she'd already walked away.

X V

t the beach now, around the dinner table, on the inland bicycle paths where he walked with Marshall in the mornings, the
thought of her distracted him unendingly, so that he felt ill-
committed to anything he was doing and found himself wandering away as soon as he could. How had it happened to him: his best
friend's sister, a girl he'd barely noticed until two days ago? The
beach went on forever and he used it as distraction. He would
leave Marshall reading a book on the porch and then set off rambling along the shoreline, not sharp in his thinking until he had
passed two or three curves on the great spits of sand and the
house had long ago vanished behind the dunes and the low stands
of trees. She lived constantly in the center of his thoughts. He
would try to think about his plans for the rest of the summer, but
his eyes would conjure up her forthright gaze; he would try to listen to the clap and rumble of the surf, but would instead recall
their conversation together on the porch, and then his kiss, and
then in return her enigmatic scolding.

He wasn't comfortable to begin with, but now he was shaken.
He knew he should leave; he should go back to New York and

reestablish himself, begin to prime his mind for next year; but there was no chance of this. He was on edge. Returning home in the afternoon, he would stop a quarter mile down the beach and stare up at the house, instantly aware which figures were moving about the deck. If he saw hers, he hurried back.

He also began to see how ill-prepared he was for this kind of life; after dinner the Emerson-Pelhams entertained themselves with Scrabble or cribbage or dominoes, parlor games he had never played before and that were unkind reminders of the fact that he had been raised so far away and could not scramble and unscramble letter tiles or calculate the odds on cards. David was the fourth for bridge one evening while Orno stood outside the circle of their chairs, calamitously drawn to Simone but so paralyzed with the thought of it that he found himself behind Professor Emerson the whole evening instead, as far away from her as he could be. He watched the hands and tried to deduce the game but his thoughts kept returning to her. It must have been obvious to everyone: his eyes seemed to travel on their own to her face. He averted them each time. Fearing Marshall would know, he could not look at him either. He took refuge on the deck instead, wandering out there repeatedly to stand alone in the yellow light from the house for as long as he could allow himself without seeming rude. He found the nighttime passage of fishing boats on the horizon luminescently beautiful. This would distract him for a few moments. Then he would return again to the gathering inside, aware like a thief of his own obviousness.

———

One evening he was sitting by himself in the dunes just before dark when she strolled down from the house. He wasn't sure of her intentions, but he found himself standing up from the sand anyway and placing himself near her path. She might have been on her way to the beach; she might have been coming out after David. But here it was again: this queer boldness. He stepped in front of her, and when she smiled he took her hand and kissed it.

This time she seemed willing, though only for a moment. Then she turned and walked back up to the porch.

He followed. He could see her parents inside. He sat on one of the Adirondacks. She hesitated, but then came over and stood next to him. "I told you," she said.

"Sorry." He sat on his hands. "It seems to have happened again."

"Yes, it does."

"You bring it out in me."

"Marshall used to tell me stories about you."

Behind her Professor Emerson came to the glass doors and looked out.

"What did he tell you about me?" he said.

She frowned at him. "That you're a cad."

"Well, he was wrong."

She studied him. "He's hardly ever wrong, you know."

"I know that," Orno said. "But he is this time."

"How do I know which one of you is telling the truth?"

"Because you have my word."

She looked at him for a long time. Then Professor Emerson opened the door and stepped out onto the porch. "Simone," he said. "I need you here inside."

———

On the beach Marshall walked up and said, "Unbelievable news, O. Guess what? They want me back in L.A. They're interested."

"Who is?"

"I just talked to my agent. There's a publisher who wants to meet me. They've arranged it. They think it's got vision. They want me to rewrite it, but she says they're definitely interested. It's great—" He shielded his eyes. "Though I guess it's not so good for you."

"When was this?"

"Well, they want me there tomorrow."

"Tomorrow? Are you going?"

"Of course."

"When?"

"Tonight. There's a flight out of Providence."

"When will you be back?"

"I don't know, O. I'll probably stay out there, if it goes well at least. I know that's not good news for you, though. Where will *you* go?"

"Of course it's good news for me." He didn't know what else to say. "I'll go home and start saving money for school."

"You're not really going to go through with that, are you?"

"Unless you plan to support me with money from the book."

Marshall grinned. "You can come back again any time you want. We'll be here next summer. Or you can come out with me to California. What about that?"

"I couldn't do that. I ought to be working anyway. I've got to start saving." He looked up the beach. He was wondering where Simone was. She might have been out there in front of him on the sand, probably walking with David Bridges. She might have been thinking of him. "I was just getting to like it out here," he said. He smiled. "God, M, it didn't take you long."

"I'll put you in it. I'll name a character after you."

"Orno the Dentist."

"The Story of O."

"You're amazing, M. Do you know that? You can do anything you want."

And that is what he thought about later that afternoon as he packed, because he didn't want to think about Simone. Back in the house, looking out over the shimmering channel, he considered the fact that, growing up here, Marshall had seen the horizon every day. The vast unknown sea—that kind of landscape must have changed him; it had to. Behind Woods Hole lay the narrow crowded neck of the Cape, but Marshall must have grown up with the sense that the great part of the world was still unknown and not yet settled, constantly hinted at over the water. He wondered briefly at what his own life might have been had he too known that feeling. In Cook's Grange there was the immense white sky but in four directions the land was the same for hundreds of miles. There he grew up imagining nothing beyond the set of larger towns that ringed them: Hale with its Cadillac dealership, Turbine with the public-housing project, Porterville and General and Level coming one after the other until one was in Hannibal finally, and then the great, wide Mississippi; and that was all he had ever imagined. He really had never dreamed of anything else. He could sell insurance; he could be a dentist. Writing a novel about America—it was not something he could have ever conceived of.

His thoughts returned to Simone, and now he felt them as a sharpness in his chest. It was probably just his leg that had drawn her to him, nothing more—just some gentle, confusing female protectiveness he'd excited; yet he couldn't help feeling that when he'd kissed her hand the second time she had softened. And then she'd spoken to him on the deck before going inside: he wondered what it was supposed to mean. But now he was leaving.

Simone was gone all afternoon, and when she wasn't back by the time the sun went down he gave up and brought his duffel out to the car. Now his chest felt hollow. He realized that he wasn't going to see her again, perhaps forever, that he was going off with little hope of returning here before she vanished down her own path in the world. He wrote a note on a scrap of paper and set it on the windowsill of her room. It said, *Write me sometime,* and because he knew David might find it he left off his name; it was dishonorable, but he saw no other choice.

That night Professor Emerson drove them into Providence. Marshall got on a plane and he himself got on the southbound commuter train; rumbling out into the dark switching yard, he had the feeling of being borne aloft again on a scattering wind.

X V I

In Cook's Grange he found work on a road crew, repairing the interstate. They worked at night under sodium lamps driven by gasoline generators that rumbled like trucks behind them, swirling with clouds of moths that bumped their arms as they shoveled heaps of gravel and asphalt in front of the graders. At five each morning they quit for the day and he slept until afternoon. He wrote a letter:

M—

So this is the difference between us. You have gone off to find your true (and great) calling, and I am here finding my humble one. Lately it's been to keep piles of pitch ahead of the pavers. I am guessing but I think a paver must weigh three tons. I'm lucky because for that reason they move slower than my shovel. I believe I must be the only Columbia graduate doing such work. (You can tell your father.) You would like it, I think: I wake up at four in the afternoon. I'm saving money, although I know it will be gone in half a semester at school. I'm looking at people's mouths. A lot of them around here are missing teeth, which might be a good sign for me. I know you don't want me to go. But I think I want to. (To each his own.) Are you finishing the book? How can I say it except that I've always had a feeling about you. I *know* it's going to be great. I've known it since freshman year. So did Phoebe Lyall. I guess now the rest of the world is going to find out. I had a wonderful time in Woods Hole. I liked your family. I'd love to come back.

Love,

O

His life at home was tentative. He didn't feel himself really there, coming downstairs in the afternoon to find his mother in the garden and Clara playing her Czerny exercises at the piano, the metronome ticking beside her. The air was heavy and he felt a cryptic estrangement from waking after the day had begun to cool. His father would return from work at six, and then when the sun went below the laurels the four of them would eat supper together. Clara was looking for a house to rent in Level, in time to begin the school year at her new job teaching social studies, and while they ate she talked about the places she'd seen. She seemed not to want to choose. His parents were urging her to leave Cook's Grange, and each time a house came open his mother went with her to see it. This was almost more than Orno could bear, that his sister wanted to stay at home, live upstairs probably, if she could, while he himself had not even told his family that he'd been accepted at the University of Missouri.

He tried to keep himself from thinking of Simone. In his free time he walked, to keep his mind occupied: each afternoon down the long hill from their house next to the Marjorrson farm to the irrigation channel that marked the division of the properties; each evening up the same hill again, where he paused to look into the dense branches of the laurels for the horned owl who kept the same backward hours he himself did. He could empty his thoughts here the way he could nowhere else in the world, loose them so that they floated into the sky that was white with heat and humidity; he felt only the slap of the long grass, the rhythmic stretch of his hips; heard only the distant rumble of tractors or the wind that made a long note at the hilltop, as though a rushing ribbon of air stretched all the way from Kansas.

The labor in darkness was welcome. Fatigue came over him naturally at midnight, but he pushed his way through it, lifting and throwing the shovel in rhythm so that by three or four in the morning a vigorous, self-propelling stamina burst upon him and an eerily receptive state of mind descended; the moon came out of the blackness and enlarged before him and if he stepped to the side of the road he could hear the smallest early-morning animals in the grass. Here again, as the summer moved on, he found himself open to contemplation, primed by some bodily chemical that the exertion had produced in him. He walked out into the roadside grass, took a soda from his bag, leaned against his shovel in the dark. But he wouldn't let himself dwell on Simone. He felt a queer sort of ecstasy, an easing of his stance in the world, and he tried to let his thoughts wander. In front of him the moths careened into the buzzing lamps. He began to think once again of God. He felt no inclination, neither toward religion nor away from it, just a sense that if he ever needed strength, this was where and how he could find it, at night and in toil.

Near the end of the summer, though, he realized he couldn't ever tell his parents about the University of Missouri; and then soon afterward he understood that this meant that from then on he was going to cast his lot elsewhere. One morning he had to walk away from the work strip and stand at the edge of the scrub pretending to relieve himself while he looked away from the highway in tears. He had the feeling he was willfully discarding familial love and kindness. His own land was one of fair exchange—work for bounty—where the difficulty was in nature and not in ambition; yet now he was going to leave it for nothing but the prickly, unnameable yearning that he'd first felt on the shore at Woods Hole. He saw himself there, his duffel on the sand of the inlet and the bus behind him, turning away toward the insistent promise of benefaction beyond the trees.

He also wondered whether it had to do with Simone. He'd managed to elude his own thoughts of her, but now once again he returned to the note he'd left on her windowsill; it was the plea of a coward. He debated it and then wrote her again, this time in care of her parents, a short note expressing general interest and alerting her that he was still alive, halfway across the continent and now and then thinking of her on the chance that she, in any way, was also thinking of him. It seemed risky. He contemplated tearing it up. In the morning, though, after holding it in his pocket all night, he mailed it on his way home to sleep.

XVII

He also wrote again to Marshall:

M—

I'm thinking about your life there all the time, about how the book is going. I'm imagining the things that must be happening: publishers and all, movie deals, starlets. What does it feel like?

Here, I've turned into one of the small animals of the night. (Looking into the scrub next to the road at any moment I can see half a dozen sets of tiny red eyes.) I'm finding there is beauty to this kind of work. On the other hand, no soap will take the asphalt off my fingers.

Please send me what you're working on. I'm getting ready to go to school and then I imagine I'll be awfully busy. I'll be living in a dorm at least for the first year. In a few weeks I leave. I do keep wondering: am I doing the right thing? (Don't answer that.)

Love,
O

A week later an envelope from Simone on the kitchen table: he brought it outside and walked with it in his pocket down to the edge of the dry mud gully where their property ended and then up along the Marjorrsons' rotting fence, taking it from his shirt and then setting it back in, sitting down at last on a slope with a view of the land. He was afraid to open it. He looked across the yard at his family's house, at Clara's bicycle standing against the drain spout, at his mother kneeling like a penitent in the garden alongside.

Dear Orno,

You seemed nonchalant in your letter, but I think I will be brave and say that I don't believe nonchalance is what you really feel. And I will be even braver and say that it is not what I feel either.

You're confusing me, but the truth is that I am thinking about you.

I wonder why if I love David I am writing you back so quickly, and why (I realize) I have been waiting for your letter since I saw you. (Did you leave a note here for me?) My father didn't tell me you were gone until the morning after you'd left (or of course I would have been there to see you off) and what I am letting guide me now is what I felt at the moment he told me, and then again when I found your note (that *was* yours, wasn't it?). I don't think I will tell you what it is until you write me back or (maybe) until I see you again. Has Marshall told you how his life is in California? And how is your leg? (asks the nurse).

> Frightenedly,
> Simone

PS—In my worst moments I think that you probably wrote me only because you are polite (I bet you send thank-you notes) and that I have over-reacted humiliatingly. If this is the case, will you please go out to a field and guffaw horribly at me <u>by yourself</u>.

His heart was pierced. The sky was dusty blue, a color he never saw in New York, and the breeze was from the south, its rare incarnation, ruffling the aspen leaves to their silver sides and giving him the rapturous feeling that if he looked eastward from where he sat on the hill holding the envelope he could make Simone think of him at the same moment he was now thinking of her. He held the letter open and looked out past their house over the plain. Then he went to his room and put it in the pocket of his jacket. That night he read it again beneath the sodium lamps during his break, watching the fluttering moths. The wall he had built between them came pitching down.

Dear Simone,

Well, it goes without saying that you were right about me. (In Cook's Grange we are not experts in guile.) I have indeed been thinking about you, although I'm sure that anyone in my position would be doing the same. You are the rarest of rare and anyone can see that. As for David Bridges, I don't know what it means either but I can tell you that he seems like a good soul, and, as I am sure you are doing, I think you need to figure out what you have between you.

When I think about what has gone on between *us*, I go back and forth between ecstasy and fear. I don't know what Marshall would think. Do you? Would he be surprised?

In a month I will be heading to Stony Brook for school, thanks partly to your encouragement. Maybe I will come up to see you, if it's okay with you.

At this moment I am looking at a stand of laurels where a horned owl lives, and I can see him sitting on a limb. It is rare to see an owl in daylight and I cannot help thinking it has to do with you.

Just as frightenedly,
Orno

The next afternoon a package in the kitchen:

O—

Ah, I find myself in the land of sin—streets paved in gold leaf and crawling with Sirens calling me toward the rocks. Los Angeles is biblically corrupt. The commerce here is in low art, if one can even call it that, although I prefer to call it corruption and bald salesmanship. The movie business is harrowingly appalling and television only aspires to that. Meanwhile the foolish Ishmaelite with the anachronistic dream works alone in the basement, doing and redoing half a page in a week—it's daunting work. I'll admit to you, I survive only by remembering that art is immortality. Sometimes I see the lure of a trade, as you have, though I still think you should reconsider and come out here to starve with me.

Here is what I am working on.

—M

The manuscript was the same length he'd sent last time. He took it outside to the hill where he'd read Simone's letter. Wrongdoing pierced him. He could think only of her.

Estophius Adams returned to the land of his ancestral past on a day of magnificence and fervent heat, his brow dotted with humidity, his legs bowed up beneath him in the metal bus-seat that had clanged and rattled two thousand miles north into Texas from the collapsing straw eaves of the barrio huts of Panama City, Panama, along a burning, glass-clear coast that looked upon two still-topped oceans. Flies were in the cabin, buzzing and careening over the seats and window tops, alighting on the sweating forearms and slack cheeks of the passengers, while the driver shooed them with newspaper and took drinks from his metal canteen.

He read on. There seemed to be very little changed from what he'd read before, only occasional words that seemed new to him, and the section ended exactly as he'd remembered. There was a dullness to it now that might have come from repetition but that easily could have been his own distracted heart. Nonetheless it worried him, because he didn't want to lie in his letter back. He thought of Marshall in the basement apartment, furnished only with a mattress and bookshelves, writing with his long view of the sea. He hadn't mentioned the publisher.

M—

Keep working. The trades are for the unbrilliant ones. As difficult as they are I cannot imagine they hold a candle to the battle you are fighting. I wish I could send you courage.

You seem to be refining the work. It reads smoothly still and often brilliantly. Keep at it.

Anything unusual happening with you?

I'll write with my new address when I have one. When I get to New York, by the way, I was thinking of calling your sister.
                                          —O (the tradesman)

Then the summer was over and he took a plane from St. Louis before he had heard back from Simone, numb with the speed of passage, rising above the rows of cornfields and drainage canals laid peacefully over the landscape as he sat still with fear. It wasn't fear of flying but of what he would find when he landed. He knew he would have to work hard again, and he tried to summon his conviction. He had told his parents as nonchalantly as he could to forward any mail. As the plane descended, he saw Long Island dense with trees, the sugar maples at the crests of hills already tinged red with the fall.

XVIII

His quarters were a single room in a modern high-rise filled with dental and medical and engineering students, its hallway carpets shabby with dampness and its small windows unwashed. The day of registration he came downstairs in the evening, feeling edgy after the autumnal sunset he'd watched from his window, and in the lounge he found his dormmates gathered around a television. He crowded in behind them, but they were only watching soap operas; his heart sank. He watched a few minutes and then went outside for a walk, thinking of The Odalisque.

The dental curriculum coincided with medicine, and for the first year they took classes alongside the medical students; in the large auditoriums—easily twice the size of anything at Columbia—he found that they quickly segregated themselves, those in dentistry sitting together in a small group near the aisle, those in medicine filling everywhere else. He was surprised at the shame he felt and tried to fight it. On the first day of class, walking up the shallow incline from the doors at the bottom of the auditorium, he felt eyes upon him. He looked up at the bright sea of seats and imagined Marshall in one of them, looking down upon his ruin. This was even more vanity on his part, however, and his shame doubled. No one there cared what he did; no one there knew this was a defeat for him. Again he thought of Marshall, this time on the beach in Woods Hole: why had he resisted his offer about medical school? Shouldn't he at least have listened to him and not ignored the suggestion as he had? Professor Emerson could have made a single phone call! His thoughts reeled. Strangely, he never really considered the possibility that it was a mistake to sell himself short until the first day he took his seat among the yellow-green, thinly cushioned chairs of the anatomy hall; then he felt it deeply.

He shuddered and looked down at the desktop folded into the armrest, already gouged with initials. There had been hundreds of others before him on this path, thousands even, and their carving seemed suddenly to be the emblem of their despondency. Why did he feel that? He'd had doubts before, but never a dread like this one, a fearful awe that seated itself in his viscera—something touching him from far back. He fought it off. He felt he had failed and had to say to himself that he hadn't, that those he sat with—Jews from Long Island, Indians and first-generation Chinese from the boroughs—had no such opinion of him, that they were doubtless bound up in the crushing load of anatomy and physiology and pharmacology whose coming onslaught their college counselors had warned them about, and warned them again. Around him as they sat waiting for class to begin they talked officiously, their voices inflected with accents, about periodontics and prosthodontics and community dentistry, about what they hoped to do four years from now in practice and in teaching, while in his seat Orno could not look up from his desk, from the names gouged one over the other into the plywood.

He uncapped his pen and in an unblemished space on the writing leaf made a small mark, an act he could never have imagined doing; and when nobody noticed him he went on, digging with the point until he'd cut *OT* into the soft backing behind the finish.

Then, distractedly, he carved *SE.* Who was doing this? He almost didn't know; but it was freeing, as freeing as first putting on the fedora, and his thoughts reeled into the future. Where did he want to be when he was done? Cape Cod? Stony Brook? Cook's Grange? Would he end up with Simone, or was this just the illusion he'd allowed to lure himself here, this day, to sit with his head down before an immense mountain of learning?

Through the small windows of the hall he could see the dark spread of Long Island Sound in the distance. Was he going to live the rest of his life here among the sugar maples and white colonials and the false nostalgia of the evenings? The fall here smelled of apples and grass and wet leaves, and all of it turned over in him a languid yearning that could not have been his own memory. In Cook's Grange the fall smelled of wheat. He had never known a dentist. There was nothing about this land, or about Simone's life or Marshall's improvident ambition, or about the human body even, that should have touched him so deeply; yet they all did. He felt oddly like a traitor.

Then the work began to roll over them. In anatomy he dissected with five other dental students, not the whole body but pieces of it—a shoulder, a hand, a pelvis—dealt out one to each group, while in the dissection hall for the medical students, a floor above, whole cadavers lay splayed on shining steel consoles; the dental students worked downstairs around circular plastic tables so that more of them could gather closer in. They joked about vultures around scraps, leaning in as one or another of them prodded painstakingly with a scalpel among the confusing sinews. The smell was rank and—he couldn't get around this—it again reminded him of failure. One night after their first week of sessions he went upstairs with his dissection partners to the empty anatomy lab to see what the medical students had been doing, agreeing volubly that their own method was far easier and a relief, to work only on a hand or a foot and not as they did up here on the whole yellowish, reeking corpse. But he went closer, raising the plastic tarp and looking into the wound—they'd already opened the chest—and he leaned over and peeked at the heart, a disappointing gray fist when he looked at it, shrunken and discolored; yet this knowledge alone, that here was the kernel of life, a small, knotty butterfly in the thorax, sent him reeling away with envy. At first he berated himself. It was unseemly—if he had maintained his discipline in college he too could have been a medical student—but then as the days went by he understood that it wasn't medicine itself he envied, not to work upstairs here beside steel tables and nonglare lights and wear a stethoscope curled around his neck; it was just the sense that so much knowledge was available in the world—so many worlds themselves existed—and all he wished was that he'd known this earlier.

———

One day there was a small ivory-colored envelope in his mailbox, forwarded by his parents:

Dear Orno,

What I felt when I found you'd left the cottage was a small stab of sorrow in my heart, and puzzlement. Sorrow because despite my pitiful attempt at being ladylike, I wanted to finish what we'd started (or at least follow just a little more on its delightful path). And puzzlement because of the timing. I was feeling bold—there were things I wanted to tell you when I saw you the next morning, and then... you were gone, just like that, pulled into thin air. That's my brother's timing for you.

You are leaving for school soon, and I've asked your parents to forward this if you've already gone. If you don't get it until after you've already started I imagine it will come as a little shock to you, a reminder from your former world. I know how that is, but please don't forget me out here, thinking about you, trying to sort out what I feel (about David, about you), wondering whether I should just get on a bus one of these beautiful mornings and come out there to watch the trees turn.

(Oh, God.)
—Simone

He went to the store and bought a card. Sitting on a park bench he wrote, *I want to see you more than anything.* Then, before he had time to consider whether it was a good idea, he walked to the post office and mailed it.

X I X

At last they learned the anatomy of the head, and for the first time they studied in more detail than the medical students. For the first time, also, it began to seem like gruesome work, abominable in its smells and details and the layered weaving of flesh that they undid with forceps and scalpels and spreaders; he was so close to the unpeeled layers of muscle and fiber that as he leaned over the dissection tray he felt like a cannibal. The neck was first, then the cheeks and orbits and sinuses; and at last the mouth, their small, blanched field of war. He regarded the dark cavity, still untouched where they had saved it for the last and greatest detail—the bloodless, barely discernible lips, the yellow incisors and sadly worn canines, the gray, corpulent tongue; the thought occurred to him again that Professor Emerson could have changed his life.

Again he put it from his mind. The first midterm approached and he welcomed it because it brought him discipline. He studied all afternoon after class let out and all evening after dinner, and on the way home from the library he stopped downstairs in the lounge where the television was tuned to *Durango* or *Dallas*, and there he tried to mingle with his classmates. They talked about anatomy and pharmacology and stared at the screen, slumped back in the assembly of institutional chairs. Again he couldn't help thinking of The Odalisque. If he allowed himself to contemplate his own life now it was dreary, so he didn't think about it. The phone rang late one night and Simone said, "You're never in your room."

His breath caught. "We have midterms. I'm studying."

"Are you sure?"

"As sure as anyone can be." He cleared his throat. "Are you coming down?"

"Well, yes, if you'd like me to."

"I'd love you to."

"When?"

"Now," he answered, surprising himself. "Tonight." It was something Marshall would have said.

"How about tomorrow?"

"You're trying to put me off."

She laughed. "I called Marshall," she said. "I just wanted to call him before I called you."

"So, what did he say?"

"Not much."

"He wouldn't mind if you came to see me?"

She paused. "He didn't seem to. But what about your midterm?"

"I'll flunk it," he said. He surprised himself again. "I don't care."

"That wouldn't be good."

"It would be worth it."

"Marshall said you were serious about your work."

"When did he say that?"

"A long time ago."

"A long time ago I was."

She laughed again, then waited. "Do you really want me to come?"

"Yes, I really do."

"All right," she said. "Maybe I will, then. I mean, I will. I actually will."

The midterm was a *practical*, the students entering one at a time into the huge upstairs dissection hall, where they were required to identify tiny structures within the opened cadavers. The bodies, a half dozen of them, lay partially covered on the long steel tables, and inside each of the cavities they'd studied—the chest, the neck, the mouth—stood three or four tiny flags, attached by red toothpicks to muscles or blood vessels or nerves. The rest of the skin was draped in cloth. Each student had five minutes at a cadaver, then the bell rang and it was time for the next one. On either side, the huge swinging windows stood open to bring in breeze from the quadrangle, where the bright morning air smelled of water. All day he had been thinking of Simone. Close up, the bodies were putrid, but as he moved through the room he caught the scent of salt gusts from the Atlantic, and each time he thought of escape. Peering into the thorax where toothpicks stood pinned into the pale thread of the recurrent laryngeal nerve and the dull gray azygos vein—or was it the superior vena cava?—he felt himself fighting his urges. Where he wanted to be was outside, in that white morning light. He leaned down into an open neck with its overlapping layers of strap muscles and he thought of walking to the beach: through the window he could see the dark isthmus of the Sound and the thick trees alongside. Simone was arriving at ten; it was not yet eight-thirty. His head swam. The bell rang, and he glanced desperately at the stiff little flags. One seemed to stand from the superior belly of the omohyoid muscle; about the other, he wasn't sure. He decided to buy her tulips.

He worked his way from table to table, trying desperately to keep his mind on what he'd studied. The morning was warm and the cadavers had begun to sag. He'd made flash cards that week and shuffled through them in all the free moments of the preceding days; but now among the stinking bodies all he could think of was his own young one, yearning to be outside. They could walk to the beach—he knew a cove accessible only through a hidden path in the trees. For a moment he thought of bringing her up here to the dissection hall, of showing her the strange, priestly sight of it. He was looking into the half-dissected mouth of an old woman; from the upper half of her face she appeared to be in her eighties or nineties, with a patrician New England set to her jaw and forehead; his mind fled again, wondering about her life, about what unthinkable benevolence had persuaded her to donate herself to this fate. It touched him. He looked up through the window again at the sun in the branches of the elms. He didn't want this; he wanted only to be near Simone. The bell rang again.

By the time he peered into the flayed neck of the last cadaver he knew he was in trouble. Of the twenty flags, he'd felt sure of only ten, had guessed at six, and on his answer sheet had simply left four spaces blank. He walked out into the bright air and began to run; he crossed the grass quadrangle and headed into the street that ascended to the top of the hill. At the crest he stopped finally, sweating, then walked over into the thick trees; he made his way through them until at last he stood looking over the Sound. New York City lay fifty miles to the west, a distant absence over the water. It was just after nine, but the air was already sweltering. He pulled off his shirt and looked down at his own body: the rectus muscles, the external obliques, the intercostals flattening with his breath. He knew he would have to struggle again, force himself through strength of discipline to cleave to this strange material; yet at the same time he was profoundly aware of the astonishing privilege of it all. His mind went again to the old woman's body, to the restful, assessing expression on her face. He knew it was just the muscles lengthened in death—first rigor mortis, their professor had told them, then this queer relaxed absence of life. It was an unearthly knowledge he now had. He made his way down through the trees to the water, thinking of a soul rising.

———

Then at ten Simone was there, holding the blowing hem of her dress as she stood on the top step of the bus, smiling shyly when she saw him.

"Tulips," she said, stepping onto the parking lot. "My favorite."

"I grew them myself."

"You did not."

"Well, I bought them myself." He took her bag.

"How was your exam?"

"Not too good."

"What happened?"

"To tell you the truth," he said. "I was thinking about other things."

"What other things?"

"You."

"You were thinking about *me*?"

"Yes."

She turned the tulips in her hand. "You were looking at dead bodies."

"No resemblance."

"You're sure?"

"Yes."

"Well, I'm here. Now you don't have to think about me anymore."

"I'm thinking about you anyway."

He took her the same way he'd just come, up the hill and through the woods to the cove. Walking down through the dense pines he watched her from behind: the ease in her joints that reminded him she was Marshall's sister, young and unabashed in the innumerable ways she registered delight. When a flight of sparrows alighted from a treetop she stopped and threw her head back, gazing up at the branches and wrinkling her nose. When she first came out on a bluff over the water she drew in her breath and covered her mouth. The cove was a narrow slip of black, as still as a lake, between two peninsulas of pine. On the shore were fallen trunks, and they walked down the hill and sat on one of them, watching a white heron nose in the shallows. He still had her bag.

"What was the exam?" she said.

"Anatomy."

"How bad was it?"

"Pretty bad. I guessed on half of them."

"That's not too good."

"No."

"Wow," she said. "Corpses."

"Cadavers."

"What's it like?"

"It's not bad."

She looked up at him expectantly. After a moment she said, "I guess Marshall *told* me you were laconic."

"A laconic cad."

She frowned. Then she laughed, and the heron in the shallows looked up at her. A fish slid from its beak.

"To tell you the truth," he said, "it's extraordinary. It's hard work, but it's an unearthly privilege. To see what we see. People donate their bodies to us. They *give* us this chance to cut them up. We were working on an old woman today and for some reason her face caught my attention. I was imagining her alive, and at the same time staring into her open neck. She'd given her body to us like that, so that we could learn. It's humbling. I don't know if I'd have the conviction to do it myself."

"So you like what you're doing?"

"I think so. It's daunting, though. I should be studying right now. We have a physiology exam, day after tomorrow."

"Let's go back, then."

"I don't want to yet."

"You're going to be in trouble."

"I already am."

"I guess that's two of us."

"How are *you* in trouble?" he said.

She looked at him and shrugged. "Oh, I don't know. I mean, what am I doing here?"

"I invited you."

"I believe I invited myself."

He stood. "Come on," he said, picking up her bag again. "Let me show you my cell."

"I want to see the cadavers."

He set down her bag again. "I don't know if you really want to. They're something, but they take getting used to."

"Then I'll get used to them." She laughed. "I can get used to anything. You'll see that about me."

"I will?"

"Yes."

He smiled. "How long are you staying?"

"There's a bus at eight tonight. I thought I would take it."

"That's not a lot of time to get used to anything."

"Well," she said. "We'll see."

He regarded her. "Maybe we can go look after dinner," he said. "When the labs are empty."

"Really?"

"Really."

"Wow," she said.

———

They spent the day walking along the coast. It was Indian summer, the sky the dark blue of autumn but the heat rising like August from the beds of dry needles among the pines. He stopped at the crest of a small hill in the woods and said, "Have you told David?"

"That I'm here? Sort of."

He laughed. "What does 'sort of' mean?"

"It means no, I haven't." She frowned. "Have you spoken to Marshall?"

"Same thing," he said.

"You mean, sort of?"

"Right."

She played with a blade of grass. "I wasn't sure there would be anything to tell David."

"Well, now do you think there is?"

"I'm not going to answer that."

"Why?"

She looked up at him. "Because I'm a smart girl."

He wanted to take her hand; but she turned and headed off down the path again. He followed, through the dappled columns of trees. They came out onto a clearing that overlooked the low spread of the dental clinics and behind it, up the hill, the broad edifice of the medical school. She stopped again. Her back was to him, the pale curve of her shoulder visible through her dress.

"I was hoping to ask you something," he said.

"What is it?"

"Something Marshall said when we were together on the Cape. I wanted to get your opinion. It's been bothering me."

"What did he say?"

"Well. It's embarrassing." He shrugged. In the distance he could see a group of dental students coming out the doors of the clinic. "He said your father could get me into medical school."

"That's what he told you?"

"Yeah."

She sat down on the path again and looked up at him. "And you want to know if it's true."

"Right," he said. He sat down next to her. "I was just wondering about it."

"What would you do if he could?"

"I'd say no."

"Are you sure?"

"Yes."

She shrugged. "Yes, he could probably do it. All his academic friends, they all do each other favors. That's how they work."

"I thought so." In the distance the dental students were pulling off their scrub masks and heading into the parking lot.

"You know what, though?" she said. "I'm glad you wouldn't do it."

"Why?"

"It just seems rare to me. Especially around here." She hugged her knees. "That's what it is. It's rare. If you did it, you'd never forgive yourself."

"How do you know that?"

"I just do."

He let a handful of pine needles slip through his fingers. He was thinking about her answer. "You sound like my father," he said.

"Your father sounds smart."

"My father certainly has his way in the world." He smiled. "He's worn the same suit every day for fifteen years."

"He has not."

"Just about."

"Well, I don't do that."

He reached over and touched her wrist with his finger. "Lunate," he said.

She didn't move.

He touched it again, further over. "Triquetrum. Capitate. Hamate."

"I like that word," she said. "Lunate."

"It means moon. It's one of the eight bones."

"Which one is it?"

"This one," he said. He leaned forward and kissed the side of her hand.

She let her head tilt back. "Hmm," she said. "Do you do this with all your patients?"

He leaned forward again and kissed her on the mouth. "Only certain ones."

"Oh God," she whispered, "I think I do have to talk to David."

X X

The next day he walked out to the cove with a pad of paper. He was supposed to be studying.

Dear M,
    I have some news.

It sounded abrupt. He tried again:

M—
    I've been meaning to write for a while. How are you?

He tried:

Dear Marshall—
    It's been so long, and I wanted to let you know what's happening here. I'm sitting at the edge of Long Island Sound.

The heron stood watching him. He crumpled the paper and sat still on the log, thinking of Simone. He wondered if she'd talked to David yet and what she would say. She'd left yesterday, right after dinner, which they'd eaten on a lawn near the bus station, her hand in his as it grew dark. But nothing else had happened; he'd felt an exquisite restraint. Now, as he sat on the log, he thought of her shoulder through her dress, on the path in front of him. He would write Marshall later, he decided, when the words came more easily. In front of him the heron had resumed its foraging. He watched it. After a time he stood, pulled off his shoes, and walked down to the edge of the water. He waded into the shallows, where the great bird eyed him, now and then blinking its wary eye. Occasionally it lifted its wings, but he moved very slowly and eventually it grew calm; he had always been good with animals. Its beak returned to the water, picking at the silt. He was able to approach within a few feet, from where he could see the odd, ancient-looking legs and the oily waterproofing of the wing feathers. Next time Simone was here he would show it to her like this, wading out into the still inlet. There was sweet mystery to the world; there was rapture in the small things around him.

———

The day before his physiology exam, he took out his textbooks. He was supposed to be studying the circulatory system, and though it was elegant in theory, the details quickly overwhelmed him. He glanced through the pages—the complex passageways of blood, arterioles and venules and capillaries; the efficient, interlinked lungs; the extraordinary heart. His thoughts drifted, to Simone on the steps of the bus; to the huge elms outside the Methodist Church in Cook's Grange—the first time in weeks he'd thought of home. He stopped on a page showing the opened ventricles: the two sides, right and left, with their different duties—at once too elegant for chance and yet too complicated for God. It was too miraculous to learn the way he knew he was supposed to. He was supposed to memorize the formulas for stroke volume and oxygen exchange; instead he gazed out the windows into the maples.

At last by evening his fear overcame him, and he stayed awake late into the night making flash cards. By morning he was thinly prepared, but he had at least read through all the pages; when he walked into the testing room he felt that with luck he could get through it. The other students milled in the hallway, discussing the material. He fled to his seat.

———

Dear Clara—

Well, the work has begun here, and now and then I have my doubts as to whether I am up to it. The other students are serious. (Serious may not even be the right word. Dedicated is what they are.) I myself on the other hand sometimes think I am wasting the time of my professors. When I look into the open bodies of the dissections I cannot help but think of our own short stay on this earth. Such thoughts do not help during exams (although perhaps they may shorten my own stay here!) How is your life as a teacher? Are you working hard? I understand that the first year is the most difficult and that then it becomes easier. Do you see Dad and Mom as often? What is your life like these days?

Love,
Your Brother

———

The next afternoon when he got back to his room the phone was ringing. "You know," Simone said, "you never showed me the cadavers."

"Come back, and I will."

"Maybe. How was your test?"

"Miserable."

"See. I'm not good for you."

"You're the best thing in the world for me."

"What would your father say?"

"He might agree with you, actually."

"I talked to David," she said.

"Uh-oh. What happened?"

"He said he knew from the moment he met you."

"Knew what?"

"What was in store."

"I don't believe that."

"I do," she said.

"How could he have known?"

"I knew, too."

"You did?"

"Yes. Why do you think I was so funny with you?"

"I thought I was the one who was funny with *you*. I thought I was bothering you."

"Well, you weren't," she said.

"Really?"

"Really." She laughed. "You don't know anything about girls, do you?"

"Well, I thought I did."

"Well, I guess you were wrong."

"Ordinarily, I would be hurt by that."

"That's because you don't realize it's a compliment."

"It is?"

"Yes."

"I guess I really *don't* know much, do I?"

"It's sweet."

"When can you come back?" he said.

"Did you flunk your exam?"

"I don't think so. At least, I hope not. When can you come?"

"Oh, God," she said. "Tomorrow."

In the morning a beige envelope in his mailbox. Again he was momentarily confused:

O—

A missive from the vast forgotten desert, sent way late but with thoughts of you. How go the chores of a tradesman? Are you learning? Can you name all those funny teeth yet?

Here, the life of art bears hard on the soul—so difficult for me but I am filled every morning with hope. It is a dreamy feeling, to walk these low-built streets, thinking of characters, thinking of scenes, like a leopard in the high snow. The world here is trippingly beautiful but locked behind sandstone walls, bougainvillea cascading over. A cryptic society, more so for its candor: the men are not to be trusted and the women to be trusted less. (Isn't that always the case?) Work remains for me a salvation, the great dreamed treasure of my life. Write with news. I struggle at the plow.

—M

He stared at the letter, feeling caught.

———

Dear M—

Your letter was welcome. I'd been meaning to write but haven't had much time here, as you might imagine. Your life sounds wonderful, difficult as the book may be. I'm envious—to be devoted to your work like that; to dream about it. That is a rare fortune.

Yes, I have learned the names of the teeth but they are probably not what you had hoped for, not named for kings or planets. They are merely numbers. The front left lower incisor, that is number 24. The right upper first molar, that is number 3. Such is it with my life, a sturdy, practical one. Nonetheless I am quite often struck by the beauty in it. Studying has been difficult for me, more so than I had imagined. I am awed at the grace of what we learn but tripped up by the details. There are mountains of them. I too struggle at the plow.

—O

Then, in the evening, she was there again, standing on the top step of the bus. He looked across the lot at her from the waiting room, afraid of not feeling what he'd felt when she'd left. But it was the same: she came down the steps, carrying a small bag, and his heart lifted.

He took her to the anatomy lab finally, after dinner, after he'd told her she wouldn't like it, that to see the bodies for the first time would shock her; he told her that it would ruin their evening together and that the smell would get into her hair. But she'd sat quietly, eating spaghetti and smiling at him, insisting she wanted to see them.

"Why do you care?" he asked.

"I just want to know what you do all day. When I go back home, I want to be able to think of you."

"Think of me in the woods."

"Plus, I want to see a heart."

"Why?"

"I just do."

"You know," he said, "I did too. When I first started, it was the thing I most wanted to see. We weren't at the chest yet, but the medical students were, so I went up to see one in their lab."

"Did you find one?"

"Yes."

"What was it like?"

"It was a disappointment. At least, at first. It wasn't what I thought it would look like, just a gray lump. But I couldn't stop thinking about it. I had dreams about it for days. In a way, it became miraculous."

"That's why I want to see one, too."

The labs were locked, but all the students had keys, and after dinner they walked up to the medical students' dissection room. When he first opened the doors she took a step in, then stopped. The fans were whirring in the walls, and there was too much formalin and antiseptic in the smell for it to be vulgar, but beneath the medicinal odor was such a strong, mortal reminder of flesh that she put her hand out against the wall to steady herself.

"See?" he said.

"No, it's okay. I just wasn't expecting it. Not this strong, anyway."

"I barely notice it anymore."

She stepped up to one of the steel tables, where a body lay flat, its flayed leg visible between two parted blue sheets. She stared at it, holding on to the table; he stood behind her. "We call it the lower extremity," he said. "For some reason nobody says 'leg.' I don't know why that is."

He pulled back the sheet and they looked. He was struck by how colorless and unrecognizable it must have seemed: the structures gray and matted, clung to by bits of debris, nothing like the illustrated plates in his textbook.

"My father used to bring home animals for Marshall to dissect," she said.

"Really?"

"They were fish mostly. Once he brought home a shark, which he pointed out to us was not a fish, really. It's something else, I guess. I forget what. It was about five feet long. He made Marshall cut the whole thing up, out on our laundry porch. The pigeons thought they'd landed in heaven. Marshall used to try to get them to carry off the whole shark. When my dad wasn't there he'd lift it in his arms and open the screens so they could fly in and peck at it. Like Prometheus." She held her nose. "Felix went crazy, too. He tried to scrape a hole in the door to get out there."

"Who's Felix?"

"He was our Siamese. A flamepoint Siamese. I was never sure whether he wanted the pigeons or the shark. He ran away after that. My father left the door open and he got out."

"I'm sorry."

"You're so sweet. I was ten."

"So that's how Marshall knew about my vein."

"What vein?"

"When I cut myself on the boat. Your dad quizzed him on the name of the vein in my leg."

"I thought you didn't say leg anymore."

"I don't, but you've got me flustered." He returned the sheet to its position and they wandered up the rows of bodies, toward one where he knew the chest had been opened. "Didn't it stink up the apartment?" he said.

"Not so badly. My father always brought them home in winter. Marshall had to wear a wool cap and gloves with the fingers clipped off to do the dissection. The laundry stairs are outside, you know, behind the kitchen. The garbagemen use it."

"I think I saw them."

"He brought home animals, too. Marshall dissected a dog once. Can you imagine doing that?"

"A dog?"

"From my father's lab. I don't know why he had a dog in a fish lab, but he did."

"Sounds kind of horrible."

"It was."

"Did you ever help?"

"No. They never let me. It used to make me really mad, too. I didn't care what they were doing. I didn't care if it was horrible, I just wanted to do it with them. That's the way I was." She lifted a corner of one of the sheets. "It's the way I still am, I guess. I suppose that's why I want to see this now." She gasped. "What's that?"

"That's just packing," he said. "They pack the bodies when they're done, to keep them fresh."

"I'm glad we already ate."

"You know, I'm envious of all the things your family did. Of growing up with so much learning. We never did that in my family."

"It wasn't as great as it sounds. Not for Marshall at least."

"Still, he learned so much. He learned to see the whole world when he was still a boy. I never had that feeling, growing up. When I got to college it overwhelmed me."

"But Marshall didn't want to be doing any of it, you know. My father used to torture him with it. He used to keep him inside until he'd dissected whatever it was. Marshall had to lay the pieces out on a cloth and name them for him. He used to smell, too. He would scrub his hands with a brush and pour aftershave on them. It humiliated him. He used to wear gloves when his friends were around, even inside."

"But he was learning. And your house was filled with books. Your grandfather was a civil rights attorney. My grandfather sold feed. Cow feed, which is hay. And pig feed, which is cows. Partly cows, at least."

"What else did Marshall tell you about my grandfather?"

"That's all," he answered. "Why?"

"Oh, my God," she said pointing. "There it is, isn't it?"

He looked. It was sitting by itself on a side table. Some other scraps lay around it, snipped remains of blood vessels and tiny yellow clumps of fat; but there it was: a heart, still clamped by a pair of forceps, resting listlessly on a steel tray. "I think I'm going to faint," she said.

"I am too."

"No, you're not," she said. "You see this all the time."

"Okay. Maybe not."

"Let's go," she said.

"Let's run."

They did, out the long aisle onto the landing, where he stopped to lock the doors; then down the stairs and to the end of the long hall again, where he caught up with her. They ran out together along the marble corridor onto the grass, then across the street and up the hill, where they slowed finally and walked. She sniffed the air. "I can still smell it," she said. "It smells like our laundry porch."

"Here, Felix," he said.

"Stop it."

"Come on, Felix! Take this damn shark away!"

She reached up and kissed him on the mouth.

"Sorry," he said.

"Don't be. *I* did that."

"I mean, sorry about Felix."

"Felix ended up mauling the shark."

"Did he really?"

"Yup. One night he got in there."

"How'd he do that?"

"I left the laundry door open."

He kissed her again. "You did it on purpose?" he said.

"Yes. I mean, *someone* had to do something. I just wish I'd given Felix more time. A shark doesn't have bones, you know. It has cartilage. Felix would have eaten the whole thing, but he ran out of time."

"It was nice of you to do that."

"For Felix and Marshall, maybe. But my father sure didn't think so. He thought Marshall let him in."

"Is that why Felix disappeared?"

"Oh, God, I never thought of that."

"I didn't mean to ruin anything."

"Well, you haven't yet."

"Did you ever confess?"

"About Felix? No. I'm not *that* nice."

"Good thing, I guess."

She looked up at him. He kissed her once more. This time, her hand went up behind his shoulders. He felt it there, pressing him to her. Her tongue, a cool surprise in a warm cup; she had a taste, chewing gum, something mint; a warmth in her fingers so that he felt each of them, even through his shirt. His own hands went to her hips, narrow, also warm; he ran them down the curve to her thighs. She pulled away. "Oh, God," she said. "I'm shaking."

"Me, too."

"Let's walk," she said. "Let's walk so we can think about this."

"I'll trip if we walk."

"I'll watch you."

"You're shaking too much."

"So are you."

He put up his hand. "I guess I am," he said.

"Come on," she said. "One foot in front of the other."

They walked up to the top of the hill again, where he kissed her once more; he could feel her in his arms, loose, as though ready to fall. Then they walked down the other side of the hill and along the water to the road. He could see his dormitory over the row of trees now, the lights in the upstairs hall. He led her that way. At the door she stopped. "This is a big step," she said.

"I know."

"Aren't you going to ask me in?"

"I was working up the nerve."

"Yes," she said. "I accept."

X X I

In the morning he woke early and watched her as she lay next to him in the narrow bed. She slept deeply, facing him on her side, one arm straight underneath her head and the other on the pillow by his cheek. He looked at her fingers: long and narrow, the tips curled gently. He took them in his mouth and kissed them; she didn't stir. Without looking, he knew it was 5:00 A.M. He rose and made coffee.

At his desk, he set out his physiology book and began to study, watching her over the top of the spine. The same chapters he'd gone through the week before, drowning in details, now presented themselves almost clearly: the physiology of the human circulatory system. He read, now and then looking up to watch her. She slept like a cat, edging into the thin slat of sun when it rose behind the shade. When she sighed, her shoulders tossed, a light-weighted seesaw that he pondered, watching her pale neck. It was miraculous—he felt his heart open up; he wanted to lift her, somehow, to raise her gently from the bed into his arms. Her eyes moved in a dream. At seven, he kissed her and she woke.

"What I was going to tell you," she said, "was that my grandfather wasn't a civil rights attorney."

"Good morning," he answered.

"What I started to tell you yesterday," she said. "I also tried to tell you this when you came to the beach this summer. My father's father wasn't what Marshall told you he was."

"I made you coffee. Do you like coffee?"

"Listen to me."

"What was he, then?"

"He was a barrel salesman, a Jewish barrel salesman. He came through Ellis Island from Vilna. From Lithuania, sometime in the twenties, I think. My father made everything up. He's made up his whole childhood."

He leaned down and kissed her. "Then why did Marshall tell me he was a lawyer?"

"Because that's what my father tells *us*."

"But it's not true?"

"No."

"And the business about Ralph Waldo Emerson?"

"Entirely made up."

"Really?"

"Really."

"Wow," he said. "Have you ever met your grandfather?"

"No. He died before I was born."

"Then how do you know who's telling the truth?"

"Because my father's sister once told me the real story. I've never met her, but she wrote me a letter."

"You've never met your aunt?"

"No. My father doesn't want us to. I don't know if something happened between them or whether he just wants to keep hiding his real family."

"What about your mother?"

"What about her?"

"Does she know the real story?"

"She usually goes along with him."

"Strange."

"I know," she said.

He went to the window. "The funny thing is," he said, "it's exactly what your father said about Winthrop Menemee Scott."

"So you remember that?"

"Perfectly. He said Professor Scott was—what was the word he used?"

"He usually says grifter."

"That's right. Grifter. He said he was a grifter and a fraud and the son of a Jewish hat salesman. I remember that. He was so angry about it. I didn't understand what was going on. It was my first time at your house. I remember you tried to calm him down."

"I'm flattered."

"Why are you flattered?"

"Because you noticed me. I was dying of shame that night."

"Of course I noticed you," he said. "You were beautiful. You were wearing a yellow dress and you had a ribbon in your hair. When we were in the kitchen together I wanted to touch it. When you were at the sink."

"I wish you had."

"I'm glad I didn't."

"Why not?"

"Because then this never would have happened."

"They might have both happened."

"If you think *that*," he said, "you don't know anything about boys."

"Don't make fun of me." She looked up at him. "This is hard. I wasn't sure I wanted to tell you."

"What did you think I would do?"

"I don't know," she said. "Lose interest." She looked down. "Run."

"I'm shaking too much."

"Be serious."

"I wouldn't run," he said. "What difference does it make to me? I'll never meet your grandfather." He walked over to the bed. "I'm not going to run."

She touched his leg, then withdrew. "Really?"

"Really," he said. He opened the window shade; the room flooded with light. "So what made you tell me this now?"

"I don't know. That's a good question." She smiled. "Truth in advertising, I guess." She leaned up and kissed him on the mouth, then withdrew and touched his lips with her fingers. "It's like he's daring us," she said.

"Daring you to what?"

"To cross him."

"And you never do."

"It's way too late, years too late. Even my mother can't do it. She knows he's inventing it. Marshall and I know. He knows it himself, at least I assume."

"Are you afraid of telling him you know?"

"I'm afraid I'm going to hurt him."

"I could see that."

"More than hurt him, actually. Crush him, you know? On the one hand he's this incredibly impressive man, but on the other hand he's so vulnerable it's pathetic. And we know that, which is why he lies and we don't say anything. And the sad thing is he doesn't need anything he doesn't already have. He doesn't need more prestige—he could give a lecture and half the biologists in America would come. But for some reason it's more important to him that those people there on the Cape—you know, people who made their money the day they were born—for some reason it's more important to him that they think he can afford our house there. Which he can't, really. It's ridiculous. They turned off our electricity last summer. He's mortgaged all the way to the deep water. But he knows enough people out there that he can borrow money to make the payments on the bank loans. I have a feeling it's all going to be taken away someday."

"That would be sad."

"For us, I suppose. But not in the big scheme of things, obviously. I don't think the world would suffer if the Emersons lost their vacation house."

"It's still sad for you to have grown up with it."

"You're sweet," she said again. "When I was a girl I used to be afraid that they would take him to debtors' prison. I used to think about it all the time, what we would do when they took my father away. Once we were pulled over by a cop for a broken headlight, and I was so sure that he was going to be arrested I hid in the backseat under a blanket. When the cop saw my shoes sticking out he shined his flashlight around the whole car. My father asked me if I was *trying* to get him into trouble." She sat up in the sheets and looked out at the sun. "I still remember that question, the way he turned around from the front seat and raised his eyebrows and asked me, because I suddenly understood that I *was*. He was absolutely right. I was so scared of him. I suppose I was scared of what was going to happen to us. And I wanted to be done with it."

"But nothing ever did happen."

"No. Not really. And I remember feeling sorry for my dad, too, even then. But more than anything, I wanted him to stop scaring us. To stop putting everything in jeopardy. I never thought other kids felt that way about their fathers."

"Most of them don't," he said.

"I know. I don't even know how I'd heard of debtors' prison at that age."

"It was probably something your mother said."

She looked at him. "Of course," she said. "Very good. She must have been afraid of it, too. But now I think we all pity my father. He scares us still, but more than that we feel sorry for him."

"I don't think Marshall does."

"I think it's different for Marshall. I don't think he's stopped by pity."

"Stopped from what?"

"From crossing him."

"Marshall says he hates him."

"Marshall wants the same things *he* does. Marshall told you the same story about my grandfather."

"That's true," he said. "How come *he* believes it?"

"He doesn't. That's the point. In some ways he's just like my father."

He went to the window and looked out. For a moment he pictured Marshall, sitting at the head of the table under the dark balcony of The Odalisque. "I don't know what to make of that," he said. "I don't believe he'd lie to me."

"Don't make anything of it, then. Marshall is sweet. He's always been sweet about most things. Sad, too. But sweet, no matter what he's done. It's always been a lot harder for him to deal with my father."

"He once told me *you* hated your father, too."

"He told you that?"

"Yes."

"No. No. He's wrong. That makes me so sad for him, you know? Sadder than anything else, really. He's always divided the world like that—the people he loves against the people he hates." She brushed the hair from her eyes. "Marshall loves me—he loves you too—so he absolutely can't understand, or maybe he just can't accept, that I would love someone he doesn't. That's why he wants me to hate my father. But I've never hated him. That's putting it much too strongly. I feel sorry for him in lots of ways, and I dislike plenty of things about him now, but to me he's just a regretful, forlorn man like all the rest of them on that beach, standing at the bar in the afternoon." She gestured out the window. "That's what the breadwinners of that generation did, and I do pity them all a little, but I don't hate my father. I really don't."

He moved next to her. "You know," he said. "You're a gem."

"Oh, come on."

"You *are*," he said.

"No, I'm not. I'm just the girl who warns the onlookers and keeps her hair pinned up while the ship is sinking."

"You're a rare gem. You have a character that's made the world."

"That's just because you're used to hay farmers."

"*Wheat* farmers."

"Hay, wheat, I thought they were the same thing."

"Hay is alfalfa or timothy or clover."

"That's so exotic, you know?"

"What is?"

"That you know that." She looked up at him, reached out and drew him toward her, her fingers on his belt. "I'll remember that now," she said. "I'll remember that forever."

XXII

Dear Orno—

I have two students like you. They are brothers, Silas and Duke Burkitt. Silas used to like to stare out into the trees when I was teaching. Duke liked to stare out a little higher, into the sky. I had a talk with Mrs. Burkitt. She told me to go ahead and use the ruler with them. I laughed.

Could that be what you need?

Love,
Clara

XXIII

Weeks later, after he'd passed his midterms with C's, and his first set of finals with B's, he finally wrote.

M—

How are you? I think about you all the time out there in paradise, now that it is turning cold in these parts. Here, the birds have left, the leaves are almost gone, and the local citizenry is putting up storm windows. I imagine it is not quite the same where you are.

Anyway, this is a hard letter to write, but sooner or later I imagined I would have to tell you the truth about what I'm about to say. It's strange—I feel I can confide in you, and I always have, but it's harder to tell you this than anything I've ever told you before. I don't know why that is, exactly. I don't think you value conventionality at all, or even propriety. But I do, and I think that what I'm writing about might be seen as impropriety, even by you. I don't want that to happen, and I don't want to put our friendship to the test. Anyway, I hope this doesn't come as too great a shock to you, but I'm writing to tell you that I've fallen in love with your sister.

We've fallen in love with each other, I guess I should say. I hope this is news you want to hear. Having my own sister, I wanted to tell you that I tried to doubt myself at every turn. It was surprising, I have to tell you, because I assumed that if Simone and I saw each other it would eventually run its course. I would turn out to be unworthy, or find myself drifting away, as I've done in every romance I've ever had before. But that's not what happened. We've spent a lot of time together over the last few months, and I for one feel a great ease around her, which may partly be related to you, and also unquenchable curiosity. Maybe this is what they mean by Cupid's arrow, but every small part of her life interests me, and every small part of my own is more interesting with her around. We can sit on the beach and talk about what we remember from the time we were five years old, and soon we're talking about the color of the willow leaves, or how flowers that don't smell are pollinated by hummingbirds, or whether children should be spanked. Then it's seven o'clock and the sun has gone down and I haven't started my work yet. (I got four C's on four midterms.) There seems to be no limit to the conversation. Have you ever had that with someone? She drinks up the world.

It's come a long way now, and I'm telling you because she's graduating next year and then she'll probably come out to Long Island and we'll get a place together. She's been visiting here all fall and I've been going up to Bard. The truth is she makes me happier than I've ever been. She has a great, calming effect and her own generous view of the world. It's different from your own view, but I can see how it must have made the two of you close. You are very, very important to her. She tells me that all the time. She was the one who encouraged me to write you now (although I would have anyway).

So here I am past only one semester of dental school and despite my embarrassing grades the tiny rebellion you put in me has already been quelled, partly by your sister. There have been times in my life when I've wondered about God, and I realize those times were the ones when I didn't know my direction. I do know it now, though, and again it's Simone I have to thank, and for me this is relief as profound as any I've ever had.

At first it stuck in my craw that I was doing something just because it was safe (during anatomy lectures I used to imagine what you would think of the whole business here) but after a while, and especially after coming to know Simone, I realized that this is good enough for me. You see, I'm not the kind to find a new world. You are, but I'm not. It was a relief to learn that.

We're starting to see patients now, and even though I have my hands in their mouths, I'm beginning to relax enough to enjoy it, and I see that there *is* something adamant and useful and (I'll say it) *graceful* about teeth. (Think of anything else, man-made or not, that lasts as long and through so much.) Anyway, the point is that my patients need me, and I may not be changing the course of history but I'm making them feel better. Simone and I go for long walks in the evenings, and I've come to understand that this is where the pleasure and reward of life occur, out along the Sound with a girl like her who sees so much beauty in the world. Not in an office, at least not for me. I discovered that if you give up your aspirations you don't miss them.

I don't think that's true for you, however. I think that when you have a gift like yours it's your duty to struggle with it and see it out. Great risk, great gain. By now you must be almost done with the book and I am waiting eagerly to see it.

Is it hard for you to hear this about your sister? If you wrote me that you were about to move in with Clara (though she's my older sister and that's different), I'd be happy that she found someone as extraordinary as you but I'd be worried that it might become uncomfortable between *us*, because at some point I'd understand that you'd become better friends with her than you are with me. I suppose that's happened already with Simone, and I'm sorry that life has handed us this situation, but I want to make the best of it, and I want you to know that I'll always be there if you need me.

Love,
Orno

He was in clinic in the afternoon, where they followed the dentists around watching them work, occasionally sitting in to help pack amalgam or guide a patient through an alginate impression; as he crossed from examining room to examining room his thoughts kept returning to Marshall. During a cavity prep he was asked about childhood enamel formation and the etiology of the dry socket and he could not bring his mind around in time: the faculty dentist looked at him with disapproval; but still he couldn't force himself to concentrate. How did anyone react to news like that? He thought back to their days together; he'd always shown Marshall that he treated girls well—he hadn't been a cad at all. He remembered standing in a stairwell on Broadway telling Marshall to be kind to Sofia. Certainly Marshall would understand that this meant he'd treat Simone well, too. Still, it was a strange thing to have happened. He wondered if Marshall would distance himself now, the way he'd done before.

XXIV

O—

Ah, to read such lovely news here in the lovely sun—I could not be happier nor wish for tidings any better than this. Simone is the most lovely dark emerald, and you—you know how I feel—you are as splendid to me in every small facet. I cannot wait to see the two of you together, to walk with the two beacons of my life, one on either side.

I send you both my love—

—M

He went to show Simone, and over her shoulder he read it again.

X X V

Snow came in January, huge drifts that covered the yards and roofs in silence; and ice came in March, rounding the angles of the land; but soon it was April and in the afternoon the eaves and limbs were dripping. Now and then he wondered about Marshall: since his letter, he seemed to have vanished again. Simone hadn't heard from him either, and from her mother she brought only vague news: the novel was almost finished; he'd moved to an apartment near Venice Beach. Orno spent every weekend in Annandale, and Tuesdays and Wednesdays, when Simone had no classes, they spent the days together in Stony Brook. When she was there he skipped every lecture he could, spending two hours at his desk before she woke each morning to read his textbooks. Again, the time was strangely clear for him. He did the rest of his work on Mondays and Thursdays and on the bus rides back and forth to see her. He felt he was certainly near the bottom of his class; yet somehow, this made him laugh. Buds were coming out on the trees; this made him laugh, also. The teaching assistants raised their eyebrows at him when they handed back his tests, but he didn't care. He heard a joke: "What do they call the guy who graduates last in his class from dental school?" He told it to other students and to the hygienists and receptionists at the clinic, despite the rush of embarrassment he felt. The answer was "Doctor."

He'd done cleanings now, worked on cavity preps in the lab, assisted in three oral surgeries and half a dozen extractions. He was proficient at the physical tasks, coming to them more easily than the other students he watched, and this served to ease him. He began to like his classmates; they were a genial, unassuming group for the most part, and they seemed to be thankful to have found themselves at this station in their lives; what they were doing was suddenly forgivable to him. They wore ties and Oxfords to class and studied in the evenings, gathering downstairs in the lounge afterward to watch the big TV. When Simone was not there he joined them now, eating pizza out of cardboard flats and passing around six-packs of beer. In May, a professor called offering him a job for the summer in his lab, and he and Simone made plans to move in together to a sublet one-bedroom a mile from the dental school. It was a small change, really, not much different from what they had already; but he was joyous.

One evening near the time of final exams he was in the dormitory lounge watching *Durango* when the credits came on and suddenly in the corner of his vision he saw the words *Written by Diogenes Mendelsohn.* He sat up: there it was. He stood and the conversations around him faded, and then he was outside on the street, walking fast to a phone. When Simone answered, he said, "Your brother's a TV writer. That's where he's gone."

"What on earth are you talking about?"

"I saw his name on the credits."

"Of what?"

"Of *Durango.* I saw a name he uses. At least he used to use it. He once told me it wasn't him, but I think he used it in college."

"What was the name?"

"Diogenes Mendelsohn. The credits said, 'Written by Diogenes Mendelsohn.' "

She laughed. "Oh, my God," she said. "Well, was it good?"

"I wasn't paying close attention. I was just sitting there, not really even watching."

"What makes you think it's him?"

"I know it's him," he said. "No wonder he hasn't sent me the novel yet."

"Come on," she said. "You don't think he's still working on *that*, do you?"

"He must be."

She laughed again. "Forgive me," she said. "But he's my brother."

"Forgive you for what?"

"For telling you this. But I'm sure he's not really working on that book of his. And I doubt there's any publisher for it."

"Why do you say that? He met with an editor last summer."

"In Los Angeles?"

"I think so."

"Which publishers are in Los Angeles?" she said.

"I wouldn't know."

"There *are* none," she said. "Didn't you know that?"

"I can't say I did."

She laughed. "I'll tell you where he was going, sweetheart. The reason he left Woods Hole was that he saw you kiss my hand."

"Come on."

"I wasn't sure whether you knew that. He didn't leave because of any publisher. When we were in the dunes, he was upstairs on the deck looking down on us. That's why I walked away. And it's why he left the next evening. So that you would leave, too."

Orno was silent, looking out at the pale buds on the trees. He could feel himself flushing.

"What's the matter?" she said.

"I don't know. I guess I don't know who to believe. I mean, then why did he write such a nice letter? I believed Marshall. Now I believe you. It makes me feel naive."

"It's not naive. You're not used to my family."

"It *is* naive."

"All right, a little bit. But that's exotic, too."

"That I'm gullible?"

"That you trust people. Where I grew up, that's a rare quality. Our family seal is a snake, twisted in knots."

"It is not."

"Good," she said.

He flushed again.

"I should have told you he saw us," she said. "I just thought you knew. I'm sorry about that."

"That's okay. It wouldn't have made any difference."

"Maybe not."

"I can't believe he's writing for TV," he said. "Do you think he's been doing it the whole time?"

"I bet he has."

"What do your parents think of it?"

"I think they think what *you* thought."

"Which is what?"

"That he was writing a novel."

"Doesn't that make them naive, too?"

"It's different," she said. "Entirely and utterly different."

———

Before he went to sleep, he called Marshall, standing by the window looking over the spread of trees to the west, trying to imagine him in his apartment. He was planning to make a joke, but Marshall picked up on one ring and surprised him. "M?" Orno stuttered.

"You shouldn't be watching so much TV," Marshall answered.

Orno laughed.

"You saw one, I guess," Marshall said, "didn't you? Shouldn't you be studying?"

"There was more than one?"

"There've been a few. I've been waiting for you to call."

"Yeah, I did. I saw *Durango.* It was good." He waited. "I mean, I wasn't paying close attention until I saw your name, but I remember it being very good."

"You sound the same. Exactly. You're lying to be nice."

"No, I'm not."

"That's the second time already. You'd do well out here."

"I was calling to congratulate you."

"Don't."

"Congratulations," said Orno. "It's amazing."

"And a great disappointment to all."

"Don't be silly."

"I didn't think I was. I'm wasting my life. That's what everyone does out here."

"I thought that's what *I* was doing."

"I was wrong. You're making something of yourself."

"Anyway," said Orno, "it's amazing to hear your voice again."

"Yours too, O."

"How's the novel?"

"How's my sister?"

"She's good." He waited. "I was thinking maybe I'd come out to visit."

"Here?"

"Yeah."

"You won't believe it out here, O."

"That sounds good so far. I'll see if I can get a ticket." In the background he heard another phone ring.

"You know, O, I would love that. I would really love it." The other phone rang again. "But I have to take another call right now. Let's think about you visiting. All right?"

"All right."

"Don't ever change," Marshall said.

"I won't."

Marshall laughed.

"What's so funny?"

"That's an expression here," he said. " 'Don't ever change.' It's just an expression. Nobody ever answers, 'I won't.' "

"But I really won't."

"I know," Marshall said. "That's why I laughed. That's why I love you."

XXVI

A week later an envelope in the mailbox: inside, a letter; inside the letter, a plane ticket to Los Angeles.

O—

You'll love it in L.A., out here among the blooming jacarandas. Have you ever seen one? They look like Alice in Wonderland in the sunshine. Purple trees!

Please accept the enclosed bequest as my meager and modest enticement. Phone first, and like magic you shall be collected at the airport (out here, this is considered an unusual favor).

—M

M—

Your generosity is quite touching. But as you see, I'm sending back the ticket. I can't wait to visit (but I'll pay my own way). Simone sends you her love.

—O

O—

Don't be silly. Here's the damn thing back. For which more worthy endeavors do you think I've sold my soul? If you don't take it, I'll be crushed.

The jacarandas are still blooming (though not for long).

—M

M—

You win. Thank you. School ends in May. Then I'll be there. I am deeply touched.

—O

XXVII

As the spring went on, and finally as the heat grew and the new leaves uncurled on the tree limbs, he began to notice a shift in how he saw the world. He'd always assumed frankness in human character, but now it was as though a flicker of deceit had suddenly become a possibility; in the smiles of others, in their words, in their small gestures and nods he began to see the shadows of duplicity. He was working on patients every day now, and he began to notice the ones with chipped incisors or gingivitis who smelled of alcohol underneath their cologne and argued with the receptionists outside. Of course there were upright people in his chair as well, mothers and fathers and workingmen, but there seemed to be any number of these others now also; and as he began to pay attention to them, their stories grew more and more suspect.

Yet to his surprise he found they also held a certain appeal. All of them seemed to struggle with an effacing self-encumbrance that brought out a generous feeling in him and led him to banter with them as he worked, though he knew they weren't exactly on the level. They liked to tell him their stories, and it amused him now, with his new views, whenever he realized they were lying. Through the reception room walls he heard them explaining why they had missed their appointments and why they were behind in their bills, and one day one of them sat down in his chair and when he put the bib over her neck she began to cry and asked him for money. Her name was Mollie Summers. She was a weary-eyed, blond woman twenty years older than he was—not unpretty, though, with red nails and dyed hair and the lined face of a cocktail waitress or one of the wives, not uncommon around there, who had been left by a husband and then found work in the tourist shops. She wore makeup like an actress. She'd been his patient once before, and when he handed her a tissue and asked her how much money she needed, she said eighty dollars. He smiled and asked her why. She told a story about her daughter's medical bills and he smiled again, but when he asked the name of her daughter's doctor she stumbled. As he turned back and forth between the chair and the instrument tray he felt a certain expansive comprehension within himself; it felt like worldliness to him, like a privileged underview and forgiveness of humanity. Her eyebrows were penciled coal-black and the remains of her glossy lipstick were on his hands. He wished that Marshall could see what he saw every day. When he finished the cleaning and pulled off the bib he told her that if she came by the next afternoon he would lend her the money.

He didn't tell Simone. They didn't have it to lend, but the next afternoon he emerged from the clinic and Mollie Summers was sitting on the steps outside the door. She stood quickly and brushed off her skirt. He asked her how she was and she smiled, giving him the opportunity to look at the work he'd done on her fronts. He asked after her daughter and her eyes turned down. She was made up again the same way, a friendly exaggeration of beauty. Then she looked up at him imploringly. He reached into his bag and took out the envelope into which he'd folded four twenty-dollar bills that morning, and when she had it in her hand she leaned forward and kissed him quickly on the cheek.

XXVIII

A week after school ended, he flew out to Los Angeles. Simone had already come down from Annandale with her belongings and they'd moved into the apartment together; it was small, two rooms, and their few possessions filled it up—she was a literature major and because they had no bookshelves her novels were lined up on a deep window seat that looked into the branches of an elm, the only charming feature of the apartment. His dentistry texts were stacked on the floor—*Preventive Dentistry, Surgical Anatomy of the Head and Neck, Accepted Dental Therapeutics*—thick, hardbound books draped in dishtowels to protect them from the sun. On the humid morning when they moved in and he stacked them there he felt a grave, tranquil covenant with the world—this formidable knowledge he now held, this girl hanging skirts in the small closet, this warm air of summer. It was the tranquillity of instinct, he thought to himself. A year of professional school was behind him and for the first time in his life he felt he knew almost enough to strike off on his own in the world. They spent a week together before he flew to California. In the evenings, the singing of the crickets was so ardent that they went to the window to look. He could not have been happier. Again, somehow, he thought of a soul rising.

As the plane moved west at the end of the week, he found himself garrulous, talking to the salesman on one side of him and the manager on the other, types that by habit he had learned to shun at Columbia. Now he saw them as the true sponsors of social equanimity—not unlike what he himself wanted to become—modest and diligent and clear-eyed about the world. He stretched his arm over the seat back. They passed over the Mississippi and he gazed down through the broken cloud cover at the black coil of river, surprising and still where it laid itself out among the fields of wheat and alfalfa. They were north of Cook's Grange—from the course of the shoreline, he guessed Rock Island or Burlington. He thought of his parents, of their eventless lives moving unnoticeably below him; his mother, kneeling in the pansies next to the drain spout; his father, washing the Chrysler because it was a Saturday. He thought of Simone back in Stony Brook, bringing in flowers to set in a glass on the windowsill. When he returned he would cook dinner for her, and after dinner they would walk into the hills.

Then they were descending over the Sierras and soon the basin of Los Angeles came into view, as far south as he could see: yellowish skyline and the dark blue reach of the Pacific. To his relief as the plane approached he felt no hesitation. Marshall had been the same twice on the phone now, relaxed and acerbic, so that both times he could imagine him present: gazing upward as he spoke, his arm out against the wall.

When Orno walked off the plane onto the ramp, Marshall said, "Who's better than you, babe?"

"I don't answer that one either, right?"

"Right."

They hugged without hesitation. Marshall looked well, but at the same time different. Older. Not in his features but in a bearing that he now had. Privileged. Each time Orno glanced sideways over his shoulder he remembered that he himself was still a student of a trade, while Marshall already had a name in the world. Marshall was dressed in khaki pants and a black shirt; waiting for his duffel, Orno noted that the pants were cuffed and the shirt was silk. "You're looking like a prince, M," he said.

"Prince of darkness, of course. Welcome to Los Angeles. Don't worry, I have a shirt for you here."

"I wasn't worried."

"Maybe you should have been."

And Marshall did have one, black like his own and the same material: he handed it over in the car. Orno had never felt anything like it: shiny black and cool on his hands. The car was an Audi, with a sunroof that Marshall opened as they sped up the freeway. When they arrived at the apartment in Venice Beach there was a pair of pants, too, hanging by the door in the guest room.

"My God, M, you're rich."

"It's what you get in exchange for your soul."

The townhouse was modern, concrete with architectural details that made it look like a ship; Orno followed him through it holding the new pants on their hanger. Small round windows like portholes as he climbed the spiral stairs to the second floor; narrow shellacked planks set in circles around the light fixtures. Through the glass wall of the living room, a walled garden of palms and huge, tree-sized ferns; from the portholes upstairs, the sea. It broke silently behind the glass, half a block away. "Wow," he said. "Last *I* knew, you were living in a basement."

"Ah, yes."

Orno pulled open the curtains in the bedroom: the hazy sky, washed of its blue; water white from the afternoon sun.

"As I was saying," said Marshall, "there's a price for your soul."

"Show me where to sign up."

"You'd never do it. I know you."

He smiled at Marshall, then looked out the window again. "My God, look at all this."

"I know. It's curious, isn't it?"

"It's amazing."

"A long way from The Odalisque."

"So what are you now, a screenwriter?"

"That and a producer."

"You're a producer? You?"

"That's right. Me. That's how it works here. You write what they want for a while. Then when you can't think of anything new anymore they put you in charge. That's what being a producer is. As soon as you lose your judgment, they make you the boss. Rats on a gangplank." He picked up a glass of wine from a shelf. "Then you read the drivel written by the other rats, who are like you were six months before. Six months is a long time here, by the way. They're still thinking about their art and about how they might write a novel one day, and they think secretly that you're an idiot who happens to have arrived the previous year, that's all, and you're telling them fine, fine, but what we need is a script." He sipped the wine. "That's the deal, basically. Chance and mystery, the unknowable course of our days."

"Sounds nice."

"But it isn't."

"Well, you seem to be liking it."

"I do actually. I'm having a party tonight. You can meet some of the other rodents."

"Who are they?"

Marshall laughed. "Sellouts," he said. "But charming ones. You'll like them."

"And what about *your* novel?"

He looked sour. "I'm still working on it. Let me show you around."

He took him through the rest of the townhouse: inlaid woodwork in the kitchen; a Jacuzzi outside; alarms on the windows and doors and gate; an assemblage of ferns and palms and cactuses in gravel beds along the backyard deck, tended by a specialist gardener. "It's quite an art," Marshall said, showing him soil beds that had been dug into the terrace. "*Roystonea regia, Phoenix dactylifera*— they're a mixture of sun plants and shade plants, not to mention desert and tropical. My gardener's the best in L.A."

"You have the best gardener in Los Angeles?"

"That's right. Tropical and desert."

"I can't believe you just said that. It sounds like a script. Like you're playing a rich man."

"Pretty close."

"In Stony Brook, we have some nasturtiums in a bottle next to the window."

"I know," said Marshall, "and down the block from here the bums are mainlining. It's a strange world. Two years ago, I never would have imagined it."

"It's hard to imagine now."

"I suppose you're right. I keep forgetting what I used to think of it myself."

"I can tell you," said Orno.

"Don't," said Marshall.

———

As soon as darkness arrived that night, the guests began appearing; their cars were parked by valets, two college students in white jackets who sprinted up and down the block. Orno was in his new clothes. He'd already had a scotch straight up with Marshall, standing in the kitchen while around them the caterers lifted sheets of foil from platters. He felt more like one of the boys parking the cars than one of the guests; even after the drink he found himself looking down when he was introduced. Women in black body stockings under short skirts, nodding at him when he said his name; he ordered another scotch. To the back the doors were opened. Guests moving in and out. He met agents and film editors and composers of film scores, and after he'd been introduced to three or four women he stopped saying he was a dental student and started saying he was a dentist. Another drink. Then another, and talking to a girl in a short dress wearing earrings that glinted though it was nearly black inside the living room, he suddenly said he was a doctor. It just slipped out; he tried not to look startled. She smiled. "What kind of doctor?"

He thought of his anatomy classes. "Surgeon."

She smiled again: difficult to interpret but it didn't seem to be doubting. It was late by now. He felt shabby in the surroundings and mystified by the drink. Yet he was spurred on by a fervid clamor for ascension; everyone in the room seemed to be taking part.

Soon the conversation faltered. The girl wandered away. Before he'd asked, the barman had poured him another scotch. He stood there a long time, talking to the garrulous types as they made their way in around him. If anyone asked what he did, he lied again, worried that he might come across someone to whom he'd already told the truth. To what low had he now sunk? Marshall had disappeared toward the back of the house; he hadn't seen him in a while, and the drink was obscuring his conscience. A few of the guests began filtering back out to their cars, collecting them from the valets; he moved to the front door to watch them drive away into the warm night. He wanted to keep telling his story. This was the surprising part. Something had taken hold of him. He was leaning against the porch post, talking to anyone who paused near him. It was easy. He knew enough to make it seem true, and he imagined that he had the bearing, especially in his silk shirt. The smiles on the girls' faces became familiar, confidential softenings of their otherwise circumspect expressions—admissions that if things went forward they would have told him secrets. That was what doctors brought out in people. He sipped his drink. Dentists brought out wariness.

The party had thinned now. Marshall finally reappeared from the back, gesturing for Orno to come outside. He followed, out onto the stone patio. Empty now except for two girls on the other side next to the Jacuzzi, cross-legged in the low chairs. Both of them beautiful: slender, dark. They raised their glasses and Marshall nodded from the doorway. He leaned to Orno's ear. "Don't worry. They're old friends." He laughed. "They're actresses."

Orno looked at him.

"They think I'm going to hire them."

"Oh, I get you," Orno whispered back. "And who do they think *I* am?"

"Doesn't matter. You're a friend of mine."

He swallowed the rest of his drink. It was early morning back in Stony Brook: Simone would still be asleep. Marshall took a cigarette case from his pocket, and the two girls stopped talking. One of them giggled and Marshall said, "This is my friend Orno."

Their names were Grace and Dee-Ann. He was trying not to feel uneasy. Marshall opened the cigarette case and Orno looked in. Cocaine. He said, "I don't believe it."

Dee-Ann sat up straight. Pulled at her skirt.

"You've tried it, haven't you?" Marshall tapped out a tiny heap onto the table and shaped it into a line. Orno had seen it at The Odalisque half a dozen times but never used it; among the arts majors it was popular and for a time he'd considered trying some: he'd never been afraid, but he'd never been asked. Marshall rolled up a bill and handed it to Grace, who leaned over the table. Then he tapped out another line. Dee-Ann leaned over. She sat back up and handed Marshall the bill, her fingers resting on his hand.

Marshall said, "Dee-Ann and Grace are actresses."

"So I understand."

"What do *you* do?" Grace asked.

Marshall smiled. "He's a surgeon." He leaned back in his chair.

Orno laughed. Sipped his drink.

"I was going to be a doctor," said Dee-Ann.

Marshall touched his forehead. "So was I," he said. "I just didn't have the grades."

"I guess I didn't either," said Dee-Ann.

Orno laughed again and Marshall handed him the bill. Another line on the tabletop. He thought Marshall didn't expect him to, so he leaned down over it; covered one nostril and tried to inhale as he'd seen Dee-Ann and Grace do, half one side and half the other; but most of it came up on the first pass. Tingling. The edges of his lips numb. He waited. Nothing more happened; that was the stolidness. Suddenly, again, he longed for Simone. She would be waking soon, next to their open window. He stood and walked to the patio door: one of the caterers in the kitchen, an old Mexican man in a bow tie, was washing shot glasses at the metal sink. *All you ever have*, his father used to say, *is yourself.* He looked down at his watch. Then he excused himself and went back into the house. He began picking up ashtrays and platters from the living room. He looked back through the glass. Marshall was still smiling, smoothing another line onto the glass; then he leaned over it, and when he sat up he handed the bill to one of the girls.

———

The next morning at breakfast, Marshall said, "Can I ask you something?"

"Go ahead."

"Does it disappoint you what I'm doing out here?"

"It's your business."

"No, really. You've never told me what you think. I know you don't like to judge people, as you like to say, but you've got to have an opinion about this."

"About what?"

"About all this. I'm rich, or at least I'm getting rich. I sold myself down the river. I bring wanna-be starlets over to the house. I do coke. Tell me the truth," he said, looking over his cup of coffee, "what do you think of it?"

"Why are you asking *me*? I'm the one who said I was a doctor."

"That's different," Marshall said. "You just figured out what you were supposed to do."

"Tell lies about myself?"

"They're not really lies. Cab drivers say they're screenwriters. Half the actresses you met last night make coffee in the studios. Everybody does it."

"Well, I don't."

"Come on. You're making the coffee cold. Relax."

"What does it matter what I think of your life?"

"It matters to me."

"Why?"

"Because *you* matter to me."

"Well, thank you."

"You do," Marshall said. "You must know how important your friendship is to me."

"Yours is important to me, too."

Marshall offered him a plate of muffins. "I've always envied your sturdiness," he said.

"You've said that before. That's ridiculous."

"Not at all. If you thought about it, it would make perfect sense. So what do you think of what I'm doing with my life?"

Orno sipped his coffee. "All a man ever has," he said, "is himself."

"What does that mean?"

"It means, what do you think of it yourself?"

"I think it's despicable," he said.

Orno went to the window. Outside, the sun had climbed above the rooftops; a desert brightness in the air, a bleached sheen of light from the waves and stucco walls that suddenly seemed hellish. "Why do you do it, then?"

"Because it's all I deserve."

"I hope you know how ridiculous that is."

"Why are *you* becoming a dentist then?"

"It's different. I have no choice."

"You're implying that I do have one."

"You do. You could do anything. You could write a beautiful book."

"Don't talk about that."

"What happened with it?"

"You still haven't said what you think of my life."

"You're doing what you want to do."

"Tell me what you think," Marshall said.

"It's not for me to say."

"Tell me you think it's despicable."

"I don't," said Orno. "I told you. It's not for me to decide."

"Say it's despicable."

"People change."

"No, they don't."

Orno didn't answer. The truth was, he had never imagined himself immune to any weakness he'd ever seen in anyone else, certainly not to the forces that played in Marshall's life; Marshall lived in a world of suspicion and appetite that towered above his own small-time dreams. And yet there was a combustive ardor to everything he did that Orno had forgotten until this moment; but now, somehow, he didn't want to rise to it anymore. All he wanted was to be with Simone. He felt her absence now as an emptiness in his chest. Marshall set two shot glasses in front of them and filled them from a metal flask that had been in the cabinet; he raised his drink, smiled at Orno, and tossed it back.

"It's a bit early for that," Orno said. "Don't you think?"

"It's already dark under the house." Marshall poured himself another. "That's what my father says." He smacked his lips. "Here's a story," he said. "Did I ever tell you about Selim Aziz?"

"I don't think so."

"The very first day we were in Istanbul, we were walking at the Koyumçu Kapişi, which is a corner of the old Bedesten where the goldsmiths work. You have to be careful there, because a lot of the gold is low quality, and the prices don't tell you which is which. Anyway, our plane had landed that morning from Kennedy, and my mother didn't want me to be afraid of Istanbul, so as soon as we unpacked at the hotel we took a taxi down to the market, then walked to the Bedesten together, just the two of us. The Bedesten is the covered part of the market, where they sell valuables. I suppose they do that because it's the only part they can lock at night. Do you want to hear this?"

"Of course I do."

"My mother kept smiling and talking to the merchants, just to show me how friendly everyone was. It was so hot and the sidewalks were the busiest I'd ever seen, much worse than New York, but I wasn't bothered by it. I kept drinking Fruko, which is a God-awful lemon drink, but my mother I guess was intent on buying me whatever I wanted, so I wouldn't be afraid. I wasn't afraid, though. What was there for me to be afraid of, at that age? There was a whole quarter of the market that just sold sandals. That was incredible. They sew them from tire bottoms, a much better use than we make of them. Anyway, my mother bought me a pair, then right before we left she bought me another pair just because I liked it better. I could tell she was worried, even though she was pretending not to be. Otherwise, she would never have done that. We bought some etli böreki to eat on the way back. The whole point was to show me how nice Istanbul was going to be. Anyway, just as we were getting ready to walk back to the hotel, we were right in front of the Koyumçu Kapişi, when a man bumped us and took off into the crowd with my mother's purse."

"Oh, no," Orno said. "What did she have in it?"

"Listen to the rest. The guy was wearing a white shirt, and I watched him run through the crowd. My mother was panicked, but as soon as he started running, another man came out from one of the stalls, looked at the two of us, and took off after the guy. But this second guy was a lot older, and I could see he was never going to catch up. The guy with the purse was most of the way up the hill, and then he disappeared into one of the alleys. I wanted to find a policeman, but my mother was so upset she took me to a bench off to the side and we just sat there, wondering what to do. At the same time, she was still trying to show me what a good time we were going to have in Istanbul, so while we were sitting there she decided we should eat the böreki. I went along, because I wanted her to feel better. She unwrapped them—they're big pastries with ground meat inside—and we sat on the bench, eating them and drinking Fruko, even though my mother had just lost her purse. I could tell she was trying to remember what was in it. She told me the passports were back in the safe at the hotel, so that I didn't have to worry. And most of our money, too. Anyway, while we were sitting there, eating böreki, the older man who'd chased the thief walked up, and he had the purse in his hand. He apologized in English, pretty good English, and gave it back to my mother. Then he went across the street and came back with a baklava for me. That was how we met." He took another drink. "That was Selim Aziz."

Orno fingered the glass but didn't lift it. "Go on," he said.

"So Selim Aziz became our protector there. All the money was still in the purse, so my mother took him out to dinner with us that night, and after some wine he told us his life story. He was a retired ferry captain from the Sea of Marmara, so he knew all about the countryside and the Princes Islands, where my mother was going to be doing her work. It was all very lucky. He told my mother about a good pensione in Heybeli and about dozens of restaurants where we had great food over the time we were there. After that we became friends. Every Saturday morning he took us for a walk in some old part of the city that we'd never have gone to on our own. He would meet us at the hotel gate and we would walk from there, sometimes for an hour or two just to get where he wanted to take us. He must have been seventy years old, but he was in great shape. He was always very polite, too—he had a British accent because he'd been taught English by a woman from Calcutta. My mother always paid for the meals, but that was expected, I guess. Selim Aziz was embarrassed by this, but there was nothing he could do. He told us the history of Turkey, mostly military history, which I had never heard before. It was such a new way to talk about the world, from battle to battle. He told us about his boyhood in the countryside. He never told us much about his family, though. I remember that. I didn't notice it at the time, but my mother did. She implied he'd had a painful past and that I should be wary of asking him about it. That was fine with me. I wouldn't have asked him anyway. I was more interested in the Turkish navy. Anyway, one day a few months later, near the end of our time in Istanbul, I was walking with Penny McRary near the Bedesten again, when we stumbled on Selim Aziz sitting at an outdoor café. He was with a young man, who he introduced as his son. As soon as he introduced us, though, his son left. I didn't pay much attention, though, because I was nervous that Selim had seen me with Penny. We weren't supposed to be away from the hotel, remember. I wasn't sure whether to pretend everything was fine, or to just take the risk and beg him not to tell my mother. It didn't matter, it turned out, because the Turks have an extra sense about those things. After we had tea with him, while Penny was using the bathroom, he winked at me and told me he would never tell my mother what he'd seen. I loved him at that moment. I really did."

"So did your mother ever find out?"

"No, she didn't. But here's the thing. By the end of our stay there, Selim became sort of a replacement chaperon for me. After Penny ran away, he took care of me a few times during the day, so that I wouldn't have to make the trip out to the islands with my mother. He'd come to the hotel in the morning and take me for walks. Or sometimes we'd sit under the blood oranges and he'd drink raki. This was at the very end of our time. He gave me a little, too. It was my first hard liquor. And I loved the taste, even then. I thought it was something my father should have done a long time ago. I remember thinking I wished I didn't have to go back and see my real father again. I wanted to stay there with Selim." He laughed and poured another shot. "It's funny how wrong you can be about a person."

"How were you wrong?"

"I never told you this, but the day before we left Turkey for good, we were entirely cleaned out. All my mother's things were stolen, for real this time—her jewelry, her cash, her camera. Our plane was leaving in the morning, so we never had a chance to report it."

"Did they take your passports?"

"No."

"That was lucky."

"I don't think so. He left them on purpose. So we'd still leave in the morning and not come after him."

"Clever, I guess."

"Selim Aziz was a clever man."

Orno broke one of the muffins. "Come on," he said. "You think it was him?"

"I know it was."

"How could you know that?"

"I'll tell you how. My mother never figured it out, but I did. Of course, she had to consider him, even though he'd been like an uncle to us, but she couldn't imagine anyone changing like that. So in the end she figured it was one of the porters in the hotel."

"How do you know it wasn't?"

"I'll tell you why. And I didn't realize this until we were back in New York. But one day I was sitting at an outdoor restaurant on Columbus Avenue when all of a sudden it came back to me that Selim's son had looked familiar when I met him. I'd been too nervous to really notice it at the time, because of Penny McRary of course, but all of a sudden I just realized that he was the one who'd taken my mother's purse. He was the thief in the white shirt. The first time, the day we got there."

"In the market?"

"Yes."

"Selim's son was the purse snatcher?"

"No, Orno. He wasn't his son. At least I don't think he was. They sure didn't look much alike. He just told me he was his son because I'd surprised them together. But he was the thief, all right. That's why I recognized him. He and Selim were working together. They had been the whole time. How else would an old man have caught up with a young guy two blocks ahead of him?"

"Come on," said Orno. "You can't be sure of that."

"But I am. There wasn't enough cash in my mother's purse, so that's why he brought it back. Then he set out to earn our trust. That's what he was doing all those months. Not to mention free dinners. He figured there was more to be had." He drank his shot. "And he was right, too. That was a real lesson. It's why I think you're wrong."

"About what?"

"About what you just said about me. That people change. I don't think they do, really. For a long time it bothered me that Selim could have changed from such a gentle man to a thief, all so fast. But that was only a childish defense on my part. Maybe I missed having a father like that. Maybe I wanted Selim to be a kindly old man who cared about me. But the point is, he was a thief and a con artist all the time. He didn't change. Nobody changes. They just reveal themselves." He fingered his empty glass. "Remember that," he said, "as you get to know my sister."

"Just a minute," Orno said. "What's that supposed to mean?"

"It doesn't mean any more than I said."

"Are you telling me to be careful?"

"That's all I'm going to say."

"About Simone?"

"That's all I want to say, O."

"I'm not sure how to answer that."

"You don't have to." He pointed to Orno's glass. "But drink that," he said. "Or else I will."

———

In the afternoon Marshall took him to his office. A bright, yellow-walled room in a sandstone building on the lot of Columbia Studios. He drove through with the top down, waving at the carpenters and set-hands by raising his hand slightly on the steering wheel. Soundstages and scenery shops and whole towns built in façade. The office had a wall of windows with a secretary in an outer hallway and a second room to the side, carpeted and set up with a long conference table and expensive chairs. The secretary was beautiful too; like one of the actresses from the night before. Next to Marshall's desk, a telescope pointing out the window. Orno went to the glass and looked over a long avenue lined with warehouses that ended at a back lot built to resemble a ghost town. Two men on ladders against one of the façades. Orno leaned down and peered through the telescope. "They're putting in a window," he said.

"Stunt glass," said Marshall. "A guy is going through it this afternoon."

"From the third floor?"

"They put down a mat."

"Do you get to watch?"

"I used to. Don't much anymore. I once watched the invasion of Earth by giant worms from this window. That was good. Nothing else compares."

"This is where you write?"

"If you call it that."

"I do call it that. Pretty interesting life."

Marshall opened the drawer to his desk. "But you don't approve."

"Why do you keep saying that?"

"Because it's true." He took out a cardboard box. "This is it," he said. "My life's work. One half-finished novel. Look." He held it up and laughed. "There's dust on the rubber band." He snapped it and a cloud rose.

"What does the publisher think?"

"They prefer them without dust."

"Tell me the truth."

"They're disappointed. They don't say that, but I know they are." He laughed and smoothed his hair. "They're still waiting patiently."

Orno stood back from the window. Across the lot a pane of glass was being lifted by a crane. "So, which publisher is it?" he said finally.

"Charles Scribner's."

Orno watched him thumbing through the pages.

"Hemingway's publisher," Marshall said, without looking up.

"Guess you're in good company."

"Hemingway and I led similar lives. I don't think he was late with his books, though."

"Were Scribner's the ones you left the Cape to meet?"

"Right."

"Well, what happened? Don't you have a deadline?"

He placed the manuscript back in the box. "You know," he said, "I was thinking about what I said about my sister."

"And?"

"Well, all I meant was that I think you should think carefully before you make any kind of irrevocable move with her."

"What do you mean?"

"I mean, she's not always what she seems." He looked at Orno. "Look—you're my oldest friend, and Simone's wonderful, but I'll just say that in my opinion you should think hard if you're trying to decide whether to marry her."

"Tell me what you mean."

"I'd rather leave it at that."

"I can't leave it at that."

"Sorry, then. I didn't mean to bring it up."

"Look, Marshall, I'll marry her if it's right. I can't say what's going to happen this afternoon, let alone years from now. But I'll do what's right."

Marshall came to the window. "Wow," he said. "I've never seen you mad before." He put his hand on Orno's shoulder. "I apologize."

"I think you should either tell me exactly what you're talking about, or you shouldn't bring it up."

"I'm sorry. I won't bring it up then. Look," he said, "the stunt man's mat." He pointed to the façade, where a yellow pad the size of a mattress lay three stories below the window. "That guy's going to fall thirty feet onto that thing. It's amazing. They're the most talented people in Hollywood."

"You keep saying sinister things about your sister, but you won't tell me what you mean," Orno said. "I can't abide that. I really can't stand here and listen to you talk about her." He moved away from the window. "It's not right."

"I'm sorry," said Marshall. "I really won't ever say anything else about it." He put his hand on Orno's shoulder again. "Forget I said it. Look." He pointed. "He's getting ready to jump."

"You make me mad when you do that."

Marshall was at the window. "Come on, O, you're going to miss it."

"All right." He moved closer and bent over the telescope. "That's the guy?"

"Yeah."

Through the lens he could see him clearly: small, surprisingly old, a slight figure in an orange jumpsuit. He watched him moving the mat, looking back and forth from the window to the ground. He let his anger ease. Cameras on dollies and men stringing power cords up to the lights. Marshall stood at the window next to him. Orno kept his eye to the telescope; he didn't want to look up. His mouth was dry and he felt heavy in his shoes. Disordered and anxious and unsure of how to act. What was Marshall implying? Should he break off his friendship with him? Was that the upright course? He peered again at the set. Simone would want to hear about it when he returned; but the details around him—the maple-handled telescope, the averted posture in which he stood, the words that came to mind to start a different conversation—all of them seemed to be implements of a sad and formal cunning: he didn't want to take part anymore. His head was still bowed to the eyepiece. And it was disconcerting that none of this seemed to bother Marshall. He'd gone back to the desk now; Orno heard the drawer open again. The thought struck him that Marshall had never in his life felt the restraint of morality. Not in college and not now. He'd never worried about the calamity and demise that to Orno were hidden everywhere, inevitable punishment for a hundred different failings. It allowed Marshall great ease in bars and expensive parties and fabricated landscapes like this one. Duplicity didn't frighten him.

The stunt man had gone through a door in the façade and now the set was still. Orno turned around: another line of cocaine on the ink blotter. For a moment Marshall looked sheepish, then he offered the rolled bill over the desk. "Tell me," he said, "what do you think are the gifts of life?"

"The what?"

"What makes you want to be alive? What gives you pleasure in the world?" He gestured with the bill.

Orno shook his head. "My God," he said. "How often do you do this?"

"I'm an addict."

"You can get help for that, you know."

Marshall laughed. "You're the sweetest person I've ever known," he said. "You know that? I don't *want* help for it."

"How often do you do it?"

"Every day. Twice every day."

"It must cost quite a bit."

"I make quite a bit."

"I see that. There are treatment programs."

"Tell me what you think the gifts of life are."

"That's a strange question."

"It seems like a good question to me."

Orno came away from the window and sat down in the chair across from him. "All right," he said. "What I get pleasure from is walking with your sister, and learning my profession, and helping people with their dental problems."

Marshall burst out laughing. "You get pleasure from helping people with their dental problems?"

"Yes I do."

"That's amazing. It sounds like the Boy Scout Handbook."

"It's the truth."

"I know it is. That's why it's amazing. You people have such an easy time with life."

"Which people?"

"You people. Midwesterners. Regular people."

"No, we don't. Not particularly."

"But you want what you're supposed to want. That's what makes it so easy. Do you know how much I've wished I was like that?"

"If you were like me you'd have none of this."

"Maybe, but you really do want a good moral road to set your life on."

"And what do you want?"

"You know what I want."

"No I don't. I used to think you wanted to be a writer."

Marshall leaned over the desk. "You're right," he said. "I used to want to."

"And what do you want now?"

"What I've always wanted."

"And what's that?"

"You tell *me*, O."

Orno looked out the window. The hellish sun again. "I think you want to destroy yourself," he said. "I mean, I think you want some kind of success but at the same time ever since I've known you you've been stabbing at self-destruction." For some reason a laugh came out of him. "I'm sorry, that's not a very friendly thing to say."

"But it's perfectly right."

"I know. Why is that? You're the most gifted person I've ever met."

"I'll tell you why," Marshall said. He pushed another heap into a line. Snorted it. "I'm not alive."

"What do you mean?"

"Like when I'm walking around or sitting here at my desk or making a show, I feel like I'm hollow inside. I feel like—how should I say this?—like a rotted piece of wood. I don't feel anything. I never do. The only times in my life I've ever felt anything are the times I've been dying." He closed the desk drawer. "That's the truth." He brushed back his hair, then bent over the desk again and snorted up the remnants. "Think about it." He looked up. "When I took those pills I was just giving in to temptation. You have no idea what that's like. It's utterly beyond something I could ever imagine you feeling, or even understanding. But you have to know it's an overwhelming force. It takes me over. I know it's dangerous, but it's what I want all the time. All the fucking time. I want to feel something. I want to feel like myself."

Orno put his hands on the desk. "I don't understand. What does that feel like?"

"I know you don't understand. That's why I like you. You're an innocent. I just want to feel alive."

"I'm not an innocent anymore, M."

"As you wish."

"You don't feel alive until you're in danger?"

"Until I'm dead."

"Come on."

"It's what Kafka said: the soul is a frozen sea. I live for the moment it thaws."

"Hurting yourself."

"Killing myself."

Orno tried to smile. "But you've never succeeded."

"Yes, I have."

"You're not making sense, M."

"I won't be able to explain it to you. I told you. But I can tell you, there are lots of other people like me, all over. There was another one at the party last night. We recognized each other. I saw her right off, and she saw me. Her sleeves were buttoned all the way down."

"And you both have the same reasons?"

"Yes."

"How do you know?"

"I just do."

Orno looked at his hands. "Are you going to do it again?"

"Do what again?"

"Try to hurt yourself."

"I don't know, O."

"Simone loves you, M. So do I."

"Thanks."

"Will you let someone know if it's going to happen? Will you tell *me*?"

"I don't *want* to be saved, O. That's the point."

Orno walked back to the window. "Then why did you call me?"

"I wanted you to visit."

"I mean, the time you took the aspirin. If you wanted to die, why did you call me?"

"Sounds like you've talked to Simone. What else did she say?"

"I haven't talked to Simone."

"I called you because I was scared, O. That's all. You never get over *that*. It had nothing to do with anything else. Despite what my sister says."

"Simone didn't say anything about it."

"Simone thinks everything's complicated."

"I don't think that's true, M."

"Of course you don't. That's what love does. It blinds you." He pretended to fire an arrow. "I love her, too, O, but you ought to know she's as empty inside as I am."

"She's not empty inside."

"As you wish."

"Neither are you."

He laughed. "If you only knew."

"I do know, M. You're an incredible, brilliant human being. You draw people to you. You can have anything you want."

"Then what I want is for you to beware."

"Why do you keep saying that? You're trying to keep me away from her. I don't know why you're doing that."

Marshall brushed off the desk blotter with his sleeve and examined it. "Of course I'm not doing that," he said. "You misunderstand me terribly." He looked at Orno. "I'd want nothing more in the world than for you two to be together. That would be my dream. But you're my oldest friend, O, and I just want to make sure you know what you're getting." He checked his watch. "I have a meeting now," he said.

"Did you really have a publisher when you left Woods Hole?"

"What do you mean?"

"Or did you really leave because you saw me with your sister?"

"That's also the kind of thing Simone would say."

"Is it true?"

"Of course I had a publisher. I still do. And I didn't know you were with Simone until I got your letter. I would have been happy if I'd seen it. And I have a meeting now, O. I really do. So let's talk about it later."

Orno moved to the door. "One more thing," he said.

"Of course. But fast."

"How come you never told me you were Diogenes Mendelsohn?"

"Oh, that?" he answered, flicking his hand. "I just always assumed you knew."

———

Orno drove the Audi out to the beach in Santa Monica; but walking on the sand in the middle of the afternoon embarrassed him. Marshall's meeting was going to last a couple of hours. He went back to the house again, driving slowly beneath the palms to speed the day along. Finally Marshall came home, striding in the back door with a bag of groceries; he was friendly again, and Orno didn't know how to react. He didn't want to argue anymore. He was thinking about Simone: he felt compelled to hide her now. Yet he needed to see her. How well did he know her, really? She and Marshall both seemed to have been buffeted by a malevolent force larger than anything he had ever been subject to himself; did that mean he *was* naive? Could she have escaped whatever had enveloped her brother?

Yet somehow, it seemed to him, she had. She was certainly aware of malice, but in some mysterious manner it had brought out sympathy in her, not cunning. An astounding turn. He himself was only the product of hardworking certainty and charitable expectation; Simone on the other hand had invented herself, benevolently and nearly entirely. Yet certainly she could not have been accustomed to benevolence. He decided not to believe Marshall. Again he was buoyant, this time with relief.

He was leaving that night. In the evening they put the Audi's top down again and drove down Sunset Boulevard through Beverly Hills, all the way to the beach. Then up into Topanga Canyon, where Marshall let him drive, pointing out the estates and laughing again about his own decline. Steep, curved streets that opened over the sea. The wind filling his new shirt. At the wheel in the warm night he felt intoxicated, and coming over a summit where the moon came into view he suddenly realized it was by wealth. He tapped the brake. He'd never wanted a life like this. Hard work and an honest standing in the world—that's what he'd been after. A wife and children. A house and neighbors. He'd wanted to be able to look his father in the eye.

"It's nice," Marshall said. "Isn't it?"

Orno was startled. "It's not for me," he answered. He wanted to be home.

X X I X

Dear Clara,
   Once again I believe you are right. Indeed I need the ruler.
                                                    Love,
                                                    Orno

X X X

Stony Brook was hot; not the desert heat of Los Angeles but closer to the moist weight of summer he remembered from childhood. The whitened horizon. The lawn sprinklers. The empty streets and dark, shaded porches that brought to mind Cook's Grange in the time before the harvest. Classes were over and he had a week before his job started in the lab. They woke late and every morning Simone made a breakfast of eggs cooked with tomatoes; then they walked down to the beach. The waterline smelled of fish from the bait schools; out in the Sound the commercial boats made their runs from the piers, their gunwales lined with rods and anglers. Seabirds flew low over the waves. Again he felt a state of suspension in the air.

At the end of the week, finally, another letter:

O—

Like a penitent I have few thoughts these long days that are not of you or my sister; this little note is to tell you how sorry I am about what I said. Nothing in the round world could make me happier than to have the two of you together, forever. I don't know if marriage is in your plans, but from your words I believe it most certainly must be—sometime, somehow—and I wanted to add my exuberant hopes to your own. And I wish you congratulations as fervent as my hopes. May the amiable gods smile upon the two of you.

Love,

M

Frankly, it startled him. He didn't show it to Simone. Instead he lay awake in the dark, watching the shadowy lights from Route 25 across their ceiling; he felt oddly like a lawbreaker, like a small-time confidence man of the heart: he was suddenly afraid. Why didn't he show her? It was nothing, a small note of goodwill; but it paralyzed him. Was he weakhearted? A breaker of vows? When it came down to it, would he falter? He rose from bed and looked again for the envelope. There it was, folded inside the pocket of his coat, seemingly straightforward; but as he held it he suddenly thought of his family meeting Simone's. His father in his brown suit. His mother in her flowered hat, walking on the Emersons' stretch of rockless beach. His father would say nothing—a scornful silence. Where was the value of work among these people? Whose labor and diligence had produced such fortune? His mother would tinker with her cheerful hat, trying to get the flowers right.

XXXI

The year passed quickly. Simone found work as a teacher's aide in a children's home, a real orphanage of the kind Orno never knew existed; it was on the outskirts of town in a run-down stone building filled with hallways upon hallways of boys. In her work with them she was sober and diligent. When he visited they were not what he thought they would be. Not sullen or angry but childishly eager for her attentions and as well-behaved as he'd ever seen children, gathering around her like birds. At the end of his second year of dental school, he began volunteering in the infirmary himself: he checked teeth and sent the boys down to the clinic for fillings and in a couple of extreme cases ortho-dontics. They were touchingly grateful for his ministrations, sit-ting back in the chair and throwing open their mouths as though they thought he was going to feed them; following his hands as he moved through their uppers and lowers with the probe. Afterward, in the evenings, he walked out to the yard to throw a football with them.

He was somehow afraid to ask Simone to marry him but he rarely thought of it now; another year started. Their lives moving.

Soon he would be done with his degree, and now he was doing good works as well. They bought a car together, a Volkswagen with a hole in the floorboard that they covered with cardboard and a towel; in winter they added a rug. They both woke early and returned late, now and then Orno driving out to the orphanage after his clinic to eat dinner with Simone and the boys. A hot summer and a bright, assuring fall, and suddenly it was winter once again and the light in their apartment was shadowed by the bare branches of the elm.

One night, as the cold waned, they were watching the Academy Awards on television. Simone pointed to the corner of the screen and whispered, "My God, look at that. I wonder if my father's watching."

He looked different, his stride stately. His eyes so dark Orno wondered if he was wearing makeup; he crossed the ribboned walkway with an actress on his arm. Orno vaguely recognized her; she was smiling off to the side, and then Marshall leaned down to hear something she said: the camera was only on him for a moment, but before it turned he looked into it and touched his hand to his forehead. Orno said, "Goddamn, I wonder how long he's been doing *that*."

"I think for a while," she answered, though she hadn't understood.

———

Now they no longer called him when they saw his name in the credits of a show. But one evening it appeared after a television movie, and they sent him a bouquet of flowers; then one day in the early spring Orno was passing a movie theater and saw it on a poster there. He wondered what Marshall's life was like now. He thought of the Audi, cresting at the view of the sea. He himself still walked to school, or waited for the bus if it was too cold. Simone took the Volkswagen, and in the winter she had to wear mittens to drive.

She never complained but he felt he should be able to give her

better. The talk among his classmates now was about practice opportunities and the changing demographics of the state, and he
began thinking about where he could go to make money. He was
seeing his patients in clinic for the last time, letting them know
that they would be assigned to someone else when they returned,
one of the underclassmen who would arrive in July to take his position. He thought incessantly about what was the right thing to
do. The bulletin board was covered with flyers. Groups upstate
that were taking on associates. Medium-sized practices in the
growing suburbs around Albany and Troy. Good home prices and
safe neighborhoods and the chance to get in early on the boom.
Practices in the boroughs that offered large salaries after
five years. Practices in the Midwest, too, but he tried not to think
about them. He stood gazing at the possibilities. The students around him talked excitedly, but all he felt was inde-
cision. He lurched out into the cold evening. His thoughts
spiraled: something entered him, a dark doubt. As he walked in
the night it grew, until, as he passed the colonnaded façade of the
medical school, the thought formed itself: Simone was an aristo-
crat. Not by birth, perhaps, but by bearing and upbringing. That
was it. It was obvious enough, and of course he should have recognized it long ago, but it shamed him suddenly to realize that he
hadn't. Was it obvious to everyone else—his frenzied pursuit of
another class? He thought of Professor Emerson, borrowing
mortgage money at a cocktail party: was that who he himself was
also?

———

The following week, when Mollie Summers came in for the last of
her checkups, he let a certain playfulness enter his banter; sure
enough, as she was taking her coat from the hook she said without
turning around that since he was leaving the least she could do
was take him out for a drink. She glanced back at him. He smiled
and said, "Sure, why not." They agreed to meet at nine that night
in a bar across town from the dental school.

———

That afternoon he wrote:

Dear Dad—

School is approaching its end and I am grateful to have gotten what I came for, a grounding in the basics of a profession that will serve me, I hope, from now forward. There are a good many practice opportunities out here in New York State and I want you to know I'm thinking about them. The suburbs here are growing and there are jobs up north. Simone is still working in the orphanage but she has said she will go with me wherever I choose. How are you and Mom? I thank you for what you have given me, this chance to make my way in the world. Graduation is approaching and I'm thinking of you both.

Love,
Orno

———

At eight he told Simone he was going to the library. Covering himself with his long coat, he walked to the bar instead. He was afraid to go in, though; he walked block after block alongside, crossing the bustling boulevard behind and the quieter neighborhood streets around it, meandering under the still-leafless maples. The hour of their meeting arrived and he tried to let some intercession of chance overcome him. Something to happen. A friend or a patient outside on the street, someone to run into. Then he wouldn't have to open the door himself and go in there like a man climbing the three steps to his own gallows. Maybe this was what Marshall meant: no feeling until danger. The wind stirring the bare branches and the stars bright with frost. He was repelled by the prospect of a drink with Mollie Summers and at the same time drawn to it ruinously. Marshall might as well have been there with him, bellowing at the lit sky. What would he have told him? Seize the day? Wind was in his hair and he was warm in the cold night. A *cad.* He pulled open the buttons of his coat. Nine o'clock gone and he was still walking, circling the neighborhood; what overcame him at last was good manners.

He found her at a table in the back, an empty highball in front of her. Next to it a full shot glass; she tossed back the shot and began to talk. Surprisingly nervous. He assumed she was a woman who'd been around the block, but before he even sat down she began apologizing: the run-down bar, the neighborhood, the cracked highball glass, the broken wooden peg on which he was trying to hang his coat. He tried to apologize in turn for being late. She called over the barmaid and he ordered a whiskey. She told him her teeth didn't hurt at all and then opened her mouth, laughing nervously and then closing it. Red lipstick on the canines. She told him he was the best dentist she'd ever had. He smiled. He thought briefly of Simone and then forced himself back. Small talk. His *patient:* the word came to mind. The barmaid wiped the table and set down drinks for both of them. She stood there and when Mollie Summers looked away he realized he was expected to pay. It turned out she'd had several drinks already. After he gave the barmaid the money his wallet was nearly empty.

Then they were alone again and the conversation paused. He found himself saying that the night was beautiful. He swallowed his drink. Then they were outside the bar—he wasn't sure who had led the way—walking the path he'd walked a quarter of an hour before. Pointing out to her for no particular reason the brimming stars and the stark outlines of the trees. She followed next to him. Down the hill to the river. The water at its edge still rimmed with a melting skin of ice. Stars burning in it like candles. She made a little sighing noise and took his arm. His heart jumped but he turned and kissed her.

Of course she smelled of whiskey and cigarettes. But there was an eagerness to her embrace that touched him. The small-town way she moved her feet between his own when they parted and looked up at his face; her two familiar incisors gleaming, yellowed from childhood antibiotics. Her lips parted in a half-smile of wretched hope. He'd thought she was a wizened old drunk, but in the moonlight she looked like a schoolgirl.

He should have been slain with guilt but as he kissed her he was surprised at his ease. Her perfume didn't hide her life; so much striving in the close-up smell of her—dust, whiskey, smoke, hair spray—and something reminiscent in it of the way his own sister's friends smelled back home. He collapsed his guard and sighed and took her hand again. He hadn't even known his own wariness until it relaxed. He wondered if this was what Simone felt around him—that he was simple and straightforward and explicable in a way her own people were not. So easy. Mollie had called him Dr. Tarcher in the bar. Now she perched at his side by the railing of the bridge looking up at his face. Waiting only for the next thing he would say or do. A girl who stood wide-eyed for a dentist.

At the corner by her building was a liquor store and on the four flights up the stairs to her apartment she held the banister all the way. She smiled in an embarrassed way and said she was going to quit smoking, but he could see the wobble in her step. He was trying to carry himself forward with the momentum of his surprise and ardor. Up through the dingy hall hung with last year's calendars and through the scuffed brown door whose lock she turned and then kicked hard to open. He wished he'd had another drink himself. The apartment small and dark. A window over nothing but the light well and fire escape—he'd seen it before, thinking briefly of Daphne's place in college. But clean and very warm from the clanging radiator. Sprawling yellow-green ivies in pots. "I could use the drink you promised," he said.

She poured it for him and then stood against the doorjamb as he drank, her shoulders pointing into the small bedroom behind her. The double bed covered with a stretched, crocheted spread of the kind he associated with old women or farm wives. The mattress sagging and on the nightstand a telephone and a single red rose in a jar—she must have put it there an hour ago. He poured himself another drink, thinking of ruin.

When he set down the glass she walked into the bedroom, disappearing behind the wall. He debated it a moment, then gathered his courage and followed. As soon as he was in the room she stepped toward him with the frank helpfulness of one of his hygienists. Reached for his shoulders. Tilted back her lips so that before he closed his eyes he had a picture of her face that he tried to hold in his head as he kissed her. Her lids half-shut in a sphinxish tease that she must have learned thirty years ago before a mirror. She led him to the bed and when they lay down he felt the spread being pulled back. She made love to him quickly. The efficient athletic manner of a woman used to an unkind husband. He tried to pay attention to her but it seemed unimportant that he did.

Afterward, he stared at the broken candelabra fixture in the ceiling, trying to summon the picture of her he'd had before. He dozed briefly. When he woke he went into the bathroom and ran the water while he glanced at the open medicine cabinet above the sink: tranquilizers in a cup and a bottle of pills for high blood pressure. He used a washcloth to clean his arms and legs and chest.

When he came out she was sitting on the bed counting out money. "I know it was a long time ago," she said. "But here's what I owe you."

"Oh, no. I couldn't take it now," he said.

"You have to." She smoothed her hair. "Especially now."

"Pay me another time."

"Does that mean I'll see you again?"

It was eleven and Simone knew the library closed at eleven-thirty. "I think so," he said.

"When?"

"I mean, maybe not." The drinks were wearing off. He didn't know what to do with his hands. She'd stopped fingering the money and was looking up at him. "Well," he said, "the truth is, I'm getting married."

She smiled. "You are?"

"Yes."

"Well, that's wonderful," she said, incredibly. He himself was reeling. "She's a very lucky girl."

XXXII

Walking home that night in the slashing cold of his own depravity: not the feeling that he'd sinned exactly—more that he'd *almost* sinned. Waking up with Mollie Summers in an overheated fourth-floor walkup was not an act of disloyalty but a contemplation of it. But far worse was that he'd told her something he hadn't even told Simone. His resolve stirred. He crossed the two miles of icy walk back to his own apartment, forcing himself to see the future: he would live apart from his family, as far away as he could. The sour reproachfulness of his own people would not interfere. He would skip the final year of training and get a job right away—in Algonquin Hills, he suddenly decided, three hours upstate. That is where he would go, out to the new settlement whose photographs he'd seen on the dental school pinboards. Dales and hills where the framed houses cut an advancing edge along the lies of streams out into the woods. It was ridiculous to think of himself as a pilgrim, moving to a suburb to tend to the teeth of merchants and aeronautical engineers, but that is what he felt like as he walked in the cold darkness. A pilgrim, infatuated with possibilities.

He'd always thought of himself as the type to go down on his knee; but that night, turning from the window where he'd been gazing at the lights of Route 25, he found Simone watching him from the kitchen table; with less fanfare than he could ever have imagined, he said, "Will you marry me?" His own father had taken his mother on a paddle-wheeler cruise on the Mississippi; ashore at dinner in New Orleans he'd paid a waiter to slip a ring into her glass of champagne. He'd heard that story a dozen times growing up and it seemed the right way to do it: reverent but with a touch of surprise. As though to promise those very things for life. But now the words just fell right out of him. No preparation or cere-mony. As soon as he said them she accepted, setting down her book. That was it, their lives unfolding. The radiator clanged and came on.

Three

he week after he graduated, they went north together, to
Preston, Maine. It wasn't Algonquin Hills—the practice had
received hundreds of applications for the three new partner-
ships—but it was only a few hours east of there in a moraine
between felled timber forests, a town on a logging river where a
dentist had died. The dead man's partner, Dr. Meansy, was an old-
time settler of the area, still strong but seventy years old himself,
and Simone pointed out that Orno might be inheriting the entire
practice in a few years if he persevered. When Dr. Meansy called
to interview him, the television was going in the background, but
when Orno told him he was from Missouri there was a pause on
the line and the television went quiet. Dr. Meansy was from
Sedalia, it turned out. Gone north to start over.

The salary was modest but he wrote that Preston was not an expensive place to live. Orno wanted to visit; but by May he'd received no other offers. The day after Memorial Day, his degree
pressed in cardboard and their belongings tied to the top of the
Volkswagen, they set out for the north.

Maine was more beautiful than the pictures even, the sweeping coast a constant astonishment as they left the settled south; but the inland views were even more appealing to him, bantam vistas truncated by woodsy hills; barns and scarecrows and farm machines in sagging disrepair. That was what appealed to him, the suggestion of a life so different from the farmer's life in Missouri, the ordered plantings and painted tractors and rows of pansies there alongside the kitchens and the drain spouts. Here sheets of plastic had been taped over the missing windows, and in the unkempt yards sunflowers stood with their heads bent, as mournful as cows. The Volkswagen rolled north. Every house seemed to be selling its belongings. They stopped at a few sales, but the merchandise was poor—a single pan, a girl's grass-stained clothes, a box of chipped filling-station plates and a tied-up wad of whittled fishing floats. That night they slept in a state park and the next morning they ate breakfast in town for a dollar each, pancakes and eggs and coffee served by a woman with a missing lower incisor. The place seemed like a different country or a different century.

When they met Dr. Meansy at last, he was a relief: a tall, affably articulate man in a bow tie and gray vest, greeting them as they came up the front walk of the office as though he'd done nothing all morning but await their arrival. The rooms were already filled with patients, two in the chairs and three in the waiting area, men in overalls who nodded and lifted their caps and after they shook hands put their hands back into their pockets. The practice seemed to be a little bit short on equipment, but there was a compressor and one of the two chairs was hydraulic; the other moved with three iron foot pedals. Things were clean, and there was a shy calico cat named Doctor Diamond, who sat on the windowsill gazing longingly out at a field full of robins. Orno kneaded the scruff of her neck and she came off her perch and rubbed his leg; Dr. Meansy said it was a good sign.

He introduced the two of them around, calling them "Dr. Tarcher and Mrs. Tarcher" as he led them before the taciturn men in the waiting room and then his receptionist, who was also his hygienist and assistant, a plump woman with a strabismic eye and a chattering demeanor like a fountain in the desert. Her name was Genevieve Crawley, and after they were introduced she reached behind her desk and offered Simone a pound cake wrapped in blue cellophane and tied with a ribbon. "You are going to love it in Preston, you two," she said, closing her eyes and pressing her fists together over her bosom. "I know it right here."

———

Dr. Meansy's office was the only one for thirty miles either way, and the road in both directions was dotted with villages, old mill towns along the Malakoot River that took in tourists in the summer and sent their men to work in the furniture factories the rest of the year. It wasn't a good living, but by and large people kept work and some of them came to the dentist. He felt like a celebrity in town. He learned more in his first month here than he'd learned all his last year in dental school. His patients didn't seem to mind when Dr. Meansy came across to the other examining room and walked him through his difficult procedures right as he was doing them, three-quarter crowns and cantilever bridges; Dr. Meansy placed one long hand in their mouths and pulled in Orno's on the other side to teach him. There was too much modesty everywhere for Orno to be irked.

On the street everyone called him Dr. Tarcher long before he knew who most of them were. Suddenly there was a miraculous feel to the commonplace—now that he was in the world for the first time, really—a clarity to the morning air and a buoyancy to the warm evenings that made him feel light, as though the rippling sunshine could lift him into the air. He worked hard in the office, changing his shirt after lunch even though the rooms were air-conditioned, and in the few moments that remained between appointments asking about families and furniture mills and hunting dogs; his patients rose and stretched their backs and spit into the drain, and when he was finished all of them came around the chair to shake his hand.

On weekends he and Simone worked in the garden around their house, which the former tenant had planted like a miniature farm: a low picket fence circling a small section of the grassy yard, strung with netting to confuse the deer and watched over by a tiny scarecrow made of a hat and sticks. Inside the fence, several neat rows of vegetables, midway to their peaks. Six heads of butter lettuce. Four struggling stalks of corn. Two varieties of tomatoes still green in their wire harnesses. A few square feet of radish stems and an equal portion of potatoes, neatly hoed. At once both pitiful and industrious, enough to eat for a week and no more—but tended faithfully, they could see, until their arrival. They in turn tended it just as closely. Weeding. Pinching off the wasted shoots. Watering sparingly to bring out the flavor. It was pleasant work. Orno surprised himself with how much he knew about the process, picked up somehow in childhood. Simone considered it a test, a trial that the town would be watching; every morning she moved on her knees among the plantings, looking for cutworms and vermin, propping up the tomato stems as they hung lower and lower toward the ground.

The yard itself circling the garden was huge, a rambling half-acre of dense bluegrass that grew from the bumpy roots of the elms all the way back to where a stand of birches marked the start of the deep forest. An ancient Sears gas-powered lawn mower stood in the garage, and when Orno pulled the cord their first Saturday in town it rumbled beautifully to life; that morning he pushed it all the way around the yard, the booming old machine throwing the clippings deftly to the side, a gridded wet carpet that smelled to him, suddenly and powerfully, of home.

"Hey, Dr. Tarcher," Simone called from the porch, "you missed your calling."

"Maybe I did," he called back. "Maybe I missed the whole point."

He took to mowing every Saturday morning, while Simone tended to the vegetables. The life was easy to like. On weekday evenings, Simone walked into town to meet him on his way home from work; in the hours that still remained before sunset they explored the rolling roads looking for the nocturnal animals in the tree line. After dinner she spent time planning their wedding, while Orno sat across from her in a rocking chair reading dental journals or a mystery. Now and then she would look up and ask him something about flowers or catered food for the reception, and he would answer with good humor, trying to seem firm because firmness appeared to be what she wanted, although in truth he cared little either way. The wedding was set for Labor Day weekend at an Episcopal Church Professor Emerson had picked, up the Cape from Woods Hole; the reception was at the Emersons' and on the beach behind. As the plans progressed, Orno felt uneasy that so much money was being spent on his behalf.

Yet Simone seemed to set about the task as though it was a necessity she would not let daunt her, the way women in Cook's Grange set about canning after the harvest. She showed him piles of brochures and menus and photo portfolios. She sat at the kitchen table silently sifting through them, making notes on a light blue pad and filing piles of paper in three packing boxes stacked on the seat by the window. She didn't seem to mind that he read his journals while she did this. By August he felt long married.

Dr. Meansy was still seeing most of the children so Orno rarely had an unwilling person in his chair. Some of his patients smelled like booze, but it wasn't the same thing here as in Stony Brook; he didn't hear arguments from the reception room. His patients brought him corn and tomatoes and whittled walking sticks and bottles of blueberry jam. He befriended Doctor Diamond by bringing her a mouse he'd made from string and a sock, which immediately solidified his reputation. He got his first paycheck and only a tiny part of it went for the rent. That weekend he took Simone to dinner at a French restaurant in Augusta, where before dessert he slipped the waiter a ring to place into the bottom of her glass of champagne.

———

Sometimes he wondered how Simone liked the life. After the wedding, she planned to look for work, but jobs in the area were scattered; the two public schools were ten miles away, and a little further out stood a military academy for wayward boys.

Otherwise there were only the two furniture factories and the last of the three paper mills. It was not even enough employment, Dr. Meansy said, for the men. In the summer, jobs appeared at the coast and at the big lakes, which were inland; but in winter, plenty of families ate turnips and, occasionally, trapped rabbits. The only other vegetables they saw were potatoes. Twenty years ago, Dr. Meansy told them, he'd seen a real case of scurvy. "Do you know what scurvy was?" he asked Simone. They were at his house for dinner.

"A disease in the novels of Melville and Conrad," she answered.

He raised his glass to her. "Very good," he said. "Indeed, as you say, a sailor's affliction. But in fact, it arose from lack of vitamin C. The British navy boarded limes to counter its onset. I suppose they lasted longer than oranges, or perhaps they were easier to get hold of. Which is why they called the British 'limeys,' by the way. Tell me," he said, "aren't you going to miss New York?"

"I came here to be away from that," she answered.

"Still, at your age, you'll need to find something to do."

"Likewise at your age," she said, raising her glass.

"Touché," he said, pleased. Dr. Meansy liked her, Orno could tell. He seemed to be proud of her, somehow, though they'd only met a month ago. Orno was proud as well.

That night in bed, Orno said to her, "How can you not be scared by this?" He pointed out the window into the black night, empty of all signs of civilization. "You don't know anybody up here. You came because *I* had a job. You grew up in a brownstone."

"But I also grew up at the ocean."

"You're a long way from that, too."

"But I love quiet," she said. "It's quiet here too, the same way the Cape is in winter. I can read. I can garden. There are all kinds of people up here for me to meet. I'll know them soon enough."

"I guess in your shoes I'd still be scared."

"I know," she said, in a matter-of-fact voice. "That's just because you've always been scared of people." She moved next to him and rested her head against his shoulder. "But I've never been."

Soon she was asleep. Next to her, he lay awake long into the night, gazing out the window. He was awed, somehow, by her presence. It was her fearlessness, really, but it was also the fact that she'd known such a thing about him. He thought of his father, hanging his suits: was he, too, scared of people? In some way, although it was impossible to say why, it struck him as fundamentally true. He hadn't even realized it about himself until she said so.

———

In August, she went home to finish arrangements for the wedding. Early one morning, he drove her to the Greyhound station, realizing as the bus pulled onto the highway that without knowing it he'd grown accustomed to his life with her, to the sun setting and rising on the two of them together. Then he drove home, and because it was not yet six, went back to sleep; when he woke again he walked into town the long way, along the old logging road, aware in a new manner of all the details around him; he ambled up over the crest of the hill where stands of young hardwoods rose along the cutting tracks and then took a side route down to the Malakoot, where the only large houses in town stood with their backs looking out at the slate-colored water. He had on a tie, loosely knotted because it was a weekend. He wore one everywhere now, partly because he suspected Dr. Meansy preferred it that way, and partly because he enjoyed it himself, the way the townspeople spoke to him attentively from behind the counters and tipped their mill caps to him if they caught his glance from across the street. He stopped up the hill just past where the water took its widest turn, where the abandoned lumber mill and the Texaco station stood at the center of the only fair-sized intersection for ten miles either way; from there he looked out over the entire town, green roofs and the short white steeple of the church, his whole world now, scattered leavings against the dark sea of treetops.

He felt his week alone before him. In Missouri, the land stretched for miles without a building, but there one nonetheless always saw evidence of man—in the straight black stripe to the horizon or the shining green slope of cultivated hills. Here, if he turned halfway around from the vista of town, no more evidence of it remained than the occasional whoosh and slap of the screen door at the Texaco station or the rumble of a pickup. He'd never felt alone in such a way before; it was a landscape neither he nor Simone had grown up with, and now again he felt like a stranger in it, suddenly unused to the endless hardwoods and the dark hills that appeared in the middle distance when he turned that way, cupping him inside a bowl of greenery and sky. It seemed that the world could easily drop out in a place like this, that there was so little memory that if things changed he could reinvent his life one more time with ease. Who knew him? What did he know himself of his own life here?

Simone was supposed to come home Sunday but on Friday morning she called and told him she wasn't finished yet and was going to stay on another few days.

"Finished with what exactly?" he asked.

"All kinds of things. You have no idea how much there is to do. I have to choose the photographer, for one."

"Let's take our own pictures. My mother loves her camera."

"Orno, this is important to me."

"How long do you need?"

"Four more days," she said. She waited. "Maybe three."

The sun was moving up over the trees. "Do you have to stay so long?"

"I miss you," she said. "I love you."

"It's funny up here without you."

"Funny how?"

"I don't know," he said. "I feel like I'm watching someone. A dentist. Up here in this town. It's hard to think it's me."

"Sweetie," she said, "we're late to meet a photographer. But when I get back I have a surprise for you."

"You do? What is it?"

"My mother bought you some silk."

"Pardon?"

"My mother bought you some Italian silk." She waited. "To make a suit."

"To make a what?"

"A suit, for you to get married in."

"Pearls before swine," he said.

"Don't say that."

"But tell her thank you."

"I already have. We'll go to Portland when I get back. She knows a tailor there."

"Will we really?"

"Yes."

"And they'll make a suit out of it?"

"Yes."

"Amazing," he said. "Okay. I'll keep pretending I'm a dentist."

"Good. And I'll be your wife."

They hung up, and he sat at the table by the phone, thinking of himself in a new suit. He owned one already, and he'd worn it only a few times; it seemed perfectly passable. But Mrs. Pelham wanted him in something different. She wore beautiful clothes, he remembered. He imagined the material would be nice. He wasn't due at the office for another hour—it was just past seven and the time stretched before him. He sat, thinking of his roots in the world.

He decided to call home. When his father answered he sounded the way he always did, unsurprised to hear from him, as though it were every morning and not once a month that he called. "We found a leak in the attic," his father said. "No doubt from an ice dam on the southern eaves. I'm planning to lay more insulation up there." He paused, and Orno heard him lighting his pipe. "Now I'm looking out the window at your mother's pansies. They're beautiful. But she's still asleep. What time is it out there?"

"I figured she was," said Orno. "It's a little after seven. I was just calling to say hello."

"Hello to you, then. Aren't you due at work?"

"In a few minutes."

"How is Simone?"

"She's good. She's in New York."

"Who's cooking, then?"

"I am."

"Are you really? I never learned. So, are you working hard?"

He'd just wanted to hear his voice, really; he found it calmed him. "Everything's good, Dad," he said.

"Good."

They hung up, and he walked to work. As he stood over his patients that morning his mind went again to his parents: to his mother, always fumbling with things—her hat, her dresses, all her signs of propriety; to his father, plugged with moral surety. He couldn't imagine his father wondering about life. Was that what he'd always thought it was—strength born of purpose? Or was it, in fact, fear? Did a man like his father gather the weak around him? Is that what his mother was, a quaking leaf blown against him? Was that what he himself had become in reaction? And was that why he was drawn to Marshall, as well? This thing he did for a living—he looked at a row of molars—it seemed the sort of concreteness to which only a wanderer would be drawn.

That afternoon he left work and walked down to the Malakoot, where as the sun moved lower he slipped into one of the swimming holes and paddled out to the middle. It was the height of summer but the water was still cold enough to take his breath away. He plunged under, opened his eyes to the meandering streams of current that flowed through the pool and tumbled away downriver over boulders; he shot out into the sunlight, shaking his head in the heat; he climbed out onto the warm rocks and stood at the side. Even among the thick maples it took him only a moment to get warm. Then he went back in again. He seemed to produce an unquenchable heat—he squatted at the bottom, his ankles snug between the slick rocks, holding his breath till it burned while the fast water at the surface churned his hair. When he came up again, a moose appeared at the edge of the trees. Preston was awfully far south for one, but it wandered down near him and drank, its broad humped shoulders rocking. He felt visited: *chance and mystery, the unknowable course of our days.* After a time it looked up at him, and he turned away so as not to frighten it; when he turned back again, it was gone, branches snapping into the woods.

XXXIV

On the last day of August they drove down to Woods Hole for the wedding. For the first part of the week they were alone with the Emersons: his parents and sister were due three days later, and the rest of the guests two after that; most of them were biologists or academics from Manhattan, uncles and aunts of the Emersons from across New England, and Simone's friends from Bard. It was an eerie time. The spit of land seemed empty to him somehow, though there were still plenty of vacationers strolling on the long flats of sand. Even the surf seemed timid, lapping quietly where he'd remembered it as thunderous; a state of suspension in the air. He saw the tiny clouds hanging tentatively at the horizon, like gloves on a mantel; he saw the marsh grass swaying and the herons waiting stealthily in the shallows. There was plenty for him to do, yet no task seemed to be particularly his own. Simone went off with her mother in the mornings, into town to talk to caterers and check on flowers and leave deposits at hotels. Professor Emerson disappeared early and Orno was left alone at the house. He walked a long way on the beach, past settlement after settlement, houses set back into the seaside scrub with flags limp and weather vanes pointing out to sea. The land seemed to be waiting for fall. Seagulls picked at the waterline. From inland came the sound of hammers.

One morning after Simone had already gone off with her mother, Professor Emerson invited Orno to fetch a load of firewood with him. He came around front in an old pickup, flinging open the passenger door and slowing down but not quite stopping so that Orno had to trot after, hop up onto the running board, and climb into the seat. Then Professor Emerson revved the engine abruptly so that they lurched out onto the road. The floor was rusted metal, and through a hole near his feet Orno could see the asphalt running by. To shift gears Professor Emerson had to pump the clutch back and forth and thrust the gear knob forward, throwing it from his hand so that the grinding didn't catch him in the palm. The chassis shook and the smell of burnt air rose from the vents. The truck must have been thirty years old. Orno thought of what Simone had told him.

Professor Emerson drove slowly, staying to the right side of the lane with one wheel on gravel so that other cars could pass. As they made their way inland, Orno was overtaken with the feeling he used to have as a boy riding Olaf Marjorrson's tractor next door, a rumbling yellow machine as big as their garage; he'd gone out on it a dozen times in childhood. Every summer after his crop was in, Olaf Marjorrson ran him along the whole perimeter of his fields talking about drainage tiles and irrigation lines and smoking a pipe that he never took from his mouth. The great axle rotated right below Orno's seat, his sneakers resting on a grating only a few inches above the huge, resolutely turning gear. The tires had grooves deeper than his hands and dropped slabs of mud as big as dinner plates as they turned downward at their peaks. There always seemed to be a point to what Olaf Marjorrson was saying, but Orno remembered never quite understanding it. He bought his insurance from Orno's father and he used to tell Orno that it wasn't right for a boy not to learn to farm. His coveralls were full of patches. This part of it was understandable enough, and Orno could remember the mixture of shame and excitement he used to feel as the tractor nosed down into the drainage gullies and his own house disappeared from view, the monstrous wheels slipping for a moment in the dampened troughs and then catching and lifting them up again. There were only a few kids in Cook's Grange who would have considered it a treat to ride a tractor. He'd always had two feelings together as he rode, that there was an undeclared distinction between his father and Olaf Marjorrson, and at the same time that he was learning something from the gruff, mumbling farmer that his father would not have been able to teach him in a hundred summers. Now, as Professor Emerson drove the truck inland along the gravel shoulder, he had the same feeling again, the same sense that he'd been brought along in a show that involved difference and rivalry and hospitality in an order he didn't comprehend. Driving the truck was complicated; Professor Emerson wasn't speaking.

"I've never told you," Orno began, "but I'm deeply grateful to you for your daughter."

"Not at all." He tossed the gear knob forward and the truck bumped. "We've been making all kinds of arrangements. I think we may have a Kennedy or two at the ceremony."

"The Kennedys are coming?"

"I can't guarantee it, but I know the senator should be on the Cape for Labor Day." He turned in the seat and smiled.

"Well, that'll be something to write home about." It was an expression of his father's and it suddenly seemed hokey. "Simone didn't tell me," he added.

"Simone doesn't know yet." He turned again and winked. "She'd accuse me of meddling."

"It's kind of you to help the way you are."

"Here's a joke," Professor Emerson said. "A boy goes to the pharmacy. He asks the pharmacist for a box of condoms, and the pharmacist says, 'Which size would you like?' The boy says, 'Well, I'm not sure.' The pharmacist says, 'Young man, they come in boxes of three, six, or twelve.' The boy says, 'Well I've got a pretty good chance with this girl tonight, so I'll take twelve.' The pharmacist smiles at him. That night the boy goes to pick up his date and he has to have dinner with her parents before they can leave. The father asks the boy to lead them in prayer and he does. He prays and prays. He puts his head down and prays and prays, and prays some more, and when he finally looks up the girl says, 'Gee, I didn't know you were so religious.' And the boy says, 'Well, I didn't know your father was a pharmacist.'"

Orno started to laugh, but suddenly they arrived at the firewood and Professor Emerson stopped the truck and jumped out. They were at the back end of an apple orchard, and he began pulling split logs from a pile and tossing them underhand over the panels into the bed. Orno jumped out to help. Nobody else was in sight, the farmhouse only barely visible in the distance. Professor Emerson worked fast, the engine running. He stood looking over the hill toward the orchard, only glancing back at the truck as he tossed, his body turned away from Orno as though facing seaward on the bridge of the boat. "You know," he said, "I used to be able to do this without looking."

"You're doing that right now."

"No. Something's happened to my balance. Did they teach you about balance in dental school?"

"Not really."

"I hope nothing's wrong with my cerebellum."

"I don't think so."

"Or my vestibular system."

"I doubt it."

Suddenly Professor Emerson brought his hand to his eyes and squinted over the horizon toward the farmhouse, still tossing logs behind him with the other arm. Abruptly he stopped throwing again and moved back to the truck. The bed was not yet full; again Orno had to hop up onto the running board after it was moving. Once they were on the highway again, Professor Emerson said, "I like that joke."

"Which one?"

"The pharmacist."

"So do I."

"You didn't seem to."

"It took me a moment to get it."

"I see. Your parents will be arriving tomorrow, then?"

"Yes, they're flying into Boston and renting a car."

"Where do they stay in Boston?"

"I don't know. I don't think they've ever been there before."

"We've put them up at the Hay-Markhams for the wedding."

"Thank you."

He looked at Orno. "Do you know the name?"

"I'm afraid not."

"Your parents will be staying in the house that the mitral valve built." Professor Emerson looked at him across the seat again. "The Hay-Markham mitral valve. You remember the valve, I'll assume."

"Oh, yes. I wasn't sure he was the one." He recalled it vaguely from his infectious-disease class: if any of his patients had a Hay-Markham valve he was obligated to prescribe antibiotics.

"Years ago I helped him out with the thing," said Professor Emerson. "In those days, Dick Hay-Markham couldn't find his way to the men's room in a medical laboratory. Now he's one of the wealthiest men in the state."

"I can imagine."

"They've got quite a splendid guest cottage on the beach now."

"That's very kind of them to let my family stay."

"Dick is glad to help me out so he doesn't have to pay me anything."

Orno nodded.

"For showing him how to prevent the ball cock from clotting." He pushed the gearshift into third. "Do you think I should go after him?"

"Pardon?"

"What's your opinion? I've always thought I ought to have my attorney contact Dick Hay-Markham about a share of the royalties. But I've never done it. Do you think it would have been wise?"

"I don't know."

"You're going to be part of the family now."

"I'm looking forward to that."

Professor Emerson looked at him again.

"I don't know what advice I could give you, though," said Orno.

"And I don't know what advice I could give *you*." He cleared his throat.

Orno looked out at the road.

"Simone has always been on her own," said Professor Emerson. "She's not like the rest of us. She's an independent spirit. Her own little island off in the sea. I could never tell her much, as you can see."

"I haven't necessarily seen that."

Professor Emerson blew his nose into a handkerchief and folded it back into his pocket. "Maybe *you* can tell her things," he said. "I hope so. But *I* can't."

"We tell each other things."

"I suppose I'm glad about that."

"And I wanted to thank you for putting together such a wonderful wedding."

"We're going to show you how it's done here."

"That's very kind of you."

"I noticed your parents had the Gutfreunds on their list. Are they a relation of the Manhattan Gutfreunds?"

"I don't think so."

"Doesn't matter anyway," said Professor Emerson. "Well, we're here," he said, and as soon as he'd pulled the truck onto the grass he was out the door. At the steps to the house he paused for a moment, standing on one foot with his arms out to the side like a tightrope walker, wobbling slightly; then he disappeared. Their firewood was stacked at the side of the porch; Orno began unloading.

In the afternoon he called his parents. His father answered and told him his mother was still packing. "We're leaving for the airport in fifteen minutes," he said, "and she's still folding her dresses. She's going to be deciding on her shoes when the plane takes off."

"I'm sure you'll be fine," said Orno. He looked out at the beach, where Professor Emerson was smoking a cigarette between the stands of dune grass. "Everything's all set for you here. They're making all kinds of preparations. You're staying at a nice cottage."

"Well, good."

"It's the Hay-Markham cottage, the man who invented the heart valve."

"I didn't know a *man* invented it."

"I mean an artificial valve. He's a friend of the Emersons."

His father was silent.

Orno looked out the window again. "Guess who else is coming?"

"Who?"

"Senator Kennedy."

His father coughed.

"They live out here," said Orno. "I guess they're friends of the family. I mean, if he's in the area he's going to come."

He coughed again. "Your mother's been packing for two days. She feels her dress isn't right."

"Which one is she wearing?"

"God help me, I don't know."

"She can buy one in Boston if she needs to."

"She has plenty."

"Mrs. Pelham bought me a suit," said Orno.

"Pardon me?"

"She bought me the material for one, I mean. I had it tailored."

There was a silence. "I thought you already had a suit, Orno."

"It's a nicer one."

"I see," said his father. "Well, we'll see you in it soon enough then."

Fishing boats were coming across the horizon in a string, heading back to port ahead of the line of a squall. Professor Emerson had come up off the beach now and was sitting on the deck pouring a drink into a tumbler. Orno said, "Well, give my love to Mom," and then he hung up and headed outside. The chilly, electric pressure of a storm was blowing in over the dunes from the north. He went back into his room and checked the suit hanging in a plastic bag in the closet. He ran his hand over it, feeling the cool charge on the silk.

———

That night, he and Simone went to the Hyannis airstrip to pick up Marshall, who'd flown in on a twin-engine from La Guardia. They followed the headlight in across the water; the plane touched down and taxied across to the terminal, and suddenly there he was, standing at the top of the staircase. He was obscured in darkness, but Orno found to his surprise that he felt great relief in the familiar back-leaning tilt of his gait and the odd military way he held his hand to his eyes to look for them. A girl appeared behind him in the door and he took her arm and headed across the tarmac.

"Welcome home," said Orno, hugging him.

"Welcome to Shangri-la," said Marshall. He had the buoyant step of his best moods. He hugged Simone and said, "This is Elizabeth. Elizabeth, my sister, Simone."

"Congratulations, you two," said Elizabeth. "You must be very excited. Nice to see you again, Orno."

She smiled at him and suddenly he recognized her: the actress from the party, he was almost sure. It was odd. Her name had been Dee-Ann.

Simone said, "Welcome, Elizabeth." She turned to Marshall and patted him on the shoulder. "*You* never tell us anything," she said.

"Elizabeth's coming to the wedding," said Marshall.

"Good," said Orno.

"We gathered that," said Simone. "And we're glad. But you're so secretive about it."

"I like mystery."

"Mystery's one thing," said Simone. "I don't know anything about your life anymore."

"There's nothing to know."

"There's all kinds of things to know," said Elizabeth. "Marshall's all over Hollywood. He's one of the big producers in town."

"See?" said Simone. "I have to hear that from your girlfriend?"

"She's exaggerating."

"No, I'm not."

"Then tell me everything," said Simone.

For the rest of the drive home she sat in the backseat talking to him, going over all kinds of gossip, friends from the Cape and relations he'd never heard of, while in the front Elizabeth sat next to Orno looking out the window. He wondered if she actually *was* Marshall's girlfriend. She looked nervous, touching her hair and adjusting her necklace. He turned to her and said, "You changed your name."

"Oh, I forgot. I might have used something else at the party. What did I say it was?"

"Dee-Ann."

"Oh," she said, and laughed out the window. "I might have said that. I'm trying out Elizabeth. Which one do you like?"

"Which one's your real name?"

"Does it matter?"

"Well, I think it does."

"It's Dee-Ann."

"Then I like Dee-Ann," he said.

She smiled at him. "Then I guess I like you better as a dentist."

He flushed.

"Don't worry about it," she said.

He drove on. He should have been embarrassed, but as the car moved through the dark he felt strangely at ease, familiar in a way that made him hopeful, persuaded by the swirling low barometer of the night and Marshall's easy slouch behind him. The twisting road uncovered itself in the bright cove of his headlights, hemmed in by the swaying leaves of the oaks. The moon peeked through above. He felt promise at the periphery of his grasp, the dizzying sensation that he could not imagine what would happen next: it was what he used to feel, he remembered, walking to The Odalisque.

X X X V

In the morning the Tarchers arrived, and that afternoon Orno and Simone drove to the Hay-Markham cottage to pick them up for lunch. His mother was sitting on the edge of the deck in a flowered dress Orno had never seen, her hat and her heeled shoes next to her, bouncing her feet in the sand. His father and Clara were reading.

They drove in to the country club, where the Emersons had already taken their seats at an outdoor table overlooking yachts in the water. Orno couldn't help feeling a weight of dread as he stood just inside the door, the maître d' glancing at his list, while across the courtyard Professor Emerson put down his drink and moved toward them. He felt strangely as though it was an attack. "Here he comes," he said.

"Goodness, he's tall," said his mother.

"He must get his height from his son," said his father.

But then he was there, and suddenly he reminded Orno of Marshall himself, ten years before in New York when they'd all met at the restaurant and his parents had never been so charmed by any of his friends. Professor Emerson was smiling. He kissed

Orno's mother and then Clara, and he shook his father's hand and then Orno's. His father liked him; Orno saw it immediately. The two of them moved off ahead, toward the table where Mrs. Pelham stood smiling. Other diners were looking up; Professor Emerson clapped a couple of the men on the shoulder.

"What can I get you?" he said when they were all sitting.

"I'll have white wine, please," said his mother.

His father smiled at Professor Emerson. "I'll take whatever you're having."

Clara said, "Ginger ale."

Orno looked at her. "I'll have whatever they're having, too," he said.

It was scotch. He'd never seen his father drink in the afternoon, but as soon as it came he took a sip and he seemed to enjoy it. The sun lit the green parasol above them and the shore breeze lifted their napkins. The conversation moved along. Simone talked with his mother; it didn't seem difficult for her. Orno was the only one without a clear partner: he was between Simone and his father, and nobody was turned to him. Now and then the talk paused while one of the sailboats heading out of the harbor let out a spinnaker or hoisted a sail that snapped sharply and sent a whooshing hiss rising to the shore. Long elliptical hulls flashed in the sun. Orno didn't mind not talking; he sat back, grateful for the ease, dumbfounded and warmed by the scotch and filled with a kind of late-day contentment that was spurred on by the shine of sails and the smell of heat on the deck boards.

When lunch was over they sat back in their chairs and the conversation opened up around the table. His father asked what field Professor Emerson specialized in.

"Taxonomy," he answered. He pointed to the water. "Invertebrate primarily. It's the centerpiece of ocean ecology, really. More important than what you and I normally think of as the life of the ocean—fish that is. Marlin and tuna and around here bluefish and striped bass."

"I have a cousin who's a taxonomist," said Mrs. Tarcher.

His father looked at her.

"Well, it's a rather small field," said Professor Emerson. "What's his name?"

"Mel Baines. Melvin Baines."

"I'm afraid I haven't heard of him. Where is he?"

"He's out of Springfield, Missouri. Or nearby there." She smiled.

The waiter brought the check covered in a leather folder and set it down in front of Professor Emerson.

Orno's father pulled out his billfold. "I'll take it," he said. "It's the least we can do."

"Don't be silly."

"I'm not being silly. You've been more than kind with the arrangements."

"Please, Drake. I'll hear nothing of it. All I have to do is sign." With a small flourish he pulled a pen from his jacket pocket and scribbled on the check, then held up the folder for the waiter. "Is your cousin at the University of Missouri?" he said to Orno's mother.

"I don't think so."

"Oh," his father said. He laughed. "I see what's happened." He laughed again. "Your uncle Mel?" he said to his wife. "You mean taxidermy, honey."

"Oh," she answered. She took a sip of wine. "I guess that *is* what I meant. That was certainly silly of me."

"Not at all," said Simone. "I used to make the same mistake."

"It must be the wine," said his father.

"It must be," said his mother with a little laugh. She took another sip, then reached up and touched her hat.

"Well," said Professor Emerson, "we've got quite a crew assembled for this little affair."

"Father," said Simone, "the Tarchers have already seen the guest list."

"Oh, tell us anyway," said his mother.

"I'm not sure I should really be speaking of it."

His mother turned to him. "Oh, go ahead."

Professor Emerson reached for his tumbler. He looked timid.

"Orno filled us in," said his father. "Senator Kennedy might be coming along."

"What?" Simone looked at her father.

"Well, it just so happens, sweetheart—"

"What is *this* about? I didn't think you were going to do this."

"Please, honey," said Mrs. Pelham.

"We don't *know* them." She looked down. "They're not going to come to my wedding."

"Oh, come on, honey," said Mrs. Pelham. "Listen to how you sound."

"I said it would be okay," Orno said. "I mean, what does it really matter?"

"Well, I'm not sure I agree with *that*, either," said Professor Emerson. "You may not realize it yet, but these men can make a difference in your life."

"What difference can he make in *my* life?" said Simone. "Does he need his teeth cleaned?"

"Simone!"

"Young lady, if I'd had the chance to meet a senator when I was your age—"

"Honey, it's going to be fine," said Mrs. Pelham.

"Well, I think it will be very exciting to meet them," said Orno's mother. She touched her hat again.

Simone looked at her mother, then down at her plate. "All right," she said.

"Dick Hay-Markham is going to approach him," said Professor Emerson. He drank again. "I thought you would like it as a surprise, sweetheart."

"We do like it," said Orno. He turned to her. "Sweetie, I kind of like the idea."

"I said all right."

The maître d' was suddenly standing next to Professor Emerson with his arms folded. "May I speak with you a moment, Professor?" He cleared his throat.

"And he'll probably bring you something very nice," said his mother.

"I already said it was all right. Really, it's fine with me." She smiled at her father. "You can say what you want."

"Professor?"

"What's this about?"

"Perhaps we can speak at the desk."

"I understand Mrs. Kennedy is quite an impressive lady," said his mother.

"Not at the moment we can't," said Professor Emerson.

"I think you're thinking of his mother," said Orno's father. "Rose Kennedy."

"Professor?"

"Oh yes, perhaps I am! It's the wine again."

"Go, honey," said Mrs. Pelham.

"Oh, all right," said Professor Emerson. He stood up from the table, bumping his chair, then strode across the plaza to the desk, where he had to wait for the maître d' to catch up to him. Orno could see them gesturing at each other.

"I can't wait to see what Senator Kennedy brings," said his mother.

His father said, "I imagine one of his aides will buy the gift."

Across the plaza of tables Orno saw Professor Emerson turn away from them and reach for his wallet in his coat. Then in a moment he was back at the table, standing next to his chair again. He looked toward the water. "Shylocks," he whispered.

"Well," said his mother, folding her napkin and smoothing it at her place in front of her. "The gift will probably be very nice." She laughed. "I can't believe I said *taxonomy*. Oh, well." She put her hands on the table. "Well, thank you, you two," she said. "It was a lovely lunch. Wasn't it, Drake?" She held down her hat. "Goodness, it's gotten windy out. Oh look, a yacht coming in!"

———

That night after dinner Simone went to sleep early. Orno ended up on the beach alone with Marshall, underneath a slivered yellow moon that threw triangles of light across the slants of waves.

He didn't know where Dee-Ann had gone. Marshall had a bottle of whiskey and they sat in the dunes drinking. There was something about him that kept Orno awake—it was like their nights above the Hudson again, the sound of water now and everyone asleep around them. "What are you reading these days?" he asked.

"I don't read books anymore," Marshall said. "Just scripts."

"I read dental journals."

"Ah, life."

"To that," said Orno, and held up the bottle. "And to this place."

"The Toasting of Idiots," said Marshall.

"Indeed."

"Some untidy spot where the dogs go on with their doggy life."

"What's that?"

"Auden. I like the next line—and the torturer's horse scratches its innocent behind on a tree."

"Who's the torturer?"

"That misses the point," Marshall said. "The point is the horse. Unknowing. Like you two."

"All right," said Orno. He didn't want to start again on the subject. They were quiet. "Then you're seeing Elizabeth?"

"Now and then."

"Her name used to be Dee-Ann."

Marshall laughed. "I didn't think you'd remember."

"I remember very well. Are you seeing each other?"

"I paid her to come with me."

"Come on."

"She's what they call an escort." He laughed.

"I don't believe that."

"Charitable of you." He drank from the bottle. "But she is. She wants to be an actress." He laughed again. "She's from your part of the country, actually. She's a farm girl trying to make it in L.A. To tell you the truth, she's taught me a lot."

"About what?"

"A lot about *you* people. There's something inside her. It's the same thing inside you. Not ambition exactly. Not lofty enough. She just wants to be a two-bit soap player the way you just want to clean people's teeth. That's not ambition, but it's drive."

"We're born with it," Orno said.

"I know. I used to laugh, but now I'd give anything to have it. It's unwavering. You can knock her off her horse and she gets back on, and you knock her off again and she gets back on and ties herself into the saddle. She's had two speaking parts in five years. But you keep scrubbing teeth and she keeps coming back to me because she wants it so much. It's amazing. You're like that, too. You're unflappable. It's what I told you in Los Angeles."

"I've just stumbled into my life."

"How can you say that? You've just inched along toward it. That's not stumbling. Now you've got a career and a house and you're about to marry my sister."

Orno closed his eyes and leaned back in the sand. There was a rawness to Marshall's friendship that was oblivious to time. "Did you ever give her a part?" he asked.

"A couple of small ones."

"Is she good?"

"Doesn't matter."

"Of course it does."

"She's all right. No worse than anyone else. But it scares me."

"What scares you?"

He drank again. "How much she wants something. It makes me know I've missed it."

"Missed what?"

"Whatever is the center of a person, O. Like, how else do you know something's wrong? How else do you compare yourself to other people? I look into the center of myself and there's nothing. If that's not frightening, I don't know what is. And I look at my father and I know he's got the same hole I do."

"You've said that before."

"And I'll say it again."

"I don't know why I have to keep saying this, M, but you've got a brilliant center."

"I've got an empty center."

"There's nothing at the center of any of us, M. Not really. Not if you keep looking."

"But *you* don't keep looking."

"I guess I don't." There seemed to be truth to that. He took a drink.

"Point closed," said Marshall.

"But you're drawn to questioning, M. You're inquisitive. You're not satisfied."

"You on the other hand *are* satisfied. That's because there's something there inside you, O. That's why you don't have to keep looking."

It was getting late. The moon moved behind clouds. "Maybe it's just my father," Orno said.

"Maybe that's right." Marshall laughed. "Maybe it's just your father in his little brown suit."

Orno drank again. "I hope not."

"Double knotting his shoes."

"God help us."

"You don't know how lucky you are, O." He held up the bottle. "Let's drink to that."

"To luck."

"To brown suits."

"Yes. To brown suits."

Marshall looked up at the hidden moon. "How everything turns away," he said. "The ploughman may have heard the splash. I like that, too. Auden again." He looked at the water. "How everything turns away."

———

Orno must have dozed, because later he seemed to wake, not sure if the sand and night heat and slip of waves had vanished completely, but aware of their return somehow, a little louder in his ears and sharper on his skin. The wind had come up. Marshall was above him, shaking his shoulder. "I've got something to give you."

"Thanks, M. That's nice of you."

"We've got to walk to it."

"I don't want to get up."

"Come on, O."

"Oh, all right."

Marshall set off across the sand, turning at the high scrub and waiting. Orno finally stood and followed. From there they walked a good distance—well down the beach, then inland over the dunes to the road that paralleled the shore. The asphalt white even under the small moon and the rustling grasses making a quivering lane into the distance. Finally, a leaning fence and a shack behind it. Marshall pushed open the gate and went into the yard. He waited for Orno at the threshold. "Go on," he said. "Surprise."

The shack was small and over the front windows a set of dark shutters was closed. Orno pushed open the door. Darker inside than out and filled with the smell of wet wood. Across the room, the dune grass again through a window; a sill that was just a white line in the moonlight. Marshall turned on a flashlight behind him; bouncing shadows obscured the room. Orno took a step in, listening to Marshall behind him in the doorway. He waited for his eyes to focus in the dark; suddenly he saw a table by the window and a girl sitting there. She didn't quite look like Dee-Ann. Nervousness.

"I came because he asked me to," the girl said. Her accent was strange. "Surprise for you, my dear Orno."

"Oh, my God," he said. "Sofia—"

"He asks me to come and see you. He said it was to be a surprise. I didn't know this kind."

Orno crossed the room and when she rose he embraced her. "Where have you been?"

"Oh, there and here. It has been many years."

Marshall said, "I'm returning her to you."

Sofia laughed.

"I am," he said. "It was a mistake."

Orno laughed also. "Oh, my God," he said, "it's been so long."

"She's yours," Marshall said. "Take her."

"You are a dentist now."

"That's right."

"I am an architect."

"Where are you living?"

"Boston."

"So you drove out here."

"Yes, I learned to drive."

"Everybody thinks I'm kidding," said Marshall.

"Was anybody hurt?"

She laughed. "It was not without difficulty." She laughed again, her Russian laugh. Deep, like a man's. "And now you get married."

"That's right."

"No one's listening to me," said Marshall. "Orno, I'm giving her back to you."

"Marshall, you are not making sense now."

"I'm giving you back."

"Marshall, you cannot give me."

"She's not yours to give, Marshall."

"I started this whole thing," said Marshall. "Now I'm stopping it. Don't you see, O? I'm making amends."

"Well it's very nice of you to bring her out."

"Let's call a spade a spade. You can take her now. We're even."

"Oh, no," said Orno. "It's got nothing to do with that."

"It sure does."

"Marshall, this is ridiculous."

"You're getting back at me for something I did ten years ago."

"Marshall, you are drunk," said Sofia.

"The expensive delicate ship that must have seen something amazing."

"You're really not making sense, M."

"You'll never make it in this world, O. This world isn't for you."

"Please, Marshall. Cut it out."

"What world are you talking about?"

"This world, O. My family. It's not Missouri."

"It's not your sister's world, Marshall."

"Oh, yes, it is."

"Your sister wants to be rid of it, then."

"She'll never be rid of it."

"You ought to ask *her* about that."

"I did," Marshall said. "You want to know what she said?"

Orno turned to Sofia. "Why don't we take a walk?"

"Yes, a good idea."

"What do you think my sister was doing in New York for a week?"

"Marshall, you're dead drunk."

"She was dating guys."

Orno had Sofia's arm; feeling along the wall for the door.

"Why don't you ask her?"

He found the door but it didn't give. "We're going out," he said.

"She was fucking guys, Orno. And my folks wanted her to. They were setting her up. They don't want this either. You shouldn't do it, Orno. It's wrong."

The door snapped open and they were in the night air, running. Sofia next to him, the asphalt streaking; the long line of shining grass tumbling ahead. They climbed a hill. Descended. Climbed again. They slowed and Orno turned around to look behind: darkness, even the shack gone. The horizon a faint arch of black. They stopped and squatted at the edge of the grass. "What do you think he's going to do?" he said.

"He is crazy." She shook her head. "How come you do not know that?"

"Maybe I'm seeing it now. He's also drunk."

"It is more than drunk. It is crazy."

"Crazy-drunk, maybe."

"Just crazy. He has been always."

"No, he hasn't."

"Oh, Orno. You never saw it."

"He was never like this."

"Yes, he was. Even years ago. He believed the same thing. Sometimes he goes over the end. Everyone is after him, to get him. He says you are going to battle to the death."

"He said that about *us*?"

"Yes," she said. "He used to be terrible sometimes. I'm afraid of him."

He looked around. Nothing to see but the outlines of the dunes. "Then why did you stay with him?"

"Oh, please. Why is it you are asking now?"

"I just want to know."

"I didn't stay with him."

"It sure seemed like you did."

"No. I knew something was wrong. Most of the time we were friends only. I was guarding myself. I was a young girl not in my own country, and he was brilliant. Terrible, too, but this was only part of it." She looked down. "Anyway, you have always believed I am stronger than I am."

He looked at her. She still stood the same way, her feet together and her hands pressed into each other. His tenderness came flooding back. He looked up the road. "Can I ask you something?"

"Of course."

"How come you came, then?"

"Because he told me we were all going to be here. He told me all of you from the old days. It was going to be a surprise. I would like to know your friends now." She stood. "I think I am the only one, though."

"It looks that way." Suddenly he had the urge to take her hand. It was confusing. Past and present, mixed in the unhindering dark. He said, "You didn't come because of me, then?"

"Oh, Orno," she said, "you are so sweet. I didn't realize—" She turned and touched his arm. "All men feel this before they are married. You are wondering if I still love you or maybe if you still love me." She shook her head. "You don't love me. We were friends only. We were convenient for each other and kind for each other. You are just nervous. You have always been that way. You have always had trepidation." She stepped back. "What are you laughing at?"

"At you," he said. "At how right you are."

"Of course I am," she said. "I always know you clearly."

It wasn't until early morning that Orno became afraid. He'd dropped Sofia at her motel in town and gone home to sleep, but before light he woke to the sound of the crashing surf; the wind was still shaking the house and he glanced in and saw the empty bed in Marshall's room. He rose and walked down to the beach, where breakers pounded at a swift slant. He went back in and woke Simone. "Where's Marshall?" he asked.

"I don't know. What's wrong?"

"Something's the matter with him."

"What's he doing?"

"I don't know. Maybe it's nothing. He was acting crazy. Accusing me. Now I can't find him."

She sat up.

"He was drinking."

"What did he accuse you of?"

"He was acting wild. There's someone here now, he brought her up. An old girlfriend of mine he knew."

"Sofia?"

"How did you know?"

"What is he accusing you of?"

"It has to do with *her*. I'd rather tell you later."

She regarded him. "She's here at the wedding?"

"Marshall invited her."

"Where is she?"

"At a motel. But I think we have to go find Marshall. I'm probably wrong. It's probably nothing. But we need to do it."

She rose and led him to her parents' room, where as soon as they opened the door Professor Emerson bolted up in bed. "What is it?"

"It's okay," Simone said. "We were looking for Mother."

"She's right here."

"We're worried about Marshall," said Simone. "He's out by himself somewhere."

"So?"

"Orno said he was acting strange."

Professor Emerson lay back down. "So are you two."

"What do you mean, strange?" said Mrs. Pelham. "What's he doing?"

Orno stepped forward. "I can't tell you exactly. It's just odd. He's not making sense. He's been drinking."

"He's a grown man," said Professor Emerson. "Let's just hope it's decent scotch. Now turn down that light."

Mrs. Pelham was already out of bed and in her robe. Professor Emerson rolled over in bed and said, "What do you propose we do?"

"Find him," said Mrs. Pelham.

"It's dark. There are hundreds of miles of beach."

"We'll take the cars. It'll be light in an hour."

"He's out having a drink. That's all. Which I wouldn't mind myself right now. His sister's getting married the day after tomorrow."

"If you don't want to come," said Mrs. Pelham, "I'll go out with the children."

"There's no need to be worried," he said. "He's just sleeping off a bottle." He pulled the covers up over his shoulders. "Do me a favor, though, please, all of you. Will you? Just don't wake up everybody on the Cape."

———

They set off in the Emersons' car, Orno driving, Simone giving directions next to him. A network of small roads crossing the peninsula. They tried all of them, passing the stately waterfront mansions from the rear as they peered down their side passages to the dark beach; inland at each intersection, past rows of smaller saltboxes on the flats and then the white colonials in the interior, hidden among the twisted, impenetrable trees. Whenever they approached the water, Mrs. Pelham shined a flashlight out the window, its flickering white cone jumping forward when it caught the dune grass amid the black expanse. The sea was whitecaps and the frothing line of breakers.

It was hopeless. After a time, Orno began skipping the inland lanes and found his way back to the beach road; he drove north toward the mainland searching for familiar signs among the hills but finding none, just a confusing run of slopes and basins, unrecognizable one from the next. Now and then he felt the lightness of panic in his stomach and his direction floundered; power poles and stands of trees and the rises of the land. The roads curved and he wondered if he'd been driving in circles, yet the ocean always lay to the left; even hidden it filled his ears. Now the light was coming up.

Then they drove over a rise and he knew they were in the right spot: a flagpole and the shack's slanted shadow against the sky. Down a footpath in the grass a hundred yards from the water. Simone was out of the car running. He followed, trailing her bouncing flashlight.

Inside the shack he saw the table again. A flashlight on one of the chairs. Nothing hanging from the three wooden pegs by the door and no sign anywhere of Marshall. "It doesn't mean anything," Simone said, sitting down.

Orno looked around. "I'm sure he's fine."

"What was he saying exactly?"

"He was drunk."

"I know, but what was he saying?"

"He was upset. It's complicated. He has this idea about our wedding."

"What is it?"

Orno shrugged. "Not worth repeating."

"It's about Sofia."

"Yes."

"Oh, come on, just tell me. He's my brother."

Orno sat down next to her. "He was saying he thought I wanted to marry you to get back at him."

"For what?"

"For stealing Sofia in college."

"Oh, I see."

"I told him it's got nothing to do with that."

"But he doesn't think so," she said. She got up and went to the window. "That's Marshall when he's scared. He used to tell me you mistreated her."

"What?"

"He said you used to mistreat her. That's the kind of thing he says."

"Mistreated Sofia?"

"I'm only telling you to show you how frightened he is."

"I don't care if he's frightened."

"Yes, you do."

"Jesus, he's treacherous."

She was next to him, her arms around his back. "I know he is."

"He's trying to destroy everything."

"He's in pain right now."

"So am I."

"No you're not," she said. "Not like him. He's in trouble now. I can feel it."

———

They drove into town first, to the four-street center, where they stopped in front of every bar and restaurant for Simone to look inside. Most of the places were dismal—dark doors held open by chairs, a piece of neon buzzing above the counter. Empty or near to empty. Simone glanced in from the doorways, then stepped quickly inside. They checked half a dozen of them, then a few tourist places, then drove back out to the beach. There was nothing else for them to do, nowhere to look that gave them any hope, not among the tangled coves of trees inland nor the vast waterline like a wall of stone.

"We should go to the police," said Simone.

"What would we tell them?" said Mrs. Pelham.

"That we're worried about him."

Mrs. Pelham touched her hair. "I don't think your father would like that."

"Of course he wouldn't, Mother. All he cares about is what people think."

"Simone!"

"It's true."

"It certainly is not. He thinks all the time about both of you. It's his wedding, after all." She laughed. "I mean, it's *your* wedding, of course. But your father's putting it on, and he cares a lot about it. Everybody's going to be arriving soon. We don't need the constable around."

"I can't believe you're saying that."

"Well, I am, honey. Marshall's a grown-up."

"He's in danger, Mother."

"At some point we have to stop worrying about him."

Orno drove on. Mrs. Pelham pulled at her coat: *We must harden our hearts.* He didn't know who was right. Simone was looking out the window, still scanning the side paths down to the water; he looked over at the shadows of the houses moving on her face and abruptly remembered the first time he saw her, stepping from the window in the Emersons' kitchen. He tapped the brake, and a crease of sadness suddenly divided him. Perhaps they should go to the police. But he felt Marshall now like a ghostly weight in the car, pulling at all of them; it seemed he had to pull back. "He might be at home," he said. "For all we know."

"That's right," said Mrs. Pelham.

Simone glared at him.

"We'll just go see," said Orno. "All right, sweetheart? We'll just go check. We can always come back to look if he's not."

When they arrived, Professor Emerson was at the kitchen table in his nightclothes with a tumbler in his hand. "Let's all go back to sleep," he said.

"Why? Did he come home?"

"No, but he's a grown man, Simone. I'm sure he's fine."

Simone stayed next to the door. "I'm not sleeping," she said. "I think we should go back out."

"And do what?"

"Look for him."

"That's just what he wants us to do, sweetheart," said Professor Emerson.

"And that's the reason you're not going to do it?" Her voice rose. "Just so you can think he isn't getting what he wants? So you're going to let him hurt himself?"

"Simone!"

"Nobody's going to hurt themselves, sweetheart."

Mrs. Pelham raised her chin. "I'm sure he's fine."

"We don't know that, Mother."

"Simone," said Orno, "there's no reason to think the worst."

"You don't believe that!"

"Here, sweetheart, let me pour you some of this."

"I do believe it," said Orno.

"I don't believe you do," she said.

"Here you go, sweetheart," said Professor Emerson.

"I don't want that!"

"It'll help you sleep."

"I'm not going to sleep."

"What are you going to do, then?"

"I'm going back out. He needs me. He needs me to look for him."

"He could be anywhere," said Mrs. Pelham.

"Simone, can't we talk for a minute?" said Orno.

Suddenly Simone said, "The boat!"

Professor Emerson blanched. "Christ almighty!" he said. He drained his tumbler, then slammed it down on the table.

———

Simone was out of the car before the engine was off, running down the dock while Orno called behind her. A gate slapping. The wind ferocious and salt spray splashing him. Then the slats flying by, bending underneath as he ran. The boats bouncing and clattering, masts and lines and jangling metal, the screech of bumpers, the hulls flashing. He made his way to the end of the jetty, guessed at the turnoff, and moved down the pier toward where the spume rose in gusts over the seawall. Simone shouted, "Here!"

She waved from the deck: he moved down the dock until he found the *Chesterton* and jumped aboard. The door flew open in the wind, then slammed shut.

"He was here," she said, leaning against the wheel.

"How do you know?" A stool next to her, fishing rods stacked against the handrail, a metal flask on the map counter. She pointed out the cabin window: ahead and behind the small decks were soaked.

"He was out tonight." She opened the flask and smelled it.

He pushed on the door again and it caught in the wind and flung itself open. The deck was slippery; he held on to the rail and moved up to the bow looking over the docks. The rows of slanting hulls, the canvas covers snapping in the wind, the masts and bridges rocking. Suddenly the motor churned on and the boat steadied in the water. Behind him on the bridge Simone was frowning. Then the engine went off. He looked over the side: they were still tied to the cleats, front and back. The door slammed again. From behind him Simone said, "He must have just come in." She leaned down and lifted a cover from a hole on the deck and poked a flashlight through. She reached her hand down and brought it up. "Yeah, he did."

"How do you know?"

"The engine came right on. It never does that. You have to prime it, then choke it, and even then it takes a while. You heard me turn it on, one turn of the key." She stood up. "And there's sea water in the bilge."

"What would he have been doing out?"

"God knows."

He looked toward the seawall, a dark row of piled rocks thirty yards across the channel; a wave erupted over its back. "It scares me," he said.

"It scares me, too. But he came back in. That says something."

They moved into the cabin and Orno latched the door. "He doesn't want us to get married, you know."

She was looking around. "I don't know about that."

"That's what he told me when he was drunk."

"That's the kind of thing he says when he's drunk. It doesn't mean it's true." She opened the storage chest under the seat. "The seas must have been huge."

He looked out at the snapping flags. "I can't imagine."

"He knows what to do in a boat."

"Still—" He sat on the countertop. "He also told me that your parents don't want you to marry me."

"What?"

"That's what he said."

"Well, it's not true. That's ridiculous. That's just the kind of thing he says sometimes. You know that. My mother adores you."

"That's not the truth."

"Yes, it is."

"Your father thinks I'm a hayseed."

"My father doesn't know *what* to think."

"He seems pretty sure to me."

She stopped looking around the cabin and faced him. "Well," she said, "that's his problem. If he wants to think that, he can. He's still hoping I'll marry a Vanderbilt." She tried to kiss him. "He thinks if he believes hard enough he can just change the way things are. Like with us." She sat up on the counter. "From his point of view, I guess I was his only hope. I mean, the man I married was his only hope."

He laughed. "And you married a dentist."

"The best thing I'll ever do in my life."

"Maybe he'll tell people I'm a doctor."

"He already does."

Orno laughed. "Doctor Vanderbilt," he said. "Working without a salary. Donates his skills because he certainly can't need the money." He moved to the window. "So, where's Marshall now?"

"I don't know, but I'm not worried anymore."

"Why not?"

"Because look, the boat's here. He came back in." She nodded toward the seawall. "If he'd wanted to do something terrible he could have headed sideways into a breaker."

"Still—"

"And you have to really think about things with him. That's the way he is. He knew we'd come out to find him. He probably knows we're here right now. He's telling me he's all right."

"Jesus," he said. "It's all so labyrinthine." He looked out at the yachts rocking in their berths. "I can't believe I like him. You know?"

"But I'm glad you do."

"He's so vulnerable you *have* to. He really moves up right next to you, even after all this time. I've always felt that." He wiped the window with his sleeve. "You know, in a way it's flattering. Maybe he doesn't want us to get married because he thinks he's going to lose both of us."

"I'm not sure he doesn't want us to get married," she said.

"That's because you didn't hear what he said to me last night."

"I know what he said, or at least I can imagine. But I know him better than you do. I'm just not sure that's what he's trying to do."

"Then what do you think he meant?"

"I don't know," she answered. She kept looking out the window. "But I have my own idea."

"Well, what is it?"

"I'm not exactly sure."

He laughed. "Now *you're* the one who's too charitable."

"Not at all."

"We should go home and go to sleep," he said.

"You *have* to like him," she answered, "in spite of everything."

"I do."

"And you have to forgive him."

XXXVI

That afternoon Orno took the pickup truck and searched the coastal road again, miles in both directions along the empty sand. He returned to the shack but it was unchanged from the night before. He drove home slowly, stopping at all the bars he passed, and at every vista of the beach. "No sign of him," he told Simone when he returned.

"He'll be back tonight."

"How do you know that?"

"I *don't* know it," she said. "But I *hope* it."

He wrapped his arms around her. She was distracted; he could feel it in her shoulders. "I don't want Marshall to ruin this," he said.

"He won't."

"But what if he doesn't come back at all? I mean, for the wedding?"

"I don't want to think about that." She shrugged and moved away from him. "But I *am* thinking about it, I guess. Aren't I? Damn him." She pursed her lips. "I think he's going to come back tonight," she said. "Tonight, after the rehearsal dinner. He'll miss that, to scare us. But then he'll come back."

"That's a rather precise prediction."

"My specialty, by now."

"Well, I hope you're right."

That evening Marshall was indeed gone for the dinner, which was held at a small waterside restaurant in East Falmouth. A half-dozen relatives of the Emerson-Pelhams, a couple of Simone's friends, and Orno's family. Orno's mother asked after Marshall, and Simone told her he wasn't feeling well. Orno's father raised his eyebrows, but what Simone had said was close enough to the truth that Orno added nothing more. The meal passed quickly. A couple of toasts, but brief ones. Professor Emerson rose, welcomed everyone, then gave a short history of their cottage, starting with the governor of Massachusetts who had expanded it and added horse stables in the nineteenth century, ending with the fire that had burned the stables after World War II; he closed by thanking the Hay-Markhams for their hospitality and the Tarchers for their long journey from Missouri. After that, Orno's father stood, somewhat shyly, and said a few words in thanks. That was all. The evening ended early.

Back at the house, Simone stayed awake late, long after Orno had gone to bed. Twice he woke and went to the living room to find her sitting by the window. "Come to sleep," he said. "It's your wedding day."

"In a minute," she answered. "You go."

He went back to the bedroom, where he fell into a fitful sleep. Finally, long into the night, Simone shook him awake. "He's still not back," she said.

"What time is it?"

"Almost four. He's not in the house or on the beach either, at least not in back."

"Were you out looking?"

"Of course I was."

"You're worried."

"Of course I am. But I've been thinking hard about it all night, and I really think he's going to be okay. But that's not the point. The point is that you and I are supposed to get married today. I'm not having a wedding while he's missing."

"You need to sleep," he said. He pulled her toward the bed. "He'll be back in the morning."

"No, he won't." She shook him again. "It *is* the morning, Orno. I've been thinking about this. Wake up."

"Well?" he said. He tried to open his eyes. "What do you want to do, then?"

"Leave."

She wasn't smiling. She poked him. "Wake up."

"Yes?"

"I want to elope."

He laughed.

"I mean it," she said. She lifted his head and pointed to the floor, where their two duffels lay packed. "Come on," she whispered. "Before my father wakes up."

———

The sun had not yet lit the horizon when they got into the Emersons' car. Simone set her duffel in the trunk and closed it quietly. It was all she took: her wedding dress could not have been inside. He felt disbelief—awe, really: this was nothing he could have ever imagined. He moved over and let her drive. She started the car and nosed it out the driveway to the gravel path, leaning close to the wheel as she steered, a posture that struck him with its mingled intimacy and forcefulness; he saw that she had a determined aspect to her that he'd never seen before. It was nice to know it.

They made it out to the road and he said, "I need to tell my father."

"They'll be asleep."

"Not my father."

She smiled. He was in love with that smile: determination and kindness in it, the two things he wanted most. She turned at the crossing for the Hay-Markham cottage.

"You didn't bring your dress," he said.

"I don't want it."

"We can still go back. You *must* want it."

"Well, I guess I do, but I thought if I had it I might weaken."
She leaned up close to the wheel. "This is something we have to
do, Orno. I know what I want," she said. "I want you."

"Are we going to look for Marshall?"

"No. We won't find him. He'll figure out what's happened. You
can bet on that."

"Then what?"

"Then we'll see."

They passed the long lagoon, where the water had calmed but
was broken everywhere by flotsam from the storm. "We can't take
this car," he said. "It's your father's."

"Oh, come on. Don't be so well-behaved. This is a crime we're
committing."

"But your folks will need it."

"All right, then we'll rent one. We can leave this one in Falmouth."

"I'll call them from there."

She laughed. "Remind me not to rob a bank with you," she said.

Now the horizon was brightening and as they drove next to the
water the shorebirds began appearing, hopping up from the dunes
as they passed. They reached the narrow two-track that led down
to the Hay-Markhams'; but as they turned into it Orno was cut by
a bolt of dread. The import of everything: his father; his job, Dr.
Meansy leaning inside the doorway to his office with his hands
clasped, blocking out the light; Professor Emerson rising panicked
in the empty house.

Simone slowed down. "Don't worry," she said.

"Are you sure we should be doing this?"

"I'm the one who should be worried."

"True enough."

She pulled over where the cottage was hidden in the dunes. "Go
ahead," she said. "I'll wait."

The sky not quite light. For some reason, he decided to take
off his shoes to walk down the path; it might have been trepidation—he got out and sat on the car bumper for a moment pulling at his sneakers. Then he set his socks inside them and placed
both on the trunk; the horizon a band of silver, the sea below

it a blind gray up to the bright crescent of the beach. Then he turned and started for the cottage; the cool of the night sand was a comfort; he curled his toes into it, feeling the spiny tickle of the short dune weeds. *We are eloping. We are leaving.* He would offer to shake his father's hand; that would make it final and not a question. *I wanted to tell the two of you so you wouldn't be hurt.* He figured it was near five-thirty. In the hedges a bird or a lizard was shuffling.

Then from inside the gate he heard his father's step crossing the patio and like a wall going down he was suddenly crushed with envy for Marshall. He stopped and leaned against the fence, out of sight of the gate in case his father appeared. They were doing this for *him;* they were changing their plans; they were disappointing people—breaking their hearts; he was going to humiliate his father and mother. And all for *him.* Out ahead the footsteps reached the gate and the latch jiggled. He could have run, but instead he stepped toward it: his father looked out into the path. "Look who's here," he said. "Good morning, groom."

"We're leaving." He put out his hand. They shook.

"All right."

"Is Mom asleep?"

"Last I looked."

He put his hands back in his pockets. "I mean, Simone and I are eloping. Marshall is gone and we don't want to get married without him here."

"Wait a minute. You can't do that."

"Well, we are. I'm sorry. We're leaving. We've decided."

His father stepped away from the fence, looked up at the horizon. Then he shook his head and whistled. "I guess Senator Kennedy will have to keep his present."

"I'm sorry, but we have to do it."

"You've already said you're sorry."

"Well, I am."

"Is Simone with you?"

"She's in the car."

"I suppose the engine's running."

"Well, no. But we *are* going soon."

His father walked up the path and leaned in the car window. Orno saw his head bobbing, and as he came around to Simone's side he saw they were both laughing.

"The engine *is* running," his father said.

"Simone was driving."

"Well," said his father. "You can count on me. I'll keep your mother occupied till you're out of the territory."

"I'd like Orno to tell *her* too," said Simone.

"No, you wouldn't," said his father. "You should take my word on this one. I'll do it for you."

"He's right, Simone."

"Well, thank you, then," she said.

His father leaned back from the window and Orno opened the driver's door. Simone moved across to the other seat. "Then you don't mind that we're going?" Orno said.

"Hell no," said his father. "I was wondering if you had any sense, that's all. I see now that you do. It's a relief."

"Thank you, Dad."

"Do what you have to do, Orno. I'll tell your mother at breakfast."

His father stepped around the front of the car and Orno leaned forward and hugged him, which he hadn't done since he was a teenager. His father was a little stiff about it. After a moment he patted Orno on the shoulder.

"Thank you," Orno said again into his ear. "I won't forget this. Tell Mom I love her."

He got in and put the car in reverse. As they edged backward up the driveway his father laughed suddenly and called out, "What about the new suit?" Then he stood there waving, his arm high over his head the way farmers waved to the road from tractors. When they reached the two-track Orno looked behind and saw the hand, still moving back and forth above the top of the dune; it broke his heart to turn again toward the road and leave it there like that, waving and waving at them.

———

In Buzzards Bay they rented a car, leaving the old one in a wharf lot, where Orno dropped a postcard in the mail to the Emersons. Then they headed north, staying on small roads, partly to hide themselves but more because he was drawn by the splendid trees. North of Boston they spent the night in a motel and the next day in a fine white morning of sunlight the feeling of being someone else that had been stirring inside him gave way to a sense of release, that he was a coil now unwound; as the car came out onto the shore of the Merrimack River he realized it was because of his father. At two in the afternoon—a day late, but the hour they had planned to be married—they pulled into a rest stop, drank root beer from the vending machine and stepped back behind the false-brick wall to kiss amid the sound of slamming car doors and rumbling trucks. In truth he was desperate with the meanness of their misdeed—he pictured Professor Emerson meeting the invited guests outside the church to tell them—but he knew enough to put on a cheerful expression and toast as romantically as he could with the root beer, not in a joking way, down on his knees on a small island of unyellowed grass. Then they said their vows to each other. Afterward they got back in the car and continued north, once again on small roads, once again in the shelter of the arching trees; his desperation tired itself out and turned to resignation and then by evening to an amnesiac relief; late that night they ended up in Portland, Maine, where he was giddy enough to stop the car at the beach and walk straight into the moonlit calm Atlantic in his pants. The next day Simone talked two waitresses into acting as witnesses, and that afternoon in City Hall they were married by a judge not even in a robe. By now he was in a state of pure surprise.

There it was: a wall inside him lifted. He would not have thought he was capable. And he would never have thought his father would have given them his blessing. But that was what he'd done in the ramshackle driveway two mornings before, probably made ecstatic by the mounting light but acting, it was suddenly clear, in a way that had been inside him all along. So he wasn't a stiff after all. He'd probably had thoughts of escape himself, maybe the same instinct toward disorder that Orno himself had tried to swim from in anatomy labs and extraction clinics and the sunlit kitchen nooks where he'd made the unchangeable decisions of his life, paddling in towing seas the way he did in dreams. "My father," he said. "The way he gave us his blessing. It made me think I've never known him."

"How do you mean?"

"He seemed happy for us. I'd have thought he would disapprove."

"I know," she said. "He was a hero."

They drove northwest that afternoon into the green interior of the state, up into logging country where the tourist cars thinned out and soon they saw only flatbed trucks laden with cut trunks and front-end loaders nosing in the two-tracks. Every now and then they came to a town, and by evening they'd arrived in lake country; small, slope-roofed outdoor camps turned to rental cottages by the townsfolk and marked on the road by hand-lettered signs full of misspellings. All of them were brown, painted dark when the wood alone would have been far more beautiful. Simone edged over next to him. They were trying to find a place to stay for their honeymoon.

"Amazing," he said. "Now I feel like everything I do is up for grabs. Whether we go home after this. Where we go home."

She put her head on his shoulder.

"Silly," he said. "It just makes me realize I've never known him."

"Of course you haven't. A child never does."

They drove for too long, hoping for a romantic wood cottage with a view of the moon over a lake bank or the misty slopes of conifers, and instead ended up waking the irate French-Canadian night clerk of a low-end tourist bungalow who didn't believe it was their wedding night or didn't care. Their cabin had one window and it looked backward into nothing, a tangle of dark evergreens dead at the bottom and covered with vines marauding up the trunks; the bed sagged and the pillows were stiff and different sizes. But at least the cabin was a distance from the others and surrounded by unthinned trees: they made love till early morning, turning it somehow into an event when really it was not one, just the legal indulgence for what they'd had for a long time now, since Stony Brook. Several times she sat up and regarded him, sitting astride him so that in the distant shine of the French-Canadian's office light he saw her as a progression of sweat-illuminated curves—hip, breast, shoulder, cheek—and the occasional narrow crescent of her smile. The sheets were cool in the hot night and to his utter surprise he actually felt transformed, the thing he was supposed to feel on his wedding night, so that when he woke in the morning he felt they'd been let deeper into each other's lives. A day ago he wouldn't have thought it possible.

She had a girlish way of mentioning it all morning—"This is the first orange juice we'll drink together married," and "This is the first drive we'll take"—and though he went along with her mostly out of goodwill, soon after he'd said it a few times himself its import seemed to take hold of him as well: from here forward there would no longer be trepidation. They walked in the afternoon. The clerk had warmed a bit to them and pointed out a path that ran down a short hillside to a lake they'd had no inkling was even there. They were the only ones around. On a bed of smoothly sloped stone that rose in the shallows they made love again, rolling into the water afterward and then crawling out again to warm themselves. He was aware that there were many things for him to think about but he slept until the sun moved behind the trees and he woke with a pleasant feeling of sunburn.

"This might not be the right moment to mention it," he said, when she woke next to him, "and I'm only wondering—I don't think it would matter either way—"

"What is it?"

"Well, I was thinking." He turned onto his side and laid his arm over her. "Marshall said you were seeing someone else when you went down to New York."

He waited. She didn't say anything.

"Maybe I don't want to know," he said.

"No, it's not as bad as you think."

"Were you?"

"Yes, I had a date, if that's what you want to call it. My father threw a scene. It was horrible. He set me up with the son of one of the members of his department. He was literally in a rage. He'd been drinking all morning. I went out with the guy just to get out of the apartment. We went out for coffee. I told him I was getting married. He was a nice guy. I told him my father wanted me to go on a date. And I have to hand it to him, he was as sweet as could be. I think he was gay, actually. That's probably why his father had sent him out with *me*. But he didn't seem to mind. We went to South Street Seaport and pretended we were tourists. It was a moment of real decency."

"Why are you crying, then?"

She covered her face. "It's nothing."

"Tell me."

"Well, it's weird. I'm trying to think about it. The thing is, I can't figure out how Marshall would have known that."

"That you went out on a date?"

"Yeah."

He considered it. "Maybe he talked to your mother."

"She wouldn't have told him. She was horrified. We were both horrified."

"So your father told him."

"I think you're right. But how would he have told him that? *Why* would he have? They barely talk at all. It seems so underhanded. He must have told him just so that Marshall would tell *you*." She lifted her hands. "That's why I'm crying. It's so byzantine. It's so desperate."

"It doesn't matter," he said.

"But I wanted to protect you from this. I didn't want you to see this. Ever."

She was crying fully now. He didn't try to stop her, but he rubbed his hand across her shoulders. "When I first told Marshall I was seeing you," he said, "he told me you were a liar. He said I would see it someday."

"There's no defense against that. He was just trying to poison us."

"I know that."

"He thinks I see things the way I want them to be. That's what he means. To him it seems like a lie—the idea that I can be normal, be happy. That I can make a life. It's so sad. He thinks I'm lying when I think that I can get away from all this." She wiped her eyes. "My mother was gone early in his life—when he was two she went to Turkey to do her fieldwork. Sometimes I think it was that. He had three or four different nannies that year before my father found Olivia, and I think my father must have just ignored him." She rubbed his head. "Think of him, two years old, my poor, sweet brother, and suddenly his mother is gone. Does he understand she's coming back?"

"I met Olivia when I came over for Thanksgiving."

"She stayed with us the longest, and now it's like she's the only person besides me that he trusts from year to year. Isn't that strange? Someone from when he was *two* years old. He almost never sees her, but when he does there's something different about him. It's the only time he's ever unguarded."

"I know what you mean."

"By the time I was born my mother stopped traveling. The smallest thing in the world, but it was everything. How else can I explain it? We had the same father. He was off in his own imagination all the time I was growing up, but that was okay because I had *her*. Marshall didn't. Marshall only had our father, and *he* was already pretending he was someone else. He wasn't the son of a barrel salesman, he was a professor at Columbia. He was making his mark. He won all kinds of prizes at first. You should have seen the way he worked. And with that kind of memory! He had tenure when he was something like twenty-seven. When we were kids one year he won a prize from the National Academy of Sciences. Marshall used to call it his *consolation* prize. I never understood that until I was a lot older. I actually thought it *was* a consolation prize."

"What was it?"

"It was a national medal of science. It wasn't a consolation, it was first prize. But Marshall was right. It was consolation for whatever it was he really wanted. Affection, I suppose. Money. I don't know. Acceptance. That's what I think Marshall meant. It's hard to know what my father wants. To *be* someone is the best way I can put it, and I used to think about it a lot. Being rich or famous isn't exactly the point. It's just being important. Regarded. So he can feel like there's something to him. He thought being rich would help with that, I guess. He thought if other people recognized him he'd recognize himself."

"Sounds like Marshall."

"I know. And Marshall was saying it about my father when he was twelve years old! Can you imagine? He was precocious even then."

"It was probably easy for him to understand."

"Probably. It's remarkable. He sees people the way nobody else does. That's his problem," she said. "He's so smart, but it's never soothed him at all."

Orno looked up. "That's why your father wanted the Kennedys at the wedding, isn't it?"

"That's right."

He rose and stood on the rocks, gazing out over the water. "What do you think he'll say to them now?"

"To who?"

"Senator Kennedy."

"Oh, Orno," she said, standing next to him. "That's one of the things I love about you. You still don't understand."

"Don't understand what?"

"My family. My father. I'm sure he never even asked the Kennedys."

———

They decided to go back to Preston that night. There were plenty of places they could have driven to—Canada appealed to him suddenly, the idea of unsettled land—but in the car as they moved east again he understood that they'd left behind too much unfinished business to go on vacation. He didn't want to bring up her father again, nor the fact of a hundred and sixty guests making it out to the Cape for a canceled wedding. When they passed out of lake country into farm country, Simone said, "He'll be there, you know, when we get home."

"Who will?"

"Marshall. At the house, when we get home."

"Our house?"

"Yes."

"What makes you say that?" He turned to her. She was gazing out the window. "Did you talk to him?"

"How could we have talked?"

"I don't know. You might have called him."

"I didn't," she said. "I just have a feeling."

"Well, I hope your father isn't there with him."

She laughed.

"Seriously. I can't imagine what he'll do."

"Don't worry. My father won't come up. He'll probably never speak to us again, that's all. Unless to ask for his money back."

"He'll understand eventually."

"Why? Because *your* father did? You're just lucky."

"I suppose I am."

"I'm going to pay him back," she said. "Every cent. I don't want to think about what he's feeling, though. You have no idea."

"He probably called the police."

"Not my father."

"Maybe not."

"I left them a note," she said.

"He's probably mystified even so."

"But what was I supposed to do? When I think about him having to tell everybody—" She started to cry. They were near land they knew now, coming into the low grass-covered hills around Preston. Sunflowers in the yards. The road sloping toward the Malakoot River valley that for the first time now, returning, had the tilt and light of home. He didn't try to stop her. It wasn't his family who'd given the wedding but he felt the sharp dishonor of his own ingratitude and an open gap of sadness for them, for their curious generosity spurned. She cried for twenty miles while he rubbed her shoulder, and she didn't stop until he drove up River Street, turned on Main, and parked the car in the shade of the two old maples in front of their house.

XXXVII

In their bedroom a new bed with a wrought-iron headboard and an antique quilt; on it, a note:

Such is the elfin hand quick and invisible that wishes you love and contentment here made of the bold darting courage of swallows (who mate for life).

Love,
M

"Strange," Orno said.

"No it's not. It's playful. He's being friendly. He wants to be forgiven."

Orno looked around. No sign of him. No bags, no food in the refrigerator. Simone sat on the bed saying it was the happiest day of her life, coming home with him to their own house and finding this gift from her brother; they lay down on it to nap. He didn't like that they were on a mattress Marshall had given them: another joke for his own benefit, it seemed. He slept fitfully. But when he woke, his ire was transformed. They lay together on the cool quilt looking up and without warning he was crying himself, great tears he didn't know he had. Simone rubbed his forehead, which brought on more tears, and said, "Tell me."

"I don't know," he answered. "The world is just such a surprise."

———

A few days later, without telling her, he wrote her parents to explain that Marshall's absence had made their situation untenable. He apologized even though he felt false doing so, that there was so much intent to their eloping that apology was nothing more than self-promotion. Yet he had no choice; and Mrs. Pelham might be comforted. He debated showing the letter to Simone, but decided in the end that it was his own business; late that night, after she was asleep upstairs, he walked out to the corner to mail it.

Later still that night there was a knock on the door, and this time when he went downstairs Marshall was standing on the porch. He came in and embraced Orno and set down a bottle of champagne. "French," he said. "Very, very good."

"I can't say I was expecting you. How long have you been here?"

"A couple of days, in and around. Wait till you taste this."

"I didn't think you'd want to be showing up for a while," said Orno. "Simone's asleep."

"She'll want to wake up for this." He winked. "It's extremely good. It's for the two of you. I have a man who gets it for me in Marseilles. I brought it as a tribute. It's more of my present."

"I guess when you show up you do it in a big way."

Marshall laughed.

Orno didn't want to wake Simone but at that moment she came downstairs disheveled from sleep and hugged Marshall, not letting go until he stood up straight and winked at Orno across the room. Then she hugged him again. "I brought this wonderful champagne," Marshall said. "Let's try it."

"This is the happiest day," said Simone.

"Yes, yes," Marshall answered. Over her shoulder he gestured toward the bottle. Orno brought out a dishtowel from the kitchen, set it over his wrist, and unwound the wire brace. Simone still had her arms over Marshall and now he was rolling his eyes to mock her, but on his face was the hint of a child's smile. Orno twisted the cork and shot it into the corner of the ceiling. Simone turned around at the sound and Marshall broke away. "How do you like the bed?" he said.

"It's wonderful," she answered.

"I brought glasses too, since I doubt you have the right ones." He went out the front door and came back in a few moments with three of them. He poured the champagne and said, "To Boldness."

"To Boldness."

They drank and he poured another round and said, "To leaving Los Angeles."

"Is that what you're going to do?"

"I don't know. Maybe. But here's to the idea."

"To leaving Los Angeles," Orno said, but he didn't drink. Then he picked up the glass again and said, "To talking in the morning."

"Oh, come on, O."

"It's two-thirty, Marshall."

"It *is* late," said Simone.

"Oh, all right."

They set up blankets on the couch downstairs and then went back up to their own bed, where Orno fell asleep with Simone talking to him about how wonderful it was to see her brother. He himself thought it was odd: Marshall was acting blameless and Simone seemed to welcome it. To Orno's thinking, Marshall ought to have been subdued by contrition, or at least empathy. He was angry. Yet the truth was, for no better reason than his memory, he was happy to see him.

———

The next day was Saturday, and he woke early and went outside to cut the lawn. Pulling the old mower from the garage, he found that his resentment had taken clearer shape; he kept thinking of the cabin at the beach where Marshall had brought Sofia. He'd been drinking then and for that maybe he could be forgiven, but then he'd stayed away and forced their hand: it wasn't innocent. Orno pulled the mower cord and it sputtered, then roared. Yet he himself had returned to Marshall's orbit as soon as he saw an opening—his own striving seemed just as unquenchable. He started across the lawn, and when he came back up the near walk alongside the house Marshall was standing on the porch with two cups in his hands.

"Coffee?"

"Soon as I'm done." The thunder of the engine made conversation impossible and Orno was glad of it: Marshall still seemed to have no contrition or even discomfort. He leaned against the fence, drinking. Orno tilted the mower up over one of the elm roots and Marshall suddenly coughed: a bright stain of blood burst on his chest. *A stone*—Orno dropped the mower handle and stepped toward him; Marshall smiled, looking embarrassed, then coughed again; this time a stream of red came up. He sat on the grass.

Orno ran to him and yanked open his shirt. Marshall coughed again into his hand: more red. He rubbed it across his arm. Orno pulled a towel off the clothesline and pressed it to Marshall's chest, then yelled for Simone; she appeared at the window upstairs; in a moment she was next to them in the yard. "I'll call the ambulance," she said. But Orno already had him up, holding him under the shoulders and pulling him to the Volkswagen. They put him in back and sped out onto the empty road. Marshall sat holding the towel to his mouth; the blood had spread to his armpits. "Beautiful," he said. "Beautiful."

"How do you feel? Are you dizzy?"

"Angelic."

"What?"

"Angelic."

"Shh," Simone said. "No talking."

"How everything turns away—"

"Shhh!"

In the emergency room an orderly put him on a stretcher and

took him inside. Orno spoke to the nurse. "He was just standing there," he said. "I never thought about it. A stone must have shot all the way across the lawn. Maybe it was a piece of the blade. I forgot to check. What did they find?" They stood at the front of the waiting room. Through the window they could see the curtain and behind it the doctors working on Marshall. Now and then the nurse came back out and looked over at them, but she didn't give them any news. Simone kept saying, "Jesus, Jesus."

"A freak thing," Orno said. "Come on, M."

Finally, the doctor came out. He gestured them back into the corridor. "Your friend," he said, "is stable for the moment. Tell me again what happened."

"He was standing near the mower and it threw something," Orno said. "I was dragging it over a root. I think it was a stone. Was it a piece of the blade?"

The doctor sat on the windowsill. "No, no," he said. "That's what I thought you said. No, that's all wrong." He was a slight Indian man with a British accent. "Your friend has bled internally, I'm afraid. There's no wound on the surface. You confused us."

"What?"

"There was no stone. Is that what you said it was? Nothing was thrown by the mower."

"What is it then?" said Simone.

"Could be several things, but most probably an ulcer that has bled. He is stable now. No more bleeding. That is the important thing."

Orno said, "What do you mean, no stone?"

"It appears to be an ulcer. Probably from drink. Am I right?" He raised his eyebrows. "It's stopped, but next time it could be a good deal worse. He'll spend the night here. Tomorrow," he said, "we'll send him to Portland, for a specialist. No, no stone at all. How well do you know him?"

"I've known him a long time," said Orno. "I thought I hit him from the mower."

"He wasn't hit by a stone. I told you. Only internal. Most likely an ulcer."

"I'm his sister," said Simone.

"He must drink pretty hard," said the doctor.

"What do you mean?" said Simone.

"That's how these ulcers usually develop."

"Well, he doesn't drink that much," Simone said. "Not really."

"I don't know," said Orno.

"If he does it's because he has to do it for his work," she said. "He's really pretty good."

Orno regarded her. It was clear to him that he was part of an unchangeable orbit now, but still he wanted to change it. It was also clear that for the entire time they'd known each other Marshall must have been drinking far too much. It was a strange revelation, an instant recasting of recollection: booze in the background of everything he could remember.

———

As Orno and Simone drove home that evening Orno's arms and hands began to tremble. "Look," he said.

She took her hands from her pockets. "Me too."

"I guess I'm afraid."

"I guess I am too."

"I thought I hit him with something. It happens with farm machines. That's what I thought happened."

"He's going to be fine."

"He must have a life we don't know about," he said. "He must be drinking a lot."

"I never thought he did, particularly."

"I think he must."

"Maybe you think so, but I don't."

Open your eyes, he wanted to say, but he knew he could have been saying it for his own ears. She was looking out the window now, her features firmed by the same sanguine diligence he'd fallen in love with himself, the day he'd cut his leg on the boat. It made him vulnerable suddenly, the source of his own comfort directed at another: he had to turn away. He knew that her diligence would now be floating the two of them as well, through whatever came upon their days; but as he drove on the darkening road he was again crushed with envy. "Sorry" was all he could say.

"The doctor said he couldn't be sure it's what it was. You can get ulcers from other things. Thank you, by the way."

"I guess you can."

By the time they were home he could hold out his hands and watch them in front of him like the hands of another, still quivering, unable to hold the glass of iced tea she brought out to him as he sat on the porch. She brought him a straw, too, and they sat together sipping, waiting for their hands to calm themselves.

———

Marshall ended up in the hospital for two days and then the doctors sent him by ambulance to Portland. Orno called him there, but his call was transferred to the charge nurse, who told him that against medical advice he had already signed out and gone home. The next morning, while Simone sat in the yard reading, Orno called him in Los Angeles. Marshall answered the phone cheerfully.

"Well, this is a surprise," Orno said.

"It shouldn't be."

"No martinis on the plane, I hope."

"Not until noon."

"What did the doctor say?"

"What do they ever say?"

Orno was silent. "You left against their advice."

"And?"

"And you should watch your drinking. You could have bled again."

"I didn't."

"Guess not." He cleared his throat. "You should find a doctor in

L.A. You were covered with blood. I thought the mower had thrown something. It was pretty horrible."

"You thought that because it's what you wished for."

"Oh, come on, Marshall. That's ridiculous. It was terrifying."

"Perhaps."

"Horrible. The worst moment of my life."

Marshall paused. "Not for me."

Orno looked out the window to where Simone was reading in the chair. "I can't believe that."

"You know how it is."

"Still?"

"It's not a question of *still*."

Orno waited.

"Don't tell my sister," he said.

"I might have to," Orno answered.

"She won't want to hear. It'll scare her. Promise me."

"I won't promise."

"Promise me, Orno."

"No."

"What were you mailing at midnight?"

"What do you mean?"

"The night I dropped in, you came out and mailed a letter in the middle of the night. What kind of letter do you mail in the middle of the night?"

"You were watching?"

"I happened to see."

"Marshall, it was an apology note to your mother."

"I see."

Orno didn't know what to say.

"I'm not drinking that much," Marshall said. "The doctor was wrong."

Orno looked at the phone a moment and then, surprising himself, hung up. He was no angrier than he'd been all week, but there was both accusation and evasion in Marshall's voice; he didn't want to respond to it. Not from defensiveness but because he didn't want to breach the curious invincibility Simone had now cast over both of them. What in God's name was Marshall implying about the letter? Did he think he was cheating on her? It was the kind of thing he might have gone along with if Marshall had said it about Daphne or Anne-Marie, winking at him on the cliffs above the Hudson; but at this moment he could not have been more in love with Simone. She was still reading outside, warped by the quaintly shimmering window. He walked out there, picturing her brother standing in Los Angeles holding the dead phone in his hand. In a moment ringing began in the kitchen. He was on the grass now, looking at the border of brown clippings thrown by the mower and not cleaned up. The phone kept ringing. He went to the garage for a rake and when he returned Simone was looking at him with her eyebrows raised. The phone went silent. In a moment it rang again but only a couple of times. He could feel Marshall in the air with them: desperation and pride. He knelt by Simone and laid his head on her knees. He didn't want the phone to ring again but he didn't want to tell Simone what had happened, nor what Marshall had said; perhaps she had already guessed. He didn't want to leave her either. Then with his head on her legs his eye fell on the coffee cups. "Look at these," he said. They were leaning against the porch and he rose and went over to them. "Marshall dropped these when he fell." One was still full and the other almost empty: he sniffed it for liquor but it seemed to hold old coffee and nothing more. "I guess I was wrong." He held it up. "Unless it evaporated." He smelled it again. "I thought there would be booze in here."

"Good God," she said. "What do you think he is?"

He shrugged his shoulders, set the cups next to the door, and went back to her. He didn't know what his answer was. He was a monster. He was a temptation. He was a force, the history of his own mixed wanderings, still all around them in the warming air.

"I'm sorry," she said. "I shouldn't have said that. I know what he is."

"He's a lot of things."

"I've been thinking that I wanted to tell you something," she said. She set down her book. "I know I'm wrong to protect him. I know that, and I'm telling you now just so you know I know it. But the thing is, I have to. It's just who I am."

"It's like that in a way for me, too. As soon as he gives me a chance I'm right back with him."

"My brother and I are like twins," she said. "Born wrapped in each other's arms."

XXXVIII

My Sister and Brother—

I'm sorry if I caused you trouble, but I think you'll see in the end that I saved you from more trouble than you realize. I'm not talking about the ulcer, which is no fault of anyone's, but about the wedding. Orno I am sorry for some of the things I said, but sometimes those things just come over me like waves one after the other, and I had the feeling of drowning that night when I said them. I didn't mean harm. I'm glad you liked the bed. It was handmade for you by an ironworker in Vermont, and if you have any problems with it you should contact me for I can contact him. That's all for now.

Love,
M

XXXIX

is parents sent them his grandmother's china, which arrived in a stack of boxes a week later, the note in his mother's clean hand addressed to *Mr. and Mrs. Orno Tarcher*. A sheet of paper inside the card cataloged the inventory and mentioned a missing soup tureen for which an inquiry had been made. That night only after they'd unpacked everything did they find the note from his father, slipped inside a box:

DRAKE TARCHER

INSURANCE—ALL KINDS

The point is that your loyalty is to each other now. Your mother and I have learned this only over many years and you two have learned it already. Good for you.

—Dad

———

They hadn't heard anything from the Emersons, and though he watched Simone, waiting for signs of what to him would have been an unbearable guilt, she showed none. It seemed easier for her to have done it than it had been for him. He made a note of it, this difference: that her family put her in the throes of deadly seas, but also freed her to live a life that if not utterly then at least essentially was her own. He, on the other hand, felt the constant twining pull of roots.

———

He went back to work at Dr. Meansy's and she took an unexpected vacancy a month into the fall semester at the parochial high school in Bell Arbor nearby, teaching English to the polite but wordless children of furniture foremen and the bigger farmers; a few of their parents were his patients and soon the two of them acquired an aura of respect in Preston that reached down to the smallest details of commerce and social exchange. Again Marshall disappeared from his thoughts. It was a happy time. Walking home from work in the evenings with the not-unpleasant smell of antiseptic soap still on his skin, he felt he'd been guided by a benevolent hand to this new period of contentment. It was Simone's hand in large part, and this cemented his serenity even more, that the agent of his happiness was now also part of it. A patch of sunflowers appeared unexpectedly in their garden, thick green stalks with leaves like cloth that came up late in the season alongside their bedroom window and soon peeked in over the sill, the flowers like staring yellow eyes watching the two of them. This time he laughed: he wondered if Marshall had planted them.

Four

X L

One morning in November, and again the next morning, Simone threw up; the following day she called Orno at work to tell him the news from the doctor in Bell Arbor: they were going to have a baby. Fall had already peaked and the cold was quicker than any he'd ever known, blowing in under the window as he stood watching the first skins of ice struggle in the river eddies; tears filled his eyes. He came home for lunch and the two of them went out for a walk, stepping on the nearly frozen carpet of leaves, bathed in their own surprise and tenderness. As he watched her step lightly on the crackling red and brown heaps, he was overcome with the urge to give her things—his arm, his open hands; he would have emptied his pockets for her; he would have emptied his heart.

Dear M,

A moment ago it seems we were meeting each other for the first time on Broadway, one morning in the rain. And today I'm writing to tell you that you are to become an uncle this summer.

Such is the circle of life. Simone and I are awed by the news. We hope that you will be too, and that this letter finds you well.

—Orno

Dear Mrs. Pelham and Professor Emerson—

I hope you aren't angry to see the return address on this letter, but I wanted to write you and tell you the news right away that this June the two of you are going to be grandparents. Simone is feeling great even though she's sick sometimes in the mornings, and we are very excited all the time by the news.

I guess there is no excusing what we did this fall, and I also wanted you to know that we are ready to see you and talk to you anytime that you think you are ready to do the same with us. Simone doesn't know I've written this note but I think she would agree: we have to start somewhere making up for what we did, and this is as good a time as any.

Yours affectionately,
Orno

———

She needed to eat at night, and he found that he loved waking for her in the brittle hours of early morning when the house was black and chilled, going to the kitchen for toast or cottage cheese and bringing it upstairs to her underneath the covers, where she'd built a little den of warmth like the fire inside a cave. He expected to be able to see a difference in her, but for a long time he couldn't. She was enveloped by a deep calm that touched him and added to his feelings of supplication; he could sit at the table for an hour watching her; she in turn could sit for an hour looking out the window at the dropping leaves and the landscape that was revealing itself slowly, deeper and deeper through the bare birches at the edge of the woods, into the dense corridors of firs.

———

One day he came home from the office and Simone wasn't in the kitchen nook grading papers; the house was silent and had the feel of emptiness. He made himself a cup of tea and sat at the table drinking it, looking out at the light snow that had gathered in the branches. He leafed through a dental journal to pass the time, more than vaguely satisfied that he now had experience with al- most all of the pathologic conditions mentioned; it made him feel that he belonged up here, among the farmers who knew the land, the furniture workers who could make a bow-back chair from a sawed log, and all the men in general, every one of whom could rebuild an engine or frame a barn or extract thick sap from the sugar maples—a skill he and Simone talked about learning. After he finished the journal he washed his cup and went upstairs to take off his tie. There he found Simone, standing before the bedroom mirror in her wedding dress. "My father sent it," she said. "It just came."

"You look beautiful."

"Poor Dr. Tarcher," she said. "His wife went crazy."

"You take my breath away," he answered. He moved behind her and kissed her neck. "You slay me."

"Crazy old bat missed her wedding. Now she stands in her bridal gown in the attic."

"What made him send it now?"

"God only knows."

"Did he send a letter with it?"

"No. Nothing."

"How do you know it wasn't your mother?"

"Because *she* would have sent a letter. And the handwriting on the box was his."

"And there was nothing else in there?"

"No."

"Well, that was nice of him."

"Oh, Orno," she said. "I hope you're right."

He looked at her in the mirror. "You are a great beauty."

"You are as sweet a man as there is on earth."

"As lucky."

"I'll never wear this in my life," she answered.

He laid her back across the quilt and kissed her again. He'd long suspected that their wedding was an inescapable dread to her; a thorn of sadness that would always pierce her. It occurred to him now that it was also that way for her father. He felt it was his duty to make it up, especially to her. He knelt at the edge of the bed, took her hands, and said his vows out loud again. Still perfectly remembered. Tears were in her eyes. Her pregnancy was all through her, not just in the rise of her belly but in the warmth of her fingers and the downiness of her skin and the heat of her neck; the fever that emanated from her arms and shoulders and breath when after a moment she leaned forward and pulled him all the way down on top of her.

———

By midwinter they could feel the baby all the time, sometimes even see its movements through her dress; they walked in the bitter cold, though it was windless in the shelter of the valley behind their house and Simone was so warm that she could unbutton her coat; the icy temperature made the world clearer, the air a constant surprise of clarity like a sheet of glass pressed up against the trees.

He worried when she drove through the snow to Bell Arbor. She slept during her lunch breaks at school, on a bench in the faculty lounge, where the other teachers could wake her before her next class. She ate apples, crackers, sandwiches he made for her when she came home tired in the afternoon; then she went to prepare her classes but usually fell asleep in the middle. In the evenings now he was awake by himself in the house, watching the snow through the dark rows of windows.

Usually he read his journals, but now and then if she was still awake he began reading poems instead. She had several anthologies left over from college and he took to browsing through them while sitting in the living room next to her. She sat on the window ledge because the house was too warm for her, and he sat in the ashwood rocker that they'd bought at a yard sale. He would open the book and settle on a stanza, a handful of lines to read over in the thin warmth of the winter sun that lay across his lap.

He thought of Marshall. Now and then he came across lines he remembered with lone clarity from years ago, the two of them walking together above the Hudson:

> *This is the end of them, three-quarters fools,*
> *Snatching at straws to sail*
> *Seaward and seaward on the turntail whale*

or

> *The portent wound in corridors of shells*

He couldn't say why certain scraps of words remained so clearly in memory or why the rest of them had vanished; but now, reading at the window, he recognized the gravity Marshall seemed to have been searching out in those days, different from what he suspected the others at The Odalisque had been reading and far removed from anything he himself would have pursued. He remembered thinking that the others were poseurs, though now they seemed nothing worse than unsure of themselves; though he was aware how easy it was to hold illusions, he also knew he himself had never really posed, even then; his days of wearing the fedora were too awkward to count for that. He and Marshall had sought each other out as refuge, it now seemed. He himself was a hayseed in the big city and Marshall was probably the real thing, a rueful heart and an ingenious mind together, a battler of his own frightening thoughts. It was something of a revelation and an explanation that touched him with longing and forgiveness; in the shelf of low winter sun now these years later he sighed and reached out to touch his wife.

X L I

One early morning in March, still in darkness, the phone rang and Simone answered. "Oh, no," she whispered.

He turned to her. "What is it?"

"Oh, God," she said. "No."

"Simone, what's happened? Where's Marshall?"

"He's a good swimmer," she said into the phone. "Oh, no. Oh, no."

"Simone, tell me—"

"We're coming down. We'll be there in a few hours."

"Tell me—"

She hung up and turned to him. He'd feared this for so long, held such a dreadful place for it in his mind, that at first when she told him he didn't understand. She shook her head and whispered, "Not Marshall. My father."

"What happened?"

"He went out in the *Chesterton*. Two nights ago. No one's seen him since. They just found the boat."

"Where?"

"In the swells."

"Oh, no," he said, and took her in his arms.

They left for Woods Hole before dawn. At rest stops and gas stations they called ahead: no news. The coast guard had sent a plane to search the coast, but it was March and Professor Emerson's only chance would have been to make it ashore at once. They drove in silence and every hour he stopped to call again. Simone stayed in the car, looking straight ahead. The landscape had been shredded by winter wind, the trees stripped bare, the snow flattened into ice at the road shoulder. As he drove he kept his hand on her belly and every now and then the baby came alive, kicking or rolling lengthwise across her abdomen in fits; he had the thought that the unborn knew grief and hoped it wasn't true.

Mrs. Pelham was ashen. A half-dozen others were there as well, residents from town sitting in the set of Windsor chairs looking out through the tall windows at the inhospitable sea. Boats out, scanning the flats. Now and then someone else came up the walk to the house, a neighbor with food or the constable with his hat in his hand, shaking his head, saying, "No news, no news." The harbormaster had seen the boat go out Tuesday afternoon; it hadn't returned that night nor on Wednesday. The weather had been rough in the evening, the southerly reach of a winter storm: thirty-knot winds and high seas. The townspeople sat in chairs looking out to sea. The phone rang now and then, but it was being answered in the kitchen. Mrs. Pelham sat upright, watching the water.

"He's wonderful with the boat," Simone said. "He'd know what to do. Maybe he's ashore."

"Oh, Simone. Sweetheart," said Mrs. Pelham. "Oh, my sweetheart."

"I know, I know. Oh, Mom."

"We have to wait and see. He always turns up."

Simone looked out the window, trying not to cry. Orno reached and touched her hand where it rested on her mother's shoulder, both of them looking out to sea. The water had lost its color and suddenly he couldn't shake the feeling that it was higher than they were, a frightful gray mass all the way to the horizon. Dread flooded him. He turned and left the room, walked to the front of the house so he wouldn't have to look anymore.

In the evening they went to Hyannis airfield to pick up Marshall. As Orno drove he looked to the south. Lines of frigid breakers fifty yards offshore. He thought of Professor Emerson steering the boat: the hull skidding sideways at the peaks when the rudder came out of the water; the frozen explosions across the bow in the trenches. Had the engine stalled? Had he tried to make his way across the deck? He remembered the slippery boards pitching below him, the terrifying slant he tried to counter with his legs against the gunwales. Outside, the wind pitched across the peninsula; he shuddered at the thought of being at sea. If Professor Emerson was alive the only explanation was that he'd come ashore beforehand; the boat might have blown loose from its mooring and drifted back out to the breakwater. But it was nearly hopeless: today was Thursday.

Marshall was plain-faced. At the airport he hugged both of them and as they walked toward the car he patted Simone's belly. At one point he stopped and leaned up against her blouse and said, "I'm your rich uncle"; but the playfulness of it was wrong to everybody and he stood again and kept walking. As they drove back they told him what they knew: a plane had run the coast all morning; the fishing fleet was out looking as well; volunteers were walking the beaches; four life jackets had been found on board the *Chesterton*, but nobody could remember how many it normally carried.

"Was there a note?" Marshall said.

Simone said, "Nobody knows what happened, Marshall."

Marshall was looking at the ocean, a gray curtain through the trees. "Nobody but me."

"Nobody including you."

"I know what happened," he said. "He jumped over the side." He clapped his hands together. *"Boom."*

Simone raised her chin, like her mother.

"What?" said Orno. "I think you're assuming an awful lot."

"What was he doing out there in March?"

"We don't know," said Simone.

"Then what do *you* think happened?" Marshall said.

"I don't know," she said. "He could still be out there."

"They came up here because he'd alienated everyone in his department in New York. He owed all of them money. What did you expect? He's been miserable for months. I happen to know that."

"So what?" said Simone.

"All right," said Marshall. He turned and looked out the window.

"The ocean was rough," she said.

"Come on. He knew rough water."

"Not with a storm coming."

"He always knew the weather, too."

"But he was always careful."

"That's true," said Marshall. "I was thinking about that. Maybe he's off somewhere warm. The Caribbean. That's another possibility. Is there any money missing?"

"I can't believe you're saying this," said Simone. She turned and tapped the window with her finger. "It's very possible our father is out there somewhere."

"I don't think he's out there *anymore*. And I do think it was intentional. That's all I'm saying. And I'm not surprised. What I told you before, Orno—we recognize each other."

"Marshall," Orno said. "There's no reason to say any of this."

Simone's face was hard. Orno wanted to comfort her, but in truth he also had a chilly feeling, the same dread he'd felt facing the sea. He turned the car on a sand path and drove some ways down it, trying to formulate the proper response. At the end he stopped in the shelter of a dune. The breakers crashing at a slant. His stomach was stone. He was thinking of Professor Emerson meeting the guests at the door to the chapel.

"When did Mom call you?" Marshall asked.

"This morning," said Orno.

"That's when she called me too. That's funny too, don't you think?"

"Sort of," said Orno.

"Marshall, what are you doing? Are you trying to hurt us?"

"Don't you think it's odd she didn't call someone Tuesday night?"

"Maybe she *did,*" said Simone.

"I don't think so."

"Marshall, it's really not the thing to say right now," said Orno.

"What do *you* think, Orno?"

"Frankly I was wondering about it too."

"What was she thinking Tuesday night when he wasn't back?"

"It's March, Marshall," said Simone. "It wouldn't have mattered."

"That's not what I'm saying. I'm saying you don't know anything about his life."

"And?"

"Let's not fight," said Orno.

"I don't understand you," said Simone.

"Yes, you do."

"There's no reason to believe that, Marshall."

"Maybe this was just another night he didn't come home."

Simone said, "Marshall, you don't have to do this anymore."

Orno put his arm over her shoulder.

"It's over, Marshall," she said.

"The man was a cad—"

"Don't. You already won. Don't you see that?"

"A cad—"

"Get out of the car," Orno said.

Marshall turned his head to the window and laughed.

"Get out," Orno said again.

Marshall looked back at him for a moment, then frowned, opened the door, hesitated, and stepped outside; he crossed over the dune onto the beach, where he looked back one more time, then headed up the sand toward the house. He had to lean forward into the wind, his hair whipping over his head and his arms out for balance. In the car Simone watched him, then turned and looked the other way, out past the breaking waves to the brutal whitecaps. "Do you know what my father's real name was?" she finally said.

"What?"

"Mendelsohn."

"Oh, God," said Orno.

"That's what he was doing."

"He's upset, just like we are."

"I've always tried to understand him. He's been cursed his whole life. He never loved my father. My father never loved him. What can ever come of that?"

"He's hurt now. He's afraid. It's making him angry."

"It's what had to happen. I always knew it. One of them or the other. Isn't that just horrible? Horrible?"

"He's just afraid."

"No, he's not," she said. "Will you stop saying that? He wanted this to happen. Don't you see that? Haven't you ever seen that?"

"Come on now."

"Stop it!" she said. "Stop trying to protect him all the time. Open your eyes!"

"He's your brother. It's *his* father, too."

"I know that," she said, and suddenly she was weeping. He pulled her to him, covered her belly with his palm. He hugged her and said, "It's all right," over and over into her ear, until finally he felt her loosen. Then he sang to her, underneath the roar of the wind, tunes his mother used to sing to him in Missouri, remembered out of nowhere.

XLII

The next morning at dawn, the constable was at the door: a man walking his dog had found the body in the surf. Mrs. Pelham sank into her chair. Simone wailed. Marshall turned and walked out the back door onto the deck.

XLIII

The following week, at the chapel where they had intended to marry, the memorial was held. It was a small crowd: fishermen and a handful of the winter residents. Afterward, just before dark, Orno and Simone and Marshall and Mrs. Pelham walked up to the bluff over the mouth of the harbor, wrapped in winter coats; they stood together in the biting cold looking out at the horizon. The empty sea now; no more boats. The last light sinking across the far side of the earth. Marshall started with a poem, Whitman, which Orno recognized but couldn't name: lines that ended with "O rising stars! Perhaps the one I want so much will rise, will rise with some of you." He reached into the urn and let the ashes lift from his whitened hand into the air.

No one moved. Orno stood silently, then realized the others were waiting for him. He was wrapped in an expensive oilcloth duster that had belonged to Professor Emerson; pulling it over his neck, he walked to where Mrs. Pelham held the urn and reached inside. His tears began to rise. Simone moved behind him and took his elbow. He brought his closed hand up in front of him and held it there; tears rose again, but what moved him finally to shake with sobs was not the line of gray that flew away into the wind but what at that moment he felt in his other hand, which Simone had pulled against her belly: the little one was kicking.

Simone followed. She reached in with both hands, kissed the fists she withdrew, then stood with her eyes closed, throwing out her arms at last like a diver at the bluff. Orno reached and touched the small of her back, crushed with fear and grief.

Mrs. Pelham moved a few feet away. She pulled out a sheet of paper from her pocket. "This was Walter's favorite," she said. It was Rilke's "Elegies," which Orno suddenly remembered Marshall reciting once in a quiet voice late at night by the statue of Kissuth. She read slowly. Marshall took a step over and embraced her, repeated the lines along with her as he reached around her back and buried his head in her shoulder. Orno took a step toward them, but Simone held him back and instead moved against him and held on, high above the dizzying sea, as though she was afraid she would fall into it.

XLIV

At the end of the week they drove Marshall and Mrs. Pelham to Manhattan. The storm was spent now. The horizon against the unmoving sea like paint against a frame. The Cape; the southern shore; the startling ribbon of highway; then the parkways and the magnificent hills of trees, coming to bud. They took a meandering route, drifting west into the land where Mrs. Pelham had been raised, all of them looking out the windows and now and then sideways at her in profile. Her chin was up, her eyes darting at the distant scenery. She seemed reflective, perhaps remembering. Grief had tired everybody. Marshall was as calm as Orno had ever seen him, eyes closed in the seat next to his mother: a boy on a car trip. Simone looked a lot like Mrs. Pelham, her glances scanning the reach of woods; Orno drove in silence at her side. He'd always been moved by the beauty of this part of the state: the walls of stone, the manors peeking through the hedges, the horses milling a hundred yards up the slope from where the traffic streamed noisily in the valley.

Suddenly Mrs. Pelham said, "I feel I should apologize. Your father was a complicated man—"

"Please," said Simone.

"He was a good man—"

"He was our father," said Simone. "He *is* our father."

"Simone," said Marshall. "Listen to Mom."

"There were times when I could have left him," Mrs. Pelham said. "I don't know. Maybe someday you'll understand the complications of that decision. I mean, I hope not, but there were certainly times when I thought that for the sake of the two of you I should have gone off and taken you somewhere else. That almost happened, you know. When you were little. Don't think I wasn't aware how difficult he made life for you sometimes. But he was also an extraordinary man. A hugely bright man. An exquisitely sensitive man. Do you understand that?"

"Yes," said Simone.

"You did what you needed to do," said Marshall. His eyes were still closed: a boy listening to a story.

"How can you ever know if what you're doing is the right thing?" said Mrs. Pelham. "I certainly didn't know then. I thought of leaving him three different times. Maybe things would have been better. Maybe we'd be somewhere else right now."

"You don't have to tell us this, Mom," said Simone.

"Where would *he* be now?" Mrs. Pelham went on. "Both of you have his sensitivity, you know. That comes from him. That exquisite sense of the world. That's his. That's what he gave the two of you." She leaned forward and began to cry. "I feel I should ask to be forgiven," she said.

Nobody spoke. Orno had to prevent himself from saying anything. He wanted to relieve her distress. Simone was looking out the window, thinking.

It was Marshall who finally answered. "You *are* forgiven, Mother," he said, opening his eyes at last and touching her shoulder.

————

Mrs. Pelham said nothing more at lunch, which they ate at a diner. Her confession had been extraordinary to Orno, a door opening on to a life he could not have imagined; but by the time they sat at the back table of the restaurant her chin had come up again, her manner with the waitress turned efficient once more. Now they were driving again, and she dozed. The car sped toward Manhattan. Chinked stone walls. Runs of hills. Warmer now: winter's last ice in the shadows as they moved south on the parkway. Then suddenly the Hudson alongside, the surprising smell of water; and at last the broad shining skyline in the sun.

FDR Drive in midafternoon. Light-swept cornices. Metal. Noise. They slowed in traffic and suddenly he remembered arriving the first time, on the West Side Highway, all those years ago, the brim of his father's homburg cutting his own gleaming sight of granite. He remembered sitting up in the seat. City of promise. All his dreams. Stepping out of the Chrysler onto the curb at 116th Street, eighteen years old, the electrifying jump at the center of the world.

Marshall said, "I still feel it too."

"Feel what?"

"What you're feeling. This city. I'll always feel it, as long as I live. That's why I love it."

"So do I, I guess."

"Did you know we're riding on the remains of London?"

"The what?"

"FDR Drive. It was built on the rubble of London and Bristol. From the Luftwaffe raids."

"Come on."

"It really was. Ships brought it over as ballast. New empire over the old, I guess. Now we're riding on it. And before that it was farms." He pointed out the window. "Imagine. The whole Upper East Side, a hundred and twenty years ago. Nothing but farmland."

They continued south, under the noisy tunnels. "Maybe that's why *I* like it," Orno finally said.

———

That afternoon the two of them walked. Years gone by but the same feelings in an instant: thirst; the stretch of time; smallness among the canyons of buildings. Yet he felt detached now, no longer a disciple. Clouds had moved in over the harbor; the air suddenly stinging. They walked fast, Orno in front. Seventy-ninth Street to Cedar Hill. Across the park. Turtle Pond. The Shakespeare Garden. The Natural History Museum as they emerged to the west, flattened by shadow. The Dakota. The San Remo. The rose glow of rock walls on Central Park West opening and closing like a bloom, the sun struggling above them in clouds. Light; half-dark; light again. Like a ship in seas. Marshall talking.

"Let's go to the Empire State Building."

"It's late, M."

"Let's."

The elevator; rope lines; then the deck—a remembered magnificence. Fifth Avenue blazing like a runway in the early dark. The chime of brakes and car horns a quarter mile below like distant water; the wind prowling in overtones. Marshall moved against the glass. "Remember I told you about Selim Aziz?"

"Yes."

"I never finished telling you the whole story."

"Yes, you did."

"No, there's more. The interesting part." He smiled. "Back in New York I kept thinking about him. I knew he was a thief, but I still couldn't stop remembering his gallant ways. There was something about him—I don't know—he was a reverent man. And that's what I admire most." He lit a cigarette. "He used to take us to a fortress called Rumeli Hisari, sometimes once a week, even though Istanbul was full of a thousand other sights. Stamboul alone could have occupied all our time. But Selim was obsessed with Rumeli Hisari, I think because of its history. It was a few miles out of town, so we used to go in a taxi. The same spot every time. He knew the drivers and one of them would pick us up at the hotel, then stop on the way north near the Dolmabahçe Palace to pick up Selim on the way. We never saw where he lived, and I'm sure he made a point of walking to a clean area to meet us. That's the way he was. It wasn't difficult to see through that kind of tactic, but at the same time it convinced us of a certain nobility. Not that he came from a good family, of course, because it was clear that he didn't. But still, it spoke to us, that he knew enough to put on a show of gentility. I know that sounds naive; but that's not understanding it. At restaurants he went through pains to adopt certain ways. He watched my mother and imitated her table manners. He was always extremely polite. He set down his knife to eat and switched his fork to his right hand. He dabbed his napkin at the corner of his mouth. In some ways they were feminine manners, but I guess he must have learned them from women. Really, it was a mark of his intelligence, I think now. Of his noble spirit. And part of it was his reverence." He snuffed out the cigarette on the window ledge. "You're a reverent person, too," he said. "That's one reason I like you."

"Well, thank you."

"But face it. He was a common thief. Even so, he used to take us to the fortress and stand there looking up at its walls, telling us the story of the conquests of the city. And don't think that's a simple story. Rumeli Hisari looks like a castle in a children's book. Stone walls and magnificent turrets, running down a hill to the water. The fortress of fortresses. It was guarding Istanbul from the Black Sea. Think of who's come down that way through the ages. Persians. Spartans. Athenians. Macedonians. Romans. Arabs. Bulgars. Huns. And that's just the start. Selim knew all of it. He would tell me the stories, one conquest at a time, while my mother sat on the rocks, half listening. That was another bit of his nobility. He was always playing the role of a father to me. He was a thief all right, but he had a great sense of majesty."

"So what's the end of the story?"

"Well, in the end I learned something. We were back in New York and I kept thinking about him. I knew for certain that he was a criminal, but I couldn't forget the grace he'd shown us. I can still picture him, sitting at an outdoor café, black eyes and black mustache, dabbing at the coffee on his lips with a napkin. He had hands like a giant. Big, wadded knuckles, but he used them gently, rubbing his palms together when he told a story. Anyway, back home I had an inspiration."

"What was it?"

"My father always kept cash in the house. I don't know why, but probably he was hiding it. From my mother, I mean. Or he might have had a hundred other uses for it. I don't know. I'd found it in his closet years ago. So one day I had this inspiration, that I was going to help out Selim Aziz."

"What did you do?"

"I sent him more money."

"You did not!"

"I certainly did. I took a couple of hundred dollars, over the course of a few weeks, and when I was pretty sure my father wasn't going to notice, I went down to Forty-second Street and bought a money order. I put it in an envelope and mailed it to Selim."

"Why'd you do that?"

"Why? I don't know. But I knew it was right."

"How did you get the address?"

"I sent it care of the Luxor. He had friends there. I just realized it was the right thing to do. That his being a thief was a small flaw in a remarkable life. That he needed my help but would never ask."

"So you sent him your father's money."

"Right. And to this day it's the greatest thing I've ever done. Maybe it's just what the Christians always knew. Turn the other cheek—maybe that's another way of saying it. For me it was learning to do the unexpected. To give when I'd been taken. It freed me. Like letting go of a rope that I thought had been holding me."

"I suppose," Orno said. He laughed. "As long as your father never found out."

"He never did. Or if he did, he must have thought it was my mother."

Orno leaned against the glass, watching the cars stream uptown. Suddenly Marshall said, "You don't believe me, do you?"

"Of course I believe you."

"I can tell you don't. But let me tell you, stranger things have happened."

"No question about that."

Marshall looked up. "The world is hard to believe," he said. "Did you know a bomber once crashed into this building?"

"Come on!"

"It certainly did. July 28th, 1945. The pilot went crazy. A B-25. Swerved all over Manhattan one Saturday morning. Then straight into the seventy-ninth floor. Killed a lot of people. One of the engines sailed clear through and fell out the other side, onto Thirty-third Street. Surprise for the pedestrians, I would imagine. The building stood, though. Nobody knows this stuff anymore." He pointed up to the sky. "A magnificent history. All hard to imagine now. Dirigibles used to tie up right there. Right to the spire. Imagine that! On top of the Empire State Building! So people could get off. Do you believe *that*?"

"No."

"Well, it's true, too."

"I don't believe it."

"It is. The absolute truth. They did. In the days of the *Graf Zeppelin*. This was going to be the pinnacle of the world. Man's great achievement." He turned from the glass. "You know? When it comes down to it, we're friends because you love this kind of thing, too. You're as moved by it as I am."

"That's true. I am."

"I know I've made trouble, O. Don't think I don't know that. But bear with me, all right?"

Orno didn't answer. He moved away from the windows and Marshall followed. Then they were in the elevator again, descending. The great marbled atrium and the busy riffraff of the street, throngs of evening walkers; dark coats hurrying. They started back north, but in the Fifties they grew tired and Orno hailed a cab. The brittle, overpadded cold seats as they sped uptown. Silence now between them. Marshall looking out at the traffic; Orno looking at Marshall. He had the feeling of an end, somehow, things played out. He'd been considering breaking with him, but now it seemed inconsequential: he would wait and see. It surprised him, speeding crosstown through the dark park: he had always expected to decide his fate the way his father had decided his; to decide his character, really—upright decisions in an upright life. But instead he had merely discovered it, merely stumbled upon the pieces and bits, laid out murkily before him. The half-lucky fortuity of his days. He was weak; he was strong. He knew his desires; he could only guess at them. Marshall, the sly instrument of his own unearthing, stared tiredly out the window into the night.

———

The next morning at the Emersons' brownstone they ate breakfast together before Marshall's flight, all of them cooking omelets in the big kitchen. Orno watched Marshall breaking eggs. Something easy in his movements now, the strain gone out of them. His plane was in the afternoon. The sun, low to the south, filled the window alcove; bright but not quite warm. The yellow maple of the countertops and floor, some particular beauty to the room exactly as he remembered it. He'd only been here twice now in his life: a strange realization. Simone set the table in the dining room, moving back and forth from where they worked.

After the meal Marshall disappeared again upstairs; Mrs. Pelham did, too: their way of vanishing. He remembered it from the first Thanksgiving. Again he was left to clean up with Simone, this time his wife. In the kitchen they kissed. He said, "I should have done this the first time."

"Or I should have," she answered.

He sat at the table in the sun. Once again the picture book: *Istanbul.* He took it from the shelf. The photographs like paintings, flagged with reds and golds and brilliant greens; the magnificent domes; the dark seas of men on the avenues; the pale stone. Kapali Çarşi. The Mosque of Süleymaniye. He turned a page: The Hamam of Roxelana. He studied the pictures, thinking of Marshall's tales. Topkapi Sarayi. The Galata Bridge, ateem with boats and men. He pictured Penny McRary there, eating pastry. He turned again. Bedesten: Selim Aziz and his accomplice, darting in the narrow aisles. At the stove, Simone brewed tea. The smell drifted. He turned another page: The fortress of Rumeli Hisari. All of it was there, one page after the next, the entire history of Marshall's days.

They said good-bye to Marshall in the afternoon and to Mrs. Pelham the next morning, and by the following night they were back in Preston. Orno kept returning in his mind to the phrase "stunned by grief," for that is what Simone now seemed, not so much saddened as dazed. She called her mother twice a day and when she wasn't on the phone she held herself close. He wanted to be able to soothe her, but he knew there was no point yet on which he could. Such a loss was still incomprehensible to him—this was the only way he could think of it, an immensity that he could not yet take in. He watched her move around the house. The best thing was to hold her and not speak, a kindness that now and again she allowed to enter her the way Doctor Diamond sometimes relaxed unexpectedly on his shoulder. Simone never cried during the day. But when he wasn't holding her she was separated from the world by a film of restraint that slowed her speech and tripped her movements; though he could not have identified a discrete feature that had changed in her, her face seemed to have been transformed all at once: not a young woman's anymore but simply a woman's. For several weeks she cried in her sleep.

But by the time spring appeared, days of thaw followed by hammer-blows of cold that formed short silvery icicles everywhere, she had begun to recover. This seemed to be less a product of time passing, Orno thought, than of the stealthy endocrine takeover occurring inside of her. The baby was due in three months, and though her carriage looked painful to him the benevolence of her physiology emerged nonetheless: a cheery rash of pinkness on her cheeks; hands rubbing the crescent belly curved below them; fingers resting on its globe like birds. She walked aimlessly in the house, half-smiling as she moved from room to room.

———

In May, Mrs. Pelham came to visit—suddenly again another woman, not quite the one he'd seen in the car. She wore sneakers and blue jeans, the cuffs brown with mud from the late rains in their garden. No fur-trimmed coat this time; no hat. Not confessional again, though, and no longer close to tears. Toughness and calm, a mannish, matter-of-fact stride that brimmed with frankness. When he mentioned it to Simone she said, "Of course, she's an anthropologist, remember? She's as brave as they come."

And he did remember, though it surprised him. He'd only seen her in Woods Hole and Manhattan, and then that single moment in the car. A whole life hidden. Here they went for walks in the woods and she led the way, setting off at an angle from the trail through the dense trees; rare slants of sunlight; deer bounding, then frozen; carpets of dark mushrooms. She cooked dinners for them and afterward went to sleep early, waking even before Orno. In the mornings he came downstairs and found her at the window, her chin in her hand. He made them coffee and they sat together watching the sun come up over the trees. She didn't always feel the need to talk. Finally he said, "What are you going to do when you get back to New York?"

"I've been thinking about that," she answered. "I think I'll make a trip to Turkey."

"Really?"

"For a while, at least. That is, once I meet the baby." She sipped her coffee. "But there's more work to be done there. And it would help to keep me busy."

"I suppose it would. Would you go back to Heybeli?"

She looked surprised.

"Marshall told me all about it," Orno said.

"I'm touched that he remembers."

She stayed a week. Watching her in the kitchen, in the muddy garden, in the unmarked woods, he kept thinking of Simone. Mrs. Pelham had the same dark eyelids, and her grief had made them ragged but not sad. Instead they gave her face a frontier toughness, an invitation to look at them in their weathered surprise. The resemblance startled Orno. He pictured Simone leaning up against the steering wheel of her father's car, driving away from her wedding.

XLVI

One day, sitting at the window, Orno said to Simone, "Did Marshall ever live in Turkey?"

"Where?"

"Turkey."

"You mean when my mom was there?" She pointed out at a pair of rabbits that had skittered out from the trees. "No."

"He never went with your mother?"

"No. Why do you ask?"

"I didn't think he did."

"That's where *she* went when he was two. But he never went along. Look at those rabbits," she said. "I hope they make it to next winter."

"I don't think I'm ever going to be surprised again, you know?"

"Why do you say that?"

"Oh, I don't know. Just because he's amazing. I was sitting here thinking about him."

She smiled at him. "He *is* amazing," she said, and there was such charity in her voice, such goodwill in the pink of her cheeks, that he decided not to say anything. He leaned close to the window and watched the rabbits flee across the open grass into the trees.

XLVII

For Memorial Day they drove to the coast. Evergreens glinting in the high sun. Bright white cumulus like mountains. They ate breakfast at a tourist restaurant above the harbor in Lincolnville, then walked to the boardwalk, where Simone leaned against the rail and looked over the water. Minnows nosing in the pilings; beards of moss swaying in the swirls of waves. "Such cold, cold water," she said.

From behind he wrapped his arms around her. "I love you," he answered.

"Marshall knew it would destroy him."

"Nobody knows what happened," said Orno.

"That's not true."

"Oh, sweetheart. What could you have done?"

She raised her chin. "I could have stopped it. I could have had the wedding without my brother."

"Oh, my love, you don't really believe that. It wasn't the wedding. That's silly. It was much more than that."

"I know," she said. "Of course you're right. But I still think about it all the time." She turned to the water. "And I still haven't talked to my mother about it."

"Are you angry at her, too?"

"Why would I be angry at *her*?"

"I don't know. For what she said in the car."

"What she told us about my father?"

"Yes."

"I've known that for years."

"But I noticed you didn't tell her you forgave her."

"Oh, that?" she said. "I just thought it was more important for Marshall to."

In the harbor, a pack of gulls was flocking over the corpse of a fish; Orno leaned across her shoulder and watched their attack. They circled and dived, baffling one another with their wings as they hovered, then dropped like stones onto the carcass. He understood that this was the normal course of the world's savagery; but even at this moment, despite everything, he understood that at the core of him he felt human beings were different. Marshall was labyrinthine and despotic, but here was Simone: a gem, slow-formed and clear. Hardship *made* character, hardship *broke* character; that was the paradox. Character to him was kindness and diligence and a certain social egalitarianism that was fundamental to society, and he still believed somehow that all three were instinctive. This, perhaps, was his unbending core. It had taken him some time to find it. And now the trustworthiness of his wife seemed to be only more evidence of its existence. She leaned her back against him, and he reached down and laid his arm over the warm rise of her belly.

XLVIII

As summer came the world shifted so that he no longer straddled it but stood fumbling at its slippery edge, while Simone became a great solid tree growing straight up from its middle. She gained an authority before him, and he found himself willingly bowing. Now indeed he did feel like a pilgrim. On weekends she liked to sleep all afternoon and as though this were a command to him he got into the bed with her and despite his nature fell straight into bright-colored dreams. When she wanted to walk with him he walked, though often this occurred in the middle of the night, when she woke and could not fall back asleep. It was warm now and the moonlit air was sharp with the smell of blooms. At his best he felt like a purposeful worker—a worker of God, he thought again, although this time with amusement and not the craving of his wandering days; and at his worst he felt peripheral. At meals sometimes he simply ignored his food and gave it to her. He himself wasn't hungry. He lost weight, only noticing by chance one day in the small mirror by the door.

At the same time Simone grew. He watched her slyly and with an effort to conceal his astonishment. What could he think? All his training, his wordly skill, his carpentry with teeth and gums, his feet-on-the-ground knowledge of the earth and men was nothing compared to this miracle that she blithely walked around with, sometimes unnoticing. He panted with amazement. It was involuntary, a succession of deep breaths that came to him on their own when he saw her across the room or next to him in bed. It sometimes seemed like fear, but he wasn't afraid.

One afternoon during her ninth month they were sitting at the living-room window when he suddenly departed his own existence and for the first time understood what it was to be her. He felt the windstorm of her family raging around her. He himself had been enraptured by Marshall because he'd seen him to full effect against his own unworldly cowardice and small-minded Missouri desire. Marshall's inevitable self-revelation had followed, and in Orno's view it had unfolded gruesomely and pathetically; but for Simone, he saw clearly at this moment, both the ascent and the decline must have been masked by time and by the fact that really they had occurred together. That was why she loved Marshall with the solidity of a generation spent together, while above all else he himself felt betrayed. Her father he saw now more than anything as destitute, bereft of the resources of humanity, a man cursed with true poverty of refuge; yet despite what Simone said about him he knew she must still see him as a figure of landscape, the great solid peak in the vista of her childhood. If anything Professor Emerson's failings would only fade for her with the passage of years. Orno would have to treat his memory kindly, and at the same time he also knew that in their future together he would have to prove again and again that he wasn't like him. Her mother, he realized—because at this moment he could feel how much Simone needed her—would eventually become their friend.

He saw this with a paternal equanimity that rendered it all at a distance. Simone was flushed even in the cool afternoon. Marshall was a continent away. Mrs. Pelham was back in New York, and he suspected her life there was not so different from what it had been before. He thought of his sister Clara in Level, Missouri, and his parents in Cook's Grange, surrounded by fields of winter wheat;

he had come a great distance in his life, and then he wondered if perhaps he would find he had come no distance at all.

———

On the night after the summer solstice Simone woke up in darkness with contractions, and when they grew regular by morning he called the doctor. They arranged to meet at the hospital ten miles away and then left in the Volkswagen, carrying the suitcase he had packed a month before and all their bed pillows, which Simone clutched around her on the unpadded seat. One of the things he decided to do when they got back was to investigate a new car. She was speaking between contractions, but when one came on she disappeared into a cave of silence that was frightening to him, though it lasted only a few seconds. He didn't want to drive too fast because the road was rough in places, but he became afraid that the baby was going to be born in the front seat of the car.

In the hospital room the contractions began to slow down, and then by midmorning they disappeared completely and she was joking with the nurses. In the afternoon she and Orno walked together, out the long corridor onto the strip of meadow against the trees; he held her there, the precarious odd shape of her in his hands that were gentle with fear. He felt suspended, lifted high into the air above his own life. Then as they stood he felt her womb tighten again, a hard wall beneath her gown; so they walked back inside together through the empty cafeteria, up the stairs to the landing; she paused while a new contraction appeared; then up to the room once more, Simone leaning on him now, to stand in the shower where the suffering started up again; this time in earnest, hard and fast, driving her to tears.

She moved back to the bed, panting and sweating. The hours passed for him without seeming really to be time. By nightfall, her eyes were no longer wet with pain but had turned inward; he tried to look into them during the lulls but they showed little, only a frightening dark anguish; she had no words, but he kept speaking to her anyway, telling her to keep going, acknowledged only occasionally by a brief turn in her cloudy gaze; some appeal he couldn't recognize. At the end of the inclined bed he knelt, holding on to her.

Near midnight the doctor left them and went to sleep in his room, saying the nurses would call him when it was time. Covered in sweat now, her skin drawn over her cheeks, she labored in long runs of silence. By early morning Orno himself was delirious with the need for sleep; and then he became afraid that something had gone wrong, that a grave event had occurred. He stepped to the window, pushed open the glass, and went to his knees in the cool air, praying. Over the treetops the night sky was making its shift to silver, and as he knelt watching the meadow alongside the hospital a buck stepped quickly out of a stand of birches. It stood at the side of the grass, turned its antlers up at him and stared. After a time Orno moved his hand to the pane; but at this it wheeled and sprang back into the dark. He couldn't say why this brought relief to him; but it did. He had always been that way. He turned back to Simone. A few hours later, in a high midmorning of light, she gave birth to their son, a slippery, angelic creature who came out into the world crying.

ETHAN CANIN is the author of *Emperor of the Air, Blue River,* and *The Palace Thief.* He is on the faculty of The University of Iowa Writers' Workshop, and is also a physician. He lives in California and Iowa.